Nichole Severn writes explosive romantic suspense with strong heroines, heroes who dare challenge them and a hell of a lot of guns. She resides with her very supportive and patient husband, as well as her demon spawn, in Utah. When she's not writing, she's constantly injuring herself running, rock climbing, practicing yoga and snowboarding. She loves hearing from readers through her website, www.nicholesevern.com, and on Twitter, @nicholesevern

Jennifer D. Bokal is the author of the bestselling ancient-world historical romance *The Gladiator's Mistress* and the second book in the Champions of Rome series, *The Gladiator's Temptation*. Happily married to her own alpha male for twenty years, she enjoys writing stories that explore the wonders of love in many genres. Jen and her husband live in upstate New York with their three beautiful daughters, two aloof cats and two very spoiled dogs.

CAUGHT IN THE CROSSFIRE

NICHOLE SEVERN

COLTON'S SECRET HISTORY

JENNIFER D. BOKAL

MILLS & BOON

First Published in Great Britain 2020
by Mills & Boon, an imprint of HarperCollins*Publishers*
1 London Bridge Street, London, SE1 9GF

Caught in the Crossfire © 2020 Natascha Jaffa
Colton's Secret History © 2020 Harlequin Books S.A.

Special thanks and acknowledgement are given to Jennifer D. Bokal for her contribution to the *The Coltons of Kansas* series.

ISBN: 978-0-263-28048-7

0920

MIX
Paper from
responsible sources
FSC™ C007454

This book is produced from independently certified FSC™ paper to ensure responsible forest management.

For more information visit: www.harpercollins.co.uk/green

Printed and bound in Spain
by CPI, Barcelona

CAUGHT IN THE CROSSFIRE

NICHOLE SEVERN

This is for you!
This series wouldn't keep going without you.

Chapter One

Your husband is alive, Kate.

Blackhawk Security profiler Kate Monroe stared at her reflection in the broken picture frame on the floor. Had it really been an entire year? She hadn't set foot in this house since the ambush, too traumatized to pull the bullets out of the walls, too sentimental to put it on the market. Everything had changed that night.

Tightening her grip on the manila folder in her hand, she couldn't ignore the truth. Declan hadn't died as she'd been told while recovering in the hospital from her own injuries. He'd survived. He'd disappeared. And he'd left her behind.

Glass crunched under her shoes, bringing her back into the moment, and the photo came into focus. Her and Declan dancing at their wedding, surrounded by smiling guests.

Burying the burn behind her sternum deeper, she stepped over the frame. Blackhawk's private investigator had found proof—a timestamped photo—of Declan taken a month ago in downtown Anchorage. She'd stared at it for hours, picked it apart pixel by pixel to fight the anger and resentment bubbling up her throat. In vain. The photo was real. Declan was alive, and she deserved to know why he hadn't come home.

There had to be something here that would lead her to his location. Setting the folder on what was left of the kitchen table, she fought back the memories of hundreds of dinners as she dragged her fingers over the bullet-riddled surface. She pulled out drawers in the kitchen, emptied the bookshelf beside the desk Declan had built for her, scattered old patient files across the carpet.

Bending to pick them up, Kate froze as the dark stains at her feet came into focus. Blood. Ice worked through her veins. She couldn't think—couldn't breathe. She closed her eyes against the memories fighting to rush forward and forced herself to take a deep breath. She'd been a psychologist. She'd helped others through their trauma—their pain—why couldn't she get past her own?

She traced over one mound of scar tissue below her collarbone, leaving the files where they fell. Swallowing against the tightness in her throat, she straightened. Gunshot wounds never healed. Not really. Six months since the last surgery, and the physical pain from three shots to the chest still lingered. Then again, she'd been lucky to survive at all. The gunman who'd opened fire on her and Declan hadn't meant to leave anyone alive.

Movement registered off to her right and she automatically reached for the Glock in her shoulder holster. Depressing the safety tab, she took aim, heart in her throat. Blackhawk Security's founder and CEO insisted his agents trained in wilderness survival, weapons, hostage negotiation, recovery and rescue and more, but she was a profiler. Not former military like Anthony. Not a former NSA consultant like Elizabeth. She'd never had use for a gun.

Her hands shook slightly as the weight of heavy steel threatened to pull her arms down. She'd never aimed her gun at another human being. "You're trespassing on private property," she said. "Come out with your hands where I can see them, and I promise not to shoot you."

The house had been abandoned for a year. Wasn't hard to imagine the homeless taking advantage of a roof over their heads, and she wasn't interested in forcing them to leave if that was the case. The house wasn't going anywhere. It took everything she had to stay here this long.

Shadows shifted across the intruder's features, and her breath caught in her throat. Hints of moonlight highlighted the familiar shape of his stubbled jaw, his broad chest, muscled arms and short blond hair. Her heart beat hard as she stood there, unsure if he was real or a figment of her imagination.

He closed the distance between them slowly, cautiously, as though he believed she might actually shoot him. She couldn't make out the color of his eyes in the darkness but pictured the ice-blue depths clearly from memory as he stared back at her.

"It's you." She suppressed the sob clawing up her throat but couldn't fight the burn against her lower lash line. Rushing forward, Kate wrapped her arms around his broad chest, his clean, masculine scent working deep into her lungs. A year. A year he'd put her through hell.

The grief, the anger. Why hadn't he reached out to her? Who had she buried all those months ago? Why wasn't he hugging her back?

Clenching her teeth to keep the scream at bay, Kate backed off but didn't holster the weapon. Why was he just standing there? "Say something."

"You're even more beautiful than I remembered." That voice. His voice.

An electric sizzle caught her nerve endings on fire and exploded throughout her entire system. She never thought she'd hear that voice again.

Declan Monroe shifted closer, the weight of his gaze pressurizing the air in her lungs. "You don't need the gun. I'm not going to hurt you."

"That's all you're going to say to me?" It felt as if someone had driven a fist into her stomach. "You've been alive this whole time, and that's all you're going to say? They told me you died in that hospital. I—" The pain of that day, of losing her best friend, of losing the man she'd intended to spend the rest of her life with, the man she'd planned on starting a family with, surged to the surface. "I buried you."

"I can't imagine what you've been through." He reached out, smoothed his fingertips down her jawline. Even with the ice of shock coursing through her, warmth penetrated deep into her bones, but his expression kept her from reveling in his missed touch.

Declan lowered his hand as he studied the aftermath in the living room. The bullet holes in the walls, the broken picture frames, the destroyed sectional and cushions. She didn't have the guts to see what'd become of the rest of the house, a home that was once their safe haven from their dark careers. "Is this where it happened?"

Confusion gripped her hard, and Kate narrowed her eyes to see his face. "What do you mean—"

"I get these flashes sometimes. Of this house, of different things." Declan motioned to his head, then his gaze locked back on her. "Mostly of you. Some days it's glimpses, other times I can see you so clearly walking through that front door with stacks of files in your arms and a smile on your face. Like it was real."

Her head jerked to the side of its own accord slightly as though she'd been slapped. Instinct screamed. This wasn't right. She took a step back, the gun still in her hand.

"But I still don't know your name," he said.

Air rushed from her lungs. She struggled to keep upright as the world tilted on its axis.

Strong hands steadied her before she hit the blood-stained floor a second time, but the gun slipped from her hold. Leveraging her weight against the desk, she pushed back stray hairs that had escaped from the low bun at the base of her neck. She had to breathe. Her pulse beat hard at the base of her throat as his hand slipped down her spine.

How could he have forgotten her name? Every cell in her body rejected the idea her husband had been walking around Anchorage without the slightest clue he'd been married, had a life, had a job. Where had he been all this time?

"You okay?" He was still touching her. Even through

the thick fabric of her cargo jacket, she'd recognize those familiar strokes. "I'll get you some water."

"No." The city had probably turned off the water a long time ago. She'd been paying the mortgage on the house in addition to the rent on her small apartment, but utilities would've been a waste. Kate maneuvered out of his reach. "I'm fine. I...need some air."

Lie. Nothing about the situation, about the fact the husband she'd lost was standing in front of her, was fine. Fresh air wouldn't do a damn bit of good.

Space. She needed space. The home they'd shared for more than half a decade blurred in her peripheral vision as she headed for the front door. Debris and remnants of their life together threatened to trip her up, but she wouldn't stop until there was at least two inches of door between them. Couldn't.

The cold Alaskan night prickled goose bumps along her arms as she closed the door behind her. She set the crown of her head against the wood, pressing her shoulders into the door. One breath. Two. She kept counting until she mentally reached ten.

None of this made sense. His surgeon had told her Declan hadn't survived the shooting. That he'd done everything he could to save her husband, but nothing worked. Declan had lost too much blood, the bullets had torn through major arteries and nobody could've saved him.

No wonder he'd suggested she take the time to heal from her own wounds before identifying the body. It hadn't been to save her from seeing her husband on a slab. It'd been to cover his mistake. By the time she'd had the strength to get out of that damn bed, it'd been too late. The hospital had released who she thought had been her husband into her custody, and Declan's former partner had taken responsibility for all of the funeral arrangements. Had anyone but the surgeon known her husband hadn't been inside that coffin?

The surgeon had lied. Why?

She swiped at her face as the tears finally fell. Declan didn't know her name?

Tires screeched on asphalt a few houses down. Headlights flared to life, but she couldn't see the driver through the truck's windshield. Probably one of the neighbor's teenagers. It'd been so long since she'd lived on this street, she didn't know who had moved away after the shooting, her new neighbors' names or if any of them had kids old enough to drive.

Wasn't important. Staying calm long enough to assess the situation, that was all that mattered now. The engine revved loud in her ears as the faint outline of the passenger-side window lowered.

The door supporting her disappeared, and strong hands pulled her inside a split second before the first bullet of many shattered through the house's main window. Kate hit the floor hard, her head snapping back as Declan returned fire. She checked her holster—empty—and recognized the gun in his hand. Her Glock.

The sound of pealing tires faded, and the gunfire ceased.

Declan barricaded them inside the house, his back to the front door as he dropped the gun's magazine, counted the rounds left and slammed it back into place.

Apparently there were some things amnesia couldn't destroy, loading a weapon being one of them.

Light blue eyes settled on her as he offered her his hand. Calluses slid against her palms as he wrapped his hand around hers and pulled her into him. "Are you hurt?"

"I'm getting tired of people shooting at me." Her awareness of him hiked to an all-time high. The pounding of his heartbeat against her palm, the pressure of his attention on her. Even the way he held her took a bit of the strength out of her knees.

She shook her head and stepped out of his reach to counteract the heat rising in her neck. He'd saved her life. The least she could do was help him recover his. "It's Kate, by the way. My name is Kate."

KATE.

That name was perfect for the blonde beauty with the shadows in her gaze. Striking green eyes, eyes that had haunted his memories for over a year, narrowed in on him. Thinner than he remembered from his memory's brief flashes of her, she shook his insides like the earthquake that hit Japan and brought down the nuclear reactors, leaving him breathless and full at the same time. A T-shirt and jeans hugged her athletic form, her frame hidden by an oversized green cargo jacket. But he knew every curve, every scar, every valley and ridge of muscle from memory.

The realization he hadn't gone crazy after waking up alone in a hospital room settled his nerves. He hadn't imagined her. Hadn't imagined this house. From what he'd been able to tell, they'd lived here. Together.

The real-life sight of her was enough to help him forget he'd just taken a bullet.

He let go of the gun, the crash of metal on hardwood loud in his ears, as his strength drained drop by drop. The driver had fishtailed out of the neighborhood a few seconds ago. No telling if that bastard would circle around for another shot at her, but adrenaline was already leaving his system. He was losing blood. Fast.

"Declan?" Those mesmerizing green eyes shot to his side as his shirt soaked through. "You've been shot."

Declan Monroe. That was his name. Not the one he'd adopted over the last year.

Her attention dulled the pain in his side. He'd find the SOB who'd taken a shot at her. He couldn't remember a damn thing about his life before waking up in that hospital bed, but he'd remembered her. She was important enough for his brain to hang on to, and he'd sure as hell do what he had to to keep her safe.

Blood spread across his T-shirt faster than he thought possible. "Isn't that supposed to stay inside my body?"

"Bullets tend to have other ideas. Lie down. I need to look at the wound," she said.

So levelheaded. So rational. She'd been shot at and now had to inspect a bullet wound. How was she able to keep this calm?

He clamped a hand over his side and stumbled as the pain reared its ugly head, but Kate kept him from collapsing to the floor when the dizziness took control. Her fingers brushed against his oversensitive skin, and a jolt of awareness chased the nerves up his arm and into his chest. The flashlight from her phone blinded him. Swiping her tongue across her bottom lip as she knelt beside him, she holstered the weapon without meeting his gaze. Had she felt it, too? The invisible pull urging him to touch her?

Lifting his shirt, she paused. "I need some hydrogen peroxide and towels to see past the blood. Don't move."

It'd taken him a year to get here, inside this house, to her. He wasn't going to lose her now. He forced himself to straighten. "No. That shooter could come back any minute to make sure he's finished the job. I'm getting you out of here."

"Big words from the man bleeding out on my floor. You're not going anywhere. At least, not until I see how bad it is." Setting her hand over his chest, she pushed him flat onto the floor. Kate disappeared from his side, everything inside of him aware of the space between them.

He focused on the sound of shifting debris and the slamming of cabinets to distract himself. In less than a minute, she crouched beside him with a stack of towels and a bottle of whiskey. "This is all I could find. If you move, you're going to wish you were really were dead."

I buried you. Her words echoed through his head.

"You know what happened to me." None of the flashbacks had revealed that particular memory. Before she stepped foot in the house, he'd gone through most of the paperwork stashed in the desk for leads, each folder detailing therapy notes by Dr. Kate Monroe, a psychologist. He'd studied the holes in the walls, the broken picture frames, the destroyed personal effects. But nothing had triggered another memory.

"You were ambushed." After dousing her hands in the whiskey, she prodded at the sides of the bullet wound. Her fingers feathered over his skin, cooling the fire spreading through his pain receptors. "One of my patients became obsessed with me, and when he discovered he couldn't have me, he decided no one should. You were caught in the cross fire."

"There are pictures of us together. I remember you." He hissed as she poured the alcohol over the hole in his side. Stinging agony rippled through him, and he fought to catch his breath. He might've been shot, but he'd gone an entire year without knowing who he was, where he came from, who he'd left behind. "Who am I to you?"

Using one of the towels she collected from the kitchen, she applied pressure to the wound. Still refusing to look at him. She reached for another towel. "We can't stop the bleeding while the bullet is inside. We need to get you to a hospital."

Anxiety accelerated his pulse. The last hospital he'd set foot inside had kept him fully stocked with enough nightmare material to last him a lifetime. Waking up alone. Four holes in his body. Not knowing who he was. There was no way in hell he was going back for another round.

"No hospitals." Declan wrapped one hand onto her forearm, and her attention snapped to his. His heart rate slowed, the pain disappearing as time seemingly stood still. He noted the slight change in her expression, the furrow between her brows deeper than a moment ago.

He blinked to counteract the darkness closing in around the edges of his vision. "You have to get the bullet out."

"I'm a profiler for a security firm." She tried pulling out of his grip, but he only held her tighter. The tension between her neck and shoulders visibly strained. "I never went to medical school. I'm not a trained medical doctor—"

"I trust you, Kate." And he meant it. Every word. Because even though he'd lost his memories from before he woke up in that hospital bed alone, something deep inside knew her as well as his body knew how to breathe. He couldn't explain it. Didn't need a reason why or how. She'd left enough of an impression that his own brain couldn't get rid of her as it had everything else, and he wasn't about to give that up. Despite the mysterious circumstances surrounding how he'd ended up in that hospital in the first place. "You can do this."

She studied him. "Blackhawk Security has a doctor on staff. She can help—"

"No." He growled. "It has to be you."

"Remember that when you bleed out all over the floor." The tightness drained from her shoulders as she shifted her weight between both knees. She swiped the back of her hand across her face. "Okay. If we're going to do this, I need to find something sharp enough to widen the wound so I can extract the bullet. Hopefully, it's still in one piece."

He set his jaw against another surge of pain and replaced her hand with his own for pressure to slow the bleeding. She disappeared deeper into the house.

His heart pounded loud behind his ears, a slow,

rhythmic beat that made his eardrums ache. The seconds ticked by, maybe a minute. They were running out of time.

When she came back, her phone's flashlight beam highlighted her supplies beside him. He used every last bit of strength to focus on her as she gently removed the towel.

"Are you sure about this?" she asked.

He nodded, quick and curt, the words stuck in his throat with the weight of pain squeezing the air in his lungs.

"Okay. Then no matter what happens," she said, "I need you to hold still."

Sirens echoed. One of the neighbors must've called the police. Cops meant ambulances, questions he couldn't answer and hospitals.

"What's one more scar, right?" She was trying to distract him, keep him focused on the present when all he wanted to do was compare the woman in front of him to the memories in his head. He'd noticed his own scars, of course, the mounds of tissue peppered across his abdominals, and from the slight dip of her neckline, he recognized a similar mass peeking out from beneath her shirt. Did that mean…

"Declan?" she asked.

"Who did that to you?" Rage—pure and hot—engulfed him, pushed the fact that someone had put a hole in him to the back of his mind. Someone had shot her. Too fast, too hard, the crack in his control started to spread as he imagined her lying in one of those bloodstains on the carpet in the dining room. Who the hell shot her? He'd tear them apart with his bare hands. He'd find the bastard and make him pay, just as he'd find the one who'd tried a few minutes ago.

Another dose of adrenaline and pain drove him to try to sit up. A dangerous combination with a gunshot wound. The quicker his heart beat, the quicker he'd bleed out.

"Declan, you have to stay still." Setting her palms against him, she struggled to keep him in place. "The bullet is too deep. If I keep digging, I could permanently damage something or kill you, and I'm not willing to take either of those chances. We have to get you to the hos—"

"No hospitals." Black spiderwebs snaked across his vision, and suddenly he didn't have the strength to keep himself upright. He collapsed back against the tile. Damn it. He'd lost too much blood.

"Fine, but you need a doctor. Blackhawk Security keeps one on site." Dim lighting illuminated her face as she raised her phone to her ear, and he blinked against the sudden brightness of her phone's screen. Her exhale brushed across his neck as she smoothed her hand across his forehead. "Anthony, track my location. I need an evacuation. Adult male, gunshot wound to the left side. I can't stop the bleeding."

No emotion in her voice or on her expression. Too clinical. Too rational. That wasn't the woman he remembered. Or had the flashbacks of her been a lie all this time?

"ETA?" Kate nodded, that brilliant green gaze he'd

dreamed about for months centering on him. "See you in ten minutes."

"You never answered my question from before." He closed his eyes for a moment. Forget the bullet. There was only one thing that mattered. He leveraged his heels into the floor and forced himself to sit straighter against the front door. Pressure released on the wound, and he could breathe a bit easier. His fingertips tingled with the urge to touch her, but a hollowness had set up residence in his gut at the sound of her emotionless conversation with someone named Anthony. Maybe they hadn't been as close as he thought after all? Maybe he'd imagined everything. "Who am I to you?"

Kate wiped the back of her hand across her forehead again. A nervous habit?

"Everything that happened the night you died was my fault," she said. "I didn't take his threats seriously. I didn't think he'd—" The flashlight from her phone streaked across her face as she turned her phone over in her free hand. And there it was. A chink in that self-controlled armor. "My patient came to the house that night because you're—you *were*—my husband."

Chapter Two

Every wound had shaped her, forced her to become a stronger version of the woman she'd been before the ambush. No one was 100 percent safe. No matter how hard she tried—no matter how much she needed—to repress the fear, the uncertainty, it barged straight back into her life the moment that single bullet tore a hole through her husband's body.

Kate ran a hand through her hair as she paced Blackhawk Security's main hall for the tenth—or was it the eleventh?—time.

Declan's body. They weren't married anymore. Once he'd been declared dead, their marriage had ended, but she couldn't lose him. Not again. She'd barely survived the first time. Having him here, alive, almost well, had given her hope. She'd been alone for so long, broken for so long, she didn't know what to do now. Should she be in there with him, standing by his side as the doctor removed the bullet and stitched him up?

"Who shot at you tonight?" Anthony Harris, Blackhawk Security's weapons expert, had planted himself against a wall and watched her wear a path in the firm's brand-new carpet.

As a former Ranger, he only cared about one thing: protecting the people he cared about. Once upon a time, that short list had only included their team: Sullivan Bishop, founder and CEO of Blackhawk; Vincent Kalani, their forensics expert; Elizabeth Dawson headed network security; Elliot Dunham, the best private investigator and the reason she was standing here at all; and her.

But now, Anthony had a family. A wife, a son. Yet he'd come within minutes of Kate's evacuation request. He was reliable. Solid. And terrifying behind those aviator sunglasses he wore 24/7. She'd shut down the urge to profile her teammates, but she had read his file. Within moments of meeting him for the first time, she understood he strapped himself with as many weapons as he could because he feared losing his support system like he had in Afghanistan. War changed people—made them desperate—and Anthony hadn't been any different.

Kate slowed her pace, released the breath she'd been holding. Her scars burned, but the sensation was only in her head. She knew that. The adrenaline lingering in her veins from the situation—almost the exact same one she'd survived a year ago—was her brain's way of protecting her. Of sending up a warning. Besides, it'd been months since her last surgery, and scar tissue lacked nerve cells. She wasn't supposed to feel anything.

She studied the small window in the door leading to

the firm's medical suite, and her insides tightened. She wasn't supposed to feel at all.

"I have no idea who pulled the trigger tonight." The shooting couldn't have been a coincidence. The chances both she and Declan would be in that house again, at the same time… There were too many variables to calculate. Especially given that Declan Monroe had legally died over a year ago. Had he been waiting for her to show? Brian Michaels, her patient who destroyed everything she'd known in the span of a minute, was still behind bars. Whoever had shot at them tonight couldn't have been him. Why come after her now? Or had she been the target at all?

"Take it easy on the carpet, Doc." Anthony pushed off the wall, hands dropping to his sides for better access to his arsenal if necessary. "Sullivan will kill you if he has to pay to replace it twice in two months."

Right. The bomb meant for their network security analyst had wiped out this entire floor two months ago. Was that her teammate's way of telling her they were never safe, even in the most protected and secure building in Anchorage?

Blackhawk Security employed the finest security experts in the world. She and her team provided personal protection, private investigating, logistical support to the US government, profiling and personal recovery. Whatever their client needed, they delivered. They did it all, and they did a good job. If the shooter had been targeting her, he'd be insane to try here.

Kate slowed her pacing, fingers tightening into fists. She was losing her mind. She was better than this. She'd been a psychologist. She'd struggled through months of grief by shutting everything down, ignored her instinctual drives, repressed the anger and hurt. What was wrong with her now? What had changed?

The door to the medical suite swung open.

Declan stood in the frame, those familiar blue eyes locking on her as he placed his hand over the new hole in his T-shirt, and everything went quiet.

The tension in her chest eased, and she stood a bit straighter. Right. Declan Monroe hadn't died after all. He'd cheated death. Twice. She took a single step toward him, caught in the gravitational pull she'd never been able to resist.

"Don't take too long, Doc. Everyone's waiting for you." Anthony crossed the waiting area filled with comfortable chairs and an empty receptionist's desk to the large oak doors of the main conference room. Swinging them open, he didn't wait for her before heading inside.

Leaving her and Declan alone.

She tamped down the anxiety clawing up her throat. "How's your side—"

"This is where you work." The smile she'd dreamed of seeing again flashed wide, hiking her blood pressure higher. So easygoing but gut-wrenching at the same time. "Good as new," he said. "Thanks."

"Good." Nodding, Kate rolled her bottom lip into her mouth and bit down, a nervous habit she'd picked up to distract herself when reality crept in. Which happened all too often. She scratched at the back of her neck in another attempt to lock it out. What was she supposed to say to the man who'd supposedly died because she failed to recognize the warning signs in her own patient? "Tell me where the hell you've been. Because none of this makes sense."

The words slipped out. She clenched her fists to ease the stress that had been building since Elliot had given her the photo of Declan in downtown Anchorage a month ago.

The stubble along his jawline shifted as he ran his hand over his face. Closing the distance between them, he heightened her awareness of him with every step. "Not much to tell. I woke up in a hospital alone. I didn't know where I was or what had happened. Who I was. I could barely move because of the pain in my chest, and no matter how hard I tried... I couldn't remember anything."

She held her breath as he raised one hand toward her face. This wasn't real. Soon she'd wake up, realize she'd been living a beautiful nightmare, and the grief would crush her again. But then he touched her. Her eyes drifted closed as he framed her face, and she leaned into his warmth. Wrapping her hand around his, she forced herself to look at him. To learn his face all over again.

"I remembered you for the first time three weeks after I left the hospital, and I knew I had to find you." Declan brushed his thumb across her cheek. Too soon, he pulled away, taking his body heat with him, and the brightness in his gaze dimmed. "I remembered other things, too. Bits and pieces. But nothing that explained how I ended up shot."

"You don't remember anything before waking up in

the hospital?" Her mouth dried. Retrograde amnesia. Partial or total loss of every memory he'd ever lived. She'd studied cases back in her doctoral program at University of Oregon, but never imagined she'd be involved in the real-life nightmare that came with the condition. But he hadn't sustained any head or brain injuries as far as she knew during the shooting. Which suggested trauma. His brain had blocked the incident as a way of protecting itself. "Your parents, your work, your favorite food?"

"Nothing. Guess that means I have a lot to catch up on." His attention drifted to the top of her shirt collar, to the largest of her scars. Declan's voice turned to gravel. "Your scar looks like mine. How many bullets did they pull from you?"

She gave in to the urge to cover up, rubbing the fabric of her shirt collar between her fingers. They were a reminder of the worst night of her life, the onset of a lifetime of pain and grief, a kind of death sentence that she'd go through the rest of her life alone.

But he wasn't dead. He was here.

His condition might let up. She'd have to dig into her research, call a former colleague to be sure, but he might remember the life they had together, the years they'd spent together. Hope spread hard and fast, and Kate gave in for just a moment. To remember what it felt like.

Bullets. He'd asked about bullets. "Three."

"They catch the bastard who did it? Your patient." The blue in his eyes turned to ice, the tendons between his neck and shoulder visibly tightening. Her insides went cold, her instincts on alert. The man she'd married—the one she'd built an entire life with—had never shown signs of aggression in front of her, despite it being a large part of his job inside the FBI's serial crime unit. So who exactly had come back from the dead? Her husband or somebody else entirely?

"My teammate, Elliot, found him a few weeks after I started working for Blackhawk Security. Nearly six months after the shooting. He's one of those people who likes to know everything there is to know about the people he works with, and I wasn't an exception."

She slipped her hands into her cargo jacket—no, *his* jacket—pockets, but the guilt she'd shouldered only weighed heavier in her stomach. She'd done this to him—to them. She'd been so blinded by her own personal life, she hadn't seen what was happening right in front of her. How many other patients had she failed? How many lives had been changed due to her negligence?

"Brian Michaels had been off his medication for a few months. Toxicology screen came back for additional medication I wasn't aware he'd been taking. The steroids only increased his aggressive behavior to the point…" She didn't need to tell Declan the results. He'd lived them, same as her. "He's in a psychiatric ward here in the city. Sentenced to twenty years for murder."

"If he's locked up, then who do I have to thank for a bullet in my side tonight?" Declan asked.

"I don't know." Kate turned toward the conference room door and the entire Blackhawk Security team waiting for her briefing. She'd almost lost him—

again—but this time would be different. Wrenching the large oak door open, she leveled her chin, more determined than she'd been in months. Whatever didn't kill her this time had better run. "Let's find out."

"LOOKS LIKE WE'VE got a new case." A heavily muscled man seated at the head of the table stood. "Sullivan Bishop. I run the place." He closed in on them, hand extended.

Shaking his hand, Declan noticed the guy moved with measured strength, and if Declan had to guess, the founder of Blackhawk Security was former military. The dirt under Sullivan's nails said this definitely wasn't a man who sat behind the desk while his team ran cases he wasn't willing to get his hands dirty with first.

"You've already met Anthony." Sullivan acknowledged the silent and armed weapons expert standing against one wall. "Elizabeth Dawson is our network security analyst."

A dark-haired woman with a heart-shaped face and leather jacket nodded.

"Vincent Kalani runs forensics." Pointing to the massive wall of muscle on the other side of Kate, Sullivan took his seat. Long black hair brushed across the guy's shoulders, an overgrown beard hiding his expression. "And Elliot Dunham here is the one who discovered you're still alive."

"Welcome back to the land of the living." Elliot extended two fingers in a wave, one foot stacked over the opposite knee. Storm-gray eyes zeroed in on Declan, making the hairs on the back of his neck stand on end.

The guy was studying him. Every move. Every word out of his mouth. Looking for secrets? Something to use? Declan checked his expression. Not happening.

"Kate's already given us a briefing on your death," Sullivan said. "Why don't you fill us in on the rest, so we can find the bastard who took a shot at my profiler tonight, Mr. Monroe?"

Declan took a seat at the large conference table with one hand positioned over the bullet hole in his side. A vast view of the Chugach mountain range was visible through the span of windows behind Sullivan Bishop. Funny how Declan could name each peak along the range but couldn't remember his own damn name, where he'd worked before waking up in the hospital or the fact he'd been married. His senses automatically settled on the woman sitting beside him. His wife. Hell, were they even still married since he'd been declared dead?

He studied the rest of the team, the weight of their attention settling on him. "What do you want to know?"

"Where'd you go after you left Providence Alaska Medical Center?" Elizabeth leaned forward in her chair, her chocolate-brown gaze flickering to Kate for a moment before she refocused on him. The laptop in front of her highlighted the dark circles beneath her eyes, the softness around her middle exaggerated by a too-large maternity shirt. New mother.

"Brother Francis Shelter." He pressed his back into his chair, stretching the brand-new stitches in his side, and braced against the table. "It's not much, but I get a hot meal every night, a place to sleep, and they don't ask questions I can't answer."

There was a soft gasp from Kate as she massaged the thin skin of her left temple.

"Anyone ever follow you, or you get the feeling you were being watched?" This one from the one Sullivan had called Vincent. Based on his line of questioning, Declan pegged him as former law enforcement. A cop? Federal agent? The tattoos climbing up the guy's neck had already started showing their age. All done at the same time. Declan guessed four, five years max, but Blackhawk was fairly new, and no cop would be able to get away with ink like that unless it'd been part of a cover identity. Undercover work then.

About two months after regaining consciousness, Declan had started picking up on those kinds of details. Small things at first. The small amount of mud on the shoes of one of the shelter's other residents. The way the same man had disappeared when Anchorage PD had cleared out Buffer Park for the night. Almost as if Declan had been drawn to the guy's activities. But there'd never been a point where he'd picked up on being watched. Nobody had followed him to that house tonight, either. He was sure of it. "No. Never."

"What about your consulting case, Kate?" Sullivan landed an assessing gaze on his profiler, fingers tapping on the gleaming surface of the table. "Or any of your other cases where someone might've left unhappy?"

"Anchorage PD and the FBI only brought me in this morning to run a profile for a serial murder case. There hasn't been time for me to make any conclusions or to

connect me with the investigation." There was little in-
flection in Kate's voice, as though she were a woman
dictating her grocery list into her phone instead of a
woman who'd nearly been shot a couple hours ago.
Shifting in her seat, she cast her gaze to the paperwork
set before her. "Given the fact I resemble all three of
the case's victims, a connection isn't impossible, but the
killer's MO includes an arrow and crossbow. No guns."

Every cell in Declan's body caught fire. She was
the possible target of a serial killer? He set his teeth
against the rising flood of possession. This was her
job, and from what he'd gathered from her notes back
at the house, she was damn good at it. Despite the fact
they'd been married, he was sitting next to a stranger
thanks to some dramatic event he couldn't remember.
He had no claim on her safety, but he would find the
bastard who'd tried to hurt her. With or without Blackhawk Security's help.

"Is Michaels still behind bars?" Sullivan asked. "He's
already proven this kind of thing is right up his alley."

"Yes, as far as I know." Kate's hand constricted
around the arm of her chair, her knuckles white against
the coffee-colored leather.

"Liz, let's follow up with Corrections," Sullivan said.
"Michaels has family, friends. One of them might not
have been too happy about the way his case was handled."

"On it." Elizabeth made a note on the small notepad
beside her. "Shouldn't take too long."

An automatic response had Declan interlacing his
fingers between Kate's. Some part of him deep down

considered her well-being more important than his own. Or was his body's response an attempt to recover even just a sliver of the memories he'd lost by physically connecting with the one person it recognized the most? A war had already erupted inside of him. Between his irrational urge to protect the wife he'd left behind, the compulsion to make her shooter pay and the need to uncover his past, Declan had to make a choice. "What about me? Could there be a threat from the time before I woke up in the hospital? Something to do with my job or family member?

Kate pulled her hand back, setting it in her lap.

Surprise infiltrated through the wall of certainty he'd built.

"Now there's where things get interesting," Elliot said. "I mean, aside from the fact your surgeon apparently tried to pass off a body in the hospital morgue as you to avoid having to answer for his patient suddenly missing from his hospital bed." He slid a file folder across the table. "Which I have him admitting to on audio, by the way. That guy isn't going to be cutting anyone open anytime soon."

Declan caught the folder before it dove off the edge, his name clearly on the tab's label. He'd run from the hospital so fast, he hadn't thought to read the patient chart in his room. For the past year, he'd assumed a different name, guessed at his age and birth date and had been searching records every week for a lead. His first instinct had been to run. He didn't know why. Only remembered the need to get as far from the hospital as possible. But this file… He had the answers he'd been looking for right in his hand.

Flipping open the cover, he skimmed the first page. "I worked with the FBI's Behavioral Analysis Unit for eight years. In their serial crime division. Special Agent Declan Monroe." A copy of his federal ID was right there in full color.

He studied Kate's expression, but she'd shut him out, intent on the design etched into the massive conference table. A profiler and a special agent who hunted criminals. Was it their work that had brought them together in the first place?

He scanned the list of his recent cases, but nothing stood out or jump-started another memory. "I don't recognize any of these old cases."

"But the perps might recognize you," Sullivan said. "Liz, get an update on Special Agent Monroe's past cases with the FBI, too. See if one of the suspects has been holding on to a grudge, and we'll work from there. The sooner the better."

"You got it." Elizabeth nodded, then stood, taking her laptop with her.

She wouldn't be the only one going through those cases. Declan's grip tightened on the stack of papers inside his file. Elliot had dug up the past, but this was Declan's job. *His* marriage. *His* life. He'd do whatever it took to get it back.

"Vincent, go back to Kate's house and dig as many bullets out of those walls as it takes to see if we can get a print, a ballistics match or anything to identify the shooter." Sullivan rounded the table as the forensics expert stood and followed Elizabeth out the door. "Anthony, tag along with Vincent in case the shooter gets an itch to finish the job. Elliot, you're on Kate's cases. I want to know if any of our current or past clients have had a problem with her since she came back from leave."

Came back from leave? Confusion rippled through Declan, which was common these days. He hauled himself to his feet as the meeting had obviously concluded. There had to be someone—other agents he'd worked with, a boss, a partner—who'd help him get his hands on his old case files.

"I admire you, Kate." Elliot straightened, nodding with a closemouthed smile. He rolled back his shoulder as though his muscles had stiffened up. "Took you two full weeks to get someone to start shooting at you. That's longer than I've gone."

"Thanks, Elliot. My client files are in my office." Kate stood, expression guarded. She pushed her chair back into the table without a single glance in Declan's direction. She nodded. "I need to start my profile on the FBI's serial case and check in with Special Agent Dominic."

Declan scrubbed his hand down his face. Name didn't ring a bell. Although, if Special Agent Dominic was working out of the Anchorage field office, he might've been one of Declan's peers before he "died." Dominic could have information relevant to tonight's shooting.

The oak doors swung open, and Elizabeth was there with her laptop balanced on her forearm. Chocolate-brown eyes wide, she shifted her attention from Declan to Kate, then onto her boss. "You wanted me to see if a family member or friend of Michaels might be holding a grudge. Well, I didn't get that far."

The network security analyst turned her laptop toward them, the photo of an older man, Caucasian with graying hair and puffy cheeks, on the screen. "Michaels was released from Holding three weeks ago due to overcrowding."

Chapter Three

Aware of the sweat that had broken out along her spine, Kate tried to swallow the sour taste of fear. She gripped the edge of her desk as hard as she could, supplying physical input to her muscles in an attempt to wrap her head around the news.

She'd taken refuge in her office. A few minutes to herself, that was all she needed, to get back the small bit of control she'd held on to these last couple weeks. She shook her head with a burst of disbelief. Control. Just a figment of her imagination.

Brian Michaels, her former patient who'd grown obsessed with having her for himself, had been released from prison. It wasn't supposed to be this way. He'd taken everything from her, and he was supposed to suffer for it.

"Michaels is never going to hurt you again, Kate." Declan slipped into her peripheral vision without warning. Soundless. He the predator, her the prey. The single lesson that'd been hammered into her brain over and over throughout her profiling years: behavior reflected personality. Declan's new behavior—the aggressive, sarcastic, seemingly unfazed kind—reflected a far different personality than the one she'd known.

His tone dipped into dangerous territory, raising the hairs on the back of her neck. "Or he'll die trying."

Overlaying her fear was a deep, deep anger. Anger at Michaels. For his release. For the shooter who'd put a bullet in Declan's side tonight. For the fact that no matter how hard she'd tried to blind herself from the truth the last few hours, the nagging feeling in her gut wouldn't disappear.

Kate raised her gaze to his, the bones in her fingers screaming for release. The man standing in front of her wasn't her husband. Same features, same body, same color hair. But the hardness in those brilliant blue eyes when he looked at her revealed Declan—*her* Declan— had died that night a year ago.

She forced her fingers to release the desk. "What's your name?"

"The federal ID in my file says Declan Monroe." That damn smile attempted to cool the burn blazing through her as he shoved his hands into his jeans pockets. "But I have the feeling you already knew that."

A humorless laugh escaped her throat as she closed Michaels's file and pushed it to the side of her desk. She wouldn't show weakness. Not now. Not ever. As far as anyone knew, she was emotionless, and she'd keep it that way. It'd been the most effective buffer for pain thus far. "I meant the name you've been using. What do you want me to call you?"

"I adopted a name after I left the hospital." His expression softened. "But Declan is fine. That's who I am, right? Gotta get used to it."

"Right." She nodded. Reaching across the desk, she gathered her client files to hand over to Elliot. Investigating her clients wouldn't do Blackhawk's private investigator any good. With Michaels's release, Kate had a pretty good idea where to look to find the shooter. After all, it was like Sullivan had said in the conference room: Michaels, who'd turned her life upside down once, had already shown a preference for guns.

She would help her team and Anchorage PD find the shooter. Then she'd get Declan the help he needed to move on with his life. Without her.

"I've already done the background check on Michaels," she said. "His sister is the only family he has left. He's probably hiding out at her property."

"Kate." Declan set his hand on top of hers holding the file, and an unfamiliar electric surge bolted up her arm.

Kate pushed away from the desk, knocking into her chair as oxygen left her lungs. The chair's wheels protested against the hard plastic beneath it, and she shot one hand behind her to catch herself from hitting the floor. Her throat swelled in an instant as she struggled to keep her balance. "Don't." She forced herself to take a deep, calming breath. "Please, don't."

"I'm sorry." Palms raised in surrender, he backed away from the desk. "I didn't mean to hurt you—"

"You didn't." She struggled to keep her expression neutral. She'd overreacted, but just as she'd discovered in the conference room when he'd reached for her hand, when he touched her, she hurt.

More than the bullet wounds. More than the grief burrowing a hole through her entire being. She'd prayed for nothing over the last year but to have her husband back, but the reality of it was he hadn't come back. He might be standing in front of her, but he didn't know her, didn't remember their marriage, didn't know the green cargo jacket she wore every day actually belonged to him. Or that she'd finally had the guts to take off her wedding ring when she came back to work two weeks ago. Giving in to those innocent touches, of letting hope that he'd remember everything between them drown out the pain, was a risk she wasn't willing to take.

Swiping a stray hair out of her face, she collected Michaels's file once again. She cleared her throat. "The shelter probably isn't safe anymore. Is there anywhere else you can go tonight?"

"I'm not leaving you." Declan came around the desk. His hand rose, but he didn't touch her. He was too close, but she fought the urge to pull away again. To prove he didn't affect her—nothing did. "Tell me what the hell just happened."

She was suddenly far too aware of his proximity, and her breath came a bit faster. His clean, masculine scent worked deep in her lungs, and her stomach twisted.

She gave in to her instinctual urge and tugged away, needing space between them. A lot of it. She lifted her chin. No point in keeping the truth from him. Didn't matter if he was the man she'd married or not. They'd be working this investigation together. "You're not him."

Saying the words made them real, made the ache behind her rib cage hurt a bit more.

"Your husband." Declan backed off, taking his body heat with him. A coldness ran through her as he seemed to sink in on himself. He scrubbed a hand over his five o'clock shadow, the bristling loud in her ears. "And here I thought getting shot in the gut was the worst that could happen to me today. If I'm not him, then who am I?"

"No." She blinked to clear her head, palms pressed together in front of her as she closed the distance between them. "I mean, you *are* him. You have his eyes. You have the same scar on your hand he got falling off his bike when he was ten and the dimple on the right side of your mouth. But you're—"

"Different?" Declan studied her office, but she got the sense it was more out of distraction than pure curiosity over how she'd decorated the space. "I read that could happen. Personality changes. Guess I didn't think much of it since I can't remember who I was from before."

The realization sat in her stomach like a rock. The small bit of air she'd been holding on to burned as it escaped up her throat. How could she have been so careless? He'd been through hell, too, if not worse. At least she'd been able to hold on to the memories of him. He... he had nothing. She had to remember that. "I'm sorry. I didn't mean... None of this is your fault. I—"

Commotion—yelling—reached her ears from outside her office.

"Kate!" a male voice yelled.

Recognition flared.

"Ryan?" Kate walked out from behind her desk, fully aware of her arm brushing against Declan's as she passed and wrenched open the door. The weight of Declan's gaze settled between her shoulder blades as a wall of black and white filled her vision.

Due to his six-foot-four height, she craned her head back to look up at Special Agent Ryan Dominic. Studying the hallway past his mountainous shoulder, she spotted both Anthony and Vincent as well as Dominic's partner, Kenneth Winter, waiting for her to raise the alarm. "What are you doing here? I got pulled onto your case this morning. I haven't started—"

"You weren't answering your phone." Ryan stared down at her with the darkest eyes she'd ever seen. Brown, almost black, but it was the control he kept over his expression that struck fear into the hearts of the violent offenders he hunted for the Bureau's Behavior Analysis Unit. Absolutely deadly. Made him one of the best agents on the government's payroll with higher arrest rates than any other agent. That technique had given him a nickname nobody dared say to his face. He was a good agent. A good friend, one she'd relied on since that dreadful night. She'd lost her husband in the shooting. He'd lost his partner.

"I had to hear about the shooting at your house from Anchorage PD." Dominic set both hands on her shoulders. "I came as soon as I could to make sure you were still alive. Why didn't you call me?"

"Good to see you again, Kate." Special Agent Kenneth Winter, in all his uptight glory, nodded around his partner's shoulder. He had medium length brown hair, thick eyebrows and steely brown eyes close to Dominic's in color. She didn't know Kenneth as well as his partner, but if the rumors she'd heard were true, Ryan had himself a go-getter on his team. Desperate to prove himself and to climb the internal ladder, Kenneth lobbied for the most violent and taxing cases. Usually with success. "This seems personal. I'm going to find a vending machine until you get your stuff sorted out."

"Thanks, Kenneth. It's fine, guys. I can take it from here." She waved toward Anthony and Vincent to take the physical tension filling the room down a notch. Pulling Dominic into her office, she closed the door behind him. "I'm alive and the team is running down leads with Anchorage PD as we speak. You didn't have to—"

"You're going to want to back away, friend." Declan moved beside her. If he'd had fur, his hackles would be raised.

It seemed every muscle Dominic owned stiffened. His hands curled into fists at his side. The special agent took a single step forward as he studied his former partner. "I don't believe it."

Declan watched every move Dominic made, blue eyes creasing at the edges like the investigator she remembered hunched over the dining room table, working his way through his most recent case.

"Right. Declan, this is Special Agent Ryan Dominic of the FBI's Behavioral Analysis Unit." She set her hand on his shoulder, throttling the warmth settling deep into her bones from the contact. "Your former partner."

PARTNER? THE AGENT standing in front of him sure didn't feel like a partner.

Declan eyed the Glock Dominic kept in the shoulder holster beneath that perfectly pressed suit. He didn't have any idea how he knew the agent's choice of service weapon, but the information was there, in the back of his head. Dominic worked for the FBI. Given the file on Declan's life, it stood to reason they'd met, but Dominic's body language said it wasn't a friendly relationship. Let alone a partnership. "You know me?"

Confusion cracked that carefully controlled expression, and the stiffness between the agent's shoulders and neck disappeared. Dominic widened his stance, hands on his hips. Close enough if he had to reach for his weapon. He brushed his jacket out enough for Declan to get a peek at his service weapon. A Glock. "I sure as hell hope so. We were partners for six years. Is this a joke?"

"No," Kate said. Her light vanilla scent clung to him, to his clothes, his skin, threatened to drag him deeper into the past his brain had barred him from remembering. The burn of her hand on his arm grounded him, kept him in the moment, but then it was gone. Again. He didn't blame her. She'd made it clear before the FBI had walked through her door. He wasn't her husband. At least, not the one she'd been expecting to come walking back into her life from the grave. "Ryan, Declan doesn't remember anything before the shooting. The trauma erased his memories."

"What?" A disbelieving laugh broke through the special agent's control but was gone faster than it appeared. Dominic ran a hand down his face and the stubble along his squared jawline. A hint of Latino heritage gave him the dark hair and eyes, but Declan pegged the agent as local from his accent. "They said you were dead. The FBI buried you, and all this time you've, what, been walking around Anchorage without any idea of who you are? Whose body is in your grave?"

"We don't know. The surgeon obviously has some explaining to do, but that about sums it up, yeah." They were wasting time here. The shooter could've already started planning another attempt on Kate's life. Could already be on the way to Blackhawk Security. Although getting through the front doors might take a small army considering how many armed operatives and security measures Declan had noted coming in, but he wasn't willing to take the chance. Not with the only lead he had to restoring his memory.

"This is unbelievable," Dominic said. "What do you remember then?"

"Ryan, it's a long story, and I promise I will explain it all later." Kate swiped the file from the edge of her desk and handed it to Dominic. "Right now, we need to find Brian Michaels and interrogate him about the shooting tonight. If he's off his meds again, I don't want him hurting anyone else. Can you pull some strings? Help us out?"

Ryan. Not Special Agent Dominic. Kate and his former partner were familiar with each other. Explained why the agent had touched her as soon as she opened the door. Declan locked his jaw against the unfamiliar rush of jealousy ripping through his chest. Exactly how close had his wife and Dominic gotten when he died?

"Michaels is out? This day keeps getting better and better." Dominic flipped through the file. "All right,

I'll help you track down your shooter, but in the meantime, I'm getting you into a safe house. From this moment on, you're officially in protective custody." That dark gaze flickered to Declan as Dominic handed the folder back to Kate. "If Michaels is responsible for the shooting tonight, there's a chance he'll keep trying until he gets what he wants. As far as we know, that's you, and I'm not going to let him shoot at you a third time."

"The FBI can't protect her." Declan closed the distance between him and Kate, a possessiveness bubbling beneath the surface. Kate had escaped a killer twice. The odds of her surviving another attempt, even while in FBI custody, went down with every second the bastard was out there. Serial offenders only got better at what they did. They learned from experience, and the shooter wouldn't stop unless he was caught or killed. "I can."

Dominic folded his arms, stance wide. "You can't be serious. You just said you can't remember anything—"

"I'm not going into hiding," Kate said, "and I'm not going into protective custody. I can protect myself, or have you both forgotten who I work for?" She tilted her chin higher, Michaels's file in her hand.

In that instant, Declan had no doubt the woman standing in front of him could give the shooter a run for his money. Not just physically but mentally, and for an instant, he sensed exactly why he'd married her in the first place. Profilers were known to put themselves inside the heads of the criminals they hunted, and that meant knowing how the suspect would think, act and what their next step would be before they made a conscious decision.

Dominic lowered his hands to his sides, took a step toward her. "Kate—"

"I'll have my profile on your serial case ready as soon as I can, Special Agent Dominic." She motioned him to the door. "Until then, thank you for helping find Michaels. I appreciate it."

Dominic's nut-brown eyes darted to Declan again. Dropping his voice, the special agent leaned closer to Kate, making Declan's blood boil. "You're making a mistake. Call me when you realize that."

Kate didn't respond as Dominic wrenched open the office door and disappeared down the hall. Tension visibly drained from her as she faced Declan, but the exhaustion etched into her features didn't lessen. "He's not going to look for Michaels," she said. "My case doesn't come with an honorary award like the Hunter's does if he solves it."

The Hunter. Was that the serial case the FBI had brought her in to profile? According to news reports, three women had disappeared over the last year, their bodies found in the middle of the woods around Anchorage with a single arrow shot to the heart. All blonde. All athletic and in great shape. Similar to the woman standing less than two feet from him. "You seem sure of that."

"There isn't enough room in Ryan's life for friends *and* his ego. He'll work the Hunter case and leave Blackhawk to find our shooter." She studied him. "You want to know how close we are. Your former partner and your wife."

Had she read his thoughts or was his face just that easy to read? "It crossed my mind."

"We're friends. Nothing more. He brought dinners after I was released from the hospital, helped me arrange your funeral so I didn't have to. Like I said, Ryan doesn't have room for real relationships. He uses people to get what he wants, which usually involves a case he's working," she said.

Declan didn't have any right to ask, but the words clawed up his throat anyway. "Has there been anyone else?"

Her bottom lip parted from the top. "Are you asking because you're worried it will affect our investigation into the shooter or because you were my husband in a former life?"

"I shouldn't have asked." Taking Michaels's file from her hand, he headed for the door.

"After you died, I used to talk to you. Like you were still around," she said.

Her voice slowed his escape, prickling goose bumps along his arms. The pain in his side evaporated as he slowly turned back to face her.

A humorless laugh bubbled past her lips. "It sounds insane. I buried you. I knew you weren't coming back, but a part of me still held on to hope. Still prayed day after day to some greater power that the shooting, losing you, had all been some sick nightmare I'd wake up from any moment. But the months went by—a year— and I never woke up."

Declan couldn't move, couldn't think. He worked to swallow the tightness in his throat, but the anguish in her expression held him frozen. If she'd sought comfort in another man's arms, he had no logical reason to give in to the unexplained jealousy simmering in his veins. He couldn't remember their marriage, had only glimpses of her in his memories. That wasn't why he'd come back into her life.

He took a step toward her. "Kate—"

"I took my wedding ring off two weeks ago, Declan. There hasn't been anyone else, but I moved on." She massaged the line of lightened skin around her ring finger as she stared down at her hand. Lifting her chin, she lowered her hands to her sides and locked out the emotion that'd been there a few moments ago. "We'll find Michaels or whoever took those shots at us tonight. I'll help you get your life back, but after that, I think it's best we go our separate ways."

An invisible fist clenched inside his gut. Get his life back. What the hell did that even mean? He'd spent the last year in a shelter, digging into as many records as he could find to uncover his past without any luck.

According to the few legal documents he'd read in Blackhawk Security's file on him—combined with the handful of memories his brain had decided to vomit at random intervals—his life was standing on the other side of that desk. Kate Monroe was the key to his past, the only person who knew him before he'd woken up in a hospital bed. His likes, dislikes, if his parents were still alive, if he had siblings, the sources of his scars, how he'd chosen a career hunting criminals, if he'd been a good man, a good husband. A father?

"I understand." A lie. He didn't. The few glimpses of memory he'd had of her had seemed happy enough. Her smiling as he came home, the echo of her laughter as they made a batch of vanilla cupcakes together and the flour had gotten on her nose and cheeks.

All of those memories combined had given him a mere fraction of the emotion burning through him now. This woman had been ingrained so deep in his neural pathways, not even amnesia had been able to force him to forget her. There had to be a reason.

Declan took in the lack of photos on her desk and forced himself to nod. He'd sure as hell find out why. "Lead the way."

Chapter Four

Her hand hovered above the dead bolt to her apartment. She'd never brought anyone here. Not the team. Not anyone, but bringing Declan here seemed too…intimate. As though she were inviting him into her life. But he'd been a large part of her life, part of her, too.

Kate shoved the key into the lock and twisted. Automatically reaching for the light beside the door, she braced for his reaction.

Stark white walls and furniture, no personal effects, packing boxes everywhere. It'd been nine months since she'd moved in, but the thought of making it permanent had almost been too much. The two-bedroom, two-bath high-rise apartment had gotten her as far across the city as she could get and still stay within range for the team if they needed her.

Beautiful mountain views commanded attention through the wall of ceiling-to-floor windows. The sun had yet to come up, so only the twinkling lights of Anchorage were visible from here. But in a few hours, red, pinks and yellows would crest over the peaks and light up this entire room. She'd never missed a sunrise in this apartment, in love with the idea of starting a new day, a new life. Then again, sunrises were hard to miss when she spent most of the night awake anyway.

He couldn't go back to the shelter, and the thought of getting him a hotel room for the night while there was a shooter on the loose pooled dread at the base of her spine. At least here, she could protect him. Kate tossed her keys onto the small table near the door as Declan stepped inside.

Stress lines, deeper than she remembered, etched across his face. He'd spent the last year in a shelter. Hadn't really known much else since losing his memories. She couldn't imagine the thoughts running through his head right now. In the past three hours alone, he'd inexplicably been drawn to a house he'd never consciously stepped foot inside, gotten shot, discovered he'd been married and met a partner he hadn't known existed. The brain could only take so much before it cracked. She understood that from experience.

"I think I have a box of your old clothes in my bedroom closet," she said. "Feel free to clean up while I look for it, and then I can make us something to eat."

"That sounds great." He studied the space, nodding, then headed toward the hallway off to the left with a backpack in tow. "Thank you."

She heard the bathroom door close, but instead of the stiffness draining from her neck and shoulders, Kate let herself slip down the wall and onto the floor.

For the first time since she'd seen him back in their old house, reality set in. Declan was here. Against all odds, he'd survived, and the breath rushed out of her.

The floor sucked at her, urging her to sink heavier into its supportive cradle, but the blood from Declan's wound had destroyed his clothes. Unless he felt comfortable walking around completely naked, she had to get up, had to find that last box full of his things she'd held on to.

Kate tapped the crown of her head against the door. "Can't stop now, Monroe."

The rain-like fall of shower water hitting tile grew louder down the hall as the bathroom door swung open. Pressure built in her chest as Declan appeared in nothing but a towel wrapped around his lean waist. Concern etched his expression as he caught sight of her on the floor, but she didn't have the strength to move. His dirty blond hair was thick and mussed as though he'd run his fingers through it. His mouth, full and sensual, pressed into a thin line. "Kate."

"I'm fine. I'm just…tired." The confession barely escaped her lips. These last few hours had ripped apart everything she'd worked for over the past year. She'd fought to control the anger pent up at having him taken away, she'd thrown herself into work in an attempt to distract herself, convinced herself she was finally moving on. She'd taken her wedding ring off before coming back to work for Blackhawk Security, but the truth was, she still kept it close.

Diving one hand into her jacket pocket, she showed him the thin gold band. She studied the inscription on the inside, their wedding date. "I thought taking this off would make it easier, but my finger feels naked without it. I feel unconnected." She closed her eyes. What she wouldn't give for a full night's sleep. "That doesn't even make any sense."

"It doesn't have to." Declan came toward her, his bare feet padding across the hardwood floor, and she couldn't help but admire the view. Wide, muscled shoulders, the ridges and valleys of his six-pack, the outline of powerful thighs through the towel.

Lowering to sit down beside her, he chased the cold from her bones as he brushed against her. "You don't have to control anything. Not with me. You've been through hell as much as I have. You want to yell, cry, punch me in the face, hate me for coming back into your life? Do it. Do whatever you have to to work through this. Suffering in silence will only tear you apart."

A small laugh burst from her chest. "Repressing things is one of my favorite hobbies."

When they were married, she'd kept it all bottled up. To the point she didn't know whether she truly was experiencing emotion or if she only thought she should. She still didn't know sometimes. Declan had dealt with so much pain, so much sorrow on the job hunting the monsters, she hadn't wanted to add to any of it. Their marriage had depended on it. She had to stay strong, be there for him when he'd needed it the most, but that left no one there for her.

"Not anymore." Declan raised his hand, fingers sliding through a strand of hair that had fallen loose from her bun. He studied her from forehead to chin.

What did he see? How empty she'd become since his death? How much she'd missed him? How it took every ounce of control she possessed not to compare the man in front of her with her husband? She gave in to the way his dimple only showed up when he smiled at her, the way the scar on the tip of his left middle finger glided across her jaw.

"I'm starting to see why you're the only one I remember," he said.

The flood of pain and repression broke through the dam she'd built over the past few months. Her control vanished as he leaned into her, setting his lips against hers.

Warmth snaked through her. Every cell in her body intensified in awareness as he framed her face between his large hands. Her heart was beating too fast, all the blood rushing to her head. His scent filled her system. Everything that had happened over the past year vanished as he deepened the kiss. The blood, the horror, the mystery behind the why. With him, right here in this moment, she let it go—all of it. And she'd never felt so free in her life.

A small moan escaped her mouth as he pulled her close, close enough her body pressed against the hard, muscled heat of his chest.

Kate fisted one hand low in his hair as pure need clawed through her. It'd been too long since she'd let someone touch her, care for her, hold her...she'd forgotten what it felt like.

He gripped his hand higher up on her arm, and she flinched as pain zinged down to her fingers.

"What is it?" he asked.

She pulled back, pulling her arm free of his hold. Studying the small hole in the arm of her cargo jacket,

Kate sat back on her rear end. She pulled her sleeve to center the hole and studied the light ring of blood.

A bullet hole?

She'd been running off pure adrenaline, trying to catch up with the new reality that had crashed through her world in the past few hours. She hadn't noticed the burn of a bullet graze across her arm. "I literally didn't know that was there until this moment."

"What?" Declan surged to his knees, concern clear in his voice. His hand wrapped around her arm, careful to avoid the wound as he studied it closer. Violence gleamed in the sea-blue depths of his eyes. "That SOB is going to pay. Here, take off your jacket. Let me see how bad it is."

Kate diverted her attention to the hardwood floor as his towel shifted, and she pressed herself flat against the wall. She'd seen her husband naked countless times, but this...this was different. "That's okay. I just realized how very naked you are."

Declan glanced down, righted the towel with a hint of pink climbing up his neck and into his face. Nice to know there were still some things that could get to him. "Right. Okay, first, clothes, then we'll have a look at that wound."

"I'm fine." She'd recovered from far worse injuries. A bullet graze was nothing compared to the three rounds she'd taken in the past. "Go. Finish your shower. Nothing I haven't handled before, remember? I can—"

"Let me." His fingers brushed over her arm, raising goose bumps even through the thick fabric of her jacket. "Please."

A tugging at the base of her spine had her nodding at his request. He looked at her as though he needed to do this for her, as though he needed to make up for something. Which didn't make sense. None of this— the shooting tonight, the amnesia, the fact she'd been grazed—was his fault. He was just as much a victim as she'd been.

Kate settled her hand in her lap. She hadn't been fully hit. The wound wasn't bleeding anymore. Shouldn't be too hard to apply some ointment and bandage the area. "Okay."

"Don't move. I'll be right back." Declan straightened, disappearing down the hallway. The bathroom door clicked once more, and the flood of heat he'd generated inside of her drained.

Shoving to her feet, she cringed against the now constant pain burning down her arm and headed toward her office. Saved by a bullet. How original. What had she been thinking, kissing him? How had she given up control so easily? The stranger currently in her guest bathroom was not her husband.

Kate located the box she needed from her office and hauled it out to the front room. Tearing away tape and flimsy cardboard, she held her breath against the sight of her husband's old things, items he'd cherished for years. She pulled the University of Alaska T-shirt from the top, the worn feel of the fabric still smooth in her hands, and stilled.

Declan had looked at her, and everything she'd worked to build to protect herself vanished. There was so much more in that blue gaze than she remembered, a warmth that hadn't ever been there before—a hardness.

Kate swallowed. She was almost afraid to find out what that more could mean. She closed the box, clean shirt in hand…afraid to hope.

STRENGTH. DARKNESS. The woman was an enigma he hadn't been able to read since confronting her in that house, but for a brief moment, it had been right there in her eyes as she'd kissed him. Desire. Warmth. The need to be cared for. And hell if his body hadn't responded. It'd been one of the most intense experiences he'd remember for years to come. Something no way in hell he'd forget.

For those fifteen seconds, Kate Monroe had let her guard down.

But even with that physical anchor to his past, nothing about her or that kiss had given him more information on the man he'd been before. Documents could only get him so far. His memories. They were all that mattered.

Declan toweled off, careful of the bullet wound, and dressed quickly, leaving his bloodied shirt in the small garbage can beside the pedestal sink. He'd taken wipe showers, eaten nothing but soup, slept on an uncomfortable cot after escaping from the hospital. But here, here in her too-white apartment, with her too-modern furniture and white tile, he felt more at home than he had anywhere else.

Because of her. What that meant, he had no idea.

Stepping out of the bathroom door, Declan's gut

growled. When was the last time he'd eaten? Twenty-four hours? More? He couldn't remember the last thing he'd put in his mouth. Didn't matter; he didn't care if she planned on microwaving a frozen dinner. Whatever she'd started cooking had his full attention. Until he set sights on her.

Standing in front of the stove, she struggled to tape a bandage over the bullet graze on her arm. Kate bit down on the roll of tape to secure the adhesive over the graze but dropped the entire thing into a pot of boiling water in front of her. "That's not good."

"Should give it a nice, glue-like flavor, don't you think?" Declan rounded the granite-top island, taking in the shrimp, mushrooms, herbs, cream cheese and garlic already prepared and waiting on its gleaming surface. She'd cooked for him. Or…had tried to cook for him.

Gripping the tongs beside the stove, he dove in for the roll of tape, extracted it from a mess of pasta and set it on the counter. "Trust me, I won't be able to tell the difference."

Her laugh reverberated through him, and he followed the hint of pink into her cheeks.

Studying her injury, she placed a hand over the graze and stepped back. "You'd think after making this dish so many times, I'd get it right someday."

"Give me your arm." He reached for her hand, smooth skin gliding over the calluses in the center of his palm. Heat lanced through him, straight down his spine at the contact. Touching her—kissing her—might not have brought back any past memories, but he sure as hell didn't regret it. He just had to be careful from here on out.

He cleared his throat around the sudden swelling constricting his airway. "You cook a lot?"

"I think my pasta boiling skills already answered that for you." The weight of her attention bore into him as he worked to save the roll of partially melted medical tape. "I mostly live off the protein bars Sullivan provides for the office, but after the day you've had, I thought you might like something comforting. Cream cheese and carbs always hit the spot for me."

"Can't argue with that." He placed the gauze over her arm and ripped a piece of adhesive from the roll with his teeth. Securing the bandage in place, he tossed the first-aid supplies back into the open kit he hadn't noticed spread on the counter until now.

First getting him to the doctor, then offering her home to clean up in, and now she was making him dinner. What was it about this woman? Aside from the fact she hadn't just crossed his mind over the past year, she'd practically set up a permanent residence, he had no reason to trust her. Yet every time he thought of getting what he needed from her and leaving, of finding that shooter on his own, his gut clenched. "You're officially patched up."

"Thank you," she said.

"No problem." He cataloged the rest of the ingredients across the counter and rubbed his palms together. "I'm not sure how good I'll be, but I'm happy to help with whatever it is you have going on here. It's the least I could do since, you know, you saved my life."

"You'll have to put a shirt on." Jerking her chin toward the living room, she pointed out a gray T-shirt draped over one of the chairs. Her smile increased his blood pressure. She rubbed her hand over the bullet's graze in her arm, then motioned to his bare chest. "No telling what other kinds of accidents are going to happen while I attempt to cook. Wouldn't want all those pretty muscles to get burned in the process."

"Probably a good idea." He closed in on the T-shirt she'd laid out, rubbing the material between his fingers. University of Alaska. It was a men's shirt, and she'd said something about pulling a box of his old things before he'd taken a shower. Stood to reason that the shirt belonged to him.

Pulling the material over his head, he flinched against the sting of his stitches. "What can I do to help?"

"You can mince garlic while I clean the shrimp." Kate grabbed a clean cutting board and a knife, setting them beside her station on the counter. Her deep purple nail polish caught the gleam of lights from overhead as she moved between ingredients, and it somehow represented everything he'd imagined her to be. Intriguing, sexy, independent.

Maneuvering to her side, he breathed her vanilla scent in a bit deeper, let it fill him with a renewed sense of appreciation. After everything this woman had been through—the shooting, the surprise of his resurrection, the exhaustion—she'd put his needs ahead of her own. Hell, if that didn't earn his respect. A woman like that was a rare creature, one that needed to be protected. She cared, she sacrificed, she pushed through.

He was the only one standing between her and another attempt on her life. He'd be damned if he failed her again.

"Why the change to profiling?" he asked.

"What?" Her hold on one shrimp faltered, and it fell onto the counter.

"You said Brian Michaels was your patient, but you're profiling for Blackhawk and the FBI now. Why the change?" Declan reached for another clove of garlic, brushing the edge of his hand against hers.

Awareness shot straight up his arm, of her shallow breathing, the way her beautiful green eyes widened slightly, the tightening of her fingers around the handle of the knife. Something inside him responded to her on a deep, instinctual level. It was probably due to the fact they'd been married, been intimate, that his brain refused to forget her even after the most dramatic event of his life. For all he knew, the hitch in his breathing and heart rate had more to do with muscle memory than any real connection between them. Because she'd made it perfectly clear: he wasn't her husband anymore.

He positioned the flat edge of his knife over the garlic and slammed his hand on top. Maybe a bit too hard. "Can't imagine putting yourself in the head of a killer like the Hunter does miracles for your outlook on life."

"Oh." Kate stared at the shrimp in her hand, rolling her bottom lip into her mouth. The tendons between her neck and shoulders strained. She swiped the back of one hand across her forehead, then shifted her weight onto her other foot. Obvious anxiety deepened the small indents between her eyebrows. She didn't want to talk about it.

"Hey, I'm sorry." He forgot the garlic, turning into her. He smothered the urge to touch her again. The intense reaction that sparked every time he laid a hand on her wouldn't do either of them a damn bit of good right now. "You don't have to tell me anything. We just met. We don't know each other well enough—"

"No, it's okay." But she still wouldn't look at him. The slight tremor in her hand settled as she set down the paring knife she'd been using on the shrimp. "As a psychologist, I encouraged my patients to talk in order to work through their issues. You'd think it'd be easy for me to follow my own advice."

Only the sound of the boiling water behind them on the stove drowned the hard pounding of his heartbeat behind his ears.

"I let my personal life get in the way of helping my patient." She busied herself by ripping a tail off the last shrimp and tossed it into the ceramic bowl with the rest. "Michaels was spiraling out of control, and I didn't have any clue. I missed the signs. I didn't know he'd stopped taking his medications."

Kate raised her green gaze to his, gripping the edge of the granite countertop. "When Sullivan approached me to work for the team, to help catch the bad guys and get justice for those who the police couldn't or wouldn't help, I said yes."

Everything inside of him went cold. He'd gotten a hint of her guilt back at the house, with her hands working to stop the blood flow from his wound. But this…

Declan closed the short space between them, unable to keep his distance any longer. Sliding his hand across the back of hers, he peeled her white-knuckled grip from the countertop and massaged his thumbs into her palm. "You don't have to carry that guilt, Kate. Michaels knew what he was doing. He would've found a way—"

"You don't understand. I didn't only lose you that night, Declan." Kate pulled her hand from his, tugging up the bottom hem of her T-shirt. Smooth, creamy skin slid beneath his fingers as he gave in to the urge to see if she was as soft as she looked. But his gaze homed in on the lump of scar tissue an inch or so under her belly button, dead center. White, puckered and angry, an exact match for the four scars he carried. "I lost our baby, too, and I'm not going to let Michaels get away with it."

Chapter Five

"You were…pregnant?" Light blue eyes slowly raised to hers. "With our baby."

"I carry a lot of guilt for what happened that night, but it only plays a small part compared to the anger." Kate lowered her shirt, turned to the pasta boiling over on the stove and flipped off the burner. She blinked back the burn of tears. She didn't cry. She didn't feel. She didn't let her guard down. She had control, and she wasn't about to break down for the millionth time in front of a complete stranger.

Except when Declan threaded his hand around her waist, pulled her into him and held her, that control shattered. In a matter of seconds, aching sobs ripped through her, but he only held her tighter, grounding her.

"We're going to find Michaels," he said. "Together. And we're going to make sure he gets everything that's coming to him."

She didn't know how long they stood there, the pasta overcooking, the scent of garlic thick on the air. She didn't care. For a split second, she wasn't alone. She wasn't standing on her own. He held her up, gave her the strength. He took that pain away.

Kate rested her head on his shoulder, her nose pressed into the column of his throat as her palm found his heart. She counted off the beats as the strong, steady drum hammered through her. For the first time since the shooting, right here, right now, safety was within reach. Which didn't make sense. She'd just met him, really, but something deep down—something she'd buried in that coffin—said he wouldn't hurt her.

"You can forgive yourself right now, angel. Michaels was in charge of his actions. Not you," he said. "That guilt is only going to destroy you."

Her breath hitched. Impossible. Kate swiped at her face and put a few inches of space between them, her fingers skimming down his arm. "What did you call me?"

He narrowed his eyes on her. "Angel."

"Why?" Desperation clawed through her as she fisted her hands in his shirt, the one he used to wear on the weekends, used to wear to bed. The one she'd recently packed away because she couldn't stand the thought of getting rid of it. "Why that name? Why angel?"

"Your blond hair, your perpetuity for putting everyone else first before yourself." Declan ran a hand through his already mussed hair. "I guess it kind of slipped out. If you're offended—"

"No. I'm not offended." She forced her fingers to release him and smoothed the creases her damp palms had pressed into the shirt. It was a coincidence. Nothing more. Nothing she should sink her nails into. Her pulse slowed as she breathed him in. Slow, deep breaths. The dam had been broken when he'd kissed her, when he'd coaxed her to relive the pain she'd suppressed for so long. She was out of control. She had to get a hold on reality. "You…you used to call me that. Before."

Once upon a time, she'd been his angel. But now…

"I'm sorry, Kate. I didn't know." He stepped into her, hands out, but every muscle in her body tightened in response.

Declan backed down, put space between them at her reaction. "It slipped out, but I'll be careful in the future. I won't call you that again."

Kate forced herself to take a deep breath. Then another. "No. It's not your fault. It's been a crazy day. Emotions are running high. I'm… I'm really tired, and it looks like dinner is ruined anyway."

She maneuvered around him, pointing down the hall toward her bedroom. Distance. She needed distance. The past eight hours had ripped her apart, but even with his attempt to piece her back together, the human body and mind could only take so much.

"I think it's best we get some rest before looking for Michaels, but you're welcome to raid the fridge and the pantry if you're hungry. Please, take whatever you need, and there's extra bedding in the linen closet."

The apartment blurred in her vision as she escaped down the hall, her chest too tight, her head spinning. She forced herself to close the door behind her softly, then collapsed against it. She didn't have the strength for this. For years, she'd helped her patients become stronger, better versions of themselves, helped them work through their trauma. Kate rubbed the base of her palms into her eye sockets. Why then couldn't she help herself?

She shoved to her feet. She needed to shower, drink a glass of water, get something to eat. There were people out there who needed her help, and she wouldn't be doing her team or the FBI any good in this condition.

Heading for the bathroom, she stripped out of her bloodstained clothing, then twisted the shower knob to hot. Steam filled the bathroom quickly, and she breathed a bit easier.

Declan hadn't done anything wrong. None of this was his fault. She needed to apologize to him, explain. They'd be working this case together. Despite her internal battle, he was as much a part of this as she was.

In minutes, she toweled off and dressed in her favorite pair of sweats and oversize T-shirt. As she reached for the bedroom door, three knocks reverberated through her.

"Kate?" Declan's voice was a soothing remedy to the panic consuming her vision, and it took a moment to center herself. Of course, he'd come to check on her. From the moment he planted himself in that bullet's path to save her life, he'd proven that part of her husband had survived the trauma. "You okay?"

Hand on the doorknob, she put the armor he'd stripped back into place. The man on the other side of the door wasn't her husband—never would be—and she had to accept that reality. They'd have to work together to find and question Michaels, she'd help him get his life established, get him out of that shelter, but that was as far as it would ever go between them.

Kate swung the door inward, faced with the sight of shrimp linguine in creamy mushroom sauce. Her mouth parted as her stomach gargled with hunger pains at the aroma. "You finished cooking it."

"Didn't want our hard work go to waste." Declan offered her the plate, complete with a fork and a glass of white wine, the muscles down his arms bunching as he moved. That gut-wrenching smile did its job as his fingers made contact with hers. What was it about touching him that had her all twisted in knots?

"Thank you." Heat penetrated through the plate into her hand, but the sensation exploding from her chest demanded her attention. Nobody had ever cooked for her before. Her own grandparents who'd raised her had worked full-time and hadn't had the time or the energy to do much else but provide packets of ramen noodles for Kate and her younger brother. But this…this wasn't ramen.

"Least I could do for you giving me a place to crash tonight." Declan nodded and turned to head back toward the living room, but Kate took a step after him, her heart in her throat.

"You don't have to eat alone." That sensation behind her sternum rocketed through the rest of her body as he slowed to a stop in the hallway. Ridges and valleys of muscle flexed along his back, then he faced her, blue eyes assessing every change in her expression. Looking for another crack in her armor? He wouldn't find it.

"I don't want to complicate things between us more

than they already are, Kate." Rolling his fingers into fists at his side, standing there as though he were ready for battle, he looked exactly like the special agent she'd known him to be. Would she ever be able to separate the two in her mind? He closed the distance between them, one step at a time. "I don't intend to start anything I can't finish."

The tendons behind her knees weakened. Air rushed from her lungs. What did that mean?

"I'll give you one more chance to decide and be sure this time." His voice graveled, raising the hairs on the back of her neck.

Her hold on the plate faltered as his exhale grazed the oversensitive skin across her collarbone. Why did it feel as though she wasn't asking him to eat dinner with her but something far more dangerous? Far more tempting?

"Ask me again," he said.

Kate rolled back her shoulders, leveled her chin. He'd saved her life back at the house, cooked her dinner, and she was an adult. She could take care of herself, protect herself. And maybe the thought of eating the pasta alone hollowed her insides a bit more now that their fates had intertwined again.

She'd been alone for so long. Kind of felt nice to have someone else to talk to outside of work.

"All right. Have dinner with me," she said.

His expression softened with a one-sided smile. Declan took the glass of wine from her, then threaded his free hand around hers. Instant warmth shot straight into her bones and counteracted the pain in her arm from the fresh wound. But this time, she didn't flinch away.

He pulled her into the kitchen, set her glass on the countertop and slid one of the two bar stools out for her. All of the mess from food preparations had been taken care of, the island cleaned.

"You didn't have to do any of this." Kate took a seat on the bar stool, surprised to already find silverware laid out. As though he'd expected her all along.

When had she become so predictable? Or was it the fact he seemed to read her better than anyone else ever had? Wasn't necessarily a bad thing. They were going to be partners for the foreseeable future. Because as much as she hated to admit it openly, she had the feeling Michaels wasn't going to be found unless he wanted to be.

"No trouble at all, but for the record, you did most of the heavy lifting. The thought of deveining those shrimp makes me gag." His deep laugh did funny things to her insides as Declan took a seat beside her, his body heat sliding up her arm. He lifted his own glass of wine, clinking it against hers. "To partners."

She wrapped her fingers around the clear crystal, the weight of his gaze on her the entire time. The decision had already been made. Her purpose—to bring the man who'd shot at them tonight to justice—would be greater than her pain.

Kate clinked her glass against his and took a heavy sip. "To partners."

SHE WAS ASLEEP in her bed—alone—her breathing heavy and slow.

Declan skimmed his fingers down the door frame to her bedroom and shut the door behind him quietly before heading back to the living room. She'd fallen asleep on the couch as they'd watched some mindless television show, and he hadn't been able to resist tucking her in for the night.

She'd been pregnant. With his baby.

Rubbing his palms down his face, he collapsed onto one of the too-white sofas. What the hell was he supposed to do with that information?

He shouldn't have pushed her for an answer. Should've minded his own damn business. Because the last thing he ever wanted was to see that woman cry again. Angels weren't supposed to cry, yet every crack in her expression had gutted him from the inside. And he'd do anything he had to to ensure nobody hurt her. Himself included.

"She doesn't deserve what you're going to do to her." He'd only brought pain and suffering into her life. Staying longer would only destroy her more.

Alone, in the dark, he took in the magical expanse of the city through the floor-to-ceiling windows. Kate had an entire team to track down the bastard who'd taken a shot at her tonight. She didn't need him. He wasn't an investigator anymore and she had everything and everyone she needed to get the job done. All he'd managed to do was mess with her head. And that kiss... He was selfish for using her to prompt another set of memories.

But she was the only tie to the past he had, the only one who could give him his life back.

The tablet Sullivan Bishop had loaned him for the investigation brightened across the room with a silent notification, reflecting off the wall of glass in front of him. Shoving away from the couch, Declan crossed the room and unplugged it from the charger. An email forwarded by Blackhawk's network security analyst to the in-box she'd set up for him and Kate's company email. Could have something to do with their case.

He pressed his thumb to the home button.

The screen flashed white, taking him directly to the original email. From Special Agent Dominic. The attachments laid out all the evidence, the witness statements, crime scene analysis, everything the FBI had on the serial killer Kate had been asked to profile, the Hunter.

Declan found himself tapping on each attachment, skimming over the details of all three victims and the scenes where they'd been left.

Dense trees, thick dried grass, out in the middle of the woods. Off the trail so as not to be found easily. Only the killer knew how many more were out there, waiting to be recovered. No meaningful connection between the victims as far as the FBI had been able to tell. They varied in age, height, weight. Nothing similar but their appearance. Short blond hair, athletic, green eyes. His heart raced, and he swiped through the rest of the attachments to clear his head of the look in their eyes as they stared up into the sky. All three women looked like Kate.

Declan sat in a nearby chair. Anchorage was as diverse a city as it could get. What were the odds the Hunter lured three Caucasian women to their deaths from the same location? Unless—

"You know, a normal person wouldn't stay up late to

review photos of bodies." Her voice penetrated through the thick haze the puzzle had built.

He closed his eyes against a surge of regret. Hell, he hadn't heard her approach, too embedded in the case. He got like that sometimes—invested—but now he understood why. He'd worked for the FBI. He'd hunted monsters. Standing, Declan faced her, his blood pressure spiking at the play of moonlight across her features. "I didn't mean—"

"Yes, you did. You were one of the best investigators the FBI has ever seen. I can understand the draw to solve one of their highest-profile cases."

The half smile on her lips warmed him to the core as she reached for the tablet. Taking it from him, she swiped her index finger across the screen to review the attachments.

"Anything you think might help the investigation?" she asked. "Or did you happen to solve the entire case and identify the Hunter on your own?"

Declan wiped his overheated palms down his jeans, studied the too-bright screen as she skimmed page after page. "I'm not an investigator, remember? You're asking the wrong guy."

"First impressions. Tell me what you thought when you looked at the crime scene photos." Green eyes sparkled in the glow from the tablet's light as she hiked one shoulder in a shrug. Kate reached to the end table beside the chair he'd taken up and switched on a small lamp. What was this? Some kind of test?

Okay. "The victims might've been hidden enough

to keep them from being found too easily, but they were staged."

Something familiar took root from inside him, the need to solve the puzzle as if his life—or someone else's—depended on it. His heart pumped hard behind his rib cage, adrenaline consuming him from head to toe. Declan stood and stepped close to her, his arm brushing against her uninjured side as they reviewed the evidence together. Her touch, like an anchor, kept him in the moment as possibilities of the way the killer hunted his victims played out in his head. He'd lure them in, maybe seduce them, then set them free in the wilderness. Had he given them a head start before he'd started the hunt?

Declan swiped his index finger across the screen and landed on a single photo of one of the crime scenes. Focusing on the surrounding damp ground and not the body where most investigators started, he pointed to a small patch of bare dirt. "See here? There are no footprints in the dirt, nothing to suggest the grass has been disturbed around her. Like she fell from the sky. The killer brought them to those locations and left them to be discovered."

"They were killed elsewhere." Kate nodded as she scrolled to the next attachment. "Makes sense. The lack of blood at the scenes backs up your theory. The victims had to have been placed after they were already dead a few hours, which means these killings were thought out. Meticulously planned ahead of time. The killer knew exactly where their bodies would end up, maybe even when they'd be discovered, because he picked the locations personally."

She was placating him. The excitement drained from his muscles, and he backed off a step. A small burst of laughter escaped as he ran a hand through his hair. The sting of his stitches pulled at him. "None of this is new information, is it?"

"No. But it can't hurt to have a second pair of eyes. There might be something in these files I'm missing that could help me build the profile on the guy." She handed him the tablet, then headed toward the kitchen and flipped on the coffee maker. Pulling two mugs from one of the cabinets, she set them out as the sound of bubbling water reached his ears. Within a few minutes, she'd poured them two hot cups of coffee.

Green eyes landed on him as she offered the second cup. "I will mention, however, that it took the investigating unit two hours to come up with the same theory that it took you two minutes to put together."

Surprise washed through him. Two hours? Seemed kind of obvious to him. He just had to look at the right evidence. Or had it been his past life as a serial crimes investigator coming into play?

Liquid heat bled through the mug and into his hand. "Dominic barely just sent you the email. How do you know how long it took them?"

"I'm in a group message with the BAU assigned to the case." A smile thinned her lips as she leaned forward, one leg tucked under the other. Her robe shifted, revealing pale, smooth skin above her collar. Under her thin shirt, the scars interrupted that perfection, but they only made her more beautiful in his opinion. Stronger.

She brought the mug to her lips, eyes on him over the rim. "You're good at this, Declan. You always have been. Investigating is in your bones. There's something still there and you know it."

There'd always been something, ever since he'd woken up in that hospital bed, that urged him to take a closer look, to solve the puzzles around him. Seemed the only puzzle he hadn't been able to solve had been his past, but now he was starting to get answers. Because he'd found her. If he could get even an ounce of the life he'd had back, maybe the cold, gnawing hole of emptiness inside would heal. Maybe he could start over.

He focused on the screen in his lap. "Tell me about the Hunter."

"My profile is far from solid. I only have bits and pieces right now." She set her mug on the end table to her left and stood. "Besides, Michaels is still out there. We should be focusing on finding him. His sister took custody of him after his release, and there's only one address on file for her. We should head out at first light. It's about a two-hour drive."

"First impressions." He echoed her own words back to her, drawing out a languid smile as he handed her the tablet.

"All right." Kate stared down at the screen but didn't seem to see the words in front of her. Her bottom lip parted from the top, and everything inside of him heated in an instant. "I think he's punishing her."

"Who?" he asked.

"The woman who broke his heart." She turned the tablet to face him, but he couldn't stand to take another look at the collage of all three victims. It was all too easy to imagine Kate—blond hair, green eyes—staring up at the sky, perfect sensual lips blue, unmoving.

They'd just met. Sure, they'd been married, but as she'd pointed out, he wasn't her husband anymore. He didn't know her, had no attachment to her other than the flashes of memories in his head. But the image of finding her as those women had been found initiated a violent chain reaction inside, starting with his head and working down to his toes.

"He chooses his victims based on *her* appearance," she said. "From the care he's put into placing them, stands to reason he's been intimate with them, maybe even dated them. He seduces his victims, then kills them, gently covering them in grass and foliage to protect their bodies until they're discovered. He can't bear to hurt the one person he wants to, so he replaces her with his victims. He takes his anger with her out on them, but the hurt never stops. No matter how many times he kills, her face is the one he can't forget."

"Then if the FBI can find her, they'll find their serial killer," Declan said. "In a city of three hundred thousand people, should be no problem at all." The excitement was back, stirring something deep within him.

First thing first. They had a shooter to find. Declan clapped his hands then rubbed them together. "Where's that address for Brian Michaels?"

Chapter Six

She couldn't change the past.

Hoping Declan's memories returned—that her husband was still in there, waiting to reemerge—was more dangerous than being in Michaels's sights again. She could heal physically. She'd done it before. But mentally? Kate adjusted her grip on the steering wheel. No. She'd lost him once. If she gave in to the hope buried deep down, she wasn't sure she'd survive the second time.

"You're dead on your feet." Declan's familiar voice charged through her system inside the too-small cabin of the SUV. They'd been driving for two hours, yet every time he spoke was a new lesson in awareness. "Did you actually get any sleep?"

"When you're the possible target of a shooter, sleeping isn't exactly a priority," she said.

Dried foliage and dead twigs crunched beneath the vehicle's tires. Reds, yellows, oranges and browns announced fall had arrived in Alaska as they inched along the dirt road heading away from Potter Creek Ravine Park, but the dropping temperatures said it wouldn't last long. Snow would cover these parts in the next couple of weeks, if not sooner, which would only make it harder for law enforcement to recover any more of the Hunter's victims and catalog the evidence.

"I've got more important things to worry about," she said.

"Exhaustion is not a badge of honor, Kate, and it sure as hell won't get us to Michaels any faster." Declan shifted his weight in his seat, one hand clamped onto the bullet wound in his side. "Speaking of which, where the hell are we going, and do you have to hit every bump along the way?"

Had that been concern in his voice? A smile spread her lips at the idea, but she forced herself to pay attention to the road and not the way the veins in his arms rippled beneath his skin. She'd been on her own for so long, getting used to someone else's concern would take a while to sink in. Sure, the team had her back. She trusted that any one of them would stand up for her, fight for her, show up if she needed them. But would they have taken a bullet for her as Declan had less than twenty-four hours ago?

"Michaels's sister has a residence about a mile north of here. She's the only living relative he has left, and court documents recorded he was released into her custody." A hard knot of hesitation twisted in her gut. She couldn't ignore the fact Michaels's sister lived only a half mile from one of the crime scenes she'd studied for the Hunter case, but it had to be a coincidence. Nothing more. "If he's hiding out, that's where he'll be."

"You didn't answer my question about the bumps,

which makes me think you're hitting them on purpose." Declan stared out the passenger side window, toward the hint of light coming over the Chugach mountain range.

The sun wouldn't rise for another hour, but her brain filled in what she couldn't see of his expression. The laugh line on the left side of his mouth, deeper than the one on the right. The damage he'd done chewing off the skin of his bottom lip. The small dark spot of brown in his right eye. Brains were funny like that. Always trying to fill in the blanks.

"Consider it payback. Before you..." Kate stopped herself from saying the words out loud again. How much more pain could she possibly expect her heart to take?

"We used to prank each other," she said instead. "Small things at first, but over the years, we got a bit more dramatic and tried to top one another. I have to admit, there might've been some pain involved." She couldn't fight the small lift of one corner of her mouth. "The last prank I played, I applied wax to your leg while you were sleeping, then ripped off over half of your leg hair on your thigh. You retaliated by setting my alarm clock to go off every hour for the next two nights."

"Well, that answers the question I had about my uneven leg hair." His deep laugh vibrated through her as he pressed his back into the seat, and every nerve ending she owned heightened in awareness. How long had it been since she'd heard that laugh? But all too soon, it bled into the background of the engine's growl.

"Hard to believe I had a whole life before this," he said. "I can't remember any of it, but you do, and you've had to face it alone. I can't imagine how much strength that took to keep going."

A sharp intake of breath burned her throat, and she sobered instantly. Not strength. Repression. Day in, day out, she committed to becoming a fraction more numb than she'd been the day before. She'd thrown herself into other people's heads, learning their habits, their secrets, *their* pain to keep the grief from carving a bigger hole in her soul. But since he'd walked back into her life, there'd been a spark, a small flame he'd ignited with that kiss, with the way he studied her, cared for her.

"Have you seen a neurologist?" she asked.

"Kind of hard to get an appointment when you don't know your real name, have insurance or employment history," he said. "Or any way to pay for it."

Right.

"I have a friend who works at the Alaska Neurology Center," she said. "She owes me a favor for having the team help her with a case last year. I'm sure she wouldn't mind running some tests. There might be something you could be doing—mental exercises—to speed up the process." Kate didn't think that kind of science existed, but it was worth a shot, wasn't it? "Your memory loss might not be as permanent as you think."

Especially when it came to investigative work.

"Thank you." The weight of his attention pinned her to her seat. "Really. You don't have to be doing any of this."

"Well, I am the reason you got shot in the first place, right?" Hollowness set up residence in the pit of her stomach. Her mouth dried. "I should at least try to make it up to you."

"I told you. Michaels is responsible for his actions," he said. "Not you."

"Doesn't matter what you believe. It's the truth. Maybe if I'd been more focused on Michaels during our sessions, none of this would've happened."

The road wound deeper into the woods, pulling them into darkness. Kate guided the SUV to a stop outside of a short brown wooden fence surrounding the property. "This is it. We're here."

Tufts of green grass sprouted across the half acre of dirt. Dried leaves from the surrounding trees covered the landscape, bare branches hanging dangerously low over the cabin's roof. The weathered planks along the sides of the structure hadn't been repaired, left exposed to the elements for what looked like years. Broken windows reflected the rising sunlight sneaking over the mountain peaks, and from what she could see from here, the front door had been left partially open.

"Are we about to be murdered?" Declan shouldered his way out of the vehicle, leaving the passenger-side door wide-open. "I'm getting the sense your patient isn't here."

"Former patient." Hitting the button to shut off the engine, she rolled her fingers into a fist to control the tremors. She hadn't seen Michaels since his last session, since before... She tucked her bottom lip between her teeth and bit down to keep herself in the moment. One. Two. She could do this. She had to do this.

Kate got out of the SUV, leaves crunching beneath

her boots. The small sign nailed to the fence said this was the address on Michaels's release paperwork. Her fingers tingled for her weapon. "This is the address his sister gave the judge."

"I think the judge got played." Declan stepped toward the thigh-high wooden gate protesting at the slightest push of the breeze. "There's nobody here. Are you sure it was his sister who showed up to claim him?"

No. She wasn't. In fact, Michaels had never mentioned a sister in the few sessions she'd had with him. He'd refused to talk about his family, despite her attempt to help him through a sudden emergence of a dissociative disorder.

Before emergency medics had brought him into the ER after he'd attempted suicide, he'd lost his job, his wife had filed for divorce and taken custody of his kids. Statistically, the disorder was brought on by trauma—abuse, combat—but his medical records hadn't shown anything out of the norm and there was no record of him serving in the military. So who would have taken custody of him if they weren't a relative and why?

Her instincts screamed to get out of there as she pushed open the gate, but this was the only lead they had to finding the person who took those shots at them last night. Reaching for her ankle, Kate unholstered the small, loaded revolver she kept as backup. "Here. You might need this."

She wasn't taking the chance of him getting shot again, unholstering her Glock from her shoulder holster.

Declan took the weapon and checked the rounds.

They moved as one toward the cabin. No lights. No

fresh tire tracks. No movement. Nothing to suggest the place had been recently occupied, but the weight of being watched aggravated her instincts. If Michaels was the shooter from last night, it stood to reason he wouldn't stop until he was caught or killed. Putting this address on his release papers could've just been a way to draw her into the trap. Bringing the prey to the hunter.

Warmth penetrated through her cargo jacket and settled deep into her bones as she brushed against Declan. She'd trained for situations exactly like this, but having him here, at her side, calmed the raging storm of uncertainty inside. Her mouth tingled with the memory of his bruising kiss, and she took a deep breath to keep herself from analyzing every moment of it.

Despite their personal situation, the plan hadn't changed. She'd find Michaels, help Declan get his life back and move on. End of story.

He positioned himself ahead of her, taking point as though he intended to protect her from any danger that lay ahead. His mountainous shoulders blocked her view into the cabin. "This doesn't feel right."

"I think we've seen enough," she said. Lowering her weapon, she swiped a bead of sweat from her temple with the back of her hand. The temperatures had dropped below freezing out here. How could she possibly be sweating?

Kate surveyed the property a second time. She still couldn't shake the feeling they were being watched, but there was nothing here. And they were out of leads. She took a step back, retreating toward the SUV. "Michaels isn't—"

There was movement to her left, the outline of a man in the trees, but in an instant, he was gone. Kate blinked to clear her vision. Sunlight had barely started lighting the west end of the property. Had it been a trick of the shadows? She searched the tree line. Nothing. She wasn't crazy. He'd been right there.

Shifting off the safety tab on her weapon, she checked back over her shoulder to gauge Declan's reaction. "Did you see that?"

"Sure as hell did." He moved beside her, the revolver gripped in his hand. Staring toward the spot the shadow had disappeared, he raised the gun. "We're not alone out here after all."

THE SHADOW IN the tree line hadn't been any ghost. With uneven terrain and minimal sunlight coming over those mountains, they were at a disadvantage here. For all Declan knew, the guy in the trees knew every inch of this property and beyond. They needed to call in Kate's team. "Let's get your team on the line—"

"I'm going after him." She moved fast, sprinting across the property, gun in hand.

"Kate!" Damn it. He couldn't let her go after the suspect alone. The fake address, the cabin—it could have been a setup from the beginning.

Declan pumped his legs hard, but all too soon, the stitches in his side ripped. The pain pushed the air from his lungs, but he wouldn't slow down. Not with the chance the bastard was waiting for her to come into range. Someone had already taken a shot at her in the past twenty-four hours. He wouldn't let it happen again.

Broken branches and tall grass threatened to trip him up as she disappeared into the tree line. Panic exploded through his system. Damn. He'd lost sight of her.

Freezing temperatures and the pain in his side battled for his attention, but he only cared about her. Declan pushed himself harder, into the darkness, past the first line of trees. Sunlight lightened the sky enough for him to navigate around a fallen tree ahead of him, but there was no sign of her.

He slowed long enough to take in his surroundings. No beam of flashlight. No sounds of gunshots. Kate had been trained to protect herself, but he'd be damned if he didn't get her out of this mess. He couldn't lose her. Not again. "Kate!"

Rustling reached his ears from the left, and he bolted that direction, his hand slick against the steel of the revolver. A shadow crossed his path ahead, moving fast, with another on its trail. Had to be her.

Gripping his side, Declan launched himself over a small stream cutting through the wilderness. A growl worked up his throat as another stitch tore beneath the gauze, but he swallowed it down as he landed boots first. She wasn't going to get away from him that easily and neither was the bastard she was chasing. Hauling himself upright, he forced himself to keep going. Branches drew blood at his face and arms. "You better be alive when I find you, angel."

He wouldn't lose her again.

The trees shifted to his right, pulling his gaze from the path a split second before a wall of muscle slammed into him. He twisted and fell, rolling into the stream. What the ever loving hell?

Cold water heightened his senses as he planted his hands into the ground and locked on the outline of a man less than ten feet away.

The shadowy bastard had doubled back and lost Kate in the process.

Or there were two of them.

Declan straightened. His attacker blocked Declan's path to Kate, planted himself directly in the center of the trail. It'd been a trap.

Swiping his thumb across the bottom of his nose, he dislodged the water dripping down his face. "All right. Let's get this over with."

The masked assailant charged.

Shifting his weight onto his back foot, Declan caught the bastard just as the shadow's shoulder slammed into his rib cage. Mud and foliage gave way beneath his boots, but he kept himself upright. Declan slammed an elbow into his attacker's spine. Faster than he thought possible, the man wrapped his hands around Declan's thighs and hiked him off his feet. The wall of trees blurred in his vision as he hit the ground, his attacker's weight pinning him to the ground.

Sunlight streaked across the wilderness floor, enough for Declan to realize the shadow above him had pulled back his elbow to strike. He dodged the first punch, but the second landed directly into the mess of blood from the stitches in his side.

As though the son of a bitch had known exactly where to strike.

"You should've stayed dead, Monroe."

The voice was distorted, unrecognizable.

Agony washed over Declan's side, and he couldn't hold back the scream clawing up his throat. He rammed his knee into his attacker's side, dislodging him long enough to gain the upper hand. Adrenaline burned through him, pushed the pain to the back of his mind and cut the last remains of his control. Blood slipped into the waistband of his jeans as he rocketed his fist into the masked bastard's face. Twice more.

But Declan wasn't through yet. Grabbing his attacker's collar in one hand, he positioned his arm for another hit. The shadow wobbled on his knees, barely upright. The suspect Kate had gone chasing after must've been a decoy. "Give it up, Michaels. You're finished, and you will never get your hands on her."

A low, uneven laugh bled through the pounding heartbeat in his ears. Clamping one gloved hand over Declan's, the masked assailant pried the grip from his collar and rose. Toe-to-toe, his attacker reached well over Declan's six-foot-two.

"Even with a second chance at a new life, you couldn't leave well enough alone, could you? You always had to be the hero."

What? Narrowing his eyes, Declan fought against the strength twisting his wrist, but the mask didn't reveal any identifying characteristics. Hell, even if it did, he wasn't sure he'd have anything to compare them to. The amnesia had stymied any chance of that. But the suspect in front of him didn't come across as a former patient diagnosed with dissociative disorder. No. This man had training, military or law enforcement if Declan had to guess. He was in control. A predator. A killer. "You're not Michaels. Who the hell are you?"

"Doesn't matter who I am." A fast strike to the solar plexus shot the nerves there into overdrive, pressurized his lungs, and Declan fell to one knee. The pain in his arm intensified as the shadow above held on to his hand. Any wrong move and the bones would shatter. The suspect had him in the perfect position to take him out of the fight altogether, and he knew it. "But you. You're just in my way."

Kate.

Every cell in his body heated. Declan craned back his head, attention focused on the bastard's dark gaze burning down on him. He ignored the pain in his side and his wrist. He'd been through worse, recovered from worse. And there was no way in hell the son of a bitch would touch Kate. "As long as I'm alive, you'll never get to her."

"I can fix that." His attacker increased the pressure.

Declan came up swinging. He landed a solid hit with his nondominant hand, hauling the SOB to the left and exposing his assailant's back. With a hard kick to the attacker's knee, Declan followed through with his elbow to the base of the neck, but the guy didn't stay down for long.

The bastard struck fast.

Declan wrapped his hand around the attacker's wrist, raised his arm over his head and targeted the man's rib cage. Once. Twice.

The woods blended into a stream of lifeless color

as Declan was shoved forward into the bark of a wide pine. Agonizing pain ripped through him from his gunshot wound, and Declan dropped to his knees. Clinging to the tree in front of him, he fought to stay upright as darkness closed in around the edges of his vision.

His attacker moved into his peripheral vision, a black shadow in a forest of brightening light. Fisting his hand in Declan's hair, he wrenched his head back as a hint of sunlight gleamed off metal. A knife. "To think, all this time, I thought you'd be hard to kill."

Blood dripped onto the dried leaves beneath him, a soft pattering in his ears. Declan clutched his side to slow the blood flow, but his heart was pumping too hard, too fast. Depending on the damage, he'd bleed out in a matter of minutes if he didn't get medical help. But not before he got to Kate. "Go to hell."

"See you there." The knife came at him fast, but Declan rolled at the last second.

His assailant's scream penetrated through the thick haze clouding Declan's head as the blade slashed across his upper thigh. Declan pushed to his feet, facing off with the masked thug and the large serrated hunting knife. Stinging pain spread through his skull, but a few hairs in the name of survival weren't anything to miss.

His strength drained with every drop of blood hitting the ground, but the moment Declan backed down, his attacker would go after Kate. Not happening. She'd already been through hell. He wasn't going to give this bastard the power to break her again. The past, his memories. None of it mattered right now. She mattered.

He struggled to stay balanced, blinked to clear the

sweat from his eyes and raised his fists. The pristine edge of the blade had been tainted with the attacker's own blood. "Want to take bets on which one of us bleeds out faster?"

"I've already won." The man lunged, a grunt filling the silence of the woods around them.

The knife made contact with Declan's arm and tore through his T-shirt into skin. He blocked the second strike, dodged the third. Throwing his weight into his arm, Declan pushed off the tree behind him and swung as hard as he could. Bone met bone, a satisfying crack. He followed the blade's path into the group of dying brush, wrapped his fingers around the handle and turned back to finish the fight.

He wasn't fast enough.

Clamping his hands on either side of Declan's head, his assailant pulled Declan's face directly into his knee.

Lightning flashed across the backs of his eyes as the world tilted on its axis. The blade fell from his hand as his legs dropped out from under him. He collapsed to his side, watching as his attacker collected the knife. His limbs refused to obey his brain's commands as the son of a bitch centered himself in Declan's darkening vision.

"I'm going to find her, Monroe. I'm going to make her pay for what she's done." The mask stretched thin across the lower half of the attacker's face, as though he were smiling beneath it. "And there's nothing you can do to stop me."

"No." Declan clawed at the dirt and leaves as the man walked away. He had to get up. He had to fight. But the darkness sucked him down.

Chapter Seven

Kate had closed in right on the shadow's tail, gun in hand.

Only now she recognized the build, the grayish-blond hair, the terrified features as he chanced a glance back at her. Brian Michaels. Branches and needles whipped at her face, but with the rising sun, there was little chance of losing him, even in the dense trees. How far were they from the cabin now? Half a mile? More? Her muscles burned with exhaustion, her lungs on fire from the frozen temperatures. "Brian, stop!"

Ten feet. She pumped her legs as fast as she could. Five feet. She could almost reach out and touch him. Kate stretched her hand forward, fingers brushing the soft fabric of his sweatshirt hood—

Her foot tangled in the bushes, and she hit the ground hard. A combination of pain and relief coursed through her muscles as she forced herself to look up. Michaels raced away from her, his footsteps fading within a few seconds. Tightening her hold on the gun, she pulled at her boot to get free of whatever'd she gotten caught it in. "Damn it."

Moisture soaked through her jeans and T-shirt as she sat up. If she hurried, she could still catch up with Michaels, but her foot wouldn't come loose. A flash of yellow revealed why.

Kate reholstered her weapon beneath her jacket. The crime scene tape woven throughout the dried weeds had caught in the metal brackets of her boots. She picked at it until she slid her foot out but didn't drop the thin plastic as she straightened. "What would crime scene tape be doing all the way out here?"

Surveying the trees, the surrounding grass, she froze. She knew this area, had seen dozens of photos of it, had memorized it to ensure she hadn't missed a single element of evidence when she'd started profiling the Hunter. Blood drained from her face, and cold worked through her. "This is where they found her."

The first victim.

Had to be a coincidence. Kate released the tape, letting it settle back into the bushes and took a single step forward. Unless...

She spun, searching the surrounding trees for signs of movement. No. Michaels didn't fit the profile. The evidence at all three scenes spoke of undeniable, unfulfilled rage that only grew with every kill, but the murders had been planned down to the very last detail. The FBI's suspect was a psychopath. Not a sociopath. He could control his emotions, hold on to them until the job was done.

Michaels couldn't string two sentences together before his disorder got the better of him. The Hunter stalked his victims, seduced them, then brought them out to the woods and hunted them for sport. Each kill had been too organized. Too detailed. Nothing like her former patient.

Then again, her entire job was to deal in opinions. One wrong assumption and an entire case could unravel.

Kate trudged through the knee-high grass, leaving the scene behind. Everything had been processed by the FBI. There was nothing left for her to analyze. Now she just had to figure out a way out of here and relocate Michaels. "Declan!"

She could've sworn he'd been right behind her. He could be anywhere now. Spinning in a complete circle, she headed west across the small open field she hadn't realized she'd run through during her pursuit of Michaels.

She'd find Michaels again. There were only so many places a man like that could go, and one day he'd make a mistake. She'd be there when he did. The bullet graze across her arm itched. She was tired of getting shot at. "Decl—"

Another flash of color caught her eye. Red this time. Kate slowed, her fingers tingling for her weapon as she proceeded through the grass. Pine cones beneath her boots broke the uneasy silence around her as she unholstered her weapon again. What were the chances…

No. Couldn't be.

The wind picked up, the undeniable scent of perfume on the air, and her stomach revolted. Pale skin and blond hair stood stark against the browns, reds and greens of the surrounding foliage as she came around a thicket of grass. The sun was high enough now to highlight the soft gleam of the red silk dress draped across the woman. The woman with an arrow in her chest.

Kate wrenched herself away from the scene as fast as she could to avoid contaminating the evidence. The shrimp linguine Declan had taken such care to make rushed up her throat, emptying her stomach in a matter of seconds.

Her heart pounded too loud behind her ears. A light breeze wove through the trees. One breath. Two. Didn't help. She could still smell the woman's perfume, still see those green eyes staring up at her. She had to call Special Agent Dominic.

The Hunter had struck again.

Shoving her hand in her jacket pocket, she gripped the phone and tapped the screen. No service. She wiped her mouth with the back of her hand. Every minute the scene waited to be discovered, evidence disappeared. Storms, wildlife. She couldn't leave the poor girl out here alone, but unless Declan found her on his own, Kate would have to trek east back through the woods to the SUV. She forced one foot in front of the other toward the woman in the red dress, covering her mouth with her hand.

The woman fit the appearance of the Hunter's three other victims. Around thirty years old, blond hair, green eyes, athletic from the look of her frame and bare shoulders. She hadn't been out here long. Maybe a couple hours judging by the presence of color beneath the skin. A fresh kill.

Kate had joined Blackhawk Security and consulted

with the FBI to prevent things like this from happening. Maybe if she'd started the profile sooner…

She closed her eyes. No. Evidence suggested the Hunter seduced his victims days in advance. This one had been chosen long before the FBI and Dominic's team had sent her the files. Kate stared at the woman's hands, pale against the backdrop of her dress, then focused on the victim's face. Memorized it. "I'm going to find him. I promise. Whoever did this to you is going to—"

Green eyes blinked back at her.

A scream escaped her control. Kate pushed away, the heel of her boot catching on a rock, and she landed hard on her back. Her breath came in small gasps as the last of her adrenaline coursed through her. Running her hand through her hair, she fumbled for her phone again—still no service—and crouched beside the woman.

The victim wasn't dead. The arrow must've missed her heart. "Hang on," Kate said. "I'm going to get you help. Can you tell me your name?"

The breath wheezed from between the woman's chapped lips. "M…ary."

"Mary." No time for more questions. Kate had to get help. Placing one hand just below where the arrow entered Mary's chest, she hit the power button on her phone five times and swiped her thumb across the screen to report her location to law enforcement. She retrieved the Blackhawk Security earpiece all operatives were required to carry from the bottom of her jacket pocket and secured it in her ear.

"I won't leave you, okay? Hang on, Mary. Help is on the way," Kate said. "Sullivan—anybody—do you hear me? I need an ambulance sent to my location."

Static reached through the earbud. Out of range. Kate wrapped her hand around Mary's and gave a soft squeeze. The fear in the victim's eyes speared straight through her. "I'm not going anywhere, but I don't have service in this spot. I need to walk around for a minute. I promise I'll be right back. I won't leave you."

Standing, she raised her phone above her head, hoping to catch a stray signal as she walked away a few steps. Where the hell was Declan? She slowed, cocking her head back over her shoulder toward Mary. If the Hunter had just deposited his latest kill—who wasn't dead yet—there was a chance...

The control she'd fought so hard to put back in place after Declan had stripped her bare cracked.

"Where are you?" she asked.

Something was wrong. Declan had been almost right behind her as she pursued Michaels through the woods.

A soft whistling broke through the silence. She searched the tree line, took a single step forward as every cell in her body tensed to that sound.

Pain erupted through her shoulder.

The momentum of the arrow wrenched her sideways, and she hit the ground. Her phone disappeared into the grass, shock overriding her normally quick reaction time.

She tried to sit up as blood trickled across her collarbone and over her neck. Biting back the scream building in her throat, she used her uninjured arm to flip onto her stomach and army crawl back toward Mary. The arrow's fletching scraped against the dirt, caught on weeds, and only intensified the agony ripping through her, but she'd keep her promise. She wasn't going to leave Mary out here alone. "Mary, we have to move."

They had to get out of here.

No answer.

The taste of copper and salt strengthened as she neared the Hunter's latest victim. Blood. The nausea churning in her gut drowned the pain for just a moment.

Mary stared straight up at the sky. No movement. No chest sounds. Nothing.

Kate's eyes burned as she wrapped her hand in the woman's once again, almost shaking her. No. No, no, no, no. She blinked against the rush of dizziness threatening to pull her under, her body growing heavier by the minute. "Mary."

Footsteps thundered through grass and dirt, loud above the frantic beat of her heart. The Hunter closing in on his prey.

She shuddered as she unholstered the gun from under her jacket. Kate ensured she'd already loaded a round. Forget the shooting. Forget the mind-screwing situation with Declan. Forget the profile. The only thing that mattered now was survival.

Because she sure as hell wasn't about to be the Hunter's next victim.

DECLAN WOULD FIND HER, or he'd die trying.

Mud gave way beneath his boots as he stumbled forward, one hand clutching his side. His shoulder rammed into a tree beside him, and he struggled to catch his breath. He didn't know how long he'd been unconscious, how much blood he'd lost. Didn't matter. He promised Kate he'd protect her, and that was exactly what he was going to do.

He strengthened his grip around the large hunting knife he'd recovered from the bushes. The bastard wouldn't lay a finger on her.

Pulling his hand back away from the wound, he stared at the bright red across his fingers, then wiped it down his jeans. He pushed himself forward, muscles begging for relief as he followed the footprints along the thin trail. The sun had risen fully, almost a bright tunnel of light straight ahead as though he were being led through the trees. A ring of black closed in around his vision, and he slowed to use a tree for support. Damn it. He'd lost too much blood. Soon, his organs would start shutting down one by one.

He had to find her before that.

"I'm coming for you, angel. Hang on, baby." Air wheezed up his throat as he soldiered forward. He'd been through—survived—worse. A single gunshot wound was nothing compared to the four he'd taken a year ago. Then again, he'd been treated by an entire team of medical professionals, he'd been declared dead by the end of surgery and he hadn't been chasing a psychopath through the woods where all kinds of infections lay in wait. "I'm coming."

If the psycho hurt her...

Rage—explosive and hot—burned through him. His assailant thought he knew him? Whoever'd attacked him had no idea what kind of monster he'd kept caged all this time. How much anger, hatred and bitterness he carried from having everything ripped away. But Declan was more than happy to show him.

A twig snapped nearby, and Declan slowed. The hairs on the back of his neck stood on end, and he turned from the edge of the meadow. No movement, but the feeling he was being watched only intensified. Strangled breathing reached his ears, pulling him to the right. The blade grew heavy in his hand as exhaustion sucked the life from his body, but he'd still do the job.

"I know you're there," he rasped. "Come out so we can finish this."

No answer.

"Kate?" His defenses dropped as panic consumed him. Had the bastard already gotten to her? The breathing grew stronger as Declan rushed around to the other side of a massive tree. His heart beat hard behind his rib cage as a pair of boots came into sight. He slowed. A pair of men's boots.

Brian Michaels. Blood from a wound in his neck stained the collar of a bright white shirt beneath his dark sweatshirt. Blue eyes called out for help. Kate's former patient had already lost too much.

Declan took a single step forward, biting down against the rush of pain in his side, and stabbed the knife straight down into the dirt. The muscles ticked in his jaw as he crouched in front of Michaels and ripped off his own shirt. He tried plugging the flow of blood with the fabric, but it was too late. Michaels had been sentenced to death the second his throat had been cut.

Blood slipped from Michaels's fingers as he reached out to Declan.

"I should kill you right now." Declan could put him out of his misery. Walk away and let whatever higher power out there decide what to do with the man. Michaels was the one who took those shots a year ago. He'd done this to Declan's memory. Taken Kate's husband from her, taken their baby and ruined their lives.

But the thought of finishing the job only hollowed Declan's gut more. He curled his fingers around the blade, drawing Michaels's gaze. "You took everything from her."

Michaels's jaw worked overtime as he set his head back against the tree bark. The shooter's graying hair and beard added to the lack of color overtaking his features. This wasn't the man who'd attacked him back in the woods. "Hired...me."

Cold worked through Declan. "Who?"

Michaels's shoulders pulsed with shallow breaths. "He'll...kill—"

"You're saying someone hired you to shoot Kate?" Hell. Declan increased the pressure on the bastard's wound. No. Michaels wasn't going to die out here. Not when they were so close to uncovering the truth. That was too easy. He deserved a life of guilt knowing how many lives he'd destroyed.

"Tell me who sent you after Kate Monroe, and I'll make sure you're put in the FBI's protective witness program." All Declan needed was a name—anything he could go off of—to end this nightmare. "He'll never get to you, Brian. I give you my word. Now tell me—"

"Already found…her." Air escaped past Michaels's lips, brown eyes staring into the trees ahead as his chest deflated.

"Michaels, stay with me. Where is she? Where is Kate?" Declan shook the body.

His head pounded as he slid back onto his heels. He threw his blood-soaked shirt to the ground. Damn it. Studying the wound on the shooter's neck, he shut down a shiver working up his spine with a rush of breeze taking his body heat.

Michaels had been the only lead they'd had. There was no doubt in Declan's mind that Kate's former patient had fired those shots last night—just as he had a year ago—but if Declan were to believe a dead man's dying words, a variable had been added. Michaels had been paid to pull the trigger both times. A contract hit.

What were the chances the shooter had died within minutes of Kate and Declan discovering his location?

Two gunshots exploded from nearby.

"Kate." Declan shoved to his feet, knife in hand. Desperation clawed through him as he burst from the tree line and into a wide space of tall grass. The sudden strike of sunlight blinded him, but he pushed himself harder. He wasn't going to lose her. Not again. Because no matter how many times he'd tried to convince himself he'd only stuck around to remember the past, he knew the truth. He didn't give a damn about his memories right now. She was all that mattered. He wasn't going to stop fighting for her.

A scream rang out off to his left, freezing him from the inside. Declan pumped his arms hard. "Kate!"

The masked man who'd attacked him spun around, pulling Kate with him. He was heading toward the trees. Kate struggled in his hold as Declan closed in, her scream still fresh in his mind. His chest burned with exhaustion. Fifty feet. Forty. The minute the attacker disappeared into the trees, there was a chance Declan would never see her again, a chance she'd become a victim.

Not happening. Adrenaline coursed through him as a hint of her blond hair swung into view. No. He'd been given a gift when she walked back into his life, a second chance. Nobody would take her away from him.

"Come any closer and I will end her right in front of you." The man wrenched Kate close to his body, using her as a shield, his hand gripped around an arrow close to her heart. "Stay where you are, Monroe."

"Tell me you're the one who shot her with an arrow, so I can rip you apart with my bare hands," Declan said, his lungs burning.

Hundreds of crime scene photos pushed to the front of his mind. The victims who looked like Kate with their blond hair and green eyes, the arrows shot through the heart and the bodies left in the woods to be discovered later. As though their killer was punishing the one woman he couldn't make himself hurt, the woman who'd broken his heart. Clearly the killer was highly intelligent, extremely organized and meticulous, knowledgeable of crime scene analysis and police investigations to succeed at staying anonymous this long.

Declan locked his eyes on Kate's, noted the undeniable pain in her expression, then focused on the suspect. "You're the Hunter."

"Declan, get out of here—" Another scream ripped up her throat as her captor twisted the arrow deeper into her shoulder.

Her agony seared into Declan's brain. He'd never forget that sound. Fire burned through his veins, and he took another step forward, fists clenched. He forced his jaw to release. "You're going to want to start running."

"One more step and she dies, remember?" The Hunter reached into his cargo pants pocket and extracted what looked like a car remote. "Besides, I think you'll be too busy trying to save yourself."

He hit the button.

A metal length of barbed wire tightened around both of Declan's feet, tearing through his jeans and deep into muscle. Pain exploded from his ankles as a mechanical hiss pulled Declan's gaze to the left. A groan worked up his throat. He reached down to relieve the pressure, but the world tilted on its axis as the trap pulled tight and hefted him higher.

"No!" Kate lunged for the trap's trigger, only to be ripped back into the Hunter's chest by her hair. "Declan!"

He reached to pry the oversize snare trap from his legs, but gravity and the fact he'd already lost too much blood stripped his strength. Droplets hit the bottom of his chin as he reached again. He couldn't get loose. Not with his body going into shock from blood loss and not without putting Kate at a greater risk of danger.

"Don't worry, Monroe. I have a feeling you won't

be in pain much longer." The Hunter closed in on his newest prey, hand back on that damn arrow in Kate's shoulder.

Sweat pooled at the base of Declan's spine as the bastard stared up at him.

"I'm going…to kill you." Declan blinked to clear his head. To memorize every inch of Kate's face before he blacked out again. As soon as he got out of this trap, he'd start a hunt of his own. Black spiderwebs crossed his vision as Kate slumped in her attacker's arms, unconscious.

"We'll see." The Hunter adjusted quickly, tossing her over his shoulder in a fireman's hold. "After all, you do keep surprising me."

Chapter Eight

No one could hear her screams.

She didn't know how long she'd been down here, unconscious, but her throat hurt from the effort, and the darkness had crept in. Still, no one had come for her. The combination of damp earth and salt dove deep in her lungs. Her fingers were sore—possibly bloodied—from clawing at the dirt walls, but with the arrow in her shoulder, she hadn't been able to climb. With the tarp above, she couldn't see well enough to determine what else could be down here. The man who'd taken her—the Hunter—had tossed her into a pit trap and left her to die.

She screamed again, her throat raw. She closed her eyes against her last memories of Declan. There'd been so much blood. His face had been covered in it. Was he still alive? Had he gotten free? Had he gotten help?

Kate forced herself to breathe evenly, to consider the situation rationally. She wasn't going to run out of air down here, and the tarp overhead would keep most of the elements at bay, but she could starve. She could die of dehydration.

Rubbing at her throat, she sank back on her heels.

From what she could tell, the circular pit was about ten feet in diameter and ten feet deep. No branches or roots protruding from the sides to help her climb, but the pain in her shoulder combined with the loss of blood had only let her survey half of the hole so far.

Screaming wouldn't help. She was trapped. Like an animal.

"Think." She had to control the fear skirting up her spine. Deep breath through her nose, exhale through her mouth. The tension burrowing in her neck almost released. Almost.

The Hunter didn't want her dead. At least, not yet. Why else would he have shielded his face and disguised his voice? Which meant he'd been reacting to having her at the scene of his last kill. He hadn't planned for her, but if she didn't get herself out of here, she was going to die. He'd only stashed her here until he could figure out what to do with her or until he could come back. But Kate didn't want to die.

She felt around, her fingers brushing against a large rock that barely fit in the palm of her hand. She couldn't do anything until she dealt with the arrow in her shoulder. Wiping her damp palm on her jeans, she clutched the rock as hard as she could. The arrow hadn't gone all the way through. She couldn't pull it out without tearing through more tendon and muscle and possibly damaging her shoulder permanently.

Tapping her head back against the wall of dirt behind her, she closed her eyes. Declan was out there, alone, bleeding. He needed her to get out of this hole, and no matter how many times she'd tried telling herself differently, she needed him. Needed his concern, his touch. She needed that gut-wrenching smile. The only way she'd get to experience any of those things again was to force the arrow all the way through her shoulder. "You can do this."

Most arrow fletchings were super glued to the end of the shaft. This one was made from feathers. Flexible enough to travel through the hole she was about to tunnel into her shoulder if she needed. Holding the rock straight ahead, she positioned it until one smooth side slid against the end of the shaft. Three. Kate swallowed the sudden dryness in her throat. Two. Deep breath. One. She slammed the rock into the arrow as hard as she could.

A strained scream ripped through her as metal pierced through flesh for the second time in a span of a few hours. She battled to stay conscious as darkness cut across her vision, and she dropped the rock beside her. Her lungs worked overtime to keep up with her racing heartbeat.

The woods went utterly silent above the tarp, then slowly came back to life as she remembered to breathe. Leaning forward, she winced as the arrowhead pulled against smaller roots and dirt at her back. She'd pinned herself to the dirt wall by forcing the head of the arrow through, but now she had to separate the arrow tip from the shaft. Still pinned, she wrenched her shoulder away from the wall. Reaching back, her fingers shook as she slipped the edge of the arrowhead. In a few turns, the blood-coated metal dropped away, and she was able to maneuver the shaft back through the entry wound.

"Stay awake. You've got to stay awake." She discarded the shaft of the arrow. Damp earth gave way beneath her boots as she pushed away from the wall, but she sank immediately back to the ground in the middle of the pit. Tightening her hold in the fine labyrinth of roots in the pit floor, she pressed her forehead to the cool dirt.

No, she had to move to the edges, had to find something sturdy to grab on to to pull herself up. Couldn't think about the physics of holding her own weight with one good arm right now. She had to try.

Muted beams of moonlight penetrated through one edge of the tarp above, but not enough for her to see. How long had she been down here? Six hours? More? Stiffness worked through her fingers as temperatures dropped, but she kept moving, kept searching. There had to be something—anything—she could use to pull herself up. "Come on."

Her boot caught on rogue roots at her feet, and she pitched sideways, landing directly on top of something soft, yet solid. The smell of salt tickled her nose as she struggled to sit up. Salt and...cologne?

Supporting herself with her good arm, she fisted her hands in what felt like wet T-shirt material. What the hell? The Hunter wouldn't have left supplies. The tarp shifted from above, allowing more light into the pit, and horror flooded her.

Shoving back as fast as she could, Kate didn't stop until her back hit the other side of the hole. Air pressurized in her lungs, but it couldn't distract her from the sight of a dead body.

Another victim of the Hunter?

The wetness on his shirt... Blood. Kate rubbed her palms into the dirt, frantically trying to wipe it away. Rationally, she knew it wouldn't do any good, but rationale had gone out the window the minute she'd been thrown in a pit. She was a prisoner for however long the Hunter wanted to keep her.

Tears burned her cheeks as the soft settling of snowflakes on the tarp filled her ears. Michaels's hideout was located far outside Porter Creek's limits. Nobody was coming to save her. Nobody would hear her screaming. Nobody walked these woods at night. She was on her own.

Too many bodies. The first three, then that poor woman in the field. Mary. And now another body here in the pit with her. Kate had dropped her phone and her gun in the grass when the Hunter had shot her. Had any of her emergency tactics gone through so law enforcement could find the Hunter's latest trophy?

She shook her head, wiped at her face with the back of her hand. Didn't matter right now. It wasn't a coincidence her former patient had been out here the same time the Hunter had made his latest kill. They were connected.

She needed to know how. She would not give up. "Get up, Monroe."

She had to finish searching for something to pull herself out. The body lay straight ahead. As much as the thought sickened her, she could use the victim as a sort of stepping stool to higher ground, a branch or root just out of reach. She followed the curve of the pit trap back around until her boot hit the sickeningly familiar feel of the corpse's bloated middle.

Moonlight shifted around the edges of the tarp, and Kate froze. Recognition flared, and her heart rate quickened. The gash across his neck revealed the cause of death, and those wide brown eyes… She was staring at Brian Michaels. The shooter she'd been desperately trying to locate was right in front of her. Only… "The Hunter found you first."

He'd made sure Michaels would never pull a trigger again.

Was she supposed to feel bad about that? Goose bumps prickled across her skin. She couldn't look away from the body at her feet. Couldn't force herself to feel…anything. Leveling her chin, she reached for the wall of dirt for balance as she stepped onto Michaels's torso. Snowflakes worked through the edges of the flapping tarp from above, catching in her eyelashes as she skimmed her fingers over the wall.

Her palm brushed over a large, protruding root, and she latched on with her uninjured hand as tight as she could. She held back the sob of relief swelling inside. She had to keep it together. At least long enough to get out of this hole, long enough until she found Declan. Then she'd trek back to the SUV, call for backup and lead the search team back for Mary's and Michaels's bodies.

She lifted one boot and slammed it into the wall for leverage. Wrapping the root around her forearm, Kate tested her weight. It held, but the tricky part came next. She bit back the groan clawing up her throat as she raised her injured arm overhead. She gripped the root hard and hauled herself up the wall of dirt, slid her hands higher and did it again. Pain ripped through her shoulder, sweat beaded above her furrowed eyebrows and dripped down her spine, but she only pushed herself harder. She was almost there. A cold breeze grazed across the back of her hands as she reached the top of the root, a sensation she'd never take for granted again.

One more foot until she reached the top of the pit. That was all it would take—

The root broke free from the wall and then she was falling. "No!"

She hit the ground hard, the air knocked from her lungs. Her lungs spasmed until she finally gulped enough oxygen to clear the shock.

The edge of the tarp above fluttered with a gust of wind, then rolled back to expose her and Michaels to the elements. Snow fell in a heavy layer now, homing her attention to the root still clutched in her hand. That was her last chance of getting out.

Flakes melted against her skin as she lay there. She barely had the strength to lift her head, let alone try to climb the wall again, but she wouldn't die down here.

She hadn't survived three bullets wounds, a miscarriage and a year's worth of grief over losing her husband to die in the bottom of a pit. She'd fight. She'd find Declan. She'd get the Hunter's victims the justice they deserved. She didn't know how to give up.

Rolling to her side, Kate shoved to her feet, approached the wall and pulled in a long, slow breath. "Help!"

"Cut him down!" an unfamiliar voice shouted. "And find Kate!"

White light brightened the backs of his eyelids, and he forced himself to open his eyes. Hands hanging over his head, he blinked to clear the haze. Five beams of light bounced in front of him. Or was it ten?

"Her phone pinged over by that fallen tree. Vincent, you're with me." Female voice this time. Recognition flared as two flashlight beams swung off to his right. Elizabeth Dawson?

"Declan, you alive?" Sullivan Bishop appeared in front of him, the reflective light from Blackhawk Security founder's flashlight deepening the very serious creases in his forehead.

"As far...as I can tell." The words barely slipped from his frozen lips. The last thing he remembered was trying to reach the knife he'd dropped when the trap had hung him upside down. After that... He couldn't remember. Which wasn't a new feeling. "Where's... Kate?"

"We're looking for her." Sullivan twisted around as another flashlight closed in. This one belonging to Anthony Harris. "Give me your knife. I need you to catch him when I cut the line."

"How did you...know..." Declan's body urged him to close his eyes, but he fought against the drugging effect of the cold. They hadn't found Kate yet. The second her team cut him down, he'd go out and look for her. He wouldn't stop until he found her.

"Kate hit the emergency settings on her phone, which pinged Anchorage PD and us. We came as soon as we got the call. Police are searching the cabin where you and Kate left the SUV. We came straight here." Sullivan disappeared from Declan's peripheral vision. The sound of something scratching against tree bark filled his ears. Sullivan was climbing the tree holding Declan hostage. "What the hell happened to my profiler?"

"He took her." Another storm of rage exploded through Declan, but he couldn't act on it. He couldn't do anything right now, but the bastard would pay for every broken hair on her head. Declan guaranteed it. "He took her. I tried to stop him. I wasn't fast enough."

"We'll find her." Sullivan's voice dipped into dangerous territory. "Trust me. This is what we do best."

"I'm trying to come up with a reason you're still alive with that much blood on you." Anthony took position directly under Declan's shoulders. "Why is it every time we meet, you're literally dying?"

"You got a better…first impression…in mind?" Every breath was agony. Cold worked through him, and the loss of blood didn't help. The wound in his side had gone numb a while ago. Hell, he didn't know how long he'd been strung up like an animal. How long had Kate been missing? Declan rolled his fingers into fists. To prove he had the strength. "I need to find her."

"You need an ambulance." The branch wrapped with trapping line bounced as Sullivan pushed out farther, knife in hand. The flashlight in his mouth skimmed over Declan's face, and Declan blinked at the sudden brightness. "You can't do anything for Kate if you're dead."

"I'm not leaving her out here alone." No way in hell. He'd made her a promise. He wasn't going anywhere until she was in his arms. Forget an ambulance. Forget the investigation. Forget the past. Declan needed to find her.

"Get ready to grab him, Anthony." The line swayed with Sullivan's efforts to cut through it. What the hell had the Hunter used? Whale line? "He's going to come down hard, and Kate might kill us herself if she finds out we let him die on our watch."

"Please drop me. I'd like…to see that." Declan braced for impact a split second before the line snapped. His shoulder slammed into Anthony's, but the former Ranger flipped him to his feet as though Declan's two hundred pounds—minus at least a liter of blood—meant nothing.

The world swayed, and he stumbled forward but quickly steeled himself. He'd been shot and left upside down for dead, but he wasn't going to give her team any reason to leave him behind during the search. "Thanks."

"Don't mention it." Anthony slipped a pair of brown aviator glasses over his eyes, voice low and even, then unholstered the gun from his shoulder holster. "Ever."

"Here, cover up." Sullivan tossed him a shirt.

"We've got something!" a voice shouted, followed by heavy breathing and footsteps. Elizabeth materialized out of the darkness, but her tone of voice indicated it wasn't because she had good news. "You're going to want to see this, boss."

Sullivan followed without a word, Declan on his trail with Anthony's support. Tall grass and weeds parted as they made their way toward Vincent Kalani's flashlight. Then he noted nothing but red silk.

A body.

"I'd say she died around the same time Kate pinged us with her phone. Six hours, give or take thirty minutes." Vincent moved his flashlight over a woman partially hidden beneath a bed of leaves and pine cones. Tossing something at his boss, the forensics expert crouched beside the victim and pointed west. "I found Kate's phone a few feet away in the grass over there. Must've hit the emergency signal when she found the body."

Sullivan checked the phone. "Then we can't track her with her phone. We'll have to go in blind. Anthony, you're with me." Sullivan tapped his earpiece and searched the tree line where Declan had been hung up to die. "Elliot, quit messing with the damn trap and find something we can track. Vincent, stay with the victim until Anchorage PD or the FBI can take custody. Liz, I want a map of this area on my phone in the next thirty seconds. We're going after Kate."

"I'm…coming, too," Declan said.

Blond hair, green eyes staring straight into the sky, athletic build. Declan's stomach lurched. He didn't give a damn how much blood he'd lost. This victim was one of the Hunter's. Serials usually had a cooling-off period, a time frame while they enjoyed their latest conquest. But not this one. Both this woman and Michaels had died at the Hunter's hand today. Kate wouldn't be next.

Blinking through another round of dizziness, Declan accepted Elizabeth's offered water bottle and downed as much liquid as he could take. "He shot her with an arrow. She's bleeding. You need as many eyes as you can get out there."

"Why do I have the feeling you won't take no for an answer?" Sullivan pegged him with that sea-blue gaze, then extracted a backup weapon, handing it to Declan grip first.

"Let's roll out." Declan checked the weapon, loaded a round into the chamber. One way or another, he was getting Kate back. "She's been gone too long as it is."

The team didn't need any more motivation than that, taking positions. Declan headed for Elliot's flashlight beam at the edge of the woods, checking the time on his wrist. Six hours. That was how long she'd been gone. Anything could've happened in that time, but his gut said she was still alive. She was out there. He ignored the burn of his damaged skin thawing around the wound. Nothing would stop him from finding her.

"Over here! Looks like she put up quite the fight." Elliot swung his flashlight beam straight at them, then back into the heavy shadows as they approached. "Into the woods I go, to lose my mind—"

"—and find my soul," Declan finished.

An apt quote. Because Kate wasn't anything less. She'd been part of him from the beginning, the missing piece. Always would be.

Declan studied the tracks, fresh drag marks leading deeper into the wilderness. He avoided stepping directly on them to preserve the evidence. The minute the news of the Hunter's latest victim hit, the FBI would descend. And he wasn't about to mess up any chance his former employer had of taking this suspect down.

The drag marks disappeared about fifty feet in from the field, leaving only one set of boot prints. The Hunter had carried her from here, but he had rushed this one. Her abduction hadn't been planned, and he'd made mistakes along the way. He'd left evidence. "This way. Stay sharp. This bastard…is good at what he does."

Declan took point at the head of their pack. Every sound, every movement raised his awareness to another level. This was what the FBI had trained him for, what he'd been good at before the shooting. There were some things he'd never forget. Hunting was one of them.

A few branches off to his right had snapped at the ends, as though someone had broken them on the way through these parts of the woods. He headed that direction.

"You sure you know where you're going?" Sullivan asked.

"Yes." Positive. Kate was counting on him. And there was no way in hell he'd let her down again. Declan slowed as silence descended. What were the chances every animal had vacated the area at the same time? Unless… He pulled up one hand, signaling the team to stop. And listened.

"Help!"

He jerked at that scream, as if he'd been struck by lightning.

"Kate." Declan surged straight ahead, leaving the Blackhawk team behind. Lights swept the area ahead of him and reflected off what looked like a tarp buried with leaves. Fresh snow crunched beneath his boots as he slid to a stop at the edge of a man-made pit in the middle of the woods.

Declan ripped back the tarp, shone his light down into the hole. And there, at the edge, Kate frantically tried to scramble out of the trap.

"Get her the hell out of there!" he yelled.

"Help!" She strained again. "Help, help, help…"

"I'm coming, angel." The team circled the pit, but he couldn't wait anymore. The anguish in her voice pulled him down the steep side. He clutched thick roots and rocks to make it to the bottom, and within seconds Declan ripped her away from the wall and into his arms.

Her bloodied fingers locked on his borrowed shirt, the sobs racking her.

"I've got you." His hands shook. Declan scanned the bottom of the pit; one of the team's flashlights pointed at a mass of clothing and flesh a few feet away. The Hunter had put her in the hole with Michaels.

Turning her away from the remains, he held her until Sullivan, Anthony and Elliot pulled her from the Hunter's trap.

Anthony then hauled Declan up to the edge of the hole and pulled him from the pit.

Declan wrapped her in his arms again.

"I thought you were dead." Her voice rasped. How long had she been screaming down there? How many times had she tried to climb the walls? Had she lost hope he'd come for her?

"You can't get rid of me that easily." He needed to get her to a hospital. The blood blooming across her shirt was still wet, sliding down her side. He'd nearly lost her, and there hadn't been a damn thing he could've done about it. Never again. She was his priority. Not recovering his memories. Not tracking down the Hunter. Kate.

"Michaels…" she said. "He was in there with me."

"You never have to worry about him again." Declan strengthened his hold on her as they trekked back the way they'd come. The ambulances would be arriving soon if they hadn't already. Intertwining his fingers with hers, he planted a kiss on the back of her hand.

As for the Hunter, Declan was only getting started.

Chapter Nine

She was going to die.

"No!" Kate shoved herself up to sit. The sudden brightness of overhead lights and incessant beeping of machinery forced panic—greedy and dark—up her still raw throat before familiar blue eyes filled her vision.

"I've got you, angel." Declan's voice triggered an automatic chain reaction within her body, urging her to relax, to trust, but the nightmare had been so real. No. Not a nightmare. A memory.

Calluses caught on her skin as he smoothed his hand down the only part of her that didn't ache. "You're safe."

"Declan." She hurt. The beeping wouldn't stop. She blinked to clear her head. She wasn't in the pit anymore. Broken pieces of memory clicked into place the longer his touch anchored her to the present, and she slipped back against the pillows of the hospital bed with his help. Her heart pounded hard behind her rib cage. "How long have I been unconscious?"

He traced the veins in the back of her hand with the pad of this thumb. A bit more color had returned to his skin, but the bruising across his face and hands stood stark against white hospital sheets. It'd been a miracle the damage hadn't been worse. Left for dead in a snare trap, stitches torn open during the fight with the man who'd shot her, but the small butterfly bandages said he'd at least seen a doctor while she'd been under anesthesia. "You got out of surgery a few hours ago. The surgeon was able to repair the damage in your shoulder, but you'll be in a sling for a few weeks."

A few hours of her life. Gone. She'd already lost so many after the surgery to remove the bullets the first time around.

Kate studied him at her bedside. He was alive. After what happened—after accepting the reality she'd never see him again—he was alive. She wasn't going to waste any more time. The brightness wouldn't lessen, but focusing on him helped the throbbing in her head.

Declan hated hospitals. Had he been by her side the entire time? "You don't have to stay here. I know how uncomfortable hospitals make you."

"I'm not going anywhere. I almost lost you, and it was worse than any trauma I've ever endured," he said.

Pressure released in her chest.

Pulling the back of her hand to his mouth, he planted a kiss on the thin, oversensitive skin. Stubble prickled against her hand, but it was the guilt in his gaze that hollowed her from the inside out. "I never should've lost track of you when you went after Michaels. I—"

"Don't." Kate moved her fingers to his mouth. He had no reason to apologize. Flashes of those terrifying seconds when she wasn't sure he'd live or die as the Hunter closed in sprinted into reality. She tried shoving it into the tiny box she'd created to survive over the last year at the back of her mind, but there were still so many unanswered questions.

Desperation burned through her. They'd almost died out there. She'd almost lost him—again—and she couldn't stand to not be touching him for another moment. Kate fisted her hand with what strength she'd managed to hold on to and pulled him into the bed.

Declan shifted closer, and she nearly collapsed into him. Settling back into the pillows, he positioned her along his side. She slipped her hand over his chest.

He pushed a strand of her hair out of her face, then framed her jaw with the palm of his hand. "I would've killed him if I hadn't found you."

"None of this is your fault. There was no way we could've known he was out there, waiting for us to spring his trap." Kate set her forehead against his and closed her eyes. His scent clung to her, spread through her system, got into her head, revitalized a part of her she believed she'd buried in his casket over a year ago. The need to be close to someone else. "The Hunter got away."

Which meant he'd be taking another victim. Their killer had shown he didn't have any sort of cooling-off period between kills. He could've already started drawing in his next prey.

"He knows those woods. He knew exactly how to vanish after stringing me up for dead. Knew where to set his traps." Declan smoothed his knuckles along her bare arms, raising goose bumps in his wake. "He had everything planned out. Even using and killing Michaels to get our attention was part of the plan."

The memories of being in that pit with Michaels's remains, of his blood on her hands, tightened the muscles down her spine. Burying her head between Declan's neck and shoulder, she counted off his heartbeat. She'd come so close to never hearing that sound again. "I tried to get out. I kept falling and the pain in my shoulder... If you hadn't pulled me out—"

"He'll never lay another hand on you." He pressed his mouth to her ear as the flood of panic rose. "You're safe now."

Safe.

Such a simple word. But for the first time in over a year, she felt it down to her bones. Because of him. Because he'd fought off death for the slightest chance of saving her life. Because he'd risked everything to ensure she'd made it out of those woods alive. With Declan, she was safe. He'd earned every ounce of trust she could give.

"There was so much blood." Kate wiped at her face. She set her head back against his shoulder, stroking her thumb across his jaw. "How did you get out of the trap?"

"Your SOS. Blackhawk Security got the signal and responded. They cut me down, found your phone. They helped me find you." Trailing his fingertips down her back, Declan planted a kiss into her hair. "Without them, I would've died out there. You have a good team."

"They're okay." A laugh escaped her control. If she didn't have this one release, she feared she might fall apart completely. Truth was, her team was more than okay. They'd kept her going. They had her back. Declan was alive right now because of them. Kate lifted her head, studied those familiar blue eyes. "Thank you for saving my life. Again."

A smile pulled at one corner of his mouth, and her insides flipped. "That's twice now. We'll have to see what we can do to start making up the difference."

Kate studied him. Would it always be like this between them? This fire? This...need to have him close? She'd loved her husband. She'd worked hard at their marriage, but because of the things they'd dealt with in their individual careers, there'd always been a distance. Out of necessity. Otherwise the darkness of their careers would've corrupted their relationship from the inside. But now... Now she saw nothing but light. Nothing but hope.

"Are you trying to hook up with me?" she asked. "I was literally unconscious three minutes ago."

The hospital room door opened with a long slow creak.

"Look who survived a serial killer. How you doing, Doc?" Sullivan Bishop flashed a bright, straight smile before moving aside for the familiar face at his back. Hiking a thumb over his shoulder, her boss scanned the room for threats like the good SEAL he was supposed to be. "Right. This guy followed me here."

"Damn right, I did. You should've called me the minute she got out of surgery." Special Agent Ryan Dominic focused on her, then Declan, and back to her. Was that concern etched into his expression? Anger? He'd spent a good amount of time over the last year helping her through the grief, but Kate had never really been able to crack the carefully modulated control the agent kept in place.

Hands on his hips, he gave them a glimpse of that federal gun and badge he was so eager to display anytime Blackhawk Security came into the equation. "Seems not a moment too soon, either. Everyone out. I'm taking Kate into protective custody."

"Like hell you are." Declan's growl reverberated through her a split second before he stood. "The only reason she's alive is because of Blackhawk Security. You're not taking her anywhere."

She reached for him, using him for balance, and stood on shaky legs. "Ryan, I've already told you. I'm not going into hiding. You hired me to profile the Hunter, and that's exactly what I'm going to do."

"Kate, you've been through hell. I understand that, but you are the only surviving witness in my serial case," Dominic said. "I need to know everything you remember about this guy. I need answers. Now."

She felt Declan tense beside her at the agent's tone. He dropped his hold on her, took a single step toward Dominic. "You have no idea what she's been through and pushing her to give her statement is going to do more damage than good. I don't give a damn if you need answers. She needs rest."

They didn't have time for a testosterone showdown.

"Declan, give me a minute with Special Agent Dominic." Her words were crisp. She might've survived an attack from one of the most complex killers she'd ever profiled, but she wouldn't play the victim card.

She'd wasted too much of her life on that path. "You, too, Sullivan."

"I wouldn't piss her off if I were you. She's studied a lot of killers. She knows how to get rid of a body if she has to." Sullivan targeted his shoulder into Dominic's on the way to the door. "Agent Dominic."

The heat of Declan's touch ran through her as he traced the column of her spine. His gaze narrowed in on his former partner. The tendons between his neck and shoulder strained as he maneuvered toward the door. "I'll be right outside if you need me."

Kate waited until the door closed before she let the exhaustion pull her to the edge of the bed. Declan didn't need to see how weak the Hunter had made her. It would only worry him more. But with Dominic? He'd already seen her at her lowest. There wasn't much that could surprise him after what he'd helped her through.

"What are you doing, Kate?" Dropping one hand to his side, Dominic scrubbed his palm down his face with a glance out the small window next to the door. His voice lowered an octave as he studied her. "The guy comes back, and within two days you're already climbing into his lap?"

They didn't have time for this.

"Did you find her?" Kate attempted to cross her arms, but the pain in her shoulder spiraled, and she flinched before setting her arms at her side. "The other woman out there? Mary?"

Dominic sobered instantly, lowering his gaze to the floor. "Yeah, we found her. Mary Lawson. Twenty-nine. Same MO as the other three. Same similarities."

"She's one of the Hunter's." Kate sank farther onto the bed. How many more were out there in those woods? How many more would be recovered in the coming weeks? Closing her eyes, she fought back the echo of Mary's shaking voice in her head. It was time to end this.

"You're looking for a white male between the ages of thirty and thirty-five, one ninety to two hundred pounds," she said. "He knows the area and might have property nearby. It's no coincidence we recovered his first victim and Mary in the same location. Those woods are his hunting grounds. He's too intelligent to leave a paper trail, so you'll have to dig into possible aliases. The Hunter isn't leaving a whole lot of evidence behind. He's familiar with crime scenes. Could have a job or career in law enforcement or is a huge fan of true crime entertainment. Have you discovered the connection between the women aside from their appearance? Where he's finding them?"

"No." Dominic shook his head. "I have Anchorage PD canvassing around their residences so we can work up a timeline and trace their last known locations. None of the women had their phones on them when we recovered them. Unfortunately, GPS is out of the question."

He slid his hands into his pockets, his shoulders deflating on a heavy exhale, and suddenly, he looked ten years older. "Let me take you into protective custody, Kate. You need to lie low until we find this guy. The Hunter is highly organized and has been a step ahead of the FBI the entire time. He knows who you are, where you live. Hell, he probably knows the route you take to work, and your running routine. And he's not going to let you walk away."

"I won't be running anytime soon with a hole in my shoulder." She shook her head, studied the dark circles under his eyes as a weak smile thinned his mouth. This case was getting to him. Getting to them all. Dominic had been there for her when she needed him the most. He was just looking out for her now. She knew that.

"I appreciate the help, Ryan. I really do, and I trust you and the FBI to do your jobs."

Movement grabbed her attention through the blinds covering the window beside the door, and her gut said her new bodyguard had kept his promise to stick close. "I'll give you my statement, I'll answer your questions, but I'm going to make finding me as difficult for the Hunter as possible. Then we're going to nail the son of a bitch."

DECLAN SLAMMED THE driver's-side door of the SUV and rounded the hood to her side of the vehicle. It'd been three days since he'd carried her into the emergency room. Three days since he'd nearly lost her, and he couldn't get the image of her in that pit out of his damn head. Of all the memories his brain had decided to kick to the surface, it had to hold on to that one.

Gravel crunched beneath his boots as he tugged her door open. She couldn't go home. Not to the house they'd shared during their marriage and not to her apartment. Her teammate, Vincent, had offered his cabin.

Declan surveyed the surrounding woods, the lack of access now that they were out in the middle of nowhere.

He could keep her safe here. Nobody—not the rest of her team, not Special Agent Dominic—knew they were out here. The Hunter would never touch her again.

"Is that a Christmas tree in the window?" Kate stepped out onto a thin veil of ice.

Snow clung to the surrounding pines and the roof of the A-frame structure, but damn, he couldn't take his eyes off her. All that beautiful blond hair, her bright green eyes. His angel.

The cabin looked to be two stories, had a small open porch, red door and sure enough, a Christmas tree covered in white lights in the front window. Crystalized puffs formed in front of her mouth as she closed the passenger-side door behind her. "It's the middle of October. Doesn't the man believe in Halloween?"

"I doubt he's going to get many trick-or-treaters out here," he said.

"Santa's still a possibility." Kate climbed the six steps to the front porch on steady legs. The past few days in recovery had done her good. Despite the fact that she'd tried to hide it from him, he'd seen exactly how much damage the Hunter had done. How close she'd come to surrendering. But the renewed fire in her gaze revealed the bastard hadn't broken her. In fact, Declan was beginning to think nothing could.

"There is a chimney," she said.

A laugh escaped as he hauled their overnight bags from the back seat, the new stitches in his side protesting with every move. No point in thinking about any of that now. Dominic had made it clear before she'd been discharged from the hospital: Kate and her team were no longer allowed near the case. For her protection, and for theirs. Perhaps for his former partner to get all the credit, but Declan didn't know. Didn't care. He might not have access to the FBI's files anymore, but it wasn't going to stop him from finding the Hunter.

"Maybe there's cookies and milk waiting inside," he said.

She smiled at him. "There better be."

Delirium clouded his head at the sight of that perfect smile. Hell, the things she could do to him. It was no wonder his brain hadn't been able to forget her after the amnesia took root.

Locking her gaze on him, she offered him her hand. "Come on. I bet he at least has some hot chocolate to warm up."

He intertwined his fingers with hers and crossed the threshold. A wall of heat hit his skin as he set the bags in the entryway and closed the door behind them. Exposed beams ran the length of the open space, a grand stone fireplace and chimney at the long end of the living room. Furs, flannels, natural light and neutral colors welcomed them deeper into the cabin with a hint of cinnamon in the air.

"Oh, wow." She released her hold on him, pulling her green cargo jacket—the one with the hole in the sleeve—from her shoulder, and hung it on the hook near the door. She closed in on the nine-foot Christmas tree snuggled a few feet from the fireplace as glittering lights highlighted the bruise along one side of her face. She feathered her fingers over the back of one of the sofas. "If I'd known Vincent owned this place, I'd have insisted he host Blackhawk's annual Christmas party here."

"That's probably why he didn't tell you." Declan hung his coat beside hers and keyed in the code on the panel to activate the alarm. Nobody in their right mind would come one hundred feet within this cabin, according to Vincent. The forensics expert had installed a top-of-the-line security system, and Declan intended to take advantage of it as long as they could.

He followed close on her heels. The shadows in her expression had disappeared for the time being. None of his memories—present or past—had her looking so beautiful as she did right now, illuminated in the glow of Christmas decorations. No exhaustion. No deep lines etched between her eyebrows. No darkness in her eyes. Just Kate.

"Christmas used to be my favorite holiday." She reached out for a strand of white lights, the bulb skimming down her long, delicate fingers. "When I was little, I couldn't wait for Christmas morning. My brother and I would nag my grandparents so much, they always put up the tree for me the day after Halloween. We'd spend all day hanging lights and ornaments together, listening to Christmas music and baking sugar cookies. After you and I got married and they all moved back east, you did whatever you had to to continue with the tradition. Even when you were in the middle of an important case, you always made time to indulge in my obsession."

The hollowness in his gut tightened his insides.

"I know it's stupid to get excited about a holiday

with everything going on right now," she said, "but those were some of my favorite memories. Still are. And having you back in my life, with all these decorations, it's…perfect. It's normal." Her voice was quiet. Calm. A genuine laugh escaped her lips, and the sound tightened the muscles down his spine. Green eyes glowed bright with help from the hundreds of lights on the tree, and he'd never seen a more beautiful sight.

Hell. He hadn't expected an angel to set his world on fire, yet there she stood.

"I know it's not the same," she said, "and it's fine that you don't remember—"

He couldn't keep his hands to himself any longer. Declan threaded his fingers in her hair and crushed her lips to his. Careful of her shoulder, he sandwiched her between his body and the large stone fireplace. Her light vanilla scent combined with the sharpness of cinnamon raised his awareness of her all the more.

His gut spiraled as she framed his jaw with her hand, urging him to deepen the kiss. His heart pounded hard in his chest, her sweet breaths barely audible over the throbbing of his pulse.

A shudder shook through her, and his fingers dug into her hips. Too rough. Too fast. But the need he'd tried to suppress had clawed to the surface the second he'd found her in that damn pit. He'd thought far too much about what could've happened if he hadn't followed the training ingrained in his head. He could've lost her. She could've died. And he would have never forgiven himself.

She pulled back, her shoulders rising on a strong inhale, but it was the return of the shadows in her eyes that sent ice through him. Fingers pressed against her lips, she slumped against the stone wall behind her. "I can't do this."

"I hurt you," he said.

Not a question. Kate Monroe was the strongest, most intelligent woman he'd ever met, but even a woman who dealt in death by getting into the minds of killers had her limits. She'd been through more the past four days—hell, the past year—than he could ever know, and he'd put his own selfish need ahead of her own.

"No. It's not you." She shook her head, rolling her lips between her teeth. She pushed her uninjured hand through her hair as tears welled, and his heart sank. A humorless laugh bubbled past her kiss-stung lips. "I... I close my eyes, and I'm right back in the bottom of that pit."

Hell. His hand slipped down her arm. He should've killed the SOB when he had the chance, should've been more prepared, put her safety first.

Her scent worked deep into his lungs, clearing his head. None of that mattered right now. This, right here. This mattered. And he'd do anything to chase the nightmares away. "How can I help?"

"Will you hold me? No expectations. No strings. No questions," she said.

The tears fell freely now, and he feathered the pad of this thumb across her cheek.

Another shake of her head. "I know I said I was fine at the hospital, but I'm not fine, Declan. I've showered, changed my clothes, I've washed the blood off my skin, but I still feel him. I'm not strong enough to do this. I thought I was, but I was wrong."

"Come here." Declan wrapped her in his arms, and she set her head against him. Right where she belonged. With a quick glance, he ensured he'd set the alarm, then positioned his arm beneath her knees. In a quick maneuver that pulled at the fresh stitches in his side, he hauled her into his arms and walked around the sofa. He'd endure a thousand ripped stitches if it meant he got to hold her like this.

He set her gently on the fur rug in front of the fireplace, taking position at her back, his arm wrapped around her midsection. He smoothed back the stray hairs around her ear and planted a kiss at the tendon between her neck and shoulder. "I'll hold you as long as you need, angel."

Stiffness slowly drained from her, and within minutes her breathing evened. Inhale. Exhale.

He didn't know how long they lay there as he counted her breaths, but night had started falling again, and he realized she'd drifted to sleep in his arms. Flames crackled in the stone hearth, shifting the shadows across her features. Exhaustion and her sweet scent pulled him closer to oblivion, to the point he couldn't fight it anymore. The echo of her scream in the woods cut through him as sleep closed in but he only held her tighter.

She was alive. She was safe. The truth settled deep into Declan's bones as he slipped into unconsciousness. She was his.

Chapter Ten

Kate shifted onto her side, hundreds of lit Christmas lights sparkling above her. A smile pulled at one corner of her mouth at the sight as she stretched her aching muscles. When was the last time she'd slept so well? Months? A year? The past four days had taken a toll, but for the first time since dodging bullets back at the house, she felt almost human. What had changed?

She raised her head at a hard thumping noise from outside, and she straightened. Rubbing her fingers across one eye, she pushed to her feet. She already knew the answer. "Declan?"

A tray with a steaming mug of hot chocolate and a slip of paper sat on the sofa cushion near the fur rug they'd fallen asleep on. She breathed in the combination of cinnamon and cocoa. How did he know she liked to sprinkle cinnamon on top of her hot chocolate? She pinched the piece of paper between two fingers.

Take your time and dress warm before you meet me outside.

Replacing the note, she picked up the mug. Heat spread through her as she sipped and chased back the chill that had settled there since she'd been tossed into the pit. Her shoulder ached, but it was nothing compared to recovering from three bullet wounds and the handful of surgeries afterward. Her favorite hot beverage helped. The IOU list she'd created in her head for Declan had already started growing out of control.

She changed into warmer clothes—harder than anticipated with a hole in her shoulder—and slid on her boots before stepping onto the front porch. The light veil of snow coating everything heralded the arrival of winter. She scanned the front yard for the source of the rhythmic sound, but there was no sign of Declan. Following the stone path around to the back of the cabin, she tamped down the need to search the trees at every movement, every sound.

She was safe here. She had to believe that. Otherwise…

Circling around the back of the cabin, Kate slowed as Declan came into sight.

He'd shed his jacket, and thick bands of muscle tightened and released down his back, across his shoulders, in his arms. Despite the cold, sweat formed a thin layer across his brow as he heaped a shovelful of snow onto a pile next to the in-ground firepit.

The longer she studied him, the more the knot in her gut eased. "I'm pretty sure Vincent doesn't expect you to shovel snow while we're here."

Declan spun, and that smile of his hiked her blood pressure higher as he balanced one hand on the snow shovel. "Good morning." Gleaming blue eyes focused on her, and the world disappeared. "I was about to come dump a handful of snow on you to wake you up."

"Is that what all this is for?" Warmth climbed up her neck and into her face as snow fell around them. He made her feel warm, safe, cared for. Then again, he'd had that skill from the moment he'd inserted himself back into her life. When he'd died, she'd felt as though she'd shattered into a million pieces, and it had taken close to a year to be able to put herself back together.

But for the first time in a long time, the pieces fit. She was starting to feel whole, to think of a future outside of grieving, outside of hunting down killers. A future with Declan. And last night, she could've sworn she fit perfectly against him.

Kate walked up to the firepit. Boxes of graham crackers, bags of marshmallows and packages of chocolate bars sat a few feet away. S'mores? "Quite the breakfast you have planned."

"You only live once. Well, not in my case, but you get the point." Flakes collected in his hair as he closed the short distance between them. For an instant, she could've sworn his pupils darkened as he studied the sling around her arm. "How's the pain?"

"Better today." She didn't want to think about the hole in her shoulder, how it got there, who'd shot her or why. She wanted the world to stop, wanted to close her eyes and for once not see herself at the bottom of that pit with Brian Michaels's remains. She wanted her life back. But the Hunter had made that impossible. No matter how many times she tried to convince herself otherwise, the man who'd trapped her wasn't finished. The world wouldn't stop just because she needed it to.

He wasn't done killing, and he wasn't finished with her.

Kate clenched her fists to hold on to a bit of warmth and forced a smile. "Did you build a snow fort?"

"Yeah. Still needs some finishing touches, but I thought it'd be fun to get some sunshine, start a fire and relive all those favorite Christmas memories of yours." Declan narrowed his eyes at her, then he hefted the shovel from the ground and faced the mound of snow he'd built. "What do you say, Monroe? Ready to make yourself sick from eating too much chocolate?"

He'd done this for her?

Kate reached to frame his jaw with her hand. His stubble scraped along her palms, and he closed his eyes as though he were committing the moment to memory. Hope built inside her, and she planted a soft kiss against his cheek. Her heart skipped a beat as a flood of need overwhelmed her reluctance. She leaned in a second time, kissing the corner of his mouth. "Thank you. For all of this. For saving my life. For…everything."

"Be careful, Kate." His gaze was on her again, filled with molten heat. Declan trailed his free hand to her hips beneath the hem of her jacket, holding her in place. "I only have so much control when it comes to you."

"If there's one thing I've learned over the past few days, it's that you won't hurt me. I trust you." She swiped her tongue across her bottom lip, and his gaze shot to her mouth.

The past four days—the past year of her life—had

been filled with nothing but fear, pain and death. She couldn't live like that anymore. Not when the man standing in front of her made her feel so much more.

Fisting her hand in his shirt collar, she pulled him into her. With her heart racing so fast and hard, she feared he might hear the chaotic beat, but she knew exactly what she was asking in that moment. A chance to forget. A chance to move on. They'd escape the pain for a bit, then she'd wake up tomorrow, and reality would come screaming back.

"Control is the last thing I want right now," she said.

Then he was the one to kiss her. He swept inside her mouth without hesitation, and she committed every ounce of her being to him in that moment. No turning back. No letting the past interject between them anymore. The Declan Monroe she'd married had died that night in their home after a fatal shooting. She'd always love him—always have memories of him—but right now, she had a second chance.

And she was going to take it.

Snowflakes burned against her exposed skin as he deepened the kiss. He discarded the shovel and his hold strengthened around her back, molding her against him. The shooting, Michaels's involvement with the Hunter, the nightmares, it all vanished as Declan's fingers pressed into her spine.

"We almost died out there, and those were the most terrifying hours of my life. I thought I was going to lose you all over again." She brushed her fingertips down his throat, over his Adam's apple. "I don't want to waste another minute being afraid, Declan."

He trailed his fingers along the back of her arm, every inch prompting new desire. Lacing his fingers with hers, he tugged her to the entrance of the snow fort he'd built. "You never have to be afraid with me at your side. I'll take a hundred more bullets, hang upside down for eternity and fight for you until my last breath if it means I get to be with you. I'm not going anywhere."

He picked up the bag of s'mores ingredients. Pulling her inside the snow fort, Declan rolled onto his back, on top of layers of blankets he'd laid out, and she did the same. "What do you think? Just like your childhood?"

"Not exactly. I wasn't allowed to have boys inside my fort as a kid." Gleaming ice surrounded them, but nothing but warmth penetrated through her clothing as she shifted beside him. "I'm thinking after the past few days we've had, we can break another rule while we're at it and have s'mores for breakfast."

"Coming right up." Declan made quick work of starting the fire in the pit outside their snow cave door as she unpackaged the ingredients. He slid back inside, claiming his roasting stick and an oversize marshmallow. Within a minute, the marshmallows were perfectly brown, the scent of fire and pure sugar in the air as they assembled their treats.

He bit into the mess, leaving a bit of marshmallow and chocolate on his chin. "All right. You've got sugar for breakfast and a guy in your snow fort. What other rules are you interested in breaking today?"

"Just one more." Reaching out, she skimmed her thumb over his bottom lip to wipe away the remnants of their sugar rush. Piercing blue eyes focused on her, and every cell in her body fizzed with awareness. Sunlight bore down on the fort, droplets of freezing water pooling at the edges of the blankets. A chunk of ice landed at her feet, but she wasn't going to rush this. "But with the fort coming down around us, I recommend we make this first time fast."

Kate set her chocolate-and-marshmallow breakfast aside and reached for her jacket. Sliding her one arm out, she tossed it aside and went for the Velcro on her sling. No more stalling. No more living in the past. The future sat right in front of her, waiting for her to make a choice she never thought she'd have to make. And she'd made it.

She planted her hand over his sternum. "Screw the rules."

Declan threaded his fingers in her hair, then shifted her onto her back as he flashed that brilliant smile. "I was never a fan of them anyway."

DECLAN SLIPPED FROM the king-size sheets they'd spent the rest of day underneath and grabbed his clothes before stalking toward the door. No more mistakes. He'd let that bastard get his hands on her once. He wouldn't let it happen again. He wasn't about to let her go, and he'd do whatever it took to protect her.

Even if it meant lying to her a bit longer.

Because once she discovered the truth, discovered he wasn't the man she thought him to be, she wouldn't want him anymore.

Oranges, yellows and reds bled through the cabin's windows as the sun set in the west. He dressed quickly, then extracted her laptop from her bag beside the door. Taking position on one of the bar stools at the granite countertop, he dimmed the screen and typed the online access address for the FBI into the browser. The window changed, demanding a login and password. That bit of memory had come to the surface while he dug out the snow fort, and he typed in Special Agent Declan Monroe's credentials.

Access granted.

Kate's teammate, Elizabeth, had been assigned to review his old case files for the BAU, but she wasn't an agent. She didn't hunt the monsters in the dark. He did, and there had to be something he could work with—a clue, anything in these old files—he could follow to nail the perp with one of his own damn arrows. Somehow, the Hunter knew him, and Declan would make him pay for dragging Kate into his sick game.

He read through countless case files, one after the other. Crime scene photos, witness statements, arrest reports. Nothing jogged his memory, none of it linked to any other cases where an arrow was part of the killer's MO. He had...nothing.

Declan rubbed at his eyes as frustration burrowed deeper. A single file on Kate's desktop peeked out from behind the window he'd been working in. Case 306-AK-4442. The FBI's internal offense code 306 categorized the file under serial killings, AK assigned the file to the Bureau's Alaskan field office and the last number was unique to the case. The Hunter's case.

Double tapping on the file folder, he scanned the evidence from the Hunter's latest trophy, the woman Kate had found in the field. Kate and Declan might've been banned from working the case officially, but the FBI hadn't ordered her to delete her case files. An oversight on Dominic's part, but Declan wasn't above taking advantage. Not when Kate's life was in danger.

Mary Lawson. She fit the unsub's MO, making her the perfect prey. But what were the chances the killer had found not two but four single women close to their thirties with blond hair and green eyes in this city? What was the connection? His rage boiled hot inside of him, a blistering fury that demanded he end the son of a bitch. "When are you going to try for her again, you bastard?"

The kitchen lights brightened, and his spine went rock hard as he closed down the file window.

"You want to go after him alone." She moved into his peripheral vision, her fingers trailing across his shoulders, and his grip on the counter relaxed. She took a seat beside him, her voice devoid of emotion. No plea to get him to stop. No disappointment in his decision. Nothing. "Even though we're off the case, you can't let the Hunter get away with what he did."

"He tried to kill you." But he couldn't think about that right now. He had to focus on the evidence, had to find a lead. Because the Hunter wasn't finished. He'd come after Kate again. He'd try to take her away. That wasn't happening. "And for all you know, I could be researching different s'more recipes."

"Okay, first, you're a horrible liar," she said.

If only that were true.

"Second, I know you, Declan." She reached across

the laptop and hit a command to bring up the Hunter's files. He inwardly flinched. "You might not have all your memories, but some things are ingrained too deep. Doubling down on a case is something you used to do as an agent, even when you only had a hunch. Third, there's no other way to make s'mores. I don't care what the internet says."

Her green gaze glowed from the laptop's brightness. She pulled her hand away as she stood. "Besides, I'm not sure he was trying to kill us. There were faster ways to accomplish the task, and he wouldn't have worn a mask or disguised his voice if that was his intention."

"What then? He's dressing up for Halloween?" he asked.

"I think he was testing us." Her thin robe fluttered around her knees as she moved to the refrigerator. She pulled a carton of eggs and a gallon of milk from the fridge and set them on the island in front of him. "He killed Michaels and broke his own MO. He's not operating out of some undeniable urge to kill like most serials. The Hunter wanted us—wanted *me*—to see what he's capable of. Maybe to prove he's above my skills as a profiler, which is certainly looking to be true for the time being."

Declan stood, coming around the countertop. "We're going to catch this guy, Kate." They had to. Otherwise… He shut down that line of thought. No. He wouldn't think about that. He wouldn't think about losing her like that.

"I let my personal problems get in the way of doing my job. Again." She twisted the cap off the milk and selected a brightly colored ceramic mixing bowl from the cabinet. She cracked one egg into the bowl, then another. "How exactly are we supposed to catch him when I can't even wrap my head around the fact you're standing in this kitchen with me?"

"You need to know, there was nothing you could've done for Michaels," he said. "He didn't become one of your patients by chance. He was placed in your path. Someone sent him to shoot you."

Her mouth dropped open, and she stumbled away from the counter. The egg in her hand fell to the floor, but she didn't move to clean it up. Eyes wide, she licked her lips. "What did you say?"

"Right before I heard those gunshots in the woods, I found Michaels." Declan lowered his voice.

It'd all been in his statement to the Anchorage PD and FBI while she was in surgery, but Kate had been removed from the case right afterward. She had no reason to believe she still had access to those files. No reason to go back and read his statement. If anything, she'd probably made the effort to avoid anything to do with the case since being pulled from that damn hole in the ground.

"His throat had been cut, but before he died, he told me he was hired to fire those shots. Someone paid him to pull the trigger a year ago and again the other day. He was a pawn, Kate. You did nothing wrong."

"You think that person who hired him is the Hunter." She worked to swallow, her gaze distant as she studied the broken egg on the floor. Her fingers went to the scar at the collar of her T-shirt, a nervous habit that had increased over the last few days.

"I guess that explains why both Michaels and our serial killer were in those woods at the same time, but that still doesn't make sense. The Hunter is the one with the fascination for blonde women with green eyes. Not Michaels." She looked up at him. "Why would he send one of my patients after me at all? And with a gun? Serial killing teams are rare, but if they were partners, wouldn't they have the same MO? They build off each other, they work hard—together—to distort the evidence and confuse law enforcement. Studies have shown they have a smaller chance of getting caught that way because police think they're only after one unsub instead of two distinct killers."

He'd given it a lot of thought since walking out of those woods with her in his arms and again as he'd traced the scar tissue across her chest while she slept. There was only one explanation. Declan rested his hip against the counter, folding his arms across as his own scars burned with awareness. "I don't think the bullets were meant for you."

She lowered her hand. "There was only one other person in that house, which means—"

"Michaels was sent to kill me." The bastard had almost succeeded. Twice. Only, Kate had gotten caught in the cross fire. Was that why the Hunter cut Michaels's throat? Had it been punishment for his partner nearly killing the target he was really after?

The feel of the cold granite kept the rage at bay. For now. Because Kate had been right. Declan wanted to go after him. The Hunter had started this battle, but Declan would bring the war. "I was there, Kate. Both times. That can't be a coincidence."

"If the Hunter wanted you out of the way to get to me, why wait over a year to try again?" she asked. "Why target those four other women when he had so many opportunities to take me?"

"Maybe he couldn't get to you, even with me out of the picture." Blackhawk Security watched their own and had an entire arsenal at their disposal. Their killer wouldn't want that kind of attention or heat.

Declan ran a hand through his hair, focusing on the bowl of milk and egg she'd left on the counter. "Or it's like you said in your profile. He wants us to see his work, rub it in our faces that we haven't stopped him before now. Punishing us." Air rushed from his lungs as the realization hit. Damn it. He should've seen it before. He should've known. "Punishing you. Because he can't bring himself to hurt you."

"You're saying I'm the focus of his kills." Color drained from her face, her rough exhale loud in his ears. Profilers didn't catch killers. She gave the men and women who did the details to accomplish their task. Being the target of a psychopath had never been part of the job description.

Kate straightened. "Those women are being hunted in the middle of the woods—dying with arrows through their hearts—because of me? Is that what you're saying?"

Declan wrapped his hands around her arms, careful of the bullet graze on one side. The lit Christmas lights deepened the shadows in her eyes, an opposite effect of the night before, and everything inside of him went cold. The Hunter had put those shadows there, and Declan would make damn sure he paid for it. "This is not your fault, Kate. Don't you dare let him get to you this way. The shooting, those women's deaths, what happened to me, none of it is on you."

"I know all that." Her words cut through him. "But this killer… He's not like anything I've encountered before, and he's good at what he does. He's gotten in my head, and I can't get him out, okay?"

Nothing but strength and determination showed in her expression, and damn if that wasn't the sexiest thing he'd ever seen. Kate Monroe had been through hell and back, but the locking of her jaw said she wouldn't be playing the part of victim anytime soon.

"You don't have to worry about my guilt," she said. "If anyone should be worried, it's him. I'm not going to let him get away with this." Kate collected a handful of paper towels and scooped the broken egg off the floor. Throwing it in the trash, she set back to work on the ingredients for their dinner. "He thinks he's better at hunting than I am, but I'm going to show him he's wrong."

Chapter Eleven

"If we accept our theory that I'm his ultimate prey, then the killer thinks he knows me. But I think finding a connection between the women needs to be the priority," Kate said.

Because there had to be one beyond just a similarity to her looks. Kate might've been the Hunter's ultimate target according to their theory, but she didn't know any of the victims. As far as she could tell, she'd never met them before. Not working as a psychologist and not for Blackhawk Security. It was too easy to assume their killer had found them on the street. So how was the Hunter coming into contact with them?

"However small," she said. "It'll tell us how he's choosing his victims and help us stop the next abduction. You and I both know he isn't finished. If anything, I believe he's just getting started."

"You read my mind." Declan spun the laptop toward her, the mess of French toast forgotten on the counter as four young faces stared back at her from the screen. "Brittney Sutherland, Holly Belcher, Carrie Fleming and Mary Lawson."

"Wait, why does that second name sound familiar?" Kate shifted closer to the screen as instinct flared. She'd read that name before and not in the files Dominic had given her when he'd brought her onto the case. It hadn't clicked until now. "Holly Belcher."

"I thought the same thing when I brought up her file. Turns out her brother went missing last year. She was all over the news." Declan scrolled through the digital file. "She and her mother were pleading with anyone who had information about his disappearance to call Anchorage PD over every news channel who'd give them air time."

A missing person case.

"I can only imagine what that mother is going through right now," Kate said. "First her son, then her daughter."

Losing Declan had been one thing. Losing two children within the span of a year? Kate swallowed as her throat swelled. Then again, she'd lost a child, too, hadn't she? She hadn't gotten to meet the tiny life that had been growing inside of her, but a life had been ripped from her all the same. Her gaze slid to Declan, across his shoulders, down his spine, and it took everything in her not to imagine what that life might look like today.

"Did they ever find him?" she asked. "The son?"

"No. No sign of him according to the FBI's report. He was finally presumed dead a few months ago by the lead investigating agent." Declan shook his head, leaning back on the bar stool as he crossed his arms over his muscled chest.

Kate eased away from the screen. "Now his sister is a serial killer's trophy."

Didn't seem fair after everything the family had already been through. Her heart broke a fraction more as she straightened. But she could still get them justice. She could stop the Hunter from taking more women.

"Michaels was a former patient," Declan said. "There's a chance the Hunter is, too."

"It's possible, but even if we knew his identity, we won't be able to get those files from their current doctors without a judge," she said. "If we were granted a warrant, any leads we get from them won't be usable in court. I'm not a practicing psychologist anymore, but doctor-patient confidentiality is still in effect."

The Hunter was one of the most complicated killers she'd studied. He was organized, intelligent and controlled. If he'd been seeing a psychologist, it would be impossible to pick him out of a stack of files due to his ability to blend in, to lie. To make everyone around him believe he was just like them.

Kate rolled her bottom lip into her mouth and bit down to keep herself in the moment. There had to be something they could use. Every victim had unknowingly attracted the Hunter in some way, brought him into their lives.

"What if he targeted Holly because of her media appearances?" she asked. "Were any of the other women in the spotlight? The more we learn about the victims, the more we'll learn about their killer."

Declan's fingers flew over the keyboard, the screen switching from the second victim to the first. The

Hunter had started with Brittney Sutherland, as far as the authorities knew. She'd been the first victim recovered, but there was a chance there were others out there. "You're not going to believe this."

"What?" Kate forced herself to look past the photo of the victim and read the FBI's report. Her heart jerked in her chest as she read through the lead agent's notes. "Is that…"

"Another missing person report," he said. "Only this is for the first victim's mother."

"Two victims, both tied to separate missing persons cases?" That was too much of a coincidence. What were the chances two of the Hunter's victims had loved ones missing within in the same time frame? "Check the others. Carrie Fleming and Mary Lawson."

The screen changed as he pulled the next two files. "Carrie was brought in for questioning when her best friend disappeared from a bar a few months ago, and Mary's roommate went missing last week."

"That's how he's finding them." She tapped the screen. Her arm brushed against Declan's, and her entire body caught fire with adrenaline. They had a lead. "The crime scenes where each victim was left are too complex, too clean. I'd originally thought he was a true crime buff, maybe studied a bit of forensics, but this points to law enforcement. Someone in the FBI is targeting women who've been brought in for questioning during missing persons investigations. It's the perfect cover."

"The FBI has dozens of agents assigned to their missing persons task force, Kate. We know the Hunter is local to Anchorage, knows the area and is a big-time hunter, but the Bureau won't ever give us access to the personnel files without a warrant. Even then, by the time we get through the files, another woman could go missing." Declan smoothed his hand over his wound. "I have your back, but we'll have to come at this another way."

Heat worked through her. She had his back, too, and in that moment, she trusted him more than she'd ever trusted anyone since his death. Over the last year, she'd fought to keep her head above water, fought for her team, fought with everything she had not to dissolve into nothingness, but with him here, it was easier. There was a light at the end of the tunnel.

"Our unsub had to be assigned to all four of our victims' cases to come into contact with them, right? He didn't choose these women at random. He got close to them during the investigations, probably talked with them a few times. Became familiar with their lives." She blinked to clear the exhaustion from her head. They'd been running on fumes and fear for the last few days. Barely eaten more than marshmallows and chocolate. Barely slept. But she wouldn't stop. Not until they identified the Hunter and brought his victims and their families justice. "Who was the lead agent?"

Scanning the reports, Declan confirmed a commonality. "Special Agent Kenneth Winter headed all four missing persons cases, but these are career-making cases. A lot of agents and officers wanted in. The chief of police included. Wait. I've heard that name before."

Her stomach sank. "He's Dominic's partner." The

BAU's newest agent had always been desperate to prove himself on the hardest cases. If he was responsible for these women's deaths, what was harder than making it look like some other perpetrator had delivered the killing shot while taking credit for the collar in the end? Winter was over six feet tall, close to one hundred and ninety pounds. Had he been the one to toss her in that pit to die?

Kate cleared her throat, shook her head to dislodge the memory. Like Declan said, these were career-making cases. Winter might be one name out of dozens all assigned to work missing persons cases. They'd have to dig deeper into each case.

"Blackhawk Security has a contact in Anchorage PD. Maybe she can give us some insight into who might've taken a special interest in the women during the investigations." Kate refocused on the dinner mess on the kitchen counter. Her body ached from tension, from being shot with an arrow, from the last four days. She grew heavy as a wave of dizziness took hold. "I'll let Dominic know he might want to take a closer look at the missing persons cases."

And his partner.

"Kate, you're bottoming out." Declan pushed away from the laptop and caged her against the cool countertop. "You need to get something other than sugar in you, shower and sleep for at least few hours. You're no good to any of those women if you're dead on your feet. I'll fill Dominic in and finish up the mess here."

"Thank you." She gripped the granite. He was right. Of course he was. If she didn't take a step back now, the Hunter would only take advantage of her weakness. But the thought of stepping away—even after Dominic had ordered her to cut ties to the case, even for a few hours—pooled dread at the base of her spine.

The Hunter had made this personal. He'd recruited Michaels to do his dirty work. Twice. He'd taken her husband's memories, taken her unborn baby, taken everything that mattered. The killer was still out there, and he wouldn't wait around for her to get herself together. He'd strike when she least expected it.

"For everything," she said. "Truth is, I feel better when I'm with you." Not scared. Not weak. Kate framed Declan's face with her uninjured hand, his five-o'clock shadow bristling against her palm. She didn't have to hide from him. No secrets. No lies. No pretending. He'd pulled her from the darkness and out into the light, given her a second chance. He'd saved her, and she trusted him straight to her core. He would catch her long before she ever fell. She'd fight like hell to keep him at her side.

"I've hunted at least a dozen monsters between my job at Blackhawk Security and consulting for the FBI, but this one…" Dropping her hand, she took a deep, cleansing breath and shook her head. "I'm glad you're here. I wouldn't want to work this case without you."

"Me, too. If for no other reason than having my own personal partner with benefits," he said. "Pretty sure Dominic and I never had that kind of relationship."

Kate pressed her lower back into the counter. Was this a relationship? Sure, they'd slept together in that perfect little snow fort he'd built out back, but it had started simply as a way to stop the nightmares, to distract her from the harsh reality crashing down around them both. Only, being with Declan had become so much more. Hadn't it?

He leaned into her, his mouth mere centimeters from hers. His exhale brushed against the thin skin of her collarbone as he studied her from forehead to chin. Sliding his hand to her wrist, he traced the oversensitive veins running up her arm. "Now stop stalling and get in the shower. Because, angel, you smell awful."

A burst of laughter escaped her lips, and she tipped her head up toward the ceiling. "Trust me when I say this, I don't smell as bad as you do." Desire pushed through her as she grabbed his shirt collar and tugged him back toward the bedroom. "But it's a good thing I have a solution for that."

DAWN BROKE THROUGH the trees, but the feel of a new day hadn't struck yet. With Kate asleep in his arms, it was easy to imagine the nightmares didn't wait outside these walls. They could lie here, waste the day away in bed, surviving off nothing but each other's body heat and whatever they could find in the pantry. But the world wouldn't stop for them and neither would the Hunter.

"I can almost see the wheels spinning in your head." Her fingers smoothed between his eyebrows. Kate pulled the sheets around her, hiking her uninjured hand beneath her head. Mesmerizing green eyes followed the path of her fingers as she reached out to trace one of his scars. "Trying to figure out how to sneak out of here without waking me up again? It won't work."

"Quite the opposite. I was devising a plan to convince you to stay in bed all day long." Taking her chin between his thumb and first finger, he rolled into her. He needed to tell her the truth. He'd become the one person in this world she could rely on, and he intended to keep it that way. Hell, he was a jerk for keeping her in the dark this long.

Her soft moan vibrated against him as she closed her eyes. "Wouldn't take too much convincing, but since you've already gone through all that trouble, I'll let you plead your case."

He pulled her flush against him with his arm. His mouth crashed onto hers, and Declan pushed everything he had into that kiss. The loneliness of waking up in that hospital room alone, the pain from the bullet wound in his side, the fear of losing her all over again. She shouldered it all and expected nothing in return. That was the kind of woman she was. Considerate, caring, honest.

Everything he wasn't.

"I'm beginning to see your point, but I think I need to hear a bit more of your defense." She smiled against his mouth, then skimmed her fingertips along his bottom lip. Setting her ear over his heart, she ran one hand through her hair. "It's also time we got on the same page. I know I said after this investigation was over it'd be better if we go our separate ways, but a lot has happened since then."

Anxiety clawed through him. "Kate, wait—"

"Please just let me finish before I lose my nerve." Straightening, she placed a hand over the gauze taped to her shoulder. "For the past year I've been lost. I've helped dozens of patients move past their trauma in my career, but for the longest time, I couldn't take my own damn advice. When it came right down to it, we were together for so long, I'd forgotten how to be alone."

She shook her head. "I hated it. I was cold inside. I'd given up hope of ever finding another person who could make me feel the way you did. I threw myself into my work because helping my clients was the only thing that made me feel alive. Until you walked back into that house five days ago."

Kate hiked the sheets farther up her body. "When you kiss me, I see a light at the end of this dark, lonely tunnel I've been stuck inside. You're the strongest, most selfless man I've ever known, and I don't want to give that up. I don't want to give you up." She smoothed her hand over his chest. "I want you to stay. I want us to try to make sense of whatever's happening between us. It won't be easy, but I think it'll be worth it." She placed her hand over his sternum. "So that's how I feel. Now you tell me how you feel."

Heat worked through him, and he fisted his hands in the sheets. Committing the past few minutes to memory, Declan filled his lungs with her sweet vanilla scent. He had to tell her the truth, pray she'd still want him despite the lie. And if she didn't... His gut tightened. Things would have to go back to the way they were. He'd rebuild his life. Without her. "Kate, there's something you need to know before we—"

A soft ringing reached his ears, and she lowered her forehead onto his chest. Her hair tickled his overheated skin as she pushed away to reach for her phone on the nightstand. "Hold that thought." Bringing it to her ear, she pegged him with a smile, and his blood pressure spiked. "Kate Monroe."

The smile disappeared, her gaze sinking into the sheets. Her tongue swiped across her bottom lip, and she pushed herself upright. She threw her legs over the side of the bed and positioned the phone between her neck and shoulder as she reached for her discarded clothing on the floor. "When?"

Everything inside of him shut down.

"Okay." Kate hauled her T-shirt over her head, careful of her wound. Slipping into her jeans, she hopped to pull them around her waist, and Declan shoved out of the bed. "I'll be right there."

She tossed the phone onto the bed, turning away from him.

"Kate?" Concern deepened his voice and ignited his instincts with battle-ready precision. "Tell me who was on the phone."

"That was Ryan. Sorry, Special Agent Dominic." She turned, biting down on her thumbnail. "He got our message about the connection between the women and started digging into any active missing persons cases the FBI is investigating." Kate ran a hand through her hair. She did that when she tried to hide the emotions fighting for release inside, but she couldn't hide from him. The tension along her spine gave her away, and he rounded the bed in order to close the distance between them. "He believes another woman has been taken. And that his partner is responsible."

"Kenneth Winter. But what makes you think Dominic isn't involved? That him pulling you back in isn't some kind of trap? They're partners. They're assigned the same cases." As far as Declan knew, Anchorage PD and the FBI were still analyzing the last scene, and the Hunter had already taken another victim? Damn it. They couldn't keep up with this guy.

"Serial killing teams are rare, but even so, Dominic's name isn't on any of the missing person reports." Kate shook her head. "I know Ryan. He bleeds red, white and blue for the FBI."

"So Dominic wants to keep this quiet until he has enough evidence to bring his partner in for questioning," Declan said. "That's why he called you back in?"

"He wants as many available eyes on this case as he can get. He's at a scene he believes is the last known location of a missing woman who fits the Hunter's MO." She reached for her green cargo jacket and slipped into her boots. "There's no rhyme or reason to this unsub's attacks, and it's only going to get worse from here. We need to catch this guy. If there's a chance this latest victim can be brought home before we find her with an arrow through the heart, Dominic is going to take the risk of losing his job to do it." Straightening, she softened her expression. "He's going to email me the details in a few minutes, but I really want to finish our conversation."

"This case has to take priority." Dominic's call had bought Declan some time. He'd tell her the truth soon, but right now, bringing down the unsub who'd set this all in motion had to come first. "Don't worry. We have time. We'll do what we have to do to get those families justice, then talk about us."

"So there's an us?" Her eyes glittered as sunlight speared through the windows. She stepped toward him, slipped her arms around his waist and stared up at him.

"I've waited a long time to find the woman in my dreams. Do you think I'm going to walk away after everything we've been through?" Twisting a strand of her hand around his finger, he set his forehead against hers. He tilted her chin higher and planted a soft kiss on her mouth. "You accept my past, support me in the present and have given me a glimpse of my future. You're my armor, and you and I will always be unfinished business."

That angelic smile of hers overwhelmed her expression, and he couldn't help but smile back. "Not sure I had a choice in those first two things," she said. "Finding out your husband isn't dead after all is kind of a sink-or-swim situation."

"Good thing your personnel file says you're scuba certified, then." His laugh rumbled through him, and for the first time he could remember, the gutting hollowness inside didn't ache. "Maybe after all this is over, you can show off some of those skills on a beach far the hell away from here."

She wrapped her arms around his neck, hiking herself onto her tiptoes. "Hot sand, cold drinks and nothing but the ocean and room service? I could get on board with that."

He nibbled at her bottom lip, sliding his arms around her waist. Kissing a trail down her neck, he locked on their reflection in a standalone mirror against the wall. This. This was what he wanted. Her, for the rest of his life. Every wound he'd incurred, every scar left behind, they all paved the way to this moment, to her. Declan would fight until his last breath to protect her.

Her tablet pinged with an incoming message, and she turned in his arms at the sound. "That's probably the details Dominic said he'd send over. Don't go anywhere."

"Wouldn't dream of it," he said.

Kate unwrapped her arms and crossed back to the nightstand beside the bed. He watched as she tapped the screen, confusion deepening the distinctive lines between her eyebrows. "That's not...right."

"What is it?" He pushed his feet into his boots, the mattress dipping under his weight as he bent to tie them. His gut sank. Had law enforcement been too late? Declan pushed upright, took a single step forward. "Did they already find her?"

"No." She snapped her attention up and tossed the device face up onto the bed.

Every muscle down his spine tightened as he studied the screen. Surveillance photos taken from outside her apartment—of Declan—dated a few weeks ago.

"Looks like we're going to have to hold off on that beach vacation," she said.

Chapter Twelve

"How did you know I like cinnamon in my hot chocolate?" The dates on those surveillance photos couldn't be right. If they were... Then Declan had been lying to her all this time.

Nausea churned in her gut. Lying about his memories. Lying about not knowing who she was. The photos of him watching her apartment and their home two weeks ago proved that.

"That's not the question you want to ask, Kate." He straightened from tying his boots, gripping the edge of the mattress, his attention on her tablet. "Ask me."

She swallowed around the bile rising up her throat. The truth dried out her mouth and pulled at her body until her knees weakened. It took everything to keep herself upright, but the air had been taken right out of her. Her scars burned as though she'd been shot all over again. Pain spread from her shoulder down through the rest of her arm. Or was it the scars in her heart tearing open again?

"How long have you had your memories back?" she asked.

"Hard to say." Piercing blue eyes locked on her, and the room spun. Was that an admission? Veins struggled to break through the skin of his forearms the harder his fingers clenched the edge of the mattress. "They still come in bits and pieces. I don't remember everything."

"But you knew who I was before you walked into our house that night, right? You knew I was your wife, and you stayed away anyway. You let me think you were still dead." Her eyes burned as betrayal hit.

Kate forced herself to take a deep breath to drown the nausea, but his clean, masculine scent filled her system instead. The grief, the pain he'd helped ebb clawed through her, deepening the fissures Brian Michaels had put there in the first place. A combination of sorrow and rage exploded inside her. Hot tears burned a path down her face. Apparently, Declan had only come back into her life to finish the job.

"Why didn't you tell me the truth? Why keep me in the dark? I could've helped you sooner," she said.

He stood, towering over her to the point she had to crane her head back to look at him. "I woke up with four bullet wounds, Kate. I had no memory of how they'd gotten there or who pulled the trigger. For all I knew, you were the reason I was in that hospital bed." He gripped his fists at his side. "I wasn't sure I could trust you. I thought if I inserted myself back into your life pretending not to know anything about you, you could help me regain the rest of my memories and get me access to my personnel file with the FBI. Which you have."

"You used me." Plain and simple. He'd wanted his

life back, and he'd done what he had to do to get the job done. She could still feel his hands on her, taste him, smell him on her skin. Her stomach rolled. She'd trusted him to help her forget, but all he'd done was make the nightmare worse. "And sleeping with me? Was that part of your sick mind game, too?"

"No. That was never part of the plan. But no matter how many times I tried to tell myself otherwise, I couldn't keep my hands off you, angel." He reached out with one hand as though he intended to comfort her. "You're the strongest, most intelligent—"

"Don't." Her order came out between gritted teeth. He'd lied to her, used her. He wasn't the man she thought he was. He'd seen an easy target and taken advantage, but she was the one filled with shame. Gravity pulled at her, urging her to sink to the floor, but she wouldn't show weakness in front of him. Never again. Another wave of loss swallowed her whole. "I'm not your angel. You don't get to call me sweet nicknames and make this all okay. You don't get to touch me. You don't get to pretend what you did wasn't wrong."

He didn't get to pretend she wasn't grieving all over again.

He dropped his hand, pulled back his shoulders. His expression locked into place, mirroring those times when he hadn't been able to talk about his work for the FBI. She should've recognized that look for what it really was before now—pure apathy. That was what had made him such a good agent, made him the investigator his superiors could rely on, no matter the case. He'd kept himself just distant enough to not let the darkness in, and he was doing the exact same thing to her now—distancing himself. "Who sent you the photos?" he asked.

"Special Agent Dominic. Looks like you weren't the only person in my life lying to my face." Dominic had obviously known Declan was alive before setting eyes on him in her office. He'd been surveilling her husband for a few weeks.

But why? Why was everyone keeping secrets? This was her life, damn it. She deserved the truth. She ripped her cargo jacket from her shoulder, biting down against the pain where the Hunter's arrow had pierced her, and shoved the coat into him on her way toward the bedroom door. "You can have this back. I don't need it anymore."

Footsteps closed in behind her, then a strong hand on her arm spun her into his chest. "Kate—"

"I told you not to touch me." She wrenched out of his grip, put a few feet of space between them. The anger distorted into an all-too-familiar choking sensation. She couldn't breathe. Couldn't think. "Whether you're the husband I buried after the shooting or the man who pulled me from that pit, I don't care. Don't follow me, don't insert yourself back into my life and don't try to apologize. I don't ever want to see you again."

She had to get out of there, away from him. Not waiting for his response, Kate headed for the front door. Hundreds of Christmas lights and decorations blurred in her peripheral vision, but where she'd had happy, comforting memories to draw from at the sight, now a tainted mass of betrayal set up residence. She grabbed her overnight bag and wrenched the thick front door open, stepping out into the freezing Alaskan night, and slammed the door behind her.

He let her go.

Her heated breath froze on the air, forming crystalized puffs in front of her mouth. Cold worked into her lungs and cleared her head.

Dominic was waiting on her. They were going to have a talk about how he got ahold of those surveillance photos of Declan. But she couldn't let the past few minutes—days—get to her. Despite the situation between her and Declan, she had a job to do, too. Another woman had presumably gone missing. She wouldn't let the new cracks in her armor affect the case. Not again.

The stairs protested under her weight as she forced her way to the SUV. They weren't far up the mountain. Once the sun rose, Declan could make his way back to the city on his own. She wasn't coming back here. She hit the button on her key fob to start the engine, and it roared to life. Climbing inside, she hauled her bag into the passenger seat and cranked the heater.

Snow popped and groaned beneath the vehicle's tires as she headed down the mountain. Every foot gained away from that cabin—away from him—released the pressure building around her heart.

But halfway down, the lights on the console flickered. Same with the headlights as the SUV's RPMs sank to zero. The engine died, and Kate pressed her foot against the brake pedal. Pitch blackness filled the interior of the vehicle as she rolled to a stop. Pressing the start button, she listened for a sign of what might be wrong with the engine. "Come on."

The battery must've died from the dropping temperatures. Lucky for her, Sullivan Bishop required every member of the Blackhawk Security team to carry extra ammunition, weapons, first aid kits, survival gear and an additional car battery. Never knew what kind of mess their clients or the weather would get them into, and it was always better to be prepared than caught unaware.

Pulling her phone from her jacket pocket, she sent a quick message to the team. She was back on the Hunter's case, at least for now, and she'd need their help. She tossed the phone into the passenger seat, then unholstered her weapon, checked the magazine and loaded a fresh round into the chamber. Shoving it back into her shoulder holster, she pushed open the door with her uninjured arm and hit the small dirt road.

With a single glance into the surrounding trees, Kate walked to the back of the SUV and squeezed the lever for the tailgate. No sign Declan had followed her. The last thing she needed was for him to come out here to try to help. The muscles in her jaw ached. He'd done enough damage for one day.

The soft hissing of the tailgate's hydraulics drowned the steady sounds of the great outdoors. Hauling the battery and an extra flashlight from the back, she swung open the driver's-side door and popped the hood, her boots slipping on the thin layer of compacted snow.

How long had he been surveilling her, studying her? Kate blinked to clear the burning from her eyes as she hefted the SUV's hood. Following her?

Streaks of green and purple painted the sky in rivulets overhead, each strand branching off from a central point as the aurora danced in full display tonight. Millions of stars peppered through the thin veil of color, only adding a minuscule amount of light for her to see the vehicle's engine. Clenching the flashlight between her teeth, she twisted the bolts of the dead battery free with a wrench.

She was scheduled to meet Dominic in thirty minutes. Every minute counted when a victim went missing, and the longer she was out here, the less chance the FBI—the less chance Kate—had of finding the Hunter's latest victim alive.

Kate wrapped her fingers around the flashlight and swiped the back of her hand beneath her running nose. Hell, it was cold. Rubbing her hands together, she blew hot air into her palms in an effort to keep circulation moving. She'd close this case, she'd move on with her life, and she'd help those clients she could. Without Declan.

Within a few minutes, the new battery was in place, and she settled in behind the wheel. Kate pushed the start button.

Silence.

"Are you kidding me?" What else could be wrong with the damn thing? She glanced in the rearview mirror, back up the road toward the cabin. She was going to have to go back up there, going to have to confront Declan again while she waited for a tow truck and a ride-share to make it to her meeting with Dominic. The other option was freezing to death.

Kate shook her head. Okay. Maybe freezing to death wasn't such a bad idea right about now.

She sensed movement from the back seat, and she automatically reached for the gun in her holster. A stinging pain pinched at her neck as a gloved hand closed over her mouth.

She wrapped her fingers around her gun's grip, but her body grew heavier with every pump of her heart. She couldn't get it out of the holster. Panic flooded her as the hand slipped from her mouth and took the weapon straight from her holster.

"Can't have you ending the fun before it begins." A black ski mask appeared in her rearview mirror as her eyes grew heavy. Darkness crept around the edges of her vision, then pulled her down into blackness as the drugs took effect.

"You're mine, Kate, and nobody is going to take you from me this time."

SHE WAS DECLAN'S WEAKNESS, always had been.

Now she was gone. She'd wanted him at his lowest, and he'd thrown it in her face. By holding her away from the truth in an effort to keep her in his life, he'd only managed to push her away.

Declan held on to the cargo jacket she'd pushed at his chest, his fingers poking through the hole over the left breast. Where their killer had pierced her shoulder with an arrow. He was still out there, still hunting. Declan rolled the side of his mouth between his teeth and bit until blood spread over his tongue. What kind of bastard did he have to be to lie to the only woman who'd been willing to help him, to trust him? He was a damn fool.

And for what? A few more details on a life that didn't

matter? He was never going to be the man she'd married. Even if every memory that'd been stripped from his head came rushing back, too much had changed since then. He'd changed.

"Damn it." She shouldn't be out there alone. If he left now, he could catch up, ensure she was safe until she reached her meeting with Dominic. Then he and his former partner could have a talk about boundaries. Sending Kate those surveillance photos had crossed a line. But in the end, he was as guilty as Dominic. He'd watched her apartment, memorized her routines, investigated her clients. He'd learned everything he could about her before stepping foot in the house that night to ensure she hadn't been involved in the shooting. It had all been part of the plan.

Only, he hadn't expected to fall for her in the process.

Declan strode to the cabin's guest bedroom, shoving his arms into his coat along the way. He'd have to make sure to thank Kate's teammate for preparing for the apocalypse next time he saw Vincent. Arming himself with a handgun, a fresh magazine and a burner phone from the stash of supplies, Declan loaded a round into the barrel, checked the safety and holstered the weapon.

Kate could still be a target. Adrenaline surged through him. He'd promised to protect her, and he'd keep that promise until the Hunter was in cuffs or dead.

He'd seen the shadows in her eyes, the fear in her movements since he'd pulled her out of that damn pit. The nightmares haunted him, too. He wasn't going to let that son of a bitch touch her. Not again.

He hit the cabin's front steps and followed the missing SUV's tire tracks leading to the one-lane route down the mountain. Snow crunched beneath his boots as the light show of the aurora borealis lit the way. Cold worked through his thick layers and straight into his bones, tensing his muscles into a constant ache. Or was it the fact he'd only ever felt warm—felt whole— when Kate was near?

Hell, he should've told her the truth before now, but it was too late. There was no going back, and he feared she'd never forgive him.

He picked up the pace. No movement in the trees on either side of the road, but he wasn't going to relax, either. Not until he found Kate.

Dropping temperatures stiffened his fingers. Moonlight filtered through the trees ahead where the road disappeared. If she'd already gotten to the main road, he'd lose her forever. No. He couldn't think about that right now.

A flashlight beam caught his notice down the road. One hundred feet, maybe less. No other movement. No sign of Kate. Declan pulled the gun from his holster and slowed his pace. The hairs on the back of his neck rose. He stopped in the middle of the road, listened. Was that the sound of an engine? Taking cover behind a tree, he stared straight into the darkness on the other side of the road and tabbed off the safety of his sidearm.

Keeping to the trees, he raised his weapon as he headed in the direction he thought the sound was coming from. But the outline of an SUV separated from the shadows, and something inside of him caught fire. He knew that vehicle, and there was absolutely no reason why it would be sitting there. "Kate."

He pumped his legs hard, lungs burning for oxygen. The driver's-side door had been left open, the flashlight discarded on the ground. His fingers trailed over the freezing metal as he slid to a stop beside the driver's seat. No, no, no, no. This was wrong. Kate wouldn't abandon the vehicle in the middle of the night in these temperatures. She wouldn't have walked away. Which meant...

Declan searched the interior of the vehicle, recovering her phone and overnight bag in the passenger seat, and a syringe in the back. His mouth dried, his breath frozen in midair. The son of a bitch had been waiting for her in the back seat. He'd drugged her. Put his hands on her.

Rage exploded behind his sternum. He snapped his attention to the tree line as he let it take control. "He took her."

It had been the sound of an engine before. The unsub was in the middle of making his escape. Pocketing her phone, Declan circled the vehicle, heading straight into the trees.

One set of deep footprints had left distinct marks in the snow but disappeared only a few meters past the tree line. The smell of gasoline mixed with exhaust hung in the air. Impossible to drive a car or SUV through these trees. But an ATV? If the Hunter knew these woods as well as he knew the ones surrounding Michaels's cabin, he could get in and out without anybody knowing.

Declan swept the flashlight beam at his feet and spotted the two lines of a distinct tread pattern. The ATV would've had to have been in position before the suspect got into Kate's vehicle. Question was, how did the bastard get her to stop at this precise location? Had he injected her with whatever was in that syringe while the vehicle was still moving? Seemed risky. She could've veered into any one of these trees, and she'd put the SUV in Park.

He twisted his gaze back to the abandoned vehicle. Smaller footprints circled around the back of the SUV. No. The attacker would have had to get her to stop some other way. The only other option was sabotaging the engine somehow.

Her abduction hadn't been rushed or a moment of panic like before. Whoever had taken her had planned this out.

Declan fanned his grip over the warming metal of the gun and headed deeper into the woods. The man would've wanted her separated from any kind of support or backup.

"I'm going to find you, Kate." Digging her phone from his jacket pocket, he sent her team an SOS message and tossed the device back toward the SUV. Blackhawk Security had the tech to track her phone. They'd do their jobs, and he'd do his. Gritting his teeth, he left the vehicle and her belongings behind.

His eyes adjusted to the shadows. Every instinct flared warning, but he pushed them to the back of his mind. The Hunter had taken his life from him, and he'd do whatever it took to get that back. "I'm not letting you go."

Branches scratched at his face and neck as he followed the treads in the snow. Thick trees barely allowed any moonlight through, but Declan wasn't afraid of the dark. He'd lived there long enough, and he'd keep living there until Kate was back in his arms. Where she belonged.

A few hundred feet past the tree line, his boot hit something solid and metal. The device snapped closed at his feet. A bear trap. Crouching down, he flipped the mass of metal upside down and moonlight glinted off another rig a few feet away. Over two-hundred pounds of force waiting to break one of his legs. The ATV's tire treads had swerved around what look like an entire minefield of bear traps. How long had the bastard been planning this?

A gruff laugh burst from Declan. He stood, shouting into the blackness ahead, "Is that the best you've got!"

Silence.

"That's what I thought." As long as he kept inside the tracks, he'd avoid getting his leg snapped in half. Question was, how many other traps had the Hunter set?

In reality, it didn't matter. He'd stay the course. He'd get Kate back. That was what partners did for each other. They protected one another, had each other's backs. He couldn't go back to the way it was before. In the dark without his memories. Alone. She'd changed all that, and he wasn't ready to let her go.

His Kate. His past. His present. His future.

The aurora above shifted, greens and purples reaching down through the trees, outlining the single man standing in the ATV's treads ahead. Black clothing, black hood over his head and the gleam of a silver blade in his hand.

"Kenneth Winter." The stitches in Declan's side stretched with a deep inhale.

The scent of gasoline strengthened, and he slowed, twisted his wrist to make the gun in his hand more visible. This wasn't going to be a fair fight. Where was the ATV? Where was Kate? She was the unsub's most prized possession. The son of a bitch wouldn't let her out of his sight for long. She had to be close by. Declan stepped forward. "I warned you not to touch her again. Now you're going to pay for what you've done."

"Care to make a bet, Monroe?" The distorted voice echoed off the surrounding trees, and Declan froze. Bet?

Brandishing the knife in filtered moonlight, the bastard cocked his head to one side. "You lost the last round. Would be such a shame if you lost two times in a row. Especially with Kate's life on the line."

"This isn't a game to me." Declan raised the gun and aimed, pulling the trigger.

One second, the suspect had been there. The next, the bullet penetrated a tree right where the Hunter had been standing. Damn it. Where was the son of a bitch?

Declan scanned the trees, taking cover behind a large pine to his right. Freezing air burned going down his throat as he listened for movement. "All right. You want to play? Let's play."

The hunt had only begun.

Chapter Thirteen

The more she swallowed around the gag in her mouth, the drier her throat seemed to get. Kate pulled at her wrists but only managed to tighten the rope around her neck. The last thing she remembered before waking up hog-tied to this chair...

The SUV had died on the way to her meeting with Dominic. Her abductor had been in the back seat the entire time.

She blinked against the brightness of the single bare bulb above her head. He'd drugged her, and she couldn't remember anything after that. Not how he'd gotten her here. Not where they were.

Studying the medium-size cabin, she memorized the layout. She'd been placed with her back to the door at one end of the main room, a table straight ahead holding a crossbow a few feet away. Exposed roof slats, cobwebs, wood-burning stove, old furniture covered in nothing but dust. Shelves lined with food cans showed their age. Nobody had lived here in a long time.

Which meant nobody would have reason to look for her here either.

Heavy footfalls shook the hardwood floor beneath her, then a gust of wind burst through the front door as it swung open. Speckles of dust clouded the air around her. "I was starting to wonder if I'd given you too much sedative."

That voice. His voice. The man who'd taken her.

Nausea churned in her gut as the door slammed shut. As far as she could tell, there was one way in and one way out. She'd have to go through him to get to it.

Kate twisted her head as far to one side as she could, but the rope around her throat only cut off her air supply further. A shiver chased up her spine, raising the hairs on the back of her neck as he moved into her peripheral vision. The fabric gag had gone soggy in her mouth, impossible to move. She forced herself to breathe evenly, to study him. To find his weakness. Because she wasn't going to die in here. She tugged at her wrists again when the gag suppressed her question. Where was Declan?

"Promise not to scream?" The Hunter crouched low on his haunches in front of her, like the predator he was, waiting for the perfect moment to strike.

The evidence suggested Special Agent Kenneth Winter had worked all four of the missing persons cases the Hunter's victims were tied to. He'd taken those women, seduced them and set them free in the wilderness before he started his hunt. The man had been in her office, gotten to know her when she and Dominic had met to discuss cases. Had it all been a means to an end? A way to get close to her?

He reached toward her, and she jerked away. "Up to you, Kate."

A groan escaped up her throat as the rope burned across the delicate skin over her neck and wrists. She wouldn't scream, but she'd do far, far worse when she got free of these ropes. The psychopath in front of her had killed four innocent women that she knew of as well as Michaels. Her former patient had been a pawn in his sick game. She wasn't going to let him get away with it.

She had to focus, had to plan. The predator in front of her matched Agent Winter's build, same low tone when he spoke, same dark eyes. This was the man who'd thrown her in that pit and hung Declan from his feet to die.

The Hunter had stayed one step ahead of her and the FBI this entire investigation, but there was a reason Sullivan had handpicked her to profile killers for his team. Kate had the ability to know exactly what they wanted. Nine times out of ten it was simply control—over their victims, over their emotions, over their own traumatic pasts. But this one… He wanted to prove himself. Prove he could beat her.

With her attention on that damn ski mask and the slight bulge of the voice distorter over his neck, she wrapped her fingers into fists. And nodded.

"That's my girl." He raised his hand again, the brush of his coarse knuckles against her cheek nauseating. The tang of cologne worked deep into her system, and her nostrils burned. Too sharp. Nothing like Declan's subtle, masculine scent. Her bottom lip rolled with the gag as he slid the soaked rag beneath her chin.

She needed him closer. Mouthing her question, she closed her eyes as though she were still affected by the drugs, and he leaned in slightly. Another inch, and she'd get her shot at knocking him out cold. The overhead light reflected off the blade holstered to his hip, but until she had her hands freed, it wouldn't do her a damn bit of good. There had to be something else she could use to cut through the rope.

"You know, I've studied you, Kate. I've gotten to know you over these past few months. I know your routines, the way you profile your targets, watched you grieve after losing your husband." The Hunter closed the small space between them as heat built in her chest. "Do you really think headbutting me is going to give you an advantage?"

"I wasn't going to headbutt you." Shoving down through her toes, she pushed herself and the chair off the hardwood floor and launched herself straight into him. They landed in a heap on the floor, but the wooden chair she'd been tied to didn't even splinter. She hit the floor hard, landing on her side. Panic flared as he stood and took position above her, one foot pressed against her shin bone tied to the chair.

Pain screamed up her leg and down into her toes, but she had to find something—anything—to cut through the ropes while she had the chance. Her fingers splayed out, grasping into thin air, desperate for contact. All she needed—

"A few more pounds of pressure is all it would take to break your leg, Kate, but I don't want to hurt you more than I have to. So, please, don't give me a reason." A deep, evil laugh penetrated the ski mask as he wrenched her upright. Fisting one length of rope, he leveled his face with hers and pulled until the coarse strands cut into her. "You know why I killed them, don't you? All those women."

"Me…" She struggled to breathe. She couldn't push the air out her mouth fast enough. Her dull rasping reached her ears. A wave of dizziness washed through her head, and all she could think about in that moment was her own survival.

And Declan. He'd lied to her, made her believe he was someone he wasn't, but every cell in her body screamed for him right now. She'd trusted him. Hell, she'd fallen for him, and she didn't want their conversation to be the last thing she ever said to him. Because when it came right down to it, he'd been the one to pull her from the soul-sucking agony of grief, to make her feel again, to care. He'd taken a bullet for her, rescued her from the bottom of that pit when she believed nobody would find her. Loved her when she was at her darkest. And she loved him, too. "To beat…me."

"No, Kate." Another laugh pooled dread at the base of her spine. He loosened his grip on the rope, and she was able to take her first full breath since slamming him to the floor. Grabbing the ski mask at the crown of his head, the Hunter pulled the fabric from his face. He peeled the voice distorter from his throat. "I killed them to show you I'm the one who can protect you from the monsters out there in the world. Not Declan. Not Blackhawk Security or your team. Me."

No longer framed by the ski mask, familiar brown eyes stared back at her. Confusion tore through her. No. It wasn't possible. The sedative had to still be in her system. It was messing with her head, making her hallucinate. There was no way he'd been behind all those attacks. "Ryan."

"Surprise." The small mole on the left side of his chin shifted with a smile, but where she'd been comforted by that smile in the past, only fear built in her gut now. "Gotta tell you, Kate, feels good finally letting you in on the truth. Now we can start fresh."

"You sent Michaels to the house." She licked her dry lips. The pieces were slowly falling into place as the sedatives burned off. She had to keep him talking. Long enough for her to form a new plan. "You made him obsessed with me to the point he'd kill Declan. Then you sent him again when you discovered Declan was alive all this time." She didn't understand. "You were my friend. You helped me through my grief, you were—"

"I was there for you, Kate. For over a year while you grieved. Then I discovered my former partner—a man who was supposed to be dead, by the way—had been walking around the city without a damn clue who he was, but I knew. I knew he'd make his way back to you and destroy all of the progress I'd made."

His voice rose. "I was the one who checked in on you every night after work. I was the one who brought you takeout when you couldn't bring yourself to get out of bed. I was the one who convinced you to go back to work, to take off that damn wedding ring, to put yourself first for once. Me. Not him."

Dominic straightened, turning toward the old woodstove, the butt of his knife within reaching distance. He took a deep breath. If she could only get her hands free…

"You know, I was so nervous when I saw Declan in your office a few days ago, I almost drew my weapon and finished the job right then and there." Glancing back at her, the special agent tossed the mask and distorter into the burning stove. "See, he suspected me back before that first shooting. I could tell. It was this look he gave me during one of our other serial cases, the kind that said he'd figured out what I like to do in my spare time, and I couldn't afford him interrupting my plans for you. Turns out, I didn't need to worry. Declan can't remember anything, and that leaves us all the time in world."

For what?

"You found the women through missing persons cases you and your partner worked," Kate said. "You got close to them, seduced them. Then you set them free in the woods and hunted them down like animals." The last word sneered from her mouth. Kate tugged at her wrists, careful not to pull too hard to engage the rope around her neck. Was that the rope loosening? Her teeth clenched against the groan working up her throat as the burns around her wrists protested with each movement. "You're a coward. That's why you brought in Michaels to do your dirty work, isn't it? You were too afraid to confront Declan on your own."

"You're trying to make me angry. Maybe hoping I'll lash out and knock you over so you can search for something to cut through your ropes," he said. "It's very clever, but you've already forgotten, I know your strategies, Kate. I know you. And I've waited too long for this to spoil all the fun in one night."

"What about Special Agent Winter?" Kate felt the rope give, and she struggled to worm one hand free. Progress. "You set him up to take the fall, didn't you? Just another pawn in your game."

"It's true Kenneth worked all of those cases, but what the official reports don't say is that we worked them as a team. I suggested he take the lead to get his shot at a nice promotion while I scouted for my next target. Win-win. You have no idea how many cases I had to dredge through to find witnesses who looked like you, because let's be honest, you're one of a kind."

Dominic hefted the large crossbow from a table to her right and loaded a bolt. He ran his fingers down the shaft. "Whether you realize it or not, Kate, our fates are intertwined. Ever since I first met you, I knew I had to have you for myself. I've got plans for you."

He lowered the barrel of the crossbow into his other hand and aimed at the floor as he closed the distance between them. "I'm not about to spoil any more surprises."

CARE TO MAKE a bet, Monroe?

What the hell had the bastard been talking about? A bet?

Sweat dripped down Declan's spine as he wound through the trees. The ATV's tracks left lighter impressions here, the ground harder with the frost, but he wouldn't give up. He wouldn't slow down. Not until Kate was safe. Exhaustion pulled at him, his breath heavier than a few minutes ago. Those words echoed through his head over and over.

The tracks disappeared in the thick of fallen foliage.

Damn it. Scanning the surrounding area, he searched for a spot they might pick up. Twenty feet out. Thirty. The ground had frozen solid. He was searching for a needle in a haystack now, in the dark. The howls of a nearby wolf pack shot his instincts into overdrive, and he tightened his grip on the gun. Sliding his hand over his wound, he exhaled hard at the feel of wet gauze and fabric. "Yeah. That looks about right."

Blood.

The wolves had probably smelled him a mile away, mistaking him for an injured animal. They weren't wrong. Hell, he barely had the energy to keep himself standing as dropping temperatures stole his body heat. The chances of a wolf attack were slim, but the addition of his wound didn't help. He had a higher chance of freezing to death at this rate, but he'd keep moving.

Serial killers are like wolves, Monroe. They'll go to elaborate lengths to get what they want, but they'll never die for their cause.

Declan slowed as recognition flared at the voice in his head. Special Agent Ryan Dominic. Right. They'd been partners before he'd lost his memory.

Crystalized puffs of air formed in front of his mouth, and he curled the fingers of his free hand to hold on to as much heat as he could. A quick flash of memory streaked like lightning across his mind.

Him and Dominic looking at a whiteboard covered in photos and evidence. A murder board. Five victim photos had been taped to the surface, lines connecting the dots between the pictured women. They'd been hunting another serial killer then. What was the moniker they'd given him?

Declan rubbed at his eyes as a dull pain filled his skull.

The Alaskan Logger. Their unsub had taken to copycatting the Anchorage Lumberjack, who was later revealed to have been killed by his son, Sullivan Bishop, aka Sebastian Warren, the founder and CEO of Blackhawk Security, of all people.

The Alaskan Logger had taken five women who'd rejected his advances, killing them with the ax he'd worked the land with, as the Lumberjack had. Declan and Dominic were closing in on the Logger's identity when the unsub went cold.

Care to make a bet, Monroe? I'll give you five to one odds the Logger isn't finished, Dominic had said. *Come on, we'll make a game of it.*

Declan snapped his head up, not really seeing the trees around him. Son of a bitch. Dominic. Reaching for the burner he'd stashed in his pocket, he dialed Blackhawk's main number. The line rang once. And again.

His heart threatened to pound straight out of his chest as more memories rushed forward from the darkness locked inside his head. Pinching the bridge of his nose, he shut his eyes tight against the pain, but the fragments kept coming. A growl ripped up his throat.

He and Dominic on the office's annual hunting trip. His partner's favored crossbow. The file Declan had started building when the first two women had been discovered shot through the heart with an arrow. Declan had connected the dots mere hours before Michaels had shot up his house. He'd found evidence. He just couldn't remember what it had been.

Another memory slipped into his mind, cutting through the violence, and the breath left his lungs. A positive pregnancy test. Kate's smile as she bounded into his arms with the news. She'd wrapped her legs around his waist and crushed her mouth to his right there in the middle of their living room.

Declan blinked against the burn in his eyes. Warmth spread through him, combating the freezing cold around him. He wiped the back of his hand beneath his nose. He would've been a father if Kate hadn't been shot.

Every minute wasted was another minute the chances of Kate returning home alive dropped, and he couldn't handle the thought of finding her out here, alone, with an arrow through her chest.

A soft click registered over the phone, and he said, "Put me through to Elizabeth Dawson. Now."

He should've seen it sooner. Taking Kate off the case, sending her the surveillance photos, setting the meeting. It was all part of Dominic's plan to get her alone. Isolated. To take her from Declan. Hell, he should've trusted his instincts the first time the bastard walked into Kate's office.

"Dawson," a familiar voice said.

A small wave of relief flooded him. "Elizabeth, it's Declan."

"Where are you? Kate's vehicle is here down the road from Vincent's cabin, but we can't find her anywhere."

Fear laced the network expert's voice. "There's a syringe, her phone is here on the side of the road, we've got two sets of footprints and the engine's been tampered with. What is going on?"

"The Hunter is Dominic. He took her. I can't go into how I know. I need you to trust me. I'm going to get her back." His lungs spasmed from the cold. He had to believe that. The alternative... Declan shook his head. No. There was no alternative. He loved her, damn it. He needed her, and there was no way in hell he'd give up on them. They'd been through too much together, and he wasn't ready to let her go. Wasn't ready to let the history between them go. "I need you to work your magic and tell me where he is."

"The FBI agent working the Hunter case is the killer? Give me a second." Static crackled across the line, then a hard thump as though Elizabeth had set the phone down. "You're on speaker. I've got Anthony and Elliot with me, too."

"Good. He has no reason to suspect we know his real identity so there's a chance he has his Bureau-issued phone on him. Also, tell me if Dominic or anyone he might've investigated has property out here," Declan said. "He took off through the woods on an ATV, but I've lost the tracks. Those things only hold a few hours of gas at a time. He couldn't have gone far."

The chances Declan would get handed a property with the killer's name on it were slim, but the phone was a promising lead. Dominic was smart, organized. He'd stayed ahead of Blackhawk Security and the FBI this entire time without raising any warnings, but his former partner had never gotten on Declan's bad side before. Chaos was about to reign.

Declan turned around, scanning the shadows. Another drop of sweat slid down his neck. He had to control his body temperature. The slightest hint of moisture could pull his system into hypothermic territory.

The line crackled again. Then silence. "Have Elliot collect as much evidence as he can from the vehicle," Declan said. "We need to have a case built when this goes sideways." Because it most definitely would. Dominic was FBI—he knew the system—and Declan wouldn't be surprised if the bastard had a backup plan to get himself out of a conviction. One that looked a hell of a lot like Special Agent Kenneth Winter taking the fall.

No answer. "Elizabeth?"

Pulling the phone from his ear, he watched as a bar dropped off the screen. He was out in the middle of the damn wilderness. Barely any coverage. He was lucky his call had gone through at all but pinning Dominic's location depended on staying in range. His fingers squeezed around the phone. "Elizabeth!"

"Got—phone." Static filled his ears.

Seconds passed. A combination of frustration and panic spread through him as bits and pieces of Elizabeth's voice punctured the white noise.

"—have his position. Declan?—me? He's—quarter mile north of you. We're on our—"

"Quarter mile north." Declan pocketed the phone and ran as fast as he could. His muscles burned with exertion, but he pushed through. Nothing would keep him from getting to Kate. Not the freezing cold. Not hypo-thermia. Not a pack of hunting wolves. And certainly not some son of a bitch who'd taken the only person who mattered to Declan in this life.

She'd brought him out of the darkness of his past, given him everything he could've imagined and more. Gifted him with her strength, with her body, with hope. He wasn't going to turn his back on that or on her.

Fallen trees and razor-sharp pieces of ice threatened to trip him up, but Declan only pushed himself harder when a single cabin came into view up ahead.

Partially obstructed by massive tress on every side, the small wood structure wouldn't have been visible in spring or summer, but because of the lack of leaves, the roof peeked through the trees. A perfect hideout for a serial killer. Off the beaten path, no longer in the resi-dential or rental rotation as far as he could tell from the state of the place.

Fogged windows decreased visibility inside as De-clan took position within the ring of trees surrounding the cabin, but a dim light inside revealed there was con-densation bubbling at the bottom of each pane of glass. Someone was home. Moss and vines climbed the dilapi-dated wood stairs, slats pulling away from the overall frame. A single step onto that tilted porch would give away his presence. He had to find another way in.

Keeping low, Declan crouched as he moved from tree to tree for a better angle, gun tight in his grip. One shot. That was all it would take to end this nightmare.

He switched off his flashlight, relying solely on the single burning bulb glowing through the south window.

No movement from inside, but that didn't mean anything. Didn't mean Dominic had already finished with Kate and moved on to his next victim. Didn't mean he wasn't here at all. Or that the cabin was a trap.

Declan sat back on his haunches and extracted the phone from his jacket. No coverage. No calling in for backup. He was on his own.

Her muted scream drove him into action.

Declan raced across the dirt and bounded up the stairs. No time to test the lock. Hiking his foot beside the rustic doorknob, he put everything he had into a solid kick. The door swung open, hinges protesting as he filled the doorway. Pain ricocheted up his thigh and into his bullet wound, but faded with one look at Kate bound in the chair, her back to him.

"Kate." He raised the gun and silently shifted across the floor. No sign of Dominic. The bastard had to be around here somewhere. "I'm here, angel, and I'm taking you home."

Chapter Fourteen

"Declan, no!" The gag had been put back in place, rendering her warning useless. He didn't understand. The entire abduction, having her here, it was all part of the plan. Part of the trap Dominic had set for him.

Kate pulled at the remaining rope around her wrists as Declan moved deeper into the cabin. She bounced in the chair, trying to knock it over, to get his attention, to do anything to make him get out of here. She could barely see him out of the corner of her eye as she twisted her head, her back to the door. Her throat burned as she screamed as loud as she could. "Stop!"

A solid kick from Dominic standing behind one of the canning shelves sent Declan's gun flying across the floor, the thump of metal against wood loud in her ears.

Drawing a noose around Declan's neck, Dominic pulled him tight against him. Canned goods hit the hardwood floor as both men struggled for the upper hand. A hit to Declan's face brought him down onto one knee, then another. Another after that. Dominic wouldn't let up.

Panic flared in Kate's chest as Declan took hit after

hit with no sign of getting to his feet. Then, swinging his leg out wide, Declan unbalanced Dominic and pushed him backward, the noose still tied around his neck.

Kate kicked at the chair, a rough growl escaping from around the wet fabric in her mouth. She kicked again, but the rope only grew tighter around her neck. She had to get out of this chair. She had to help him. She scanned the dusty table for a weapon or something she could use to cut the rope, but Dominic had taken the crossbow to wait for Declan. Blood-chilling silence filled the cabin, and she wrenched around for a better look.

Dominic held on to the noose, one hand at the base of Declan's neck pressed into the wall, the other pulling the rope taut. The sound of glass shattering filled the cabin, heavy breaths barely noticeable over the hard pound of her heartbeat behind her ears.

Declan threw one punch, which Dominic dodged, and hauled his elbow back for another. Dominic landed a solid hit, and Declan fell backward against the canning shelves, giving the Hunter another chance to tighten the rope around her husband's neck.

"Leave him alone!" Another garbled shout. She couldn't see them well. Swinging her head from side to side, she struggled to get Declan back in her sights, but the binds around her body made it impossible. Clawing at the rope around her wrists, Kate ignored the stinging pain of burned skin.

A hard thump broke through the air, then another. Nausea churned in her gut. She forced herself to breathe, to think.

Movement pulled her attention to one side as Dominic dragged a bloodied and swaying Declan into her peripheral vision. No. She wasn't going to lose him again. Not like this. Not ever. Rough exhales flared her nostrils. "Declan, get up!" she tried to yell. "Get up!"

"You couldn't beat me before you lost your memories, Monroe, and you can't beat me now." Dominic stared straight at her, waited for her full attention as he slammed her husband into the floor. Dominic dragged Declan back toward the door, throwing the noose over one of the exposed beams running through the cabin.

Rage exploded through her, and she snapped her head to face front. Dominic had taken everything. Her psychology practice, her confidence, her house, her baby. He wouldn't take Declan from her, too. Clenching her fists, Kate pressed her toes into the floor and rocked back on the chair's hind legs. She used the momentum to rocket her forward, just as she'd done when she tackled Dominic to the floor. Forcing one bound foot in front of the other toward the table on the other side of the room, she turned ninety degrees.

No, no, no, no.

Inhaling deep, Kate shoved off with everything she had, sending the back of the chair straight into the edge of the table. A scream worked up her throat as pain splintered down her spine and across her shoulders. The chair shattered around her, loosening the ropes. She pulled the gag from around her mouth and dove to wrap her hand around one of the chair legs as the ropes fell to the floor.

Strong arms wrapped around her, constricting her movements. "I'm not finished with you, Kate."

Slamming her head back into Dominic's face, she took advantage as he dropped his hold, and swung the chair leg as hard as she could. Wood met bone in a sickening crunch.

She lunged for Declan, but then the Hunter nearly tackled her to the floor. Her muscles burned as she battled to stay upright. Gripping his two middle fingers, she wrenched them back as hard as she could with one hand and swallowed a pain-filled scream as she swung the chair leg into his side. The arrow wound in her shoulder cried for relief, but Dominic was using his weight against her.

She hit the floor hard and kicked upward, landing a hit to his chest. "Ryan, please. You don't have to do this. We can get you help. I can help."

But it wasn't enough. The Hunter stumbled backward. A growl ripped up his throat as he reached for her, but a rope sliding around his neck cut him off.

Declan hauled his former partner into him, blood dripping down his face. "You don't get to touch her."

Relief surged through her at seeing Declan alive, but it was short-lived.

Lifting his legs high, Dominic threw his weight forward as she'd done with the chair. The bare bulb above highlighted the sweat across Dominic's brow as he flipped Declan over his shoulder and flat on his back on the floor.

The rope fell into a pile at Dominic's feet. Faster than she thought possible, he wrapped his hand around her throat and hefted her into him. "What I need, Kate, is for you to start running. That's my favorite part, you know. The panic in their sobs as they scream for help. The fear in their eyes, but sooner or later, they realize there's nowhere they can hide. Not from me."

"You...broke...them." She couldn't breathe, but one thing was clear as the lack of oxygen took hold: she'd already lost everything that mattered and survived.

Her gaze flickered to the wall of muscle rising behind Dominic. Kate slammed her arm into his forearm, struggling to get free as a distraction, but her injury took the strength out of each hit. Wrenching her elbow back, she went for his face, but he only blocked the hit. She turned as much as she could and thrust her leg backward to escape his grip. In vain. "You can't break me."

"Let's test that theory, shall we?" Violence swam through Dominic's dark eyes a split second before a glass bottle broke against the side of his head. His fingers loosened from around her throat, and Kate stumbled back against the shelf near the door as Declan charged the special agent full force.

Her fingers hit metal on the shelf. The crossbow. Adrenaline fueled her enough to heft the weapon from the shelf, and she took aim. Her hands and wrists burned as feeling came back, but she slipped her finger over the trigger.

Both men battled for the upper hand, each covered in blood. She didn't have a shot. Declan was too close. Locking her jaw against the pain in her shoulder, she blinked to clear the sweat dripping into her eyes. One wrong move and she'd pierce him instead of Dominic. "Declan, move!"

Her partner ripped away from his opponent and ducked.

Kate pulled the trigger.

A soft whistling filled the cabin, and then Dominic's scream filled her ears as the arrow tore through the muscles in his shoulder. Right where he'd shot her. He folded in half.

Pulling back his elbow, Declan slammed one final hit into the Hunter's face.

Dominic crumpled to the floor, the thick layer of dust disturbed from a hard exhale escaping his lungs as he sank into unconsciousness.

The crossbow grew heavy in her hands, and she let it sink to her side as exhaustion took control. Her lungs heaved, trying to keep up with her racing heartbeat.

The nightmare was over. They'd apprehended the Hunter, and he would serve out the rest of his life behind bars for what he'd done to all those women, to Brian Michaels.

"Kate…" Declan stumbled forward, his voice weak. Blood dripped from his nose and mouth as he reached out for her. He collapsed against her, arms wrapping around her neck, but she kept him upright through pure force of will. "Did he hurt you?"

"No." Gripping the crossbow, she rested her chin against his shoulder and closed her eyes. He was alive. They'd survived. Together. She blinked back the tears as fear, resentment, rage, every emotion she'd held on to over the last year broke free. He'd saved her life—

again—but the hurt was still there. The lie he'd forced her to believe was still there. "You came for me. Even after I told you not to."

"I promised to protect you. I might not remember much, but I do remember that." His words rumbled through his chest and vibrated down to her bones. The ache in her body eased as he pressed his hands against her spine, fitting her against him.

"Thank you." Kate pulled away. He'd saved her life, but everything else? The security she'd felt with him, the connection? The trust? It had all been destroyed. She swiped at her face with her free hand and stepped away. "How did you know where to find me?"

His shoulders sank away from his ears, exhaustion and disappointment clearly etched into his expression. He rolled his lips between his teeth and cast his eyes to the floor. "I remembered something Dominic said to me during an investigation we headed as partners. Then a whole lot more stuff I can't really explain in a way that would make sense. I called your team."

He locked brilliant blue eyes on her. "And I remembered the day you told me about the baby. How happy I was. You told me I was going to be a dad, and I remember thinking life couldn't get any better than that moment. But I was wrong. These last five days, having a second chance…" He stepped closer to her. "You're everything to me, and I don't want to lose you."

Kate shook her head. He already had.

"The worst feeling in the world is knowing you were used and lied to by the person you trusted most in the world," she said. "That's not just going to be fixed with an apology, Declan, and I think the best thing—for both of us—is space. You need to figure out who you are again, what you want to do with your life now that you have that second chance. I need to do the same. I need to learn how to be on my own. Alone. Without grief hanging over my head."

His expression shut down, and she tried to swallow through the hollowness building inside.

Kate swiped at her face again, catching a stray tear on her cheek and backed toward the door. Dominic wasn't dead. He wouldn't stay down for long. "We should call the FBI and Anchorage PD. I need to let my team know what happened."

Declan lifted his hand as though he intended to reach out for her but kept himself in check. "Kate—"

A murderous bellow pierced through the haze clouding her head as Dominic shoved off the floor and lunged.

Her heart caught in her throat, but Declan closed the distance between them, wrapped his fingers around hers and the crossbow and helped her lift the weapon up.

She pulled the trigger.

THE HUNTER WOULD never take another victim again. Would never come after Kate. Special Agent Ryan Dominic was dead.

What was Declan supposed to do now?

He and Kate had had an agreement from the beginning. They would work the case together, then move on with their lives. But this couldn't be it. Not after everything they'd been through. Not after what they'd shared.

Red-and-blue patrol lights highlighted the bruises and scrapes across her angelic face as Declan stalked toward the ambulance where the EMTs checked her wounds. She had to understand. He knew exactly what he wanted. Her.

FBI and Anchorage PD had taken control of the scene. Blackhawk Security was on standby, each member of Kate's team giving their statements. The victims' bodies would be released to their families for burial now that the case of the Hunter was closed. Declan's job was done, but he couldn't leave. Not without her.

"Declan Monroe." A wall of muscle dressed in a suit stepped into his path, hand outstretched. One of the FBI agents sent to clean up the mess. Cornflower blue eyes scanned him. A five-o'clock shadow and tousled brown hair were evidence of the amount of sleep lost on this case, but somehow Declan knew this agent had never let something as simple as sleep affect his job, which meant they'd known each other. "Special Agent in Charge Mitchell Haynes. You probably don't remember me—"

"You were my boss." Before Declan's entire world had been ripped apart. He remembered that, remembered taking his suspicions about his partner to Haynes only to be told to find hard evidence before making accusations against one of their own. Declan shook the man's hand.

"That's right. Glad to know some of those memories of yours are coming back." Haynes slipped his hands deep in his pants pockets. Mitchell Haynes, the man who'd partnered him with Dominic in the first place.

The guy ran an entire team of agents who hunted violent serial offenders on the FBI's most wanted list, but didn't seem to have aged a day over the last year. "I read yours and Ms. Monroe's statements. Everyone else's, too. You successfully tracked and brought down a killer who made it his mission to not leave evidence behind."

"I remember a lot. Have to wonder if you hadn't listened to me before now, none of this would've happened. None of those families would have to bury the women they loved over the next few days." Declan scanned the scene until his gaze landed on Kate, then nodded toward her. "And she gets the credit here. Couldn't have done any of it without Kate."

Declan maneuvered around Haynes, holding tight to the path to his future. To Kate. Of all the options out there, he didn't want a life that didn't include her. His guardian angel. Over the course of the last five days, she'd become his armor, a part of him, and nothing was worth the cost of losing her.

"Yeah, well. We all make mistakes, right?" Haynes's voice came from behind. "Besides, I knew you'd get your guy, Monroe. You always have. You were my best agent before you got shot. It'd be a shame to see that talent go to waste."

Declan slowed, turned his attention back to the SAC. "What's that supposed to mean?"

"Bringing down the predators is what my team does best, and it's what you're good at." Haynes spread his hands wide, as if that answer was obvious. His voice dropped into graveled territory. "Come back to the FBI, Declan. Help me save hundreds more families the pain of having to lose their loved ones to the sick, violent people set on destroying lives. Help me prevent more women like these four from being abducted, brutalized and murdered."

"You want me to work for the FBI after I killed one of your own men who turned out to be a serial killer?" The weight of Kate's attention squeezed the air in his lungs. This was what he'd worked so hard for over the past year. Finding his place, getting his life back. Remembering who he'd been. Hunting the most violent criminals had been part of him for so long, the idea of settling back into that role bled excitement down his spine.

"You were the only one who suspected Ryan Dominic for what he really was back then. You know the monsters are real, and you're not afraid to face them, Monroe. Only this way, you get to do your job legally." Haynes handed him a card, flashed his straight, white teeth and backed away toward a waiting SUV. "I'll try not to partner you with a serial killer this time. See you in Washington, DC, within the week."

Declan stared at Haynes's name on the small piece of embossed cardstock but couldn't absorb the letters on the card.

"Looks like you got everything you've worked for." Kate still sat at the ambulance, arms folded across her chest. The rope burns had been treated and dressed, but the fact they'd needed treatment at all resurrected the rage for the son of a bitch currently being wheeled out on a stretcher in a body bag from the cabin. "Your memories, your old job. This is great. I'm happy for you."

Not everything. Not yet. Curling his fingers around the card, Declan ignored the chill of the dropping temperatures as her light vanilla scent filled his system. Just one inhale and the fiery burn of revenge ebbed. Would she always have that effect on him or had exhaustion finally caught up? They'd been running off fumes for so long, his body had gotten used to the high doses of adrenaline. But now... Now he wanted nothing more than to take her back to her apartment and sink into bed for the next several weeks. Taking her hand with his, he ran the pad of his thumb over her bandages. "Do they hurt?"

"Not as bad as it looks." She wouldn't have admitted to the pain either way. Always determined to stand strong, always in control. But Declan knew the truth. Despite her hardened exterior and attempt to bury her emotions, in reality, Kate felt entirely too much. "How's your side?" she asked.

"Medium rare." In truth, he didn't know how the wound had fared during his fight with Dominic. He'd refused treatment until Kate had been checked over first, and his stitches ached with awareness. The bastard had tried to execute him, but more important, Declan had almost lost her. Again. He'd failed to protect her from the Hunter, and he'd have to live with that knowledge for the rest of his life, but knowing he was the reason she might walk away now... He couldn't handle that.

"Kate, I'm sorry I lied to you. I didn't want this to end. I didn't want to lose you. I didn't want..." he had to be honest with himself "...to be alone again."

The rawness of that admission broke through in his voice.

She nodded, gaze focused on a point over his shoulder. "You know, my team has been through a lot over the last year. Elliot's been shot twice, Sullivan almost died from his injuries and had to be airlifted to the hospital, Anthony's son was kidnapped and Elizabeth was abducted when she was four months pregnant with Karina."

She rolled her lips between her teeth as patrol lights reflected off the thin line of water in her eyes. "But no matter what's been thrown at us, we've survived, and we come out on top the next day. Because we trust each other, we rely on one another. Even at this very moment, my team is standing over there waiting to help me with whatever I need from them. There aren't any secrets between us. We all know and have experience with secrets putting lives at risk. I can trust them."

His gut clenched as she turned those green eyes on him, and everything inside of him went cold. This wasn't the woman he'd built the snow fort for, the one he'd taken to bed, the one who'd given him a reason to keep going. No. That woman had a warmth to her gaze. The woman standing in front of him had closed herself off and retreated to the point he wasn't sure he'd ever see that warmth again.

"So we go back to the way it was before? We—" He curled his fingers into his palms, forced himself to breathe through the next words. "We move on."

"That was the plan, wasn't it?" she said. "We'd finish the investigation and continue on like nothing had ever happened." She lifted her chin. "You saved my life—more times than I can count now—and I'll always be thankful for that, but we were partners, Declan. Partners are supposed to trust each other. There shouldn't have been any secrets between us, and I don't think you can promise me there won't be more in the future."

Declan opened his mouth to answer, but no. He couldn't promise her that.

She wiped her hand beneath her nose as she sniffled.

"I thought Ryan Dominic was my friend. Turned out he was a serial killer. I hope you understand that I can't handle any more secrets." Her uninjured shoulder rose on a shrug, the corner of her mouth lifting on one side. Uncrossing her arms, she stepped close to him and placed one hand on his chest, right over his heart.

She lowered that beautiful gaze to his hand and extracted the business card Haynes had left with him. Studying it for a brief moment, she slid it into his pants pocket. "Go get your life back, Declan. You deserve to be happy."

Her fingers feathered over his arm as she stepped around him, her soft vanilla scent still on the air, in his system, becoming part of him. But she'd always been part of him, hadn't she? That wouldn't change. No matter how much distance she put between them.

"Kate." He spun around, his breath icy on the air. "We'll always be unfinished business. Remember that."

Another half smile thinned her lips. "Not this time, Special Agent Monroe."

And then she was gone.

Chapter Fifteen

Six weeks later

She rubbed at the dry skin around her wrists. The Hunter had left his mark. On her body, in her nightmares. Kate stuffed another handful of debris into a large black garbage bag. How many did that make? Sixteen? Seventeen bags?

With the connection between Brian Michaels and Special Agent Ryan Dominic established, the FBI had taken everything they needed to wrap up their investigation, but she still hadn't been able to salvage anything from the house she once considered home. Not even the couch's decorative pillows had survived.

She shoved a featherless pillow into the bag with a little more force than needed, swallowing back the sudden dryness in her throat. It was going to take a lot more than a few garbage bags to get this place ready to sell. She took a deep breath.

Broken glass crunched under her boots as she straightened. A small sting of pain lanced through her shoulder, but the hole from the Hunter's arrow was almost completely healed. Swiping the back of her hand across her forehead, she inhaled deep to clear a rush of dizziness. Exhaustion pulled at her, and bile worked up her throat. Nightmares and heartburn. Great.

She stared out over the remnants of the living room. Not a single piece of furniture, item of clothing or dinner plate had survived both shootings. Insurance would cover the majority of the damage, but this was the second time she'd have to explain why her house had become a crime scene. What a mess—

"Kate," a familiar voice said.

The hairs on the back of her neck rose. Heat flooded her, and she exhaled hard to keep the burn under control. The hits kept on coming. She stuffed another handful of garbage into the sack but didn't turn around. No point. He wasn't staying long. "I figured you'd be across the country by now, assigned to another case."

"I turned down the FBI job." His deep, reserved voice resonated through her, sending a bolt of electricity up her spine. The shifting of broken glass and debris sounded loud in her ears—too loud—as he closed in on her.

"Oh?" The weight of his attention burned between her shoulder blades, but she couldn't face him. The moment she gave in to the urge to lock her gaze on his, the heartache she'd buried over the last month and a half would take control. No. She was just starting to heal. She couldn't do this again—wouldn't.

Crossing to the other side of the room, Kate scooped the remaining items off her desk into the bag. Broken perfume bottles from his travels all over the world, fractured picture frames holding evidence of the life they once shared. She didn't want any of it. Not anymore. "I thought getting your life back was what you wanted. Going back to the FBI was supposed to help with that."

"It was." Whispers of his exhale tickled over her heated skin. She hadn't heard him move so close. Her body flooded with awareness as his clean, masculine scent worked deep into her lungs. "Until I realized taking that job would mean keeping more secrets from you. And that's the last thing I want."

Air caught in her throat. He'd turned down the job for her? She sagged against the desk, her fingers gripping the edge for support.

"Kate." Declan's fingers fanned over her arm—too familiar, too comforting—and she wanted nothing but to sway into his warmth, trust him, rely on him as she got rid of the evidence of their marriage. But she couldn't. "Look at me."

Her heartbeat thundered behind her ears. Hard to breathe with him so close. His scent filled the space he'd cornered her in, and she couldn't get it out of her system. In all honesty, she hadn't been able to get him out of her system. Not since she'd walked away from him back at the crime scene. It had taken every ounce of energy to keep her distance, to force herself to focus on the next case for Blackhawk, not to wonder if he was safe. If he was alive.

"You're my life, angel. Not getting the rest of my memories back, not some job for the federal government or hunting monsters." His hands circled her waist, pulling her against him. His back pressed against her spine, the even beat of his heart pulsing into her.

She should fight back, but she was just…tired. And he felt so good. His mouth skimmed the shell of her ear. "I stayed away as long as I could to give you the space you wanted, but I choose you. I'm committed to you. No more secrets. No more lies."

Liquid warmth pooled in her stomach and melted her from the inside. That was all she'd ever wanted. Honesty. Safety. Love.

Kate spun in his arms, locked her gaze on those piercing blue eyes. She loved him. More than she'd ever loved another human being. Not the husband she'd buried, not the man who'd saved her life during the investigation but the combination of both. Each had their own strengths, their own weaknesses, but together they formed the man she'd dreamed of spending the rest of her life with. Raising a family with. "What do you want me to say to that?"

"Say yes, Kate." His short burst of laughter ruffled her ponytail. "Say you'll give us a chance to get it right this time."

She stepped out of his reach. Kate bit back the shock of seeing him for the first time in weeks. Dark circles had taken up residence under his eyes, but his blue gaze remained bright and focused on her. "No more secrets."

"No more secrets. You have my word." His Adam's apple bobbed as he swallowed hard. He locked his fingers around her arms. He stepped in close, his heat tunneling through her thin tank top and deep into her still-sore muscles. "I'll never hurt, betray or disappoint you ever again. I want us to last. No matter how hard things get, I have always and will always need you in my life. I'll spend as long as it takes to prove you can trust me again."

Sincerity deepened the lines carved into his forehead and at the bridge of his nose. He held her steady when all she wanted to do was collapse into him. He meant every word. His expression, his eyes, his hold on her, they all said he wanted this to work, and for the first time since he'd come back into her life, she believed him.

A weak smile curled one corner of her mouth, and she set her palms against his chest. "I haven't slept since that night. I miss having you there in my bed when the nightmares…"

She closed her eyes.

"You don't have to miss me anymore." He pushed a strand of hair behind her ear, urging her to look at him. "I'll be there. Every night to soothe you back to sleep. Every morning to sprinkle cinnamon over your hot chocolate, even when I think you're crazy for drinking it in the summer. I'll be there to decorate the Christmas tree and build you a snow fort. I'll do anything to have that chance again."

"I live in an apartment. I don't have a yard," she said.

A genuine laugh rumbled through him, and oh, how she missed that sound. Missed him. His heart beat strong under her hands, constant, assuring. She focused on the highest mound of scar tissue beneath his T-shirt, the one identical to hers.

"You say all this now," she said, "but I know you,

Declan. Even with amnesia, you ran straight at the first monster until you brought him down. It's in your blood. You might've turned down your dream job, but what if another violent criminal is running rampant in Anchorage? What then?"

"Whatever happens, we'll survive, just like we have for the past year. Together." He lifted his hand to her jaw, bringing her gaze up to meet his. A slow burn simmered in her veins at his touch, and it took everything inside of her not to melt against him. His voice dipped an octave as warmth swirled in his eyes. "I told you when Dominic thought he could take you from me—I'm not going anywhere."

She narrowed her eyes. "Are you sure about this?"

"Yes." Declan dropped his hands to hers. "You and I can officially live out our lives without our house getting shot up."

"Wouldn't that be nice? Maybe then I'd stop getting nasty looks from the garbage man." She surveyed the disaster zone that was supposed to be their living room. Focusing on Declan, she curled her fingers in his shirt collar. He'd saved her life, sacrificed his future for her, promised to be honest and open from now on. He deserved the truth, too.

"During our marriage, you dealt with such horrible things, I didn't want to add to any of it. So I kept everything bottled up until it had nowhere else to go. I can't do that again. No matter what happens, I promise to be honest with you, too."

"Then we have a deal?" he asked. "We'll both be

honest with each other and try not to mess this up a second—no, wait—a third time?"

"On one condition." He'd sacrificed so much for her already. She didn't have the right to ask for anything more, but he didn't have to give up his dream job. Not for her.

He lowered his forehead against hers, closing his eyes. He untangled his hands from hers, skimmed her lower back and pressed her closer as though he never intended to let her go. "As long as we're together, I'm in."

"Come work for Blackhawk Security," she said. "With me."

Declan pulled away, eyes on her. "What?"

"We made a good team when we worked the Hunter case together. I think we could do it again. Besides, you're too good of an investigator to quit the serial killer business for good. This city needs you. Blackhawk could use another investigator now that we're expanding." She jerked him toward her. "And I need you close."

"You're serious." Excitement brightened his features.

She ran a hand through his tousled brown hair. They'd survived bullet wounds, arrow wounds and had taken down one of Anchorage's most violent serial killers. Together. She could only imagine the possibilities in their future. "I don't want you to resent me down the road. You saved my life, and I know how much that job meant to you. The least I could do is return the favor."

He crushed his lips to hers, penetrating the seam of her mouth with his tongue and thrusting inside. Planting a hand on the back of her head, he seemed intent on making them one. He spread hair-raising pleasure throughout her system. She'd missed his touch, his taste, his warmth. Missed him. He bowed her back into him, her hips level with his.

Her phone pinged from the dresser, and she tore her mouth from his. A reminder. Was it time already? Reaching for her phone, she swiped the reminder off the screen before he had a chance to read it. Yep, right on time. "Besides, Blackhawk will need someone with your particular skill set in a few months when I put in my notice."

She curled her fingers into fists. Why was she so nervous?

"What? It's not the arrow wound, is it?" His hand slipped to her shoulder.

"No, it's not the wound. My injury is healing fine. This is…something else." Kate untangled herself from his arms. He had the right to know. Getting rid of him wasn't going to be easy anyway. Not with that suspicious look on his face. She inhaled deep. "I'm pregnant."

His bottom lip dropped, then his eyes crinkled at the edges. Tension spread from his shoulders down to his toes. A new kind of brightness engulfed his blue eyes. "What? How…how—"

"Are you asking me how we made a baby?" She couldn't read past his shock. Was he excited? Terrified? Both? "Because that should've been something we discussed before we slept together in the snow fort you built in Vincent's backyard. Which we're never going to tell him about."

"No. I remember that very clearly." A smile tugged at

the corners of his mouth. He slid his hands around her hips. His warmth permeated her clothing and soothed the bubble of nervousness spreading through her. Mouth a mere inch from hers, he asked, "How far along?"

"Almost six weeks, and I have my very first appointment with the doctor in thirty minutes if you want to come." But Declan still hadn't shown any kind of sign of what was going on inside his head. Nervous energy built behind her sternum. "Okay, you're going to have to tell me what you're thinking. I can't read you right now."

"This is the best day of my life." He pulled her to him and set his mouth against hers once again. "When do we need to leave?"

Heat flooded her system with every pass of his mouth over hers. Wave after wave of blistering arousal swamped her thoughts. She threaded her fingers in his hair at the back of his neck. Not close enough. Dropping her hands to the hem of his shirt, she stepped out of his arms and tugged his shirt over his head.

Deep purple bruising surrounded the bullet wound in his side, but the injury itself had sealed shut. Her insides burned for him. Her husband. Her partner. The love of her life.

"I think we've got enough time to see if the water's been turned back on in the shower first."

* * * * *

COLTON'S SECRET HISTORY

JENNIFER D. BOKAL

To John, you are my forever and always

Prologue

The sun had not crested over the horizon, yet the sky was lightening by degrees, from ebony to charcoal to a smoky gray. The streetlights that lined Main Street had gone dark. The stores had yet to open. The town of Braxville had yet to wake.

For Julia Jones, it was the best time of the day.

She waited in her car, the engine idling and the heat turned to full blast. A sacked lunch, packed by her mother, sat on the passenger seat. And Julia herself held a pen and notebook. The solitude was a blessing and she began—as she always did—writing a letter.

Luke,
It's been months since we last talked, but I want you to know that I love you still. I know that neither one of us can help our separation. I miss you just the same. Yesterday, I saw a commercial—the one with the cat playing the piano. Have you seen it? Do you think it's all done with computers or was the cat trained? Either way, it made me laugh. And whenever I'm happy, I think of you.

When do you think we'll be able to see each other again? I know you're busy, but I just miss you so much and would do anything to be with you right this minute.

I'll write you again tomorrow.

As always, you have all of my love,

Julia

She ripped the page from her journal. After folding it into thirds, she shoved the paper into an envelope and opened the door. Julia ran across the street, the sound of her footfalls on the pavement mingled with the *ding, ding, ding* of her car's sensor.

A blue mailbox sat on the curb. Julia set her purse atop the box as she found a pen for addressing her letter.

"Luke Walker," she wrote, before adding several hearts around his name.

From her bag, she also removed a roll of tape. A piece of tape was placed at the top of the envelope, and she stuck it to the front door of Walker Hardware. Her hand lingered on the plain white envelope as her heart raced.

"I will always love you, Luke," she said, her whispered words forming into a cloud of steam.

Her work done, Julia returned to her warm car and waited.

Like always, Luke Walker exited through the door next to the hardware store that led to several apartments. Though she'd never been invited to his house,

Julia knew that Luke lived above the store—along with three other apartments he let out to rent.

Luke wore a red sweatshirt and a pair of black running shorts—an inadvisable decision given the morning's chill. Julia reached for her journal and made a note that she needed to remind Luke to dress for the weather.

Reaching his arms overhead, he twisted his torso. Left, right. Right, left. He bent at the waist and touched his toes. Slipping earbuds into his ears, Luke took the first few steps of his jog.

Julia pressed her hands to her mouth, breathless with excitement. This was the moment.

Luke stumbled to a stop. His blue eyes narrowed, his gaze directed at the letter.

He removed the envelope from the door and the paper from the envelope. Rubbing a hand on his days-old beard, he scanned the page before crumpling both in his fist. He took off at a jog once again and threw Julia's letter into a garbage can as he passed.

Her eyes filled with tears.

He'd seen her letter. He'd read it.

They were connected and he loved her still.

It wasn't the way it had been the last time, when Julia felt such a strong connection to the handsome actor in all the spy movies. She'd met Luke Walker, an important man in Braxville. Luke had taken her to the movies and to play mini-golf and out for ice cream.

Nor would this relationship end the same way it had with the actor.

Where Julia had gone to the Southern California

studio, then to an agent's office, then to the actor's home. Her visit had ended when the police came and found her sitting on the kitchen floor. She was covered in blood, like hot silk, and pressed the knife to her own chest.

After that, she went to the hospital in California where days turned to weeks and weeks became months. Eventually, the scars on her wrists were nothing more than silver threads.

Her mother never said anything to anyone. Nobody in Braxville knew where she'd gone—or why.

She was home now and better than ever.

Using the side-view mirror, she watched Luke sprint down the street. Even from the back, she could tell that his blond hair was damp with sweat. His strides were long. He was taller than the actor. And sure, there were other differences—Luke's teeth weren't as straight or as white. His arms were toned, but not as well muscled as the actor's. Yet, they shared the same dark blond hair color. The same shade of eyes. The straight nose and well-defined jaw. In fact, there were so many similarities that they could be brothers.

The doctors had been right about relationships. Julia had to *personally* know someone in order to love them—and to be loved in return.

And, oh my, she did know Luke Walker. She knew his schedule. She knew how he liked to play the same game with her every morning. He'd always read her note quickly, careful to throw it away and keep their affair a secret. That was how Julia knew the two of them were fated to be together.

Moreover, Julia also knew that nothing and no one would ever keep them apart.

Chapter One

Bridgette Colton stood in her childhood bedroom and rubbed her forehead. It wasn't yet 7:30 a.m. and a headache had started. Already, she knew her day was going to be tumultuous. Through the floorboards came the clear sound of her parents arguing.

"I see here that you've ordered thirty half-racks of ribs?" said her father, Fitz Colton, bringing the topic around to the menu for the Colton barbecue and bonfire. "Are you expecting the family or a battalion from the Kansas National Guard."

Her mother, Lilly, replied, "We have all six kids coming. Jordana and Brooks both have new romantic partners and plan to bring them. Markus Dexter and his wife, Mary, will be here. Shep is back in town. You and me. A few neighbors. Other friends. Colleagues from your work. That's a lot of people to feed, Fitz."

Her father said, "Did you see what the caterer is charging for all of this?"

"Fine," said her mother. "I'll call back and switch the order to chicken. It's only half of the price."

"Well, then we look cheap."

"You are being cheap," her mother replied, her words an arrow hitting the target.

Bridgette groaned. It was a Tuesday, the day after the October holiday and the beginning of her work week.

Beyond being back in her parents' home—and not in her apartment in Wichita—the day was far from typical. Her newest assignment as an investigator with the Kansas State Department of Health began today. She'd been tasked with discovering why so many men in Braxville had developed a rare esophageal cancer over the years.

Discovering what had caused each illness was more than finding a needle in a haystack. It was locating the right haystack in the first place.

"What do you mean we can't order a dessert?" her mother asked, Lilly's voice an octave below shrill.

Bridgette had yet to unpack her suitcase. Setting it on her unmade bed, she rummaged through her belongings until she found a bottle of OTC pain reliever. She swallowed pills without the benefit of water. As they landed in her gut, she thanked her lucky stars that she was meeting her sisters, Jordana and Yvette, for breakfast. It gave Bridgette the perfect excuse for leaving early.

Bounding down the stairs, she entered the kitchen. Her mother still wore her plaid dressing gown and sat at the long, wooden kitchen island. A mug of coffee was cupped between her hands. Standing as Bridgette entered, she set the cup aside. "Good morning, darling. You look so pretty today."

Pretty? In khakis, a cream blouse and a rust-colored cardigan, she hoped to look neat, professional, competent. Then again, her mother always had a ready compliment and Bridgette's chest filled with affection. "Thanks, Mom," she said, accepting the praise.

Her mother asked, "How did you sleep?"

"Pretty good," she said. "But I have to get going. It's a long drive into town."

"You can't leave without breakfast," said Lilly. "I'll whip up something in no time. What do you want? Pancakes? I picked up everything for French toast, if you'd like."

"Actually," said Bridgette. "I'm getting breakfast in town."

Her mother's smile faded. "Oh."

Guilt gripped Bridgette's heart and squeezed. She tried to understand her parents' situation. It was easy to imagine that with all six kids grown and gone, her mother and father had nothing to do besides ramble around in the big house and gripe at each other.

It was a problem she would fix if she could.

Then again, even if she couldn't repair her parents' marriage, she could certainly spend more time with her mother. "Hey, Mom. Can I come home at lunch tomorrow? We can look over the menu you're planning for the bonfire."

Her mother's smile returned. "I'd love that, honey."

Her father, sitting at the kitchen table, looked up from the Wichita morning paper. "Notice how she didn't offer me pancakes or French toast?"

"That's because you said you were on a diet," her mother snapped. "Would you like pancakes or French toast?"

"Nope, but it would have been nice to have been asked."

Their arguing was a constant drumbeat, and Bridgette was never going to get rid of her headache if she stayed. At thirty years of age, she really was too old to be living at home. What had she been thinking by moving in with her parents—albeit temporarily? "I really do need to get going," she began, while reaching for her tote bag, which had been draped over the back of a chair.

"What is it that you're doing at work?" her father asked, flicking his gaze at her from over the top of the paper.

As if she were in middle school, obedient and looking for approval, her hand grazed the strap of her bag before she let it fall to her side. Her father already knew why she was here. This was his way of getting even more information. "It's a cancer cluster. The state thinks it's caused by something in the environment."

"Back in my day," her father began, "if you got cancer it was just bad luck. Now, everyone has to blame someone, or something, for all their problems."

"This is a rare cancer," said Bridgette. "One that is a little more than bad luck."

"It could be all the plastics. Your mother was telling me we need a new washing machine with a special filter. Says all of our clothes are made from plastics and little fibers come out in the wash."

Lilly nodded. "It's horrible, Bridgette. The plastic ends up in the rivers and is eaten by the fish. Then we eat those very same fish—and the bits of plastic."

Her father harrumphed and folded the newspaper. "I say it's a hoax started by the washing machine people to fleece folks out of their hard-earned money."

Her mother countered with, "I say there is no price tag on a healthy environment."

"Okay, well, I love you both. Have a great day." She quickly grabbed her bag and turned for the door.

"Honey, you forgot these." Her mother held up a plate covered in tinfoil. "I gave you half a dozen muffins. You can share them at work."

Share muffins? Maybe her parents really did think she was still in middle school. Still, it was a sweet gesture, and everyone loves food. Arriving with a plate of homemade muffins would help Bridgette with her new coworkers. "That's very thoughtful, Mom." Placing a kiss on her mother's cheek, she continued, "I do love you both. I have to get going."

Bridgette walked from the kitchen and through the foyer. She opened the door and stepped outside, drawing in a deep breath.

She'd come back to Braxville to discover what was causing all the cases of cancer in the area and that was still her top priority. Yet, now she had a new and more immediate goal. Bridgette had to find an apartment to rent—and soon.

Thank goodness she was meeting her sisters. They both worked for the Braxville Police Department and knew the area. Hopefully, Jordana or Yvette could help. Because Bridgette knew one thing for sure—she could not stay at home.

LUKE WALKER STOOD behind the counter and stared at his computer. The screen was filled with his spreadsheet for last month's sales at Walker Hardware. The numbers didn't lie. Income was down for September, no doubt about it. What happened if the trend continued—especially since the upcoming winter months tended to be lean?

Then again, the downtown businesses were less than two weeks away from hosting the annual fall-themed Braxville Boo-fest. Last year, he made more on that single Saturday than he did the whole month.

The success spurred him to get involved, and he was the chairperson for this year's costume parade. Aside from having an event for all of Braxville to enjoy, Luke hoped to draw a crowd from Wichita, which was only an hour away. He also hoped that those from the city would make a return trip—and shop.

A knock at his front door interrupted Luke's thoughts. Stacey Navolsky, owner of the bookstore, stood outside. Hand to the glass, she peered through the window.

Tucking the tail of his flannel shirt into his jeans, Luke hustled to the door and undid the trio of locks.

"Stacey," he said, opening the door. "You're up and out early this morning."

The bookstore, like the hardware store and most

every other business on Main Street—save for the coffee shop, La Dolce Vita—didn't open until 10:00 a.m. Luke hadn't looked at the clock, but it couldn't be much past eight in the morning.

Stacey was a petite woman in her fifties, with streaks of gray in her golden hair. Her typically bright blue eyes were rimmed with red. "I've had the worst night, Luke. You know how George has been sick the past few months. Well, we finally figured out what's wrong." She paused. "He has esophageal cancer."

The floor seemed to shift under Luke's feet. Memories from his youth, and of his dad's illness, came rushing back.

Gripping the doorjamb, Luke pushed away the past. "Stacey, I'm so sorry. What do the doctors say? What can I do to help out?"

"We have to go to see a specialist in Wichita next week. After that, we'll know more. As far as helping out..." Stacey paused. "I really can't chair the Boofest anymore. I was thinking about posting on social media and asking someone to step up. But I wanted to speak with you first to see if you're able and interested. People like you, Luke. They trust you. You're a natural leader."

Luke interrupted, "I appreciate all your praise, but you don't have to butter me up, Stacey. I'll take over as the chairperson. Besides, you have bigger things to worry about than a downtown festival."

"Are you sure?"

"Positive," said Luke. His head began to ache. He needed a double shot of espresso. Then again, cash flow was down, and he didn't want to spend money he didn't have. "I've got everything under control."

"Here," Stacey said, and withdrew a large, three-ring binder from a canvas bag she had draped over her shoulder. "This is the outline of everything I've done so far."

Luke accepted the heavy tome, realizing too late that he'd taken on a bigger job than imagined. Maybe, just this once, he'd splurge on a coffee. He didn't know how he'd get through all the information without one. "Thanks," he said, flipping through the first few pages. "This looks very thorough."

"Well, I better get going," said Stacey.

"Absolutely." Luke walked with her, pulling the door open. "Give George my best. Again, if you need anything, let me know."

"You're doing more than enough," she said. Rising to tiptoe, she placed a small kiss on his cheek. "You are a great guy, Luke Walker. I hope some smart woman snatches you up—and quick."

At thirty-one years of age, Luke heard comments about his bachelorhood all the time. It wasn't that he wanted to be perpetually single. He had yet to find the right woman.

Stepping out onto the street, Stacey gave one last wave before turning toward her bookstore.

Luke followed and remained on the sidewalk. A breeze blew, sending a piece of paper skittering down the street. He picked up the rubbish and placed it in a bin. Gooseflesh rose on his arms and it wasn't just from the weather.

Luke felt a tickling at the back of his neck, just a whisper of pressure, as if he were being watched—and he knew by whom.

Casting a glance over his shoulder, he searched for the ever-present dark blue sedan. It was there, just as he knew it would be, parked across the street. The pale face of his ex-girlfriend, Julia, was unmistakable in the driver's seat.

Maybe the term ex-girlfriend was a little too generous for their relationship. Luke had dated her briefly over the summer. They'd had no more than half a dozen dates before he ended the relationship.

Soon after, she started watching the store and his apartment upstairs. At first he tried being honest—telling Julia that their romance was not meant to be.

She disagreed.

He blocked her phone when she continued to call and text.

He blocked her again when she changed her number.

He threatened to contact the police—something he never intended to do.

His warning changed nothing.

He threw away the letters she left in the morning and vowed to never look in her direction.

Eventually, she'd get bored, right?

So far she hadn't.

Without another glance in Julia's direction, Luke stepped back into the store. Despite his need for coffee, he didn't want to cross the street and risk a confrontation with Julia. Taking his time, he re-engaged all three locks.

What had started as a long day had just become a lot longer. Then again, Luke wasn't the kind to complain.

He was invested in Braxville's success as more than a business owner, being a lifetime resident, as well. So, yeah, there wasn't much of anything he wasn't willing to do—even become the last-minute chairperson of the festival—for his hometown.

BRIDGETTE PULLED HER car next to the curb, taking a spot behind a blue sedan. Main Street in Braxville was like walking into a page from a history book—coming from a time when life was simple or at least seemed that way. The street was lined on both sides with small shops and restaurants. Most were built of brick, pressing cheek to jowl with one another and only rising three stories from the ground. Glass storefronts gleamed in the morning sun, and light posts of wrought iron stood on every corner.

It was hard not to smile.

After stepping onto the sidewalk, she strode up Main Street and cast a glance at the blue sedan. A dark-haired woman gripped the steering wheel with knuckles gone white. Her gaze was locked on the front door of the hardware store.

The woman took no note of Bridgette, yet her stare left Bridgette walking a bit faster.

Walker Hardware. Now that was a place Bridgette hadn't thought of in years.

While growing up, the dad of her friend had owned Walker Hardware.

For a moment, she wondered what had become of

Luke Walker. Was he still in Braxville? Or was he just another ghost from her past that haunted her still?

Pulling open the door to La Dolce Vita, she was greeted with the earthy scent of roasting coffee beans. Several round tables filled the center of the room. A glass-and-chrome pastry case separated the restaurant from the area where coffees and other beverages were prepared. Her older sister, Jordana, a detective with the Braxville Police Department, already sat at a table near the window.

She stood as Bridgette approached and pulled her in for a big hug. "How are you? I'm so glad that you're home."

"It's good to see you," said Bridgette, embracing her sister in return. Jordana was as tall as Bridgette, five feet nine inches. Her older sister wore her hair in a loose bun and had donned a long jacket in olive green that brought out the auburn highlights in her hair. Years ago, Bridgette learned that Jordana's clothing choices had nothing to do with fashion and all to do with function. Without a doubt, the jacket had been chosen to cover her sister's sidearm. Bridgette continued, "Then again, I'm not sure that I'm actually happy to be back. It's been a rough morning already. Do Mom and Dad get along at all?"

"No," said Jordana honestly. She returned to her seat. "They fight constantly. It's a bit tiring."

"A bit?" Bridgette asked with mock incredulity, while sitting across from her sister. "Can I be candid? I don't think that I can stay at the house while I'm in town. Do you know of any place I can rent?"

"Rent? Be serious. You can live with me. Clint is around a lot, but you'll really like him."

"Live with you and your new boyfriend? No, thank you. I'd rather stay with Mom and Dad." She winked to show that she was teasing, yet the last thing Bridgette wanted was to interrupt her sister's newest romance.

"Sorry I can't be more helpful, but I really can't think of any place on the market." Jordana paused. "Maybe Yvette knows some place that's available."

"Speaking of Yvette," said Bridgette. "Where is our baby sister?"

"She's running late. There's a big case."

"What happened?"

Before Jordana could answer, a server arrived with two cups of coffee and chocolate croissants. "I took the liberty of ordering for you," said Jordana. "I hope your tastes haven't changed while living in the big city."

"There's nothing better than Megan Parker's pastries," she said, mentioning the coffee shop's owner. After taking a big bite, Bridgette continued, "Besides, my tastes haven't changed at all. I live in Wichita, not on the moon."

"And how is life? Really?"

Bridgette knew what Jordana was asking. It had been nearly two years since Bridgette's husband, Henry, died in a car accident. The food turned to sand in her mouth, and she washed it down with a swallow of coffee. "Work is good," she said.

"There's more to life than work."

"I belong to two book clubs," said Bridgette. "I attend a yoga class three times a week and volunteer at the local dog shelter every other Saturday. I have a life, thank you very much."

"Anyone cute at the dog shelter?"

"There is this adorable lab-mix, but he was adopted last month." Bridgette took another bite.

"Har-har," said Jordana. "Anyone cute who walks on two legs? Preferably a human."

"None that I've seen."

"Have you even bothered to look?"

"Honestly," said Bridgette. "No. And before you try to get all big sister on me and boss me into having a relationship, I'm not good at romance. Period. End of story."

Jordana reached for Bridgette's wrist and squeezed lightly. "You are too young to give up on love. Henry was a great guy. We all thought so and we all miss him, too. He's gone and that's tragic, but I don't want to see you alone for the rest of your life."

"That's the point," said Bridgette. She pulled her arm away and reached for a napkin. After wiping her mouth, she continued, "It's my life."

Jordana lifted a hand in surrender. "I get it. I'll back off."

"You get what?" Yvette asked, standing next to the table. Yvette had the same dark hair and eyes as Jordana, but the similarities ended there. Then again, Bridgette was a triplet and she looked nothing like her brothers, Brooks and Neil. Yvette continued, "What'd I miss?"

Standing, Bridgette embraced her baby sister. "Nothing, really," she said, not wanting to share the almost quarrel with Jordana. Bridgette didn't know what she would do if both of her sisters teamed up and tried to force a new man into her life.

"Mom and Dad argue too much," said the eldest Colton daughter. She stood and hugged Yvette. "Bridgette's looking for an apartment. Know of anything?"

"I might, actually," said Yvette. They all took their seats. "Let me talk to a few people and get back to you."

"Thanks so much," said Bridgette. She took another bite of her pastry. "Jordana said that you're working a big case. What happened?"

Yvette gave their older sister an unmistakable side-eye. "We really aren't supposed to talk about work, but two bodies were found in the walls of a building that Dad's company is renovating."

Bridgette choked on her coffee. "What?" She spluttered. "Never mind. I might be a Colton, but I'm not a cop." She glanced at her smart watch. It was 8:20 a.m. "Shoot, I didn't realize that it was so late. I need to scram. How much do I owe for breakfast?"

"It's on me," said Jordana.

Bridgette didn't have time to argue with her sister. "I'll treat next time," she said, while grabbing her bag and heading for the door. Luckily, Bridgette's temporary office was located in City Hall and only blocks from where she had parked her car. If she hurried, she could go back to her auto and grab the plate of muffins her mother had prepared. That would help smooth over any rough edges a minute of tardiness might cause.

As she hurried down the street, Bridgette marveled

that the Braxville of her childhood had changed very little. Yet, it seemed as if the quaint downtown, the tree-lined streets and the well-kept homes were little more than a facade.

There were bodies buried in walls. Clusters of cancer cases. And the woman from before still sat in her car and stared across the street.

Despite the charm of her hometown, Bridgette knew that Braxville was hiding the answer to more than one mystery.

Chapter Two

The Kansas State Department of Health had set up their temporary office in City Hall, located across the street from the town park and only a few blocks from the coffee shop where Bridgette had parked her car.

She took the stairs to the second floor and found the suite of rooms assigned to the DOH at the back at the building. Juggling her bag and the plate, Bridgette pushed the door open with her hip. A round clock hung on the wall. Not only was she on time for work, she had made it with four minutes to spare.

The office was a single room with several workstations around the perimeter. A large conference table sat in the middle of the space. A dry-erase board filled half of one wall. On it was a list of names. Several windows overlooked the back street and Bridgette could see the roof of her father's office, Colton Construction, in the distance.

Two men, at separate workstations, held phones to their ears. A single woman sat at the table. A pile of folders was stacked at her elbow. She looked up as Bridgette crossed the threshold.

Holding up the plate of muffins, Bridgette said, "Morning, folks. I brought food."

The woman stood. "Welcome. You must be Bridgette Colton. I'm Rachel Shaw, I went to school with your brother, Tyler." She pointed to one of the men, an African American with a goatee, "That's Adam Stevens and the other guy is Carson Mathews."

Carson wore a short-sleeved shirt covered in a tropical print. He turned his seat. With the phone still to his ear, he waved and mouthed, *Good morning.*

Adam ended his call and moved to the table. "Food?"

Bridgette set the plate down and removed the foil. "Homemade muffins," she said. "Help yourself."

Adam took a bite. "You are quite the cook."

"Thanks," said Bridgette. "I'm staying with my parents until I find an apartment in town, so they're compliments of my mother."

"Good job, Mrs. Colton," said Adam, finishing his last bit.

Carson ended the call. He moved to the table and took a muffin from the plate. "Nice to meet you."

Bridgette made a mental note to thank her mother. Lilly had been right—food had helped to make inroads with her new coworkers. "Since we're all here," she began, taking a seat at the table, "let's get started."

For the next twenty minutes, Bridgette was briefed about the cancer clusters. In short, a study showed that twenty years ago, six men had developed esophageal cancer. Two died, and four were either in remission or struggling with the cancer's return. Then, more recently, another group of men had been diagnosed with the same exact cancer.

"What are your thoughts?" Bridgette asked.

"It's too specific to be random," said Adam, helping himself to another muffin.

"So, it's not bad luck," said Bridgette, echoing her father's earlier sentiment.

"No way," said Rachel. "It has to be environmental. The men aren't related."

"Smokers?" Bridgette asked. "Other tobacco use? Are they all heavy drinkers?"

"Two men from the first group smoked more than a pack of cigarettes each day," said Carson. "No other tobacco use is listed. A few admitted to regularly consuming more than three drinks a night before becoming ill. If this was caused by alcohol or tobacco, why aren't more people sick?"

"That's a good point," said Bridgette. She rose to her feet and walked to the dry-erase board. "Are these all the cases?"

"It's everyone we have so far," Adam said. "The original names are on the left. The newly diagnosed patients are on the right."

Bridgette scanned the list of names. Her gaze stopped on a name she knew from her childhood.

Ernest O'Rourke.

For years, he had been her father's foreman.

Bridgette asked, "Do you have contact information for all of the men?"

"Sure do," said Rachel. She pulled the pile of folders toward her seat.

"Can you find this one?" asked Bridgette, pointing to Ernest's name.

Rachel flipped through the files. "Here you go," she said, holding out a manila folder.

Bridgette looked at the information. The address was still the same. For a moment, she was transported to years before. She was sitting on the bench seat of her father's truck. A meal, prepared and packed by her mother, sat between them.

Her father tapped the steering wheel, keeping time with the latest song on the country station. At the chorus, both father and daughter bellowed the words. As the song ended, Bridgette dissolved into peals of laughter. For her, it had been one of the few perfect moments spent with her father.

What if there was more than she remembered or more than she'd been told?

Had Ernest been sick then? Was that why they were delivering food?

"I'm going to start with this case," she said, holding up the file. "In fact, I'll interview him right now."

"Now?" echoed Adam. "We usually make an appointment first. Otherwise, we don't know if the patient has time—or the inclination—to speak with us."

What Adam said was entirely true—and DOH policy. "Ernest O'Rourke will have time for me."

"How can you be so confident?" asked Rachel.

"Because," said Bridgette, "I've known him my whole life." Lifting her bag from the floor, she slipped the file inside. "I'll be back in a few hours."

Bridgette walked back to the ground floor and

started up the street toward her car but slowed her gait. Just like it had been when she arrived, the blue sedan was still parked at the curb. The same woman still sat in the driver's seat and continued to watch the hardware store. The woman's intense gaze left Bridgette feeling as if she'd been grabbed by an icy hand, and a shiver ran down her spine.

FOR THE SECOND time in a single morning, a knock on the store's front door interrupted Luke's pre-opening routine. He looked up. Standing on the sidewalk, Yvette Colton waved.

Luke hustled to open the door. "Hey, stranger," he said. "I haven't seen you in months. Is there anything I can help you find?"

"Do you still own all those rental properties?" she asked. "I know someone who needs a place temporarily—for a month or two."

"I sure do," he said. "When would they need the place?"

"Soon," Yvette said. "Like today, if possible."

Today? Aside from the hardware store on the ground floor, Luke owned the whole building, including the two floors above. Over the years, he had renovated the space into four apartments, two on each level. "There's one apartment open," he said. "Right across the hall from me. You're in luck, the last tenant moved out over the summer. It's been freshly painted and comes fully furnished."

"Sounds perfect," said Yvette. "Can we see it at lunchtime?"

Luke paused. The noon hour was one of the busiest

for the store. Did he really want to risk losing customers by closing down at lunch? Then again, filling the vacant apartment would help make ends meet. Moving to the counter, he found a set of keys along with a copy of a boilerplate lease he always used. Sliding the keys and lease toward Yvette, he asked, "Can you show the apartment? If your friend likes it, they can just sign and bring me this copy later today."

"Are you sure you don't want to meet the new renter?"

"I've known you your whole life. If they come with your recommendation, then that's good enough for me." Yvette took the keys and paperwork while Luke continued, "Take the door to the left of the store. Second floor, apartment 2A. Only door on the right."

"Thanks, Luke. I'll keep you posted."

Yvette pushed the door open, passing a newly retired homeowner as she left.

"Glad to see that you've opened early," said the older man. "The missus just told me that we have company coming for Thanksgiving. She gave me a honey-do list longer than my arm."

The store didn't officially open for another half hour. Yet, Luke wasn't going to quibble about time. The day had started, promising nothing but problems, and in short order it had turned around.

"Show me that list," said Luke to the customer. "Let's see what you need."

He led the older man down the paint aisle and wondered about the possible tenant. Should he meet with whoever Yvette Colton brought to the apartment? After all they would be a renter, and his neighbor, as well.

There were other thoughts that were harder to shake. It was impossible to see anyone from the Colton clan without thinking of his long-ago school buddy, Bridgette. Then again, Bridgette had been more than his friend. The summer between high school and college, she had been his first love—his first lover.

At the time, he had hoped their relationship was more than a fleeting romance.

He'd been wrong. Bridgette went to college. A few years later, he heard that she was getting married. Then later came the news that Bridgette had been widowed.

As he explained all the choices for interior paint, Luke couldn't help wondering what had happened to Bridgette Colton?

BRIDGETTE KNEW THE way to Ernest O'Rourke's house by heart and had no need to use her GPS for directions. The brick ranch seemed smaller than she recalled. Then again, the last time she was here, Bridgette was a kid and so her perspective had changed. The trim around the door and windows were in need of a coat of paint, and a carpet of leaves covered the yard.

She stepped from the car and slammed the door shut. After grabbing her bag from the back seat, she turned to the house.

"Beautiful Bridgette Colton," a voice boomed. Ernest stood on the threshold. Like the house, he was smaller than she remembered. This time, it wasn't just her memory. The once robust foreman was stooped and shriveled. He continued, "I recognized you the minute you pulled onto the street."

"Hi, Ernest," she said. "It's good to see you."

"What did I do to get a visit from my favorite Colton?"

While striding up the walkway, she said, "I should've called before stopping by, but your name came up with work." She paused, not sure what to say next. Lifting her bag higher on her shoulder, she continued, "Here I am."

"You don't need to call, you know that." Turning for the house, he gestured for Bridgette to follow. "Come in. I'm happy to help you with whatever I can."

The welcome was more than Bridgette had hoped to get. Ernest led her to the kitchen and pointed to a round wooden table. "Have a seat. Can I pour you a cup of coffee? Do you want a cup of tea?"

One professional rule that Bridgette kept as sacrosanct was to always accept any hospitality offered by a person involved in a study. Despite the fact that she wasn't thirsty, she said, "A cup of tea would be nice."

Ernest filled a kettle with water from the tap and placed it on the stove. "Won't take a minute to boil," he said, sitting in a chair across from Bridgette. "How's your mom and your dad?" he asked.

The argument from earlier came to mind. "Good," she lied. "Same as always."

"Now, you said that my name came up in connection with your job. How'd that happen?"

Bridgette had set her bag on the floor, next to her feet. She reached for the folder and set it on the table. "I'm in Braxville to look into a cluster of cancer cases."

Ernest sat back in his seat hard, as if she'd kicked him in the gut. His face turned the color of used paste. "Esophageal cancer, I bet," he said.

Bridgette nodded just as the whistle on the teakettle let out a long, shrill blast. "Let me get that," she said, rising to her feet. Mugs were already placed on the stove. A canister set lined the back of the counter. One of them said *tea*. It took her only a moment to prepare a cup for each of them.

"Here you go," she said, setting a steaming mug in front of Ernest.

Wrapping his hands around the cup, he asked, "Can I ask you a question?"

"Of course."

"I had cancer two decades ago. Why are people interested now?"

Bridgette blew on the tea before taking a sip. "Cancer of all kinds is to be expected in any given community. When there are more cases than anticipated, it's considered a cluster. The DOH has mapped out nearly a dozen cases in Braxville. You are in the first group, those from twenty years ago. There is another group that has formed more recently and that's what makes us nervous."

"Why's that?" Ernest asked, giving Bridgette time to collect her thoughts.

"Simply put, it means there's something causing everyone to get sick."

"You don't say," said Ernest. "We used to joke Tom, Bill and me—that working with your dad was what gave us cancer."

Cup halfway to her mouth, Bridgette froze. "What'd you say?"

"Back when I worked for your dad, two other guys on our crew got sick at the same time as me."

Setting her cup aside, Bridgette withdrew a pad of paper and a pen from her bag. "Bill? Tom?"

"Bill Warner and Tom Cromwell."

Bridgette wrote down the names. She had yet to commit all the men from the cluster to memory but knew that these names were already on the list. "Do you keep in touch with Bill and Tom?"

"They both passed away." Ernest stared at the cup in his hands and shook his head. "The cancer took Tom about eighteen years ago. Bill had a heart attack four years back. So, his death wasn't cancer related. Then again, Bill was always sick after what he went through." He took a sip of tea and set the cup back on the table.

"It sounds like you knew both of the men well."

"We grew up together. Went to school from kindergarten to graduation. We hunted in the fall. Fished in the summer. I got them both jobs at Colton Construction."

Bridgette placed a hand on the older man's arm. His skin was dry and paper-thin. "Can I ask you some questions? If not now, I can make an appointment and come back."

"I hope you come and visit an old man while you work in Braxville, but I have nothing else to do right now. Ask away."

Tapping her pen on the pad, Bridgette wondered

what question was most pertinent. Her mother's desire for a new washing machine with a filter came to mind. As did the report that plastic ends up in the river, where filaments were ingested by the fish. And then the fish eaten by humans. There was no scientific evidence linking the plastics to cancer, but it did bring up an interesting question. What else might be in the water?

"Do you still fish a lot?"

"Whenever I get the chance."

"You always catch something?"

"I'd be a poor fisherman if I didn't."

"How often do you eat what you catch?"

"Never," said Ernest. "I'm a catch-and-release kind of guy."

Still, it would be prudent to test the river's water. She made a note.

"Have you ever smoked, Ernest?"

"As a teenager, sure. Everyone did."

"I have a few questions and I want you to think back to your life before you were diagnosed with cancer when answering."

"Got it."

Bridgette had a long-practiced set of questions she asked everyone involved in an investigation. She began by asking, "Did you ever drink excessive alcohol? Take drugs not prescribed by a doctor? Finally, how would you describe your exercise routine?"

"Did I ever get drunk as a young man? Sure," said Ernest with a shrug. "In fact, most every Friday we'd all go out and have one too many after work. Take drugs not prescribed a doctor—never. In fact, I didn't go to the doctor regular-like before I got sick. Now, I have to go twice a year, whether I think I need to be there or not. And exercise? I can't say I was ever a runner or a gym rat. I carried roofing tiles up and down ladders for a living, so I'd say that counts as being fit."

"I'd say you're right," said Bridgette, copying Ernest's statement, word for word. Before she got a chance to ask her next question, her phone pinged with an incoming text. She glanced at the screen. It was from Yvette. Bridgette wasn't about to interrupt an initial interview to reply to her sister. Silencing her phone, she returned to her list of questions for Ernest.

By the time she was through, Bridgette had taken over ten pages of notes and drunk three cups of tea. Her first morning of working in Braxville was almost gone.

After asking her last set of questions, Bridgette rose to her feet and placed her notepad and pen into her bag. "Thanks for taking the time to speak to me, Ernest. I appreciate it. Will you call if you think of anything else?"

"Only if you promise to come out and visit again."

"Of course," said Bridgette, giving the older man a hug.

Walking back to her car, Bridgette fished her phone from her bag and read the text from Yvette. I found a place. Fully furnished. In downtown Braxville. I can show you today at lunch.

Bridgette sent her sister a reply. You're the best. Meet in 1 hour?

Yvette replied with a thumbs-up emoji and an address on Main Street.

With her problem of housing hopefully solved, she focused on what she'd learned from Ernest. There was something he said that bothered her more than she'd let on. Three of her father's employees had esophageal cancer. She didn't have time to do the math, but she knew the odds of that being a coincidence were pretty lousy. Could there really be a connection between the men who developed cancer and Colton Construction?

Chapter Three

Bridgette still had an hour until meeting her sister to look at the apartment. With time to spare, she drove to the offices of Colton Construction. Her father's large white pickup was parked in a reserved place next to the front door. She maneuvered her car into a spot several rows back and turned off the engine.

Walking to the front door, Bridgette couldn't help but marvel at the business her father had built. When she was a child, it had been a family-run operation—dad and grandpa building houses. Decades earlier, the old office had been a single trailer—drafty in the winter and sweltering in the summer. Grandpa kept lollipops on hand in case any of the Colton kids stopped by.

Now the offices had a metal roof of cobalt blue. The glass-and-brick building sat on the same dusty parcel of land at the edge of town, but now took up over 10,000 square feet. Behind the office were several outbuildings. The original trailer had been converted to a mail room. There was a warehouse as large as an airplane hangar. A garage held the fleet of construction equipment. The staff had grown, as well. What started as two men and a handful of full-time employees had grown to a full office staff, dozens of construction workers, plumbers and electricians. Her father had even hired a full-time architect and planned to expand by bringing a civil engineer onto the staff, as well.

Business was definitely good for Colton Construction.

Pulling open the front door, Bridgette couldn't help wondering what her grandfather would think of all the progress. Would he be proud? Or would he not see the expansion as an improvement?

A receptionist sat behind a large glass desk and looked up as Bridgette entered. "Can I help you?" the woman asked.

How long had it been since she'd visited her father at work? Long enough that Colton Construction had a new receptionist. "I need to speak to Fitzpatrick Colton."

"Can I tell him what this is regarding?"

"I'm Bridgette," she said. "His daughter."

The woman blushed slightly. "Your father mentioned that you were back in town. It's nice to meet you."

Bridgette smiled. "It's nice to meet you, too. And my dad, is he available?"

"You can go right on back."

After thanking the receptionist, Bridgette found the office.

Her father sat behind a large wooden desk. He wore a quarter-zip sweater over a golf shirt. Pen tapping on his bottom lip, Bridgette's dad leaned back in a leather desk chair. Her dad's partner, Markus Dexter—otherwise known as Uncle Dex—wore a gray blazer and a pristine white shirt open at the collar. He was situated in an armchair across the desk from Fitz Colton. The two men looked up, glaring, as she entered.

Bridgette had no idea what they'd been discussing, but the tension was palpable, almost a physical thing.

Tripping to a stop, she paused on the threshold. "Morning, Daddy. I need your help. Is now a bad time?"

"It's never a bad time to see you," said Dex, while rising to his feet. He placed a kiss on her cheek. "I'll let you and your dad catch up. Fitz, we can talk later."

"See you at the bonfire on Friday," said Bridgette.

"I heard your mom is serving ribs," said Dex. "I wouldn't miss it for the world."

She waited until Dex was gone before dropping into the chair he had just vacated. "Is everything okay? You and Uncle Dex seemed upset."

Her father waved away her question. "There's a police matter at a site we're renovating for the city. It's never good if the police are involved."

Bridgette recalled her sisters mentioning just such an issue this morning. She struggled with what, if anything, to say. In the end, she decided on discretion and said nothing. "I saw Ernest O'Rourke this morning."

A look passed over her father's face. What had it been?

Surprise? Sure, but there'd been more. What was it? Hurt? Anger?

In the end, she decided it was a look of regret. It

was gone as quickly as it came, and Bridgette wasn't positive that she'd seen anything at all.

"How's Ernest these days?" her father asked. "I haven't seen much of him since he retired a few years back."

"Did you know that he had esophageal cancer two decades ago?"

"Sure," said her dad. "It was awful. Your mother and I were torn up over his illness. He wasn't able to work for a few months while getting treatment. Of course, Ernest is a tough old bird and he kicked the cancer in the nuts—excuse my language—and came back, good as new."

"He said that two other employees of Colton Construction had the same illness at roughly the same time."

Her father shook his head, "I don't think so. I would've remembered something like that. Must be that Ernest is mistaken."

"He was really good friends with these men." She removed the notebook from her bag, scanning her notes for the names. "Bill Warner and Tom Cromwell. Do you remember them?"

"Can't say that either of those names ring a bell for me," said her father. "But that was a long time ago. People come and go in the construction business, you know that."

"Ernest said they grew up together and he was the one who got them both jobs." She paused and chewed on her bottom lip. How could she ask her father the next question without being rude? She knew the answer—there was no way to bring up the subject without being impertinent. Then again, she was doing her job—her relationship with the company notwithstanding. "Any chance that the men were exposed to carcinogens on the job?"

"You think the men got cancer from working for me?" Her father poked the top of his desk with his pen. "Bill Warner was a large guy with a heart condition who never exercised. In fact, he would rather eat a dozen doughnuts than look at an apple. Tom Cromwell was the reason the phrase *smoked like a freight train* was invented. I don't know what happened to Ernest, but neither of those other men were overly healthy when they worked for me." Tossing the pen onto the desk, her father continued, "And I always made sure those boys had health insurance, even if they couldn't work."

"I thought you said that you didn't remember either Bill or Tom."

Her father sat back in his seat, his eyes wide. "I don't," he began. "Or rather, I didn't. Then when you mentioned that they were good friends with Ernest and grew up together, I knew who you were talking about. I just didn't remember their names at first."

Her father's answer made complete sense. If that was the case, though, why had a hard knot dropped into her middle? "Is there any chance I can get employee records to cross-reference with all the other names I have on the list?"

"From twenty years back?" Her father scratched the back of his head. "Sweetie, I'd love to help you out with your job, but I don't think I've kept any records that go back that far. I'm sorry."

Before Bridgette could say anything else, her phone started to ring. She glanced at the screen. It was her baby sister and—what's more—Bridgette was late. "I have to go," she said. "I'm meeting Yvette downtown."

"Go," said Fitz. "I'll see you at home tonight, okay?"

The phone quit ringing as the call went to voice mail. "I'm not sure about that, Daddy. I'm looking at getting my own place. I love you and Mom, but—"

Her father interrupted, "You're thirty years old and living with your parents is sad."

"I'm glad you understand," she said. Her phone started to ring again. It was Yvette, blowing up her cell.

"Your mother will be disappointed," said her father.

"I know," said Bridgette. "I don't want to hurt her feelings."

"Let me talk to her. She seems to be upset with me all the time, so I can handle a little more heat from your mother."

"You're the best, Daddy," said Bridgette. While swiping the call open, she turned from her father's office and retraced her steps toward the reception area. To Yvette, she said, "I'm on my way. Sorry to be late."

While rushing to her car, Bridgette wished she had time for a leisurely drive or a long walk. She felt as if she had learned important information during the morning. It was as if she'd been given only a few pieces of a puzzle, and without time to think, she'd never be able to see how everything fit together.

BRIDGETTE MADE THE return trip to Braxville in record time. She found a parking place at the curb, next to the address provided by Yvette's text. It was near where she had parked earlier in the day. Stepping from her car, she looked for the blue sedan along with the driver and her intense and chilling stare.

The woman and her car were gone.

Thick gray clouds rolled across the sky and sun. It seemed as if the vibrant colors had been leached from Braxville and the town had been reset in tones of sepia. Yvette stood in front of the hardware store with her arms folded across her chest against the gathering chill. She wore a bright red scarf around her neck. The color made her brown eyes appear a shade darker.

"Don't you look stylish," said Bridgette, almost teasing. "Anyone in particular you want to impress?"

"Can't a girl just want to look good for herself? Does my appearance have to be about a guy?"

In Bridgette's estimation, it almost always had something to do with a man. Yet, her sister was right. Yvette was entitled to look good for herself. "You said there was an apartment for rent? What are we doing at the hardware store?"

"It's above the store. Owned by the store's owner," said Yvette, while working a key into an adjacent door's lock.

The store's owner? When Bridgette was in high school, that had been Luke's dad, Paul. How would she feel about renting a place from her old boyfriend's father? Could things get worse than living at home?

As Yvette pulled the door open, Bridgette asked, "Does Paul still own Walker Hardware?"

"Paul?" she echoed with a shake of her head. "No, the owner isn't named Paul."

Bridgette didn't press for more information—like what happened to Paul Walker. Or if his son was still in town. And if Luke was around, was he married? Or happy? Did he ever wonder about Bridgette, or why she slipped quietly from his life—and his mind—forever?

The door from the street led to a narrow landing, with a bank of mailboxes on the wall. There was also a set of stairs that led upward. The steps were clean. There were no odd odors hanging in the air.

As they climbed the first flight, Bridgette couldn't help being hopeful.

"Let's see," said Yvette as they reached the landing. "He said it was apartment 2A, on the right. That's this one." She had another key, for another lock. Opening the door with a flourish, she said, "Voilà!"

Bridgette stepped inside and smiled. The floors were wooden. The living room was furnished with a sofa, chair and coffee table. The kitchen had enough room for a small table. High windows overlooked Main Street, and from where she stood she could see La Dolce Vita.

Pointing to the coffee shop, Bridgette said, "Next time we meet, you can just wave when you arrive."

"Or I can get takeout and come up to your place."

"Even better." There was a single door off the living room that led to a master suite. Bed. Dresser. Chest of drawers. The closet was small, but she'd survive. A bathroom was set off the bedroom. Shower, tub, sink. It was everything she wanted—and more.

"It's perfect," she said. "I'll take it."

"You can think about it, maybe negotiate for a lower rent since this place has been vacant for a few months," said Yvette.

"I've thought about it enough," she said. "And I'd pay extra to get out of Mom and Dad's house. I love them both, you know."

"They don't get along and their fighting makes everyone miserable," Yvette finished for her. "Don't forget, I'm the baby. I had to stay at home after everyone went to college."

"I'm glad you understand," said Bridgette. "I hope Mom does, too."

"Well, if you're sure you want the apartment, I have a copy of the lease." Yvette held up several sheets of paper.

Bridgette scanned the information. The rent was low in comparison to what she paid in Wichita, but still top dollar for Braxville. On the final page she found a line for her signature. After signing, she wrote a check for the first month's rent. Handing both to her sister, she said, "If your job as a crime scene investigator doesn't work out, you might have a future in real estate."

"Thanks," she said. "I'm going to deliver this to the owner now. If you want, I'll introduce you to your new landlord and neighbor."

Bridgette consulted her phone for the time. It was one thirty. "I'd love to, but I've been out of the office all morning. I better get back." She added, "Thanks for finding me an apartment."

"What are little sisters for?"

"Aside from rummaging through my closet, you mean?"

"Hey, that was a long time ago. But I am excited to see what all you've brought with you. I haven't decided what to wear to the bonfire this weekend."

After giving her sister a quick hug, Bridgette left her new home.

Now that Bridgette had her own place, she could focus on her job. It was odd that three men, close friends since childhood, ended up developing the same cancer. Certainly, they had much more in common than working for her father's company. It would take all of Bridgette's investigative skills to figure out what it was.

Jogging down the stairs, she opened the door leading to the sidewalk and stepped outside. The gathering clouds had darkened, and the wind held a chill. She predicted rain tonight. After buttoning up her jacket, she glanced into the window of Walker Hardware. Her reflection was superimposed on the glass, and the store was filled with people. Her mouth went dry as she scanned the crowd.

He wouldn't be there, she knew. Why then, was Bridgette looking for her old love, Luke Walker?

WHAT STARTED AS a lousy day had turned around for Luke Walker. The hardware store had been busy. During the midday rush, Yvette Colton delivered a signed lease for the apartment upstairs—along with a check for the first month's rent. He hadn't had time to look at either.

After the store closed, he turned off the lights and left through the main entrance. While locking the door, a tickling ran up his spine. He'd become accustomed to the sensation. Still, the hairs at the nape of his neck stood on end. Using the front window as a mirror, he glanced over his shoulder.

Just as he expected, Julia, his ex-girlfriend, stood across the street. Streetlamps shone on every corner, bathing downtown Braxville in a golden glow. By mid-block, the darkness took over and left everything in shadow.

Julia stood in one of the dark places. Luke wasn't sure if it was a trick of the light or the distortion of the glass, but it looked as if Julia had no eyes—just empty, black sockets. He swallowed. Maybe his decision not to involve the police had been too hasty.

The apartment building was next to the hardware store. With the feeling of Julia's sightless gaze still on his back, Luke fumbled with the keys as he unlocked the dead bolt. After stepping inside, he shoved the door closed with a *crack*.

The uneasy feeling slipped away as he climbed the stairs. On the landing, he paused. The softly crooning voice of a country-and-western singer came from inside the newly rented apartment. It was six thirty and not an unreasonable time to visit—especially since he owned the building.

Lifting his hand, Luke rapped his knuckles on the

wooden door. From inside, he heard the sound of footsteps and a woman's voice. "Just a second."

The door opened.

For Luke, time stopped. His pulse began to race, filling his skull with the *whomp, whomp* of rushing blood.

He shook away the numbness.

Of course, it all made sense. Yvette Colton coming to him. A tenant who needed a place for a few months. It's just that Luke never would have guessed, although he probably should have known.

"Bridgette," he said. For the first time in ages, he smiled, and the expression wasn't forced. "Wow. I mean, I didn't expect you to have rented the apartment." He still held the envelope with the lease and the check, realizing only moments too late that he should have taken the time to at least glance at both before knocking on the door.

She lifted one eyebrow. "Luke Walker. What in the world are you doing here? Yvette said your dad sold the hardware store years ago."

It was hard to miss the ice in Bridgette's tone. Sure, it had been years since they had last spoken. Their final conversation had been cordial, if not friendly. She had called to say hello. His father was sick. Luke was worried that his dad's cancer had returned. Bridgette had listened and then disappeared from his life.

"My dad did sell the store—to me," he said in answer to her question. "And then I bought the rest of the building, too."

"You're my landlord?" she asked, her question dripping with incredulity. "This isn't going to work, Luke."

"What won't work? You can't rent an apartment from me for a few months?" Then again, it had been years. A lot had changed. Through distance and time, whatever feelings they once had for each other were gone.

"You know what?" he said, holding out the envelope that held the lease and Bridgette's check. "Yvette dropped this off at the store. You can have your money back and tear up the rental agreement. I'm not sure why we're enemies, but I'm too old for any idiocy from high school."

Outside, rain started to fall. A thousand tiny arrows hitting the windowpane.

Bridgette dropped her gaze and chewed on her bottom lip. "You're right, Luke. Whatever happened between us is ancient history. I guess I was surprised to see you, that's all."

"It seems like finding me on your doorstep was more than an unpleasant surprise. I really don't want you to stay if I make you uncomfortable."

"Are you kicking me out?"

"Of course not," he said before considering her question.

"Can I apologize for being rude? Is there any way we can start over?"

Bridgette's hostile reaction had stung, but Luke wasn't the kind to hold a grudge, and he found himself saying, "Sure. Of course."

"Thanks," said Bridgette, giving him that same smile she always had—the one that sent his heartbeat racing and left his palms damp.

Chapter Four

Bridgette placed her hand on the closed wooden door, her heartbeat racing. In all honesty she never thought she'd see Luke again, much less find him living across the hallway. Then again Braxville was a small town, and she had to be prepared to see people from her childhood.

Yet, could Luke really be living across the hall?

Despite the fact that she knew it to be true, it was all unbelievable. Her small apartment became cramped with ghosts from her past.

Henry and their promise of a life together—cut short by a car accident.

Her parents and their marriage. To Bridgette, the relationship had seemed so perfect as a child. Now it was fractured. Was the marriage broken beyond repair?

Then there was Luke and that long-forgotten memory. It had risen to the surface at the sight of him and left a stabbing pain in her chest.

The sound of a bubble bursting caught Bridgette's attention and drew her gaze into the kitchen.

Another bubble burst, splattering tomato soup atop the range.

"Damn." Rushing to the kitchen, she removed the pot from the stove. A grilled-cheese sandwich sizzled in a frying pan. She flipped it over, the cooked side dark but not burned. At least she hadn't ruined her dinner—or burned down the building.

After pouring the soup into a bowl, she set the sandwich on a plate. True, it wasn't the fine meal her mother would have prepared. Then again, it was *her* food prepared in *her* kitchen. Setting the steaming bowl on the table, Bridgette took a seat.

She'd seen her mother briefly, when she went to the house after work and picked up her bag. Her mother had been undeniably disappointed but loving all the same. It almost made it impossible to leave her parent's house—almost, but not completely.

Spooning a bite into her mouth, she shuddered.

The curtains were open still. The world outside the rain-streaked window was black as pitch.

Suddenly she felt exposed.

Wiping her mouth with a napkin, she rose from the table and crossed the room. Bridgette looked out of the window, her breath fogging on the glass.

There, on the deserted street, sodden with rain, was the same woman she'd noticed in the morning.

Bridgette recoiled, as if burned by the glass. True, she hadn't lived in Braxville for years, yet some things were universal. A woman standing in a storm and constantly staring at a building wasn't normal.

What should she do? Call the police? Call her parents?

Pulling her curtains shut, Bridgette knew there was really only one person she should tell. It was Luke Walker.

She went across the hall and knocked on the door. It was answered almost immediately. Luke stood on the threshold. He'd stripped out of his flannel shirt and only wore a skintight T-shirt in faded green. Through the thin fabric, the muscles of his arms, chest and abs were unmistakable. His short hair was tousled, and for the span of a heartbeat Bridgette clearly remembered the feeling of his mouth on hers.

"Hey, what's up?" he asked.

For a moment, Bridgette couldn't recall what had been so important. "There's a woman standing in the rain and staring at the building. What's more, I saw her earlier today, parked on the street and watching this building. I'm no mental health expert, but behavior like that is odd."

Luke heaved a sigh. "You're right. It is odd."

A new idea settled on Bridgette, like snow on an undisturbed landscape. "You know the woman?"

"Her name is Julia Jones. We dated over the summer. It was only a few dates and I knew it wasn't going to work. I told her we were done. Apparently, she doesn't agree."

"She's your ex-girlfriend?"

"Hey, not all my exes are as beautiful, smart, talented and stable as you," he said.

Bridgette couldn't help but smile. "Gee, you know how to make a girl feel special and creep her out all at the same time."

Luke shrugged. The shirt rode up from his waist-band, showing a sliver of rock-hard abs. "What can I say," he asked. "It's a gift."

"Shouldn't we call someone about your ex? She can't just keep staring at your building and... What does she want?"

"To be honest," said Luke. "I'm not sure. Trust me, I've talked to her more than once and tried to explain that she and I are no longer an item. Until now, I've blamed it all on her age. She's young—or youngish. Twenty-three years old."

"What about the police? There are laws against stalking, you know."

"I threatened to call the cops, but really I felt too much like a heel to file a complaint." Luke leaned on the doorjamb and crossed one foot over the other.

His legs were long and strong. Bridgette remembered the feeling of his thighs between hers and, despite herself, she blushed. "There has to be someone to contact and ask for help. Family? Friends?"

"Julia lives with her mother," said Luke. "Maybe now is the time to give her a call."

"Too bad Julia couldn't find someone else to like—someone who likes her in return."

"That's what I keep hoping will happen. That, or she'll get bored watching this place day after day."

The conversation reached a lull. Bridgette figured her soup was now cold and her sandwich had gotten soggy. "If you need me to do anything," Bridgette said. "Let me know. I'm happy to help."

"Sure," said Luke. "Hopefully, her mom will talk sense into Julia."

"Hopefully," said Bridgette. She gave Luke a little wave and returned to her apartment. She closed the door and pressed her forehead into the wood. Her heartbeat hammered against her ribs and her breath came in short gasps. It wasn't knowing about the slightly unhinged woman that left Bridgette agitated.

It was Luke.

Over the years, he had turned from a nice-looking boy into a handsome man. He was strong, smart, funny and caring. In short, Luke Walker was everything that Bridgette wanted in a man—that was if she wanted a man at all.

With him so near, she'd have to keep her emotions in check. It would be too easy to fall for Luke Walker a second time—and he was one mistake she refused to make twice.

Luke stared at the door to Bridgette's apartment long after it shut. She had been less than happy to see him at first, that was for sure. Had it been, as she claimed, shock that came out sideways and only appeared to be displeasure? Or had seeing him truly left her upset? For some reason, Luke would bet on the latter, although he didn't know why he'd place that wager.

Shaking his head, Luke stepped into his apartment and closed the door. At the window, he looked at the street below. There, soaking wet, was Julia. She stared up at his apartment. For a moment, their gazes met. She stepped forward, her hand outstretched.

He closed his curtains.

Bridgette was right. Julia staring at his apartment and store day after day was peculiar. Moreover, it was time her obsession ended. Lifting the phone from the charging stand, he used an app to find a number for Julia's mom. He'd only met Nancy Jones once. During that brief introduction, she appeared to be a caring woman, one who was truly concerned for her daughter's well-being.

He placed the call and it was answered on the second ring. "Yes?"

"Hi, Nancy. This is Luke Walker." He paused, not sure how to categorize his relationship with Julia.

Thankfully, Nancy saved him from thinking too hard. "Of course, I remember you, Luke. I'm sorry to say, but Julia is working late tonight."

"Working?" he echoed.

"Yes, she just called an hour ago and said that her boss needed her to stay late."

Luke pulled back the curtains and peeked through the seam between fabric and wall. Julia still stood on the street. Rain dripped from her dark hair and her clothes were soaked.

"Nancy, I hate to tell you this," said Luke. "But Julia isn't at work."

"No, you're mistaken. She called me."

"I'm not mistaken," said Luke. "Honestly, I wish I was. Julia has been watching my business and home for the past month and a half. She comes early in the morning and returns later in the day."

"Are you sure?"

"Positive," said Luke. "In fact, I'm looking at her right now. She's standing on Main Street and looking up at my apartment."

Nancy sucked in a breath. "I hoped that things had gotten better for Julia. That she was…well, better."

"Really, ma'am. I am so sorry. I didn't know what to do besides call you."

"No need to apologize," said Nancy. "You did the right thing. I'm going to call her now and see if I can talk her into coming home."

"Good luck," said Luke. Nancy had already ended the call and the line was dead.

JULIA STOOD ON the street, staring at the building and the closed curtains. Her phone, tucked into her jacket pocket, began to vibrate and trill. She glanced at the screen. It was her mother. Tucking the phone back into her pocket, she ignored the call.

She didn't have the time to be distracted.

Luke had made contact. The games they'd been playing were done and it was time to begin anew.

Rain fell in sheets. Julia's breath froze into a cloud before being washed away by the storm. Earlier, she'd started shivering. Now she couldn't feel her fingers or toes. Soon Luke would come to her. He'd bring her tea or maybe soup. He'd invite her to get warm and dry in his apartment.

It was almost like a scene in a movie—the same one the actor had been in.

Yet, this was not pretend. They were kindred spirits—soul mates, if you believed in that sort of thing.

And, oh, Julia believed with every breath she drew and every beat of her racing heart.

Her phone shimmied again, shaking her jacket and sending a rivulet of rain streaming down her neck. It would be her mother again. Still, Julia couldn't leave. Not when Luke was coming down the stairs and would open the door right…now.

Or now.

Or now.

The door remained closed.

Maybe he was starting the kettle for tea. Or perhaps he was drawing a bath for them both. He'd be down any minute, like…now.

Her phone stopped ringing.

It began an instant later.

Julia fished the phone from her pocket and swiped the call open. "What, Mother? I am working."

"No," her mother said, her voice hoarse from crying. "You aren't. You're lying to me and—what's worse— lying to yourself."

Julia's face went numb. Her fingertips began to throb. How could her mother know? For months, Julia told her mother that she was employed as an administrative assistant at Colton Construction, working for Mr. Colton personally. The story was almost true. Julia did work at CC, just part-time and in the mail room. One day soon, though, she'd be noticed and promoted. "I'm in a meeting, Mother. I told you that already."

"You aren't working," said her mother, steel in her watery tone. "You are standing on the street in the pouring rain and staring at Luke Walker's apartment."

Julia's chest tightened, making it impossible to breathe. "Who told you such a lie?"

"Luke just called and said you've been stalking him."

"No," said Julia. "Luke will come to me any minute."

"He won't. Your relationship with that man is over. You need to get home now."

"I won't," said Julia, stomping her foot. She splashed a puddle, frigid water washing over her leg and shoe.

"Sweetie, you need to come home on your own right now, or I'm going to have to call the police. From there, you'll go to the hospital. You know that."

Not the hospital, with the piss-yellow floors and walls the color of a cloudy day. Not the hospital, where she had to take handfuls of pills that made Julia feel as if she was watching her pathetic life and not living it. Not the hospital, where the orderly told Julia she was pretty—beautiful, really—and left his hand on her thigh long enough for her skin to crawl.

She wasn't crazy. She didn't need to be locked up.

What she needed was Luke.

He was on his way—she could feel it in her bones. He was about to open the door...now.

Nothing.

"Julia," said her mother. "Answer me right this minute. If you don't, I'm hanging up and calling the police. Julia, are you there?"

"Yes, Momma. I'm here."

"Now, there's a good girl. You need to come home, you know that."

"Yes, Momma."

"Are you on your way?"

"Yes, Momma."

"And, Julia?"

"Yes, Momma."

"I do love you, honey. I only want what's best."

Julia ended the call and walked back to her car, her shoes squelching with each step. She started the engine, turning the heater to the highest setting. A blast of cold air shot from the vents.

Damn car.

The engine wouldn't be warm enough to make heat until she got home.

She sat behind the steering wheel, wet and trembling.

What had changed?

Had Luke really called her mother?

Did she dare to think—to hope—that her mother was lying?

Then again, if he had called, why?

And that brought her questions back, full circle.

What had changed?

Julia knew most every move Luke had made. Today was no different from any other. There were a few customers at the store early. She figured that had made him happy.

Why then was he angry at her?

If only they could talk.

That would have to wait for another day. If Julia didn't get home soon, her mother would make good on her promise to call the police.

Julia recalled little of her drive, and soon she turned

onto the quiet street where she lived with her mother. She pulled into the driveway as a thin tendril of heat leaked from the vent.

"Figures," Julia grumbled while putting the gear-shift into Park.

Her house sat at the back of a small yard. A single tree stood near the street. The branches were already bare and dripped rainwater onto the sidewalk. Twin lights in sconces on either side of the door were ablaze, washing the front stoop in a warm golden glow. She was home.

Yet, she knew her homecoming would be less welcoming than the front of the house.

Her mother would be furious at Julia for lying.

Too bad she couldn't sit in the car forever. Then again Julia was cold, wet and hungry. A little ire from her mother was a small price to pay for a warm house and a hot meal.

The storm had passed and a fine mist hung in the air. Shuffling from the car, Julia opened the front door. The air was warm and the savory scent of beef stew greeted her. Standing in the foyer, Julia slipped out of her coat and hung it on a stand. Rain dripped from the sleeves and gathered in a puddle on the floor.

The faint glow of the TV filled the darkened den. She didn't pause and try to find her mother in the gloom. Tiptoeing past the doorway, Julia hoped that tonight she'd get lucky. Maybe, she could get a bowl of stew from the kitchen and sneak into her room, never speaking once to her mother.

Stepping into the kitchen, Julia flipped a switch,

filling the room with light. There, at the table, sat her mother. An oxygen tube ran from her nose to a small tank that was hooked to the back of the wheelchair.

It was years of smoking that had left her mother's body shriveled and racked with illnesses. The worst of it was that, despite her illness, Nancy's mind was fully intact. Years before, Julia's father had left to get cigarettes and never came back.

It was then that Julia's mother vowed to smoke forever. Though Julia never understood how that made her mother fearless or bold.

"Sit," said her mother, pointing to a seat opposite at the small table.

"I'm really wet and tired, Momma. I just want some stew. Can't I eat in my room, just this once?"

"You know I don't like food in the rooms—it brings about pests. I also don't like fibs. Lies. We need to talk."

Julia opened her mouth to argue but could think of nothing to say, and she dropped into the seat. Her mother wheeled herself to the stove. Slowly she lifted to standing. It took several minutes for Nancy to move along the kitchen counter, collecting a bowl, spoon and slices of bread.

Her stomach contracting painfully with hunger, Julia waited. Her mother liked to cook and prepare dinner. It gave her a sense of purpose, a glimpse into her former life.

Nancy placed the food in front of Julia with a *thunk* of crockery on faux wood. Brown broth sloshed over the bowl's lip, disappearing into the floral-patterned place mat. She set down sliced bread on a plate.

Dropping back into her chair, Nancy took deep gulps of air, as if she were drinking from a garden hose. It gave Julia a moment to eat before having to speak to her mother.

"Tell me the truth," said her mother after a moment. "What's going on."

Julia ripped a piece of bread and trailed it through the stew. "Nothing's going on."

"Let's start with the job. Is that made up? Do you work for Colton Construction—or anywhere at all?"

"I do work for Colton Construction," said Julia. "You've even seen my pay checks."

"But you aren't Mr. Colton's personal assistant, are you?"

Julia took a bite of bread. She swallowed, gagged and rushed to the sink for water.

"You aren't Mr. Colton's personal assistant, are you?" her mother asked. There was a sharp edge to her words.

Now, more than ever, Julia felt as if she walked on the razor's edge. She didn't know what to say. Leaning over the sink, her hair fell forward, a damp curtain shielding her from the rest of the world. She slurped from the faucet long after her thirst was sated.

Her mother asked, "What do you do at work?"

Wiping her mouth with the back of her hand, Julia said, "I'm in the mail room from ten o'clock in the morning until everything's delivered. Sometimes, I make copies or stuff envelopes. It's nothing glamorous."

"It's honest work. And you've been there since this summer?"

Julia nodded. "Yes, Momma."

"Sit down. Finish your stew and tell me about work."

Julia returned to the table and picked up her spoon. "I'm glad I can be honest with you, Momma. I wanted you to be proud of me, and assistant to the boss seems more important than sorting mail."

"I am so proud of you, Julia. Working and holding a job is hard—and look at you, honey. You've been employed for months." Her mother paused. "I wish you would have told me the truth from the beginning."

"I guess I should have," said Julia.

"We also need to talk about the boy."

"Boy?"

"Luke Walker."

"Momma, he's not a boy. He's a man."

"You can't hang around his apartment and store anymore."

"Listen, Momma," said Julia. "I just need to talk to him. If we speak, we can work out this misunderstanding."

Nancy placed her hand on Julia's wrist, the touch halting Julia's words. Her mother's fingers were gnarled, her skin thin and dry. "You have to let him go. Much as you like him, he has moved on. Do you hear me?"

"I hear you," said Julia. A sheen of grease floated on top of the stew and her stomach roiled.

"I'm glad we had this talk. Remember, you can tell me anything."

Julia stood and placed a kiss on her mother's cheek. "I always remember." And then she said, "Do you want me to clean up the dishes?"

Nancy shook her head. "While I can still do a few things, I will. You go and put on something warm and dry. You must be cold—your lips are trembling."

Julia walked down the short hallway and slipped into her bedroom. She pressed the door closed with just the whisper of a sound. Her room was her sanctuary, a place her mother never entered. Standing in the dark, Julia stripped out of her damp clothes. With the cool air kissing her skin, she turned on the light. Every inch of her walls was covered.

There were photos of Luke Walker. Selfies of them both taken on each date—their smiling faces side by side forever. Then there were other pictures taken of Luke, those for which he hadn't posed. The one where he ran past Julia, shirtless and covered in sweat. There were several of Luke walking from the hardware store to the coffee shop, hands in pockets and gaze cast at the road. Or his return trip with a paper cup. There was one taken from across the street and through the front window of the hardware store. In that picture, Luke was nothing more than a shadow.

There was more than the pictures. Julia still had the stubs from the movie he took her to see. She had a napkin from the time they went to get ice cream and another from a roadside barbecue stand.

Tucked beneath her pillow and out of sight was a shirt Julia found draped over a ladder on the day that

Luke cleaned the windows of Walker Hardware. She'd worn it to bed every night for months.

Much as her mother thought that Luke no longer cared, she was wrong.

Julia knew that she and Luke were meant to be together. Not just now, but always.

Chapter Five

Bridgette woke to sunlight streaming through sheer curtains. She stretched, taking up the whole bed. For the first time in years, she missed waking up in the arms of a man. She froze, mid-stretch. Breathless, she waited for the stab of guilt or the heaviness of grief to overtake her.

Neither came.

Was she ready to move on with her life even if it meant leaving memories of Henry behind?

More than that, was she ready to trust and hope and love for a second time?

Bridgette knew those kinds of thoughts were too deep to parse through without the benefit of coffee. Throwing back the blankets, she stood, stretched once more and padded to the kitchen. Last night, in her haste to move into her apartment, Bridgette had done only the most rudimentary shopping at the market. Cans of soup. Cheese. Bread. Cold cereal. Milk. Instant coffee.

Instant coffee and cold cereal seemed like a horrible way to start her day, especially since La Dolce Vita was right across the street. After pulling her hair into a ponytail and dressing in jeans and a sweatshirt, Bridgette pocketed her keys and credit card.

After taking the stairs to the ground floor, she stepped onto Main Street. Last night's rain was long gone, leaving behind a sky of robin's-egg blue, without a cloud in sight. The breeze still held a chill, and Bridgette was thankful for her sweatshirt. Jogging across the empty street, she pushed open the door to the coffee shop.

It was early, not yet six thirty, and still more than ten patrons filled the small shop. Megan Parker, the owner, looked up. "Morning, Bridgette," she said. Megan was nearly ten years older than Bridgette, and mother to several teenagers. A pleasant-looking woman with dark hair, Megan continued, "I'm glad to see you're back in town."

"Thanks," she said. "How's your husband and the kids?"

"The kids keep us busy, but my husband's been sick lately. Lots of doctor appointments while trying to figure out what's wrong. I'll tell you what, your dad's a saint. Chuck has been home more than on the job site and your father keeps paying our health insurance. Without Fitz, we'd be on the hook for everything."

Another employee of Colton Construction with a mystery illness? It couldn't be a coincidence, could it? "Has your husband been tested for cancer?" Bridgette asked.

"Oh, yeah," said Megan. "Cancer. Thyroid. Liver failure. Heart disease. So far, nothing's been positive."

"You'll keep me posted?" Bridgette asked. It was

more than being polite—his diagnosis could very well shape her investigation.

"Enough about me. How are you? Will you be in town long?"

"Only until my job is done," Bridgette said. "Then I go where the state of Kansas sends me."

"Must be nice to be around your folks. Your brothers and sisters."

Now that Bridgette had a place to call her own, she was able to honestly say, "It is nice to be back in Braxville. Nobody in Wichita has coffee as good as yours."

"Nobody?"

"Nope."

"That's quite the compliment. What can I get for you, then?" Megan asked.

Bridgette was about to order and then Luke came to mind. Certainly she owed him more of an apology for how she'd acted—or was that, overreacted—last night than a grumbled *sorry*.

"I'll take my usual and—" she paused "—what does Luke Walker typically order? I've rented an apartment in his building and want to drop off a little thank-you. He's being super flexible with my schedule."

"I know just what to fix," said Megan. "It won't take me a minute."

Bridgette moved to the end of the counter. A discarded newspaper from Wichita sat on an empty table. Picking up the paper, Bridgette scanned the headlines.

A set of bells chimed as the coffee shop's door opened. Her middle filled with a fluttering and she looked up from the paper. Immediately Bridgette knew that she was hoping to see Luke. And just as quickly she wondered why.

It wasn't him.

The person who walked through the door stole Bridgette's breath all the same.

It was the woman who'd been stalking Luke, his ex-girlfriend. Julia.

"Here you go," said Megan, holding two paper bags—one with Bridgette's croissant and the other with Luke's breakfast sandwich. There was also a drink tray with two cups. "Tell Luke I said hello."

Julia let out a hiss of surprise. Balling her hands into fists, she turned and glared. Anger radiated off her in a wave of heat.

Bridgette's instincts rose to the surface—fight or flight. With the bags in one hand and the tray in the other, she walked across the coffee shop. The slap of her soles on the tile floor kept time with her racing heart.

She reached for the door, her fingers brushing the cold brass handle. Then she paused. Hadn't Bridgette been stuck in the past, pining for a relationship that she'd never have? Moreover, she knew what it meant to be young and in love, possibly for the first time. Maybe this chance encounter was a way to help Julia get over Luke.

But how?

The answer came immediately. Hadn't Bridgette said that a new relationship always helped ease some of the pain of the old one? Actually, she had said that Julia needed to find a new man. What if Luke's ex believed that he'd found a new woman? Would that be enough?

Sipping her coffee, Bridgette turned. "You're Julia, right?"

"Yes."

"I thought so. Luke mentioned you last night."

"Me?" she squeaked. "What'd he say?"

"Just that you dated briefly, and things didn't work out."

Bridgette expected the other woman to look crest-fallen—a necessary evil to get on with her life. She didn't. Her eyes flashed with an emotion so hard that Bridgette couldn't find a name.

"When did you speak to Luke?" Julia asked, her jaw clenched.

"Like I said, it was last night," Bridgette continued, knowing full well that she was alluding to time spent with Luke, which hadn't and wouldn't happen. She held up the twin bags of food. "I gotta go or breakfast will get cold." Bridgette stepped away.

"Hey," Julia called as Bridgette pushed the door open with her hip. "How well do you know Luke Walker?"

"In some ways, better than I know myself. We grew up together and were friends all the way through school. We dated toward the end of our senior year, but things unraveled when I went to college. I'm back for work." She shrugged. "We'll see how it goes."

Without another word, she opened the door and stepped into the bright morning. A line of cars passed, forcing Bridgette to wait at the curb. She glanced over her shoulder. There, at the coffee shop's window, stood Julia. The other woman splayed her palms against the glass. Her breath, collecting into a fog, obscured her face.

Despite the sun, Bridgette went cold.

With the traffic gone, she jogged across the street. At the door to the apartments, she worked the key into the lock. Every second seemed an eternity as Bridgette imagined the pain of a hand grabbing her from behind. The key slid home, turning the tumblers. She opened the door and stepped inside before kicking it shut with her heel.

For a moment, she stood in the silent foyer and listened to her racing heartbeat. Sweat dripped down her back and dotted her brow.

Without a doubt, Julia Jones was terrifying.

Moreover, Bridgette's chest was tight with worry. Had she taken a bad situation and made it worse?

Taking the staircase to the second floor, she paused briefly on the stoop before knocking on Luke's door.

Nothing.

She waited a minute and then a minute more.

Knocked. Waited.

Bridgette rapped her knuckles on the door for the third time. As she waited, she swore that she would knock no more. She didn't know Luke, at least not anymore. She didn't know his life or his schedule. He could exercise in the morning. Or already be at work. For all she knew, he actually had a girlfriend and never spent the night at his own place.

The bag in her hand became heavy. More than that,

she felt ridiculous holding a tray with two cups when she'd obviously be eating breakfast alone.

She pivoted and strode to her own door.

"Hey, was that you?" Luke stood at his opened door. Speaking around a yawn, he continued. "I heard some knocking."

"I've woken you up. I am so sorry."

Luke's hair was tousled with sleep. His cheeks and chin were covered with the shadow of a beard. But what was worse—or maybe better—Luke wore only a pair of sleep pants that hung low on his hips. His pecs were covered with golden hair, before narrowing to a strip in the middle that dove straight down into the waistband. His abs were tight. His shoulders were broad and the muscles in his arms were well defined. He had the sexy V thing happening at his hips.

"I'm usually up at dawn for a run, but last night I had a hard time sleeping and skipped the workout." Rubbing sleep from his eyes, Luke asked, "What's the matter? Did something break?"

At least he'd been too tired to notice that Bridgette had been staring at—ogling, really—his bare chest.

"I brought over breakfast."

Luke blinked several times. "Breakfast?"

"You know, the first meal of the day. I also have coffee." She paused. "Besides, I owe you for how I acted last night. Really, it wasn't my best moment."

"I can't remember the last time anyone brought me a meal. That's really sweet of you."

"It's also really early and I've woken you up. I can just leave this for whenever you're ready."

Luke pulled the door open wider and stepped aside. "Don't be silly. Come in and eat with me. It gets old eating alone all the time."

Luke was right—solo meals were the worst. Bridgette stepped into Luke's apartment. It was the mirror image of her own yet with a lived-in feel. Several dirty dishes sat in the sink. Clean dishes stood in a strainer. A pile of old newspapers sat next to a rubbish bin. A thick binder was open on the coffee table.

"Have a seat," he said, and gestured to the sofa. "Let me put on something less comfortable. Then I'll get plates and mugs."

Luke disappeared into what she knew to be the bedroom. Sitting on the sofa, she peered at the binder. It was open to a page that listed vendors for the Braxville Boo-fest. Braxville Boo-fest? There was also an itinerary. Costume parade at 9:00 a.m. Hayrides from 10:00 a.m. until 4:00 p.m. Pumpkin lighting at 7:30 p.m. along with cider and doughnuts. Family-friendly haunted house during the hayride hours in the Ruby Row Center. Then there were plans for a scarier version that began after the pumpkin lighting.

Luke returned with both breakfasts plated, along with silverware rolled into a paper napkin. He'd changed, now wearing a pair of jeans and a faded T-shirt from KSU. Even with his chest covered, Luke was still undeniably fit.

"Here you go," he said, setting Bridgette's croissant in front of her. As he sat, his arm brushed her thigh. A shiver of something akin to anticipation traveled up her leg, taking root in the pit of her belly.

"Thanks," she said, taking a sip of her coffee. Pointing at the binder with her pinky, Bridgette asked, "What's this? I grew up in Braxville and have never heard of the Boo-fest."

"It's a new festival sponsored by the downtown businesses. This is only our fourth year. Basically, one Saturday in October we have a Halloween-themed fair. The stores decorate for the season. Kids and families can have fun and make a few nice memories. It brings people to the downtown who hopefully do a little shopping."

"Sounds like a great idea."

"It's a lot of work," said Luke before taking a bite of a breakfast sandwich. He chewed and swallowed. "I used to just be in charge of the parade. Line up judges for the costume contest. Get local businesses to donate prizes. You know the drill."

Bridgette didn't, yet she nodded in agreement.

"But then—" Luke took another bite and chewed slowly "—our chairperson up and quit yesterday, leaving me in charge of the whole event."

"Yikes."

"And I couldn't say no, even though I really feel like this is out of my league. And what's worse, there's less than two weeks for me to get up to speed and make it all happen."

Memories of Julia standing on the street corner and in the rain came to mind. Was Luke such a nice guy that he'd never deny a request regardless of how difficult it was to fill? "Why can't you pass on the responsibility?" Bridgette asked.

"She has a medical emergency in the family."

"Oh. I guess you really can't turn her down, can you?"

Luke shook his head before sipping his coffee. "What I really need is someone to take over the parade. Doing two jobs while running the store is more work than even I can handle."

"I'm sure it'll be easy find someone willing to volunteer. Who wouldn't want to see all the adorable kids in costume? Oh, and you could do a pet costume parade, too."

"You could do it," said Luke.

"What? Me? No way. I'm busy. I have work."

"We all have work. But our job is to make Braxville a great community," he said. Nudging her with his shoulder, Luke winked and continued, "Besides, didn't you say you owe me?"

Certain he was teasing, Bridgette teased in return. "Owed. As in past tense. That's what your breakfast is for."

"Too bad," said Luke. "Your pet costume parade is a great idea."

Bridgette popped the last bite of croissant into her mouth before reaching for the binder. She scanned the duties for the parade chairperson. Organize a setup crew. Clean up. A big variety show was planned at the parade's conclusion in the mall. It looked like most of the plans had been made and volunteers already placed in time slots.

Maybe she could find an animal shelter to bring some pups to the parade. It would be a great way to help some dogs find their forever home. "I'm not saying that I'll chair the parade, Luke. But I can probably help out, at least a little."

"Really? I mean, thanks."

"Do you have one of these binders for the parade?"

"Me, put together a binder?" Luke snorted. "Not likely. I do have some papers with notes. How's this, we have a meeting tomorrow night at seven o'clock. It's at La Dolce Vita. Why don't you attend? You can get an idea of what's involved and then decide if you want to take on a leadership role."

Bridgette had come back to Braxville for work—not to get re-involved in life around town. Then again, even with all its imperfections, this place was her home. "Sure," she said, rising to her feet. "I'll check it out. Thanks."

She turned, reached for the door and pulled it open. Had less than a half hour passed since Bridgette had stood on the threshold, her heartbeat racing because of the encounter with Luke's ex-girlfriend.

Did the words exchanged with Julia warrant repeating?

She didn't think they did, especially if the other woman got the hint and left Luke alone.

"See you tomorrow night," she said. After giving a little wave, she stepped onto the landing.

"Hey, Bridgette."

She turned. Luke stood on the threshold.

"Yes?"

"You are full of surprises, you know. I'm glad that you came home even if you'll only be here for a little while."

Full of surprises. The phrase left her cold and light-headed. If Luke knew the secret that she'd kept all these years he might not think her so charming, and he definitely would not be happy to have her back in Braxville.

JULIA'S STOMACH ROILED and felt as if she might retch. Gripping the mail cart's handle, she trudged down the hall. Each step was a struggle, as if she were wading through mud. Her thoughts were like a handful of pebbles in a stream, a jumble that tumbled over one another again and again.

Had Luke started dating someone else?

Had he really forgotten Julia?

Had the woman, Bridgette, really replaced Julia in Luke's life and in his heart?

And most important, how could she get him back?

A stack of letters lay atop the pile. All of them were addressed to Mr. Colton. As were her orders, Julia was to leave all correspondence with Mr. Colton's assistant. Today, her chair was empty.

The door to the boss's office was open. Sitting at his desk, head bent over a sheet of paper, Mr. Colton examined the report. Julia moved closer, as if drawn by a magnet. Was this her chance to meet the great man and perhaps impress him by showing diligence to her job.

She knocked softly. Mr. Colton looked up.

Julia held the stack of mail. "These are for you," she said. "Your assistant isn't at her desk and I wasn't sure…"

Before she finished her sentence, Mr. Colton dropped

his eyes back to the report while holding out his hand. "I'll take them."

Stepping forward, she placed the mail in his outstretched palm. Her eye was drawn to a credenza at his back. The wooden top was filled with photos in expensive-looking frames of silver and gilt.

The largest one, set in the middle of the arrangement, was filled with smiling faces, all of them bearing a resemblance to each other and to Mr. Colton. Without question, it was a family photo. Right in the middle, smile wide and bright, with her arms wrapped around Mr. Colton's neck was Bridgette—the bitch.

Julia gasped.

Mr. Colton looked up from his desk. The overhead light reflected on the spot where his hair was thinning. "Can I help you with something else?"

Damn. She'd been caught staring. "That picture," said Julia. "The one with your wife and kids, I guess."

Mr. Colton spun around in his large leather chair. "This one?" he asked, picking up the frame before facing front.

"Yeah," she said. "I know that girl, the one in the middle."

"Bridgette? Did you go to school with her? Were you in her graduating class?"

If Bridgette and Luke were the same age, then they were both seven years older than Julia. She tried— not successfully, though—to take no offense that Mr. Colton thought she looked to be over thirty years old.

"School? No, I think she's friends with my friend."

Mr. Colton set the picture on the corner of his desk. "Really? Who?"

"Luke Walker."

"Luke Walker. He was a good kid. Almost as smart as Bridgette. Damn shame his dad got ill. I always thought that Luke should've gone to engineering school. He was good with math, that one."

He was a good kid. Even though his daughter, an obvious slut, was spending the night at his apartment?

"It looks like you've got a lot of mail to deliver and I won't keep you," said Mr. Colton.

Julia knew when she'd been dismissed. "Have a nice day," she said, backing out of the office.

"Uh-huh," he said, not bothering to look up.

At first Julia thought she hated Bridgette for stealing Luke. But she had been wrong—she loathed the other woman. Bridgette's life was everything that Julia's should be.

Walking away, her thoughts focused to a razor-sharp edge. What Julia needed was a way to get rid of Bridgette Colton. But how?

Chapter Six

Bridgette spent her morning at the office and with the local staff. Going on much of the information provided by Ernest, her father's previous foreman, the team brainstormed possible causes of the cancer. The waters of nearby Lake Kanopolis. A naturally occurring carcinogen in the soil. Asbestos in the old elementary school. To Bridgette, none of the theories carried the ring of truth.

If it were something as common as lake water, the soil or the school, the number of illnesses would be at the level of an epidemic and not merely a cluster. Besides, each person in the case was male and of a similar age. There had to be something more that connected the men to one another.

Still, each theory needed to be examined and tested. With the team gathered around the communal conference table, Bridgette ended the meeting by giving out assignments. "Adam, I want you and Carson to collect water and soil samples. Send them to the state lab and tell them we need the results stat."

"We're on it," said Adam.

With a nod, Bridgette continued, "Rachel, can you do some research on the old school? Are there other types of cancers that we're missing in the area, and if so, what are they?"

"What will you be up to, boss?" Carson asked.

"I'm going to look into the lives of each of the men on our list. My guess, there's something connecting them all. Something small. We just need to find that needle buried in the haystack."

After her coworkers left to do their respective jobs, Bridgette spent a few hours researching on the internet. There were eleven men in total, but she focused on three—Ernest O'Rourke, Bill Warner and Tom Cromwell.

Tom Cromwell had passed away long before the age of social media. Bill Warner had no presence on the internet, so there were no posts for her to stalk. Bridgette was able to access the archives for the Wichita paper, and there she found the obituary for each man. Bill Warner was divorced and survived by two children, who were both teenagers at the time of his death. She scribbled the names of the children on a piece of paper and made a note to look them up later. Tom Cromwell had been married when he passed away and had four children, ages ranging from five years old to preteens. Bridgette wasn't sure how much the kids, who now were all adults, could add to her investigation. But if Tom's widow was still alive, she certainly could.

A quick internet search gave Bridgette the widow's name and phone number. Since the office phone showed up on any caller ID as the Kansas State Department of Health, Bridgette used an old handset and placed the call.

The call was answered on the second ring. "Hello?" a female asked. Her voice was thin, and Bridgette guessed she was speaking to Cromwell's widow.

"My name is Bridgette Colton, with the Kansas State Department of Health," she began, official as always. "Is this Mrs. Cromwell?"

"It is."

"I'm calling in regard to your late husband, Tom. I'm in Braxville, looking into a cluster of cancer cases. The name of your former husband has come up in our investigation."

"Cancer? That was years ago."

"I know it was, ma'am, but the state of Kansas has some follow-up questions."

"It's been two decades and now you care?"

Bridgette had expected some resistance, but what was she supposed to say to that? "Mrs. Cromwell, I work out of Wichita, but I grew up right here in Braxville. Something has made several of our community members sick and I'm determined to find out what it was." Or is.

"What'd you say your name was?"

"Bridgette. Bridgette Colton." Small towns being what they are, she added, "I know your husband used to work for my father. I spoke with Ernest yesterday. He said that your late husband was one of his best friends."

"I suppose you could stop by," said Mrs. Cromwell, her reluctance beginning to wane.

"When?" asked Bridgette.

"I have an appointment at noon," the woman began.

Glancing over her shoulder, Bridgette looked at the wall clock. It was 9:45 a.m. "I can get to your house by quarter past ten," she said. "I swear to be gone by eleven thirty." In fact, the timing worked out perfectly for Bridgette. After all, she had promised to have lunch with her mother today.

"Well, I suppose that would be all right. Let me give you my address."

Despite the fact that Bridgette had used the state's database to find the woman, she waited patiently as the widow repeated the street name and house number. "I'll be by in a few minutes," said Bridgette, ending the call.

A cloudless Kansas sky stretched out before disappearing over the edges of an endless horizon. The Cromwell house was located on the edge of Braxville, where farmland and town meet. The home was a small square, with two windows on the second floor. The front door was in the middle of the ground level, along with a stoop, round and edged with brick.

As Bridgette pulled onto the gravel shoulder, she couldn't help but notice that the front of the house looked like a surprised face. As if the home itself was shocked by her arrival.

The door opened and a woman stood on the threshold. Until now, Bridgette had a mental image of an elderly woman with a home perm and a floral housecoat. Mrs. Cromwell was tall—nearly as tall as Bridgette—with jet-black hair. She wore a pair of jeans and a long-sleeved striped T-shirt. A golden cross hung from a chain around her neck.

"You must be Bridgette," she said, extending her palm to shake. "You look a good bit like your mother."

"I'll take that as a compliment, Mrs. Cromwell," said Bridgette, shaking the woman's hand.

"You should. Lilly is good people." Pivoting toward the door, she continued, "Come on in and call me Trish."

The front door led directly to a small living room. There was a floral sofa, coordinating recliner and a brick fireplace. A wooden coffee table sat in the middle of it all. A flat-screen TV hung above the empty hearth. Trish lowered herself onto one end of the sofa. Bridgette settled into the recliner.

A stack of papers and photo albums sat in the middle of the coffee table. Trish picked up the top item in the pile. It was a clipping from an old newspaper. She handed it to Bridgette. "That's my husband's obituary. He died almost eighteen years ago. Sometimes it seems like he's been gone a century. Other times," she said, and shrugged, "I forget that he won't be coming home."

Although Bridgette's job was to be investigate the cancer cases, not get involved with the subjects personally, her chest contracted as she listened to Trish speak. "I lost my husband, too," she said. "Car accident, two years ago. I can't count the number of times I've seen something that would make him laugh or heard something he'd find interesting. I'll pick up the phone to call. Then it hits me that he'll never answer, and it's like losing him all over again."

"I can't say those moments ever go away, but they don't happen as often." Trish reached for a photo album. Pressing the book to her chest, she stroked the cover. "Time never heals any wounds, but it does dull the pain."

"Thanks," said Bridgette. Her eyes stung and she blinked away the tears that were threatening to fall. "That means a lot to talk to someone who knows—really knows—what it's like."

"Look at us," said Trish. A single tear snaked down the side of her face. She wiped it away. "Spending the morning feeling sorry for ourselves. And you with a job to do. You said you wanted some information about my husband, so I dug all of this stuff out." She handed Bridgette the album. A date, twenty years prior, was written in faded marker on the cover. "Back then, I was into scrapbooking. I took pictures of everything, then glued them into these things with little stickers and such. Anyway, that book is from the year he got sick."

Bridgette flipped through the pages as Trish spoke. The first page was filled with pictures of a New Year's Eve party. She recognized Ernest's living room as not much had changed over the decades. In the middle of the page was a picture of Ernest, Tom and Bill. Arms were draped over one another's shoulders. The trio were glassy-eyed, and more than a dozen beer bottles sat on the table in front of them. A banner over the photo read: The Three Amigos.

But was there more? By summer, all of these men would be seriously sick. Was there a hint of the illness that was to come even as they rang in the New Year?

Bridgette flipped through a few more pages. Family

photos, mostly. Snowball fights. A Valentine's party in an elementary school classroom. There was also a picture of Tom at work, his hair and face covered with plaster dust. He stood outside of one of the old Colton warehouses that became the downtown mall, Ruby Row Center. Bridgette remembered that project. It was the first big venture for Colton Construction. It launched the business from a small family-run company into the behemoth her father now ran.

The next picture was taken at the park near City Hall. Tom stood in front of a tree with branches covered in fluorescent green buds. It was obvious that he was ill. His face and arms were thin. His pallor was gray. His eyes were surrounded by dark circles.

"When was the first time you noticed your husband being sick?" Bridgette asked.

"He'd gotten what we thought was a cold around March. Aching. Sore throat. A cough that wouldn't go away. He started missing work. Ernest tried to cover for Tom, but in the end your dad had to let him go."

"I'm sorry," said Bridgett.

"Don't be. A man can't work, he can't expect to get paid. Anyway, your dad's a good boss and Tom was lucky enough to be able to keep his health insurance. We went to the doctor, who figured out it was cancer right away. He got treatment in Wichita and the cancer went into remission. Then it came back a few years later. Well, I guess it was then that Tom's luck had run out."

"Your husband and his two best friends ended up

with a rare cancer at the same time. Did they have any theories as to what caused their illnesses?"

"They used to have a few jokes," said Trish. "Gallows humor, you'd call it."

"I know, Ernest told me. They thought that my dad was such a difficult boss that it gave them all cancer."

Trish gave a wry smile. "Ernest shouldn't have said that to you. It was bad of him to tease you about your dad."

"Don't worry," said Bridgette with a smile of her own. "I'm Fitz Colton's daughter. I understand that he's a hard man to please." She paused. "Back then, what did you think?"

"Honestly, I thought that they were so close—closer even than brothers—that one couldn't suffer without the others sharing the burden."

"That's very poignant," said Bridgette. Too bad it lacked a shred of scientific evidence. "Tell me about your husband's other jobs. Aside from Colton Construction when he got sick, where else did he work?"

Tom had a long list of jobs in manual labor. Most were in Kansas, but for a short while he had worked in Mississippi on an oil rig. The petroleum industry was notorious for using carcinogens in their processes, especially decades earlier, before awareness for worker safety had been raised.

While that might account for Tom developing cancer, it could hardly explain why anyone else had gotten sick. After spending an hour with Trish Cromwell, Bridgette had gotten a full history of the case. Still, she was no closer to solving the mystery of why so many in Braxville were stricken with cancer.

BRIDGETTE PULLED INTO the circular drive at her parents' home and parked the car. Sure, her mom and dad's constant arguing had spurred her to find her own place, but as she turned off the ignition she had to admit that it was nice to be home.

Bridgette was lost in thought. The reason for all the cancer cases was close, she could tell. But it was like looking for something she dropped in the grass on a foggy morning.

She opened the door without knocking and stepped inside. Even from the foyer, Bridgette could hear the raised voices of a man and woman in the midst of an argument. Was her father home? She hadn't seen his truck.

Setting her bag by the door, Bridgette walked toward the sound. They were coming from the kitchen.

"I just really wish you'd stop pressuring me about this, Shep," said her mother. "It's none of your concern."

Oh, so it was dad's half-brother, Shepherd, newly retired from the navy, with whom her mother was arguing. Then again, that brought up a whole new set of questions. What did Uncle Shep want her mother to do? And why was it none of his business?

She approached the kitchen and watched them from the doorway. Her mother had her back to the breakfast bar, her arms folded across her chest. Shep stood just feet away from Lilly. Hand lifted, he reached out to touch her mother. He hesitated, letting his palm linger above her shoulder.

"Hey, guys," said Bridgette a little brighter and louder than was necessary.

Her mother wiped her eyes quickly before turning. A smile lit up her face. "Oh, honey, you're home. I made us grilled chicken salads and, for dessert, apple tarts. I hope you're hungry."

"If I wasn't before," said Bridgette. "I would be now." She stepped into the kitchen and leaned into a hug from her uncle. "How's the guesthouse?" she asked.

"Nicer than a lot of other places I've lived."

"Shep just offered to move out and get an apartment in town so you could move back here," said Lilly as she arranged chicken and greens on two plates.

"You stay where you are," said Bridgette. Is that what had caused the quarrel? The fact that she'd moved from home when she would have stayed if the guesthouse were empty. Wanting to smooth any rough edges between her mother and uncle, she continued, "You're already settled. Besides, being in town and close to work makes my life easier."

"Thanks for understanding," said Shep. "I better get going, I told your dad I'd stop by the office."

He left the room. Lilly stared at the door even after Shep was gone. It left Bridgette searching for something to say. "Everything okay, Mom?" she asked after a moment.

"What?" Lilly asked. "Oh, of course. Everything's fine."

"You sure? You seem a little off."

"I've been a little tired lately. I might be coming down with a cold."

"Do you want to cancel the bonfire?"

"No, I'll feel worse if the whole family doesn't get together." Lilly patted the bar stool. "Have a seat. Can I get you tea? Coffee? A soda?"

"Just water," said Bridgette as she scooted onto the seat.

"Water it is," said Lilly, filling up two glasses with ice and filtered water from a dispenser in the fridge. "Here you go," she said, handing a glass to Bridgette.

As Bridgette took a sip, her mother slipped onto the bar stool to her left. Lifting a sheet of paper from the counter, Lilly said, "This is the quote I have from the caterer."

Bridgette scanned the list of food, drinks and desserts. Her mother certainly had ordered a nice meal for family and friends. Yet, Bridgette had inherited a good bit of her father's practicality and she choked a little as she looked at the total. "What if you changed the order to half ribs and half chicken, Mom? That way you give folks a variety and costs come down."

"I guess I could do that," said Lilly. "And maybe take away the green beans since I already have roasted squash and corn on the cob. Nobody expects too many vegetables at a barbecue, right?"

Scribbling numbers on the paper's margin, Bridgette added up the new total. "That's a number even Dad won't complain about," she said, setting the menu aside.

"Trust me," said Lilly with a wry laugh. "Your father can complain about anything."

"You know, Mom. I'm worried about you and Dad. You really don't seem to get along at all."

Lilly picked up her fork and pushed a piece of chicken across her plate. For a moment, Bridgette was left to wonder if her mother was going to say anything at all.

"I guess that's what happens to old married couples," she said at length. "It's funny, but for years I was the bookkeeper for Colton Construction. It was a struggle. I had all of you kids to look after. A house to keep and a husband who loved his work." She shook her head. "Those days, your dad and I would dream about having a big house and lots of money. Then it finally happened and look at us. We're closer to miserable now than when we had nothing." She dabbed at the corners of her eyes with a napkin and gave a wan smile. "I guess that's the definition of irony."

Reaching for her mother's hand, Bridgette said, "I'm sorry, Mom. Maybe you and Dad should take a vacation. You know, spend a little time together and reconnect."

"Maybe," said her mother in a way that made Bridgette think Lilly would do no such thing.

It seemed as if their conversation was at an end, and Bridgette hadn't even finished half of her salad. But her mother had mentioned something that piqued her interest personally and professionally.

She said, "I didn't know you used to help Dad with Colton Construction."

Lilly lifted one slender shoulder and let it drop. "It was cheaper for me to do the work than it was to pay someone else. In fact, I was basically the office manager. I sent out the invoices, paid outstanding debts and processed all the paychecks. I even did the taxes for the first few years."

"Do you have those old files?" Bridgette asked.

"Of course. You know how your father is about making sure we keep everything. Little good it would do. Technology is so much more advanced now. I don't know of any computer that can read a floppy disk nowadays."

Lilly's statement left Bridgette cold. Yesterday she'd asked her father for employee information. His answer was that he didn't have records from twenty years ago. Had her father lied? Or maybe he'd simply forgotten?

"Do you know where the disks are?"

"Sure do," she said. "Your father stored them in the crawl space of the guesthouse before Shep moved back."

"Can I have the disks?" Bridgette asked. "They might help me with something at work."

Lilly sat up straight. "Why would you want a bunch of old disks?"

Why? It was a reasonable question. First, she suspected that her father had lied about having access to old employee information. Which meant what? Bridgette didn't know, but she was determined to find out.

Chapter Seven

Thursday morning, Luke began before dawn as always with his regular run. There was no note from Julia taped to the door. Nor was she or her car anywhere to be seen. Did he dare to hope that the call to her mother had solved all of his problems?

And if that was true, why in the hell had Luke waited so long?

The rest of the day unfolded. The store was filled with customers from open to close. Despite the constant activity, more than once he glanced at the clock, willing the day to end. Time passed slowly, minutes becoming hours.

As the sun dipped below the horizon, turning the sky orange and pink, he flicked off the lights and locked all the doors.

Finally, it was 7:00 p.m.

Time for the Braxville Boo-fest committee meeting. Moreover, it was another chance to see Bridgette Colton.

Carrying the binder given to him by Stacey under one arm, he strode across the street. As he crossed,

Luke glanced up and down the road. He searched for Julia lurking in a doorway. Or her blue sedan parked at the curb and belching fumes.

She wasn't there.

As he pulled open the door to La Dolce Vita, all thoughts about his ex-girlfriend ended.

Standing at the counter was Bridgette Colton. The collar and cuffs of a white blouse were showing under a bright blue sweater. Her dark blond hair was pulled into a high ponytail and hung to the middle of her back. A pair of jeans hugged her hips and rear. She laughed, throwing back her head, and he got a glimpse of her throat.

For a moment, he had a clear vision of placing a kiss on Bridgette's neck.

Was it a memory from the summer they dated? Or was it a much more adult fantasy?

At the back of the room, several tables had been pushed together. Half a dozen people had already filled seats. Taking a to-go cup from the counter, Bridgette moved to the table and sat. A single chair remained at the head of the table.

Luke placed the binder on the table before sitting. He waited for a moment as the crowd got settled.

He began, "I'd like to thank everyone for coming. However, I have some bad news. Stacey isn't able to chair the Boo-fest anymore. Her husband's having some health issues and needs her attention. I've agreed to be the festival chairperson and want to introduce Bridgette Colton. She's considering taking over my old position and being in charge of the parade. We spoke this morning and she has great ideas."

All eyes turned to Bridgette.

She waved the tips of her fingers. "First, I want to say that the parade looks like a lot of fun for families. I'd like to add something to the day. In Wichita, I volunteer at a local animal shelter. As you may guess, it's hard to find forever homes for pets in need. So, something like the Boo-fest and the parade are perfect ways to introduce homeless dogs to families. If chair, I'd work with a local shelter to make sure we get exposure for the animals."

"Great idea," said Megan Parker. "We adopted our dog, Skippy, a few years ago and he's definitely part of our family."

"I agree with Megan," said Luke. "It is a great idea. In fact, I'm a little jealous, Bridgette. You've had only a few hours to think about the parade and have come up with a fabulous idea. I had a whole year and never once thought to include a charity." Everyone chuckled. "Moving on, let's start with committee reports. Gladys, do you have anything new for the bake-off?"

An hour later, Luke was certain that all the correct permits had been filed with the city. Moreover, everyone knew their roles and all necessary plans were in place. "Today is Thursday. The festival is next Saturday. That gives us a little more than a week between now and then. Trust me, we're all going to be busy," Luke continued. "But if we all chip in, we can make this a Braxville Boo-fest for the history books." There was one item that Stacey had yet to address. Luke hated to burden anyone further, yet it could make a difference for everyone in the downtown. "We need media coverage," he said. "I'm sure the local paper will cover the events, but that only comes out once a week. We need a connection to the Wichita market. Any suggestions?"

Luke looked around the table. Nobody met his gaze.

Bridgette lifted her hand. "I know a producer for one of the TV stations. She was my college roommate. I can't make any promises, but I can send her a message."

"That's great," said Luke. "Does this mean you're officially in charge of the parade?"

Bridgette already had her phone in her hand and was tapping on the screen. "I guess it does," she said as she sent the text. Her cell pinged immediately. "She says she's interested. I need to give her a press release. Do you have one?"

"No," said Megan. "We never tried to get any media coverage before."

"That's okay," said Bridgette. "I've done a few for work. Luke, if I can get some information from you, then I can put a release together."

The meeting was adjourned, but nobody left. Like always, Megan served coffee and cookies, giving everyone a chance to visit. Several people congratulated Luke on a job well-done. Yet, he wanted to talk to one person in particular—Bridgette.

The bake-off chairwoman, Gladys Soames, sat next to Bridgette at a table by the window. Carrying a plate of cookies, he approached as the elderly woman was saying, "Now, make sure to tell your mother about the bake-off. She makes the best apple tarts in the world and would win for sure."

Bridgette said, "When I see my mother next, I'll encourage her to enter the contest."

Gladys rose from her seat. "Thank you. You are certainly a dear."

Luke sat in the seat Gladys had vacated. He set down the plate and slid it toward Bridgette with the tip of his finger. She took a cookie and lifted it to her mouth. Before taking a bite, she said, "That went well. You're a natural leader."

He shrugged. "And you're a natural idea generator."

"I guess we make quite a team," said Bridgette with a smile.

"It's always been like that," he said.

Her smile faded and she looked out the window. Night had fallen, and the front window reflected the room—and Bridgette. An emotion filled her face, but in the glass he couldn't name what it was. Pain? Despair? Regret? Was she annoyed that he'd brought up their past?

All those years ago they'd been good together. Was that why he felt there was more to their relationship than a youthful folly.

She turned back to Luke. "When would you have time to work on a press release? I'm sure you have everything in that big binder of yours."

"I haven't looked through it all yet," he said. "I'm sure Stacey, that's the old chair, knows more than what's here, but I don't want to bother her, not with everything she's going through."

"What's going on?" Bridgette asked. She took a bite of cookie. A crumb clung to the corner of her mouth and she licked it away. How could she make eating a cookie look sexy?

"Stacey's husband has cancer," said Luke. "He had it a few years ago, but it seems as if it's come back."

"Cancer?" Bridgette's eyes went wide. "What kind?"

"I don't know what he has now, but a few years ago it was esophageal."

"Are you sure?"

"About Stacey's husband having had esophageal cancer? I'm positive."

Bridgette set her half-eaten cookie on a napkin and dusted her fingertips together. "What did Stacey's husband do for a living?"

"George is kind of a jack-of-all-trades. He does a little painting and home repairs. I think a lot of the older folks in town used him for maintenance—Gladys Soames, included."

Bridgette leaned forward and lowered her voice. "Do you know if Stacey's husband ever worked for Colton Construction?"

Answering her question with one of his own, he asked, "Did he work for your dad?"

"Yeah."

Luke knew that answer, as well. "He did, six or seven years ago, I think."

Bridgette stared, openmouthed, at Luke.

"Are you okay?" he asked.

No reply.

"Bridgette, are you feeling ill? What's the matter?"

Rising from her seat, she mumbled, "I have to go."

"What? Why? Is anything wrong?"

She shook her head but said nothing more. Without a backward glance, she left the coffee shop. Luke moved to the window and watched as she hustled across the street. She unlocked the door leading to the apartments, stepped inside and disappeared from sight.

CELL PHONE IN HAND, Bridgette took the stairs two at a time. She pulled up her contact list and placed a call before reaching the landing. Her heart hammered against her chest as the phone rang and rang and rang.

"This is Rachel. I can't take your call. Leave a message and I'll get back to you." *Beep*.

"Dammit," Bridgette cursed. She hung up and called again.

It was answered on the first ring.

"Bridgette, hi. Sorry I missed you. I was just washing up after dinner," said Rachel, the technical expert in her group.

"I have something for you and it's important."

"Sure. What can I do for you?"

Working the key into the lock with one hand, Bridgette held the phone with the other. She opened the door, stepped into her apartment and flipped on the light. There, in the middle of the coffee table, was the box provided by her mother. "I have some floppy disks that I need opened. Can you do that?"

There was a long pause. "Floppy disks?"

"Yeah. I have a theory about what might tie everyone in the cluster together, but it's all on disk."

"What kind?"

Bridgette read off the serial number.

"I have a friend who collects old computers. Let me talk to her and see if she has the right tech. If so, we'll be in business."

"And if not?"

"The disks can be opened. They just have to be sent to the state office. It'll take a while."

"What's a while? Days? Weeks?"

"Try months, like three or four."

"That's too long. See what your friend says and let me know."

Bridgette ended the call and dropped onto the sofa. She lifted a disk from the box and examined it from every angle. The little piece of plastic held the power to prove Bridgette's theory, and if her guess was right, then Colton Construction was at the center of the cancer cases.

For the first time in her life, she hoped that she was wrong.

JULIA STOOD IN a darkened doorway and watched. Her chest ached with longing and hatred. Had Luke Walker really replaced her with Bridgette Colton? What was it that Bridgette had that Julia didn't?

A fancy last name? A college degree? An important job?

Bridgette only had the luck of her birth. It's not

hard to be successful when every opportunity has been given to you.

What Julia had was grit. Life hadn't been kind to her and yet she persevered.

Luke had to see that. Right?

Only moments before, Julia had watched as the other woman left the coffee shop and raced across the street, going through the door that led to the apartment building where Luke lived. A moment later, a curious thing happened. The lights had come on in the apartment across the hall from where Luke lived, the one that had been vacant for months. The shades were drawn, so Julia didn't know if Bridgette Colton had turned on the lights, but she felt safe in her presumption.

There was something else interesting about Bridgette. As she ran across the street, her shoulders had been hunched. Her complexion had gone pale. And Julia could have sworn that she'd seen tears in the other woman's eyes.

It brought up an interesting question. With a life as blessed as that of Bridgette Colton, what could possibly cause her any grief? Had she gotten into an argument with Luke?

This morning, Julia had assumed that Bridgette had spent the night with Luke and was possibly living with him now. But the lights in his apartment were dark. Was she only a neighbor?

Had picking up his breakfast been a polite gesture made by a woman brought up with impeccable manners?

Besides, that morning Mr. Colton had mentioned

Bridgette being in Braxville temporarily for work. If her stay was short, why was she living downtown? Why not stay with her parents?

Julia had seen pictures on Google Earth. The Colton house was huge. It was the kind of place that Julia would kill to call home.

A minute later, Luke emerged from the coffee shop, as well. He carried a large binder and kept his head down while walking. There was a pull in her middle, like her soul was tethered to his, but Julia stepped back farther into the shadows.

He was the one who had called her mother and ruined everything.

What's worse? Julia knew that call had been placed at the behest of Bridgette Colton.

After looking both ways for traffic that never came downtown this late at night, Luke crossed the street. Breathless with anticipation, she watched and waited. A moment later, Luke's apartment erupted with lights. Julia laughed out loud.

He wasn't living with Bridgette, after all.

It meant that Julia still had a chance with Luke, so long as Bridgette wasn't a rival for Luke's affections.

That spoiled bitch needed to leave downtown Braxville not just for now, but for good. The sooner Julia could convince Bridgette to go back to her parents' house—more like mansion—the better it would be for everyone.

DROPPING THE BINDER onto the table, Luke flopped down on the sofa. As a small business owner, his work was never done, and that included making sure events like the Braxville Boo-fest were a success. He'd barely had time to look at more than a couple of pages, and if he was going to be the chairperson, then he was ultimately responsible for everything that happened.

More than that, his store needed attention. There were invoices to file, orders to place, shelves to stock.

Tonight, he lacked the motivation for them all.

And he knew the reason why.

It was Bridgette Colton. She'd been back in his life for less than forty-eight hours, and already she was under his skin. He itched with the need to see her, to speak to her, to touch her. More than once throughout the day she had come to mind. He read an article in an online paper and wondered about her opinion. A song on the radio brought back memories of the night they had spent at her family's cabin. The scent of coffee left him wondering if she'd make it a habit of stopping by his apartment every morning.

For the first time, his apartment felt too small. What was worse, Bridgette was too close. He grabbed his phone and walked back down the stairs to the street, placing a call as he went.

"Luke." The phone was answered after the fourth ring by his friend, Reese Carpenter. "What's up?"

"Got time for a beer?"

"With you? Absolutely. When and where?"

"How about now, at the pub near my place."

"Now? I thought you were like Cinderella and turned into a pumpkin after dark," said Reese. "You never go out because you have to be in the store at dawn."

"Are you going to bust my balls about working hard now?" Luke asked.

"You know I'd never give you a hard time for everything you do. You're my favorite workaholic."

"Maybe you should consider a career change to comedy," said Luke, returning the good-natured banter. He'd walked while speaking on the phone and was now at the pub. While pulling open the door, he said, "I'm here. I'll save you a seat."

The crowd for a Thursday night was light and only half of the tables were filled. Several TVs on the walls were tuned to a football game. He slid onto a bar stool and the bartender looked up. "What'll it be?"

Luke ordered a beer and an order of buffalo wings.

"Make that two," said Reese, taking a seat next to Luke.

"Thanks for meeting me, man," said Luke, offering his hand to shake.

"I figured this was either a celebration or a commiseration. Either way, I'm here. So, which is it?"

The bartender set two glasses with amber liquid at their elbows. Luke took a sip, letting the beer settle in his middle before answering. "I need some levelheaded advice. It's about a woman."

"The dark-haired girl from this summer?"

"No, I broke it off with her almost as quick as it began."

"Who then?"

What was Luke supposed to say about Bridgette? More than being Luke's friend, Reese was an officer with the Braxville police force and Jordana Colton's partner. Did he want to put his friend in a position where he had to keep a confidence. "I ran into an ex-girlfriend," he said.

"And how'd it go?"

"At first, she was really upset to see me. Then, this morning she stopped by with coffee to apologize. I saw her tonight and she was friendly until…" He paused. "Hell, I don't even know what happened. She said she had to go and ran out the door. It's like her mood changed—" he snapped his fingers "—like that."

"So she's mercurial?" Reese asked.

Luke took another swallow of beer. "You could say that."

"Was she that way when you dated her before?"

"No way, man. She was caring, smart, funny, beautiful, driven."

"And now?"

"She looks better now than she did when we dated, and that's saying a lot. She's still smart, driven and caring. It's just…" Luke stopped talking as the bartender set down plastic baskets filled with saucy and spicy wings. Plunging a wing into a side of ranch, he shook his head.

"It's just what?" Reese asked. "You don't know what you want?"

"Something like that," said Luke, taking a bite of his wing.

"And you haven't seen this woman for years, right?"

"A decade, at least."

"As far as I'm concerned," said Reese, "that makes the two of you strangers. You want my advice? Avoid your old love. No reason to make yourself crazy over someone who means nothing to you."

If Reese was right, that left Luke with only one thing to do. He had to avoid Bridgette Colton at all costs.

Chapter Eight

Friday morning, Bridgette arrived before any of her coworkers. She'd brought the dusty old box of disks with her and it sat in the middle of the communal conference table. Heart thundering, she stared at it with as much dread as she might a bomb.

If her suspicion was right and the cancer cases were linked to her father's company, the news would be explosive.

The office door opened and Rachel, red-faced and sweating, stood pinned between the door and the jamb. She held a large box.

Bridgette rushed to her coworker's side. "Looks like you can use a little help," she said, propping the door with her foot and taking the box. Immediately, the weight of the box pulled Bridgette forward. "Jeez, this is heavy. What did you bring? Bricks?"

"This is one of the old computers I told you about. I thought it would be easier to bring it to work and see if we can get into the disks here than wait for me to take them to my friend."

Bridgette set the box on the table with a *thunk*, her

arms and back thankful that she'd set down the burden. Lifting one of the flaps, she peered inside. There was a tangle of wires alongside cubes of almond-colored plastic. "What is that?"

Rachel set a coil of wires on the table. "This is a computer circa 2005."

"Technology certainly has come a long way," said Bridgette. "What can I do to help?"

"You can start by telling me why we need this beast in the first place."

Bridgette removed one of the disks and waved it as she spoke. Over the years, her mother had written on each of the labels with her neat handwriting. The ink, once black, had faded with the passage of time to gray. "I want to cross-reference the names of our cancer victims to the names on these."

Taking the disk, Rachel read, "'Employee Tax Information, Colton Construction.'" She paused. Lifting an eyebrow, she turned to Bridgette. "Colton Construction—as in your family's business? What does this have to do with the cancer cases in Braxville?"

Bridgette hesitated. At the moment, all she had was a theory—less than a theory, really. It was more like a hunch. What if she was wrong, something she hoped with all her heart? Was she really willing to jeopardize her family's reputation on a guess?

Then again Bridgette was here to do a job. Besides, how could she ask her coworkers to trust her if she wasn't willing to trust them?

"On Tuesday I noticed that my father's old foreman, Ernest O'Rourke, was on the list of cases. I spoke to him and he mentioned that two of his buddies, both of whom had worked for Colton Construction, also developed esophageal cancer." She approached the whiteboard with all the names of the cancer victims. Using a dry-erase marker, Bridgette circled Ernest's name, along with his two compatriots. She continued, "Both of these men have since passed away. One died of cancer and the other had a heart attack."

"That's peculiar," said Rachel.

"Then last night," said Bridgette. "I learned that George Navolsky also worked for Colton Construction."

"We have a dozen men on the list and four of them used to work for Colton Construction," said Rachel, summing up the issue. "Thirty percent is a lot."

"Exactly," said Bridgette. "And these disks have information about the employees over the years. Once we access the data, we can cross-reference it with our list."

"I hate to ask, but how'd you get the disks?"

"My mother used to be the office manager," said Bridgette. "She kept everything organized by year. I asked for the disks and she gave them to me."

"I don't want to be overly nosy, but did you tell her why you needed employee data?"

Bridgette bristled at Rachel's cautious tone. "I said it had something to do with work." Already she could feel her shoulders tightening with the need to defend her actions. "Since she didn't ask for any further explanation, I wasn't obliged to give her one. Besides, I spoke to my father about Ernest and his friends already. He's aware of the possible connection."

"It could also be said that since these people are your parents, you owed them complete transparency."

"Are you saying that I'm a bad daughter?"

"Of course not," said Rachel quickly. "But you know how these cases go. There can be lawsuits. Fines levied by the state."

Until now Bridgette had been concerned only about the impact the investigation would have on her relationship with her father. She could almost convince herself that if Colton Construction was somehow involved, he'd want to know. After all, there was nothing more important than the safety of his employees. Right?

True, it was naive not to worry about the optics of Bridgette Colton investigating Colton Construction. Who would believe that the inquiry had been fair and impartial?

It was then that Rachel voiced Bridgette's deepest fear. "Can you do it?" she asked. "Can you really investigate not just the company your father owns, but that defines your whole family, as well? Can you honestly be impartial?"

"I have a job," said Bridgette. "It's finding out what's causing all the cases of cancer in Braxville. I intend to conduct this study fully and professionally, following all leads." She gestured to the box of disks. "I brought those in, didn't I?"

Rachel shrugged. "I guess you did."

"If it will make you feel better," Bridgette continued, "I'll speak to both of my parents. I'll be seeing them later this evening."

"It's settled then," said Rachel, looking into the large

box again. "I'll get this computer set up and we'll see if we can access the disks."

Bridgette moved to the whiteboard and studied the names of each of the men on the list. They were more than victims of their disease. They were fathers, brothers, husbands and friends. Countless lives had been altered by their illnesses. In the silence of her heart, Bridgette vowed to make things right for each of the men. Then again, what would she do if it meant putting herself at odds with the entire Colton clan?

GETTING INFORMATION FROM the old disks had proved harder than Bridgette hoped. By the end of the day, her team was no closer to reviewing the data. Late on Friday afternoon, she called the team together for a meeting to wrap up their progress for the first week.

"For now," said Rachel. "I'll continue to work on opening the disks. I have several more things I can try before I really am out of options."

"How long will that take?" Carson asked.

Picking up a pen, Rachel tapped the tabletop. "Two days," she said. "Maybe three."

"So, you keep working on your end until Wednesday. If we haven't made progress then the disks will be sent to the state office," said Bridgette.

"Sounds like a plan," said Rachel.

"Carson and I have taken samples and sent them to the state labs. We'll have results by the end of next week," said Adam.

"But we did a little investigating as well and found something interesting," Carson added.

"Do tell," said Bridgette.

Adam opened a file folder and spread out photocopies of old news articles. "It seems that twenty-two years ago, there was a massive flood in downtown Braxville. One of those once-in-five-hundred-years kind of flood."

Twenty-two years ago, Bridgette would have been in elementary school—probably second grade. She lived outside of town. Yet, she had a vague memory of school being canceled for several days because of a flood. Was it the same one? It seemed as if it had been. "Go on," she urged.

"The entire town was affected, including an old petroleum station that was never reopened. The cleanup effort was massive. From reading these old articles, it seems like the townsfolk pitched in." He pointed to the whiteboard. "It's our theory that those on the list all helped."

"So, what's your conjecture?" Bridgette asked.

"Carcinogens were released in the floodwater," said Adam. "And then people were exposed during remediation."

"There's a problem with your theory," said Bridgette. "Lots of people helped rebuild downtown Braxville, correct?"

"There were truly hundreds involved," said Carson.

"Then, why aren't they sick, as well?"

"A combination of factors—gender, age, working after the flood—that came together to make a perfect storm," suggested Rachel.

"Or," said Carson, "maybe they all worked on removing debris from the same building. Could be something in the materials. Safety back when Braxville was founded isn't the same as it is today."

"Or maybe they didn't wear the proper gear for the type of cleanup they were doing," said Rachel.

Bridgette nodded. "I think you have found a trail worth following. Keep it up and let's see where it leads. We've only been on the case for a week, and a shortened one at that. A lot of progress has been made. Good job, everyone."

"Thanks, boss," said Adam.

"Then if there's nothing else to discuss," said Bridgette. "I want you all to have a great weekend and I'll see you on Monday."

Bridgette's coworkers packed up tote bags and briefcases before saying goodbye. Bridgette remained at her spot.

Carson stood at the door. "Aren't you going home, too?" he asked.

"I'm going to reread these articles you found. I grew up right here in Braxville but don't remember anything about a big flood."

"How old would you have been two decades ago?" he asked. "You were a kid. Unless your house was flooded, you might have no memory."

What Carson said was true. Then again... "I feel like there was a lot I overlooked as a kid and am trying to find all the missing pieces."

"I'm going," said Carson, gesturing to the hallway with his chin. "As long as you promise to follow your own orders."

"Oh, yeah? What are those?"

"To enjoy your weekend."

"I will," said Bridgette. "I promise."

"Why do I feel as if you're planning on working every day?"

"My parents have a bonfire and barbecue every year in the fall. Mom sets tables out on the yard, right near the lake. Then we have too much food and too many drinks. Tonight's the night, so I can't stay too long at work even if I wanted."

"All right then," said Carson. "See you Monday."

Then it was Bridgette alone. She read all of the news coverage about the flood and the effort to rebuild and revitalize Braxville. To her, it seemed to be precursor to the Keep Braxville Beautiful initiative. Her father was mentioned in more than one of the articles. And in the quiet office—in the silence of her heart—Bridgette was more than a little relieved to have a lead that wasn't connected to Colton Construction.

Her phone pinged with an incoming text from Yvette. Are you almost here?

Bridgette glanced at the time. It was 6:30 p.m.

Damn. She was running late.

Tapping out a reply, she rose from her seat. On my way.

After rushing from her office, she made her way down Main Street. As she walked, Bridgette couldn't help but imagine what downtown Braxville must have looked like during the flood. With water chest high, every building would have been submerged. She could well imagine the toxins that ended up in the waters.

Was the flood to blame? Were the men who got sick sadly victims of being good citizens? Was it really what her father had said from the beginning—just bad luck?

The sun had dipped below the horizon, leaving the downtown in shadows. A breeze blew down the sidewalk, carrying a chill and the scent of rain. The door to her apartment was just ahead, but as she walked closer, Bridgette decided not to stop. She was late enough already and didn't have time to waste with changing out of her work attire.

Her car was directly in front of the hardware store. The convenient parking spot was a perk of renting the apartment from Luke. She cast a glance at the store as she passed. The lights were off, but that didn't stop her from searching the dim interior.

He wasn't there.

It was then that she caught sight of something in her periphery. The handle of a broken kitchen knife lay in the gutter. She knew what it meant before seeing anything further. Her tire had been slashed.

Bridgette rounded her car, her anger a hot flame that burst into an inferno. It wasn't just a single tire that had been cut. All four of them were completely flat. Replacing one flat tire with a spare was an inconvenience. Finding replacements for all four wheels, especially after six o'clock on a Friday night was damn near to impossible.

LIKE HE DID every Friday, Luke closed the store at five thirty. It didn't mean his work was done, or even close.

Preparing for the busy weekend, he always spent the evening stocking the shelves.

"One hour in," he said, glancing at the clock on the stockroom wall. "I'm almost halfway done."

Sure, there was nobody to hear him speak.

And true, stocking shelves was a lame way to begin his weekend, especially since he was thirty-one years old and single.

Grabbing a box of washers from the shelf, Luke walked back to the store. His eye was drawn to the window and the street beyond. Even with her back to him, he recognized Bridgette Colton. Her dark blond hair. Her long legs and shapely rear. He couldn't look away even if he wanted. Then again, there was more to see than her nicely shaped female form. All four tires of her car were flat—an unlikely accident.

For Luke, it was impossible to ignore someone in need. Setting the box on the counter, he opened the door and stepped onto the sidewalk. "Need some help, Bridgette?" he asked.

"All of my tires have been slashed," she said, gesturing to her car. "I guess some kids thinking they're being funny."

"I can fix one tire," said Luke with a shake of his head. "But not all four. You'll have to get it towed in the morning. The garage should get it back on the road in a few hours."

"Tomorrow? A few hours?" Leaning on her car, she sighed heavily.

Luke told himself that he didn't care. He'd sworn not to get involved with the complicated Bridgette Colton.

He knew all of that to be true, so why then did he ask. "Did you need to get somewhere? I can drop you off, if you'd like."

Bridgette waved away his offer to help. "It's at my parents' house. I can't ask you to take me. You'd waste an hour with the round trip. I can't ask you to ruin your Friday night on my account."

"Would it matter at all if I said you aren't ruining anything? I didn't have any plans, so this will at least get me out of the apartment."

"You're kidding?" She turned to face him. "A good-looking guy like you without a date on Friday night? I find that incredibly suspicious, Luke Walker."

Good-looking guy? Was she flirting with him? To be honest, he wouldn't mind if she was so long as he remembered that her moods were as changeable as the Kansas weather. "Honestly," he said with a laugh. "I haven't had a date in months."

"Months? What do you do to keep yourself busy?" Bridgette held up her hands. "Forget I asked. My sisters, especially Jordana, are always pushing me to date more, get out more, get over…well, the past more. I understand that she cares, but at times it can be a touch intrusive."

"Is that sort of like all the well-meaning customers who want to know if I'm dating anyone. Or when I plan to get married. Or if I want to get married at all."

"Ugh." Bridgette made a sour face. "You, too?"

"Still," he said, "I can give you a ride to your parents' house. It's not a problem."

"Sure," she said. "So long as you do me one favor."

"Anything," he said.

"Stay at the bonfire. There will be lots of food. Barbecued ribs and chicken. My parents will be happy to see you. All my siblings will be there. You can catch up with Brooks and Neil."

"Really," said Luke. "I shouldn't." He hooked his thumb toward the hardware store. "I've got lots to keep me busy."

"I mean, sure. I get it. You have responsibilities. But, really, I won't make you drive me all the way to my folks if you aren't staying. Maybe someone else is running late and can give me a ride. I'll send a text or something."

Had Luke just turned down an invitation to go to the bonfire? Hadn't he just been feeling sorry for himself and his lack of a social life? Had he said no just to avoid spending time with Bridgette, someone he wanted to be around a lot more?

Then there was her mention of the past. Of course, he'd heard how her husband died in a car accident. Even as kids, Bridgette had never been one to share her feelings. Perhaps the fact that she was friendly or not had more to do with being a young widow than anything else.

"On second thought," said Luke. "If the offer for the party still stands, I'd love to stay."

Phone in hand, Bridgette was typing out a message. "Are you sure? I mean, I'd love for you to come and would really appreciate the ride."

"Give me one minute to lock up the store and we can get going."

"Speaking of the store." Bridgette followed Luke to the front door. "Do you have any security cameras that might have caught whoever slashed my tires? Something I could turn over to the police?"

"Braxville is still a pretty safe community, so I've never needed the extra security of cameras," he said. Then again, he didn't think that local kids were involved. In fact, Luke was almost positive that he knew what happened to Bridgette's car.

The question was why would she be a target?

SITTING IN THE front seat of her car, Julia watched the scene unfold. As Luke held the door to his pickup truck open for Bridgette and she slipped into the passenger seat, Julia's chin began to quiver. It was unbelievable that her plan had utterly failed.

Luke rounded to the driver's side. He started the engine and the truck pulled away from the curb. Slamming her hand on the steering wheel, Julia said, "No. No. No."

Bridgette was supposed to be upset by the damage done to her car.

Luke wasn't supposed to care.

And they sure as hell weren't supposed to leave together.

Julia slumped lower in her seat as they drove past the corner where she'd parked. Turning her gaze to the side-view mirror, she watched until their taillights were little more than angry red eyes piercing the gathering darkness.

Starting the ignition, she hesitated only a moment

before pulling onto the street and rounding the corner. Luke's truck was more than a quarter of a mile ahead of Julia's car, but he was easy to follow.

They left Braxville, passing farmland and open fields. He turned toward the newly developed area where the houses were newer, larger, with long and winding driveways in front and pools in the back.

Even without a map, she knew where they were going. To Bridgette Colton's house.

As she drove, Julia's phone began to ring. A bracket held the cell in an air vent. Her mother's image and number appeared on the screen. Dammit.

She swiped the call open. "What do you need, Mother?"

"When are you coming home?" her mother asked, her voice all but drowned out by the road noise and the engine's whine.

"I'm going to a friend's house," Julia said. "One of the girls from work, Bridgette, invited me over for dinner."

"Are you sure?"

Julia ground her teeth together. True, she was telling her mother a lie, but what cause did her mom have to question where she was going or what she was doing? "I'm positive," she said, her teeth still gritted.

"Where does she live?"

Julia repeated the Coltons' address for her mother. She'd memorized it from all the times she looked at the house on the internet.

"All right," said her mom. "Well, I hope you have a nice time."

"I will," she said, as Luke pulled into the driveway of the Coltons' large and modern house.

The Colton home was in a private community, one that Julia couldn't enter. Eyes trained on the road, she passed the large gates and guard shack. She turned onto a frontage road and found a spot behind a large tree that gave her a perfect view of the Colton house.

She'd stowed a set of binoculars that had belonged to her father in the glove box. After removing them, Julia looked through the ocular lens, and the home came into view. With lights illuminating on the brick-and-wood facade, the home was more breathtaking in person than it had been in the pictures on the internet.

Holding her breath, Julia knew better than to hope. Could it be that Luke was only bringing Bridgett home? Was he simply a ride, a glorified taxi?

At almost the same instant, both doors opened. They jumped from the truck and Bridgette pointed to the side of the house. In the distance, sparks from a bonfire rose into the night.

Luke and Bridgette walked side by side. From her vantage point in the car, Julia was able to observe them, seeing things that she doubted they even saw. Luke stole glimpses of Bridgette, and she of him. She noted even more than their sly observations. Both Bridgette and Luke regarded each other with affection, attraction...love.

Julia refused to lose Luke.

Still, it brought up interesting and important questions. How far was Julia willing to go to keep Luke? What was she willing to do?

Chapter Nine

Bridgette led Luke to the backyard. Side by side, they were so close that their hands brushed as they walked. His skin was warm. A tingling began in her fingers and traveled all the way up her arm, until her heart began to race. Folding her arms across her chest, she vowed to forget all about the sensation.

The scent of woodsmoke, along with the sounds of voices and laughter, filled the evening air. Her family was gathered at the back of the house. A long table with a white tablecloth was filled with food. Closer to the water's edge were several round tables, already filled with family, friends and neighbors. Candles of different heights and colors flickered on every surface. At the edge of the lawn was a community lake. The bonfire burned near the water, sending sparks into the sky, where they mingled with the stars before burning out.

Her mother, dressed in slim jeans, a turtleneck sweater and barn jacket, looked up as Bridgette approached. "There you are, honey," she said. "I was starting to get concerned."

Leaning in to kiss her mother's cheek, she said, "I

had car trouble." Sure, her excuse wasn't the whole truth, but she didn't want her mother to worry or insist that Bridgette move back into the house. "You remember Luke Walker? He gave me a ride."

Luke stepped forward with his palm outstretched. "Pleasure to see you again, Mrs. Colton."

"You can call me Lilly," she said, pulling Luke into an embrace. "And here, we hug."

"You can count me out on that one." Bridgette didn't need to turn around. It was one of her triplet brothers, Brooks. Brooks and Luke had played baseball together in high school. "But it is good to see you, Luke."

"Good to see you, too," said Luke, as the two men shook hands and exchanged slaps on the back.

Brooks gave Bridgette a kiss on the cheek. "Good to see you, sis."

"You, too. You look good. How's work?"

"I'm still trying to figure out how two bodies ended up buried in the wall in a building in downtown Braxville."

"Aren't the police involved?" Bridgette asked.

"They are, but I've been hired to figure out what happened. How about you?" he asked. "What brings you to Braxville?"

"Work," she said, giving away nothing. Sure, she was being cagey. And true, Brooks might have heard rumors about the cancer cases and connected her to the investigation. All the same, Bridgette lived by a simple rule to never mix work and family.

"Obviously, it's work. You're also avoiding my

question," Brooks continued with a smile. "Or is it a big secret?"

Sure, her brother was teasing. All the same, he was closer to the truth than anyone would have ever guessed.

Bridgette was saved from answering any more questions when the other triplet, Neil, along with the eldest Colton sibling, Tyler, called out, "Walker? Is that you?" He ambled over from the bonfire to greet Luke.

Her older sister, Jordana, approached. She wore a red sweater and jeans. Her sister's casual look left Bridgette wishing that she had taken time to change out of her slacks, blouse and blazer. Next to Jordana was a man, with dark hair and dark eyes.

Since she'd never met the man, she guessed that the guy was Jordana's new love, Clint.

"Looks to me like Luke's popular," Jordana said, hitching her chin toward the knot of men, all now with beers in hand, talking and laughing. "Our brothers wouldn't be more excited if you'd brought a puppy to the party."

"Luke's a good guy, that's for sure. Without him, I wouldn't have made it here at all."

"Bridgette, I want to introduce you to Clint," said Jordana. "This my sister Bridgette."

"It's great to meet you," Bridgette said. "You've made my sister very happy."

"Your sister is the one who's made me happy. More than that, your family is one of the nicest I've met. And Braxville is a special little town."

The mention of Braxville brought Bridgette's

thoughts around to her car and the flat tires. "Jordana, you're a cop."

Her sister laughed. "Last time I checked, at least."

"Have you heard anything about kids slashing tires downtown?"

"Not a thing," Jordana said with the shake of her head. "Is that what's wrong with your car? Someone cut your tire?"

"Try tires. All four of them were completely flat."

"We haven't gotten any complaints, but I'll ask around and let you know if I hear anything." Tilting her head toward the house, Jordana said, "You want to come with me and help Mom inside? It looks like Brooks's newest girlfriend is inside, too."

"Brooks brought his girlfriend?" Bridgette asked, happy that her brother had finally found love. "I have to meet her." As they walked toward the house, their father's business partner, Uncle Dex, arrived with his wife, Mary.

"Bridgette, Jordana. Good to see you both. Where are you off to?"

"Helping Mom," said Jordana.

At the same moment, Bridgette said, "Going to meet Brooks's new lady friend."

Dex lifted his eyebrows. "About time Brooks found someone special. What'd you say her name was?"

Jordana answered the question. "Gwen," she said. "Gwen Harrison."

Dex went pale.

His wife gripped his arm. "Are you okay, Markus? You look like someone just walked on your grave."

"Just a little light-headed, that's all. Maybe I should grab a bite to eat. I'm sure that'll help me feel better."

Bridgette watched Dex approach the group of men and accept an offered beer. He most certainly didn't look piqued anymore. Was it her imagination or had Dex reacted badly to the mention of Brooks's new girlfriend?

Then again, she had more pressing concerns than anyone's opinion of her brother's latest love interest. Like, what had actually happened to her car?

Was there really a connection between the cancer cases and Colton Construction?

And, finally, how could she tell her parents—her father, especially—that their business might play a prominent role in her investigation?

After a few paces, Jordana stopped and turned to Bridgette. "Are you coming?" she asked. "Or what?"

"On my way," she said, jogging to catch up to her sister. To Bridgette, it seemed like everyone in Braxville had a secret. Walking into the bright and warm kitchen, she wondered how far people would go to keep those secrets hidden?

IN ALL HONESTY, Luke enjoyed spending time with the Colton clan. It was a large and loud family, and completely different from what he had grown up with—just his parents and himself.

"Remember that time," said Ty. "I think you guys were all seniors in high school and it was the quarterfinal game for state baseball championship."

Luke groaned. "Don't remind me, please."

They were all laughing at the memory. Ty continued, "You two were in the outfield." He slapped both Luke and Brooks on the back. "The batter hit the ball. It was headed for the fence. You both were looking at the ball—not each other. Then, smack, you ran into each other, knocking yourselves over."

Brooks and Neil roared with laughter at Ty's retelling of the tale. Luke couldn't help himself. With a shake of his head, he joined in the laughter.

"There you two were, lying on the field. For all we knew, you'd knocked each other out cold. Then Luke lifts his hand, straight in the air. Plop. The ball lands in his glove. The batter is out. The inning was over."

"Too bad we were down by four runs and never had a chance to make them up," said Luke.

As kids, Luke was always friends with the Colton boys. As men, they were people to be admired and respected. Why then, did he keep glancing over his shoulder, looking for Bridgette? More than that, where had she gone?

"To this day, that play is the best—and worst—I have ever seen in my life," Ty concluded, wiping his eyes with the back of his hand.

"Hey," said Neil. "I heard a rumor that you're now in charge of the Braxville Boo-fest, Luke. How's that going?"

"Thankfully, the former chair had a good bit of planning done. Since it's next weekend, I'll have a busy few days, that's for sure. Still, if everyone pitches in it'll be a success."

"I'm glad to see that the downtown businesses are coming together," said Ty. "It creates a sense of community."

"That's what we're all hoping," said Luke, before finishing the last swallow of his beer.

"You need another drink?" Neil asked. "I'll get you one. The cooler's empty so I'll have to grab you one from inside."

Luke's gaze traveled to the house. Through a kitchen window, he spied Bridgette. She was smiling and shaking her head. She looked over her shoulder, said something and laughed. What Luke remembered best about the quarterfinal baseball game was that his single well-timed catch had given him enough confidence to ask Bridgette to prom.

She'd been at the game. All the Coltons had come to watch Brooks. Walking through the parking lot, Bridgette had lagged behind the rest of her family. Luke had left his parents and jogged to her side.

"Bridgette. Wait up," he had said.

Even now he recalled how his heart had thundered against his chest. It was the same feeling he had every time he saw her—anticipation, excitement, along with the promise of something better.

"Sorry about the game," she said. "You played really well."

His mouth went dry. His palms were damp. "So, now that baseball season is over, I guess we have to move on to what's next."

"Like finals. Graduation. College."

"I was thinking about prom."

She had shrugged and looked over her shoulder. Facing him again, she said, "I'm not going."

Luke's heart dropped to his shoes. "Why not?"

"First, nobody has asked."

Before losing his nerve, he said, "Want to go with me? I mean, I can take you. I mean, I'd love it if you wanted to go with me, too."

Crossing her arms over her chest, Bridgette had planted her feet on the ground. "Did my brother put you up to this?"

"Who? Brooks? No, never."

Eyes narrowed, she asked, "Why are you asking me?"

Luke had been deaf to every sound other than the pulse that roared in his ears. "Because I like you. You're cool."

She'd smiled and Luke no longer cared about the baseball game. Making Bridgette happy—that's what mattered. She dragged her toe through the gravel and nodded.

"Is that a yes?" he asked.

"Yeah," she had said. "I guess it is."

"Hey, Luke," Neil asked again, bringing him back to the present. "You need another beer?"

Bridgette still stood beside the window. He felt a pull like a magnet to steel, but a thousand times stronger. "I'll go grab them. Four?"

All the Colton brothers nodded, and Luke walked across the darkened lawn toward the house. He opened the door just as Lilly Colton arrived with a tray of steaming and saucy ribs. He held the door as she passed. "Thank you, Luke."

Yet, Lilly was just the first in a long parade of those carrying food. Jordana had grilled chicken, Yvette, a large salad, and an auburn-haired woman—who he guessed was Brooks's new girlfriend—held a large tray of corn.

As the women walked through the gathering darkness, Lilly looked over her shoulder. "Dinner's being served, Luke. See if you can't get Bridgette out of the house so we can eat."

"I'll do my best," said Luke before slipping inside. The door to the patio led to a large dining room, complete with a brass-and-crystal chandelier. Through a narrow archway was the adjoining kitchen.

Just like he'd seen from outside, Bridgette stood at the sink. She looked up as he entered. Her arms were in soapy water up to her elbows. "The caterer didn't send flatware for serving, so I'm washing some of Mom's."

"Do you need help? I'm pretty handy with soap and a sponge." Good Lord, had he really just said that? It was undoubtedly the cheesiest line known to man.

Bridgette tilted her head toward a dripping pile of silverware lying on a towel. "You can dry those off," she said.

He reached for another dish towel at the same moment that Bridgette yelped and drew her arm from the water. She cradled it to her chest.

"What happened?" he asked. He reached for her injured hand and wrapped it in the towel, squeezing enough to apply pressure.

"I nicked myself on the tines of a fork, I think," she said.

Luke removed the towel and wiped away the blood. A small gash on the side of her pinky finger wept blood. Bridgette's breath washed over his shoulder. The heat from her body warmed his skin. To see her wounded filled him with a desire to make her better and always keep her safe.

He ignored it all, and said, "Looks like you did get cut. Do you have any antibiotic ointment and a bandage?"

She pointed to a cabinet with her free hand. "In there."

A first-aid kit sat on the second shelf. As he rummaged through the contents, Luke tried not to think about how much he liked holding Bridgette's hand. Or how having her close brought back memories of a time when he was younger and anything was possible.

With bandage and ointment in hand, he turned back to Bridgette. "Got it," he said.

"Thanks." Bridgette took a moment to wash and dry her injury. Then she reached for the tube of ointment and applied a dab. After opening the bandage, Bridgette tried to center the adhesive tabs on the side of her hand. "Do you mind?" she asked. "Getting this bandage on is awkward."

"Not at all," said Luke, a little too fast to be anything other than eager to touch her again. "I'm happy to help if you need it."

"Thanks," she said.

Luke smoothed the bandage over the cut. "There,"

he said. "Good as new." Yet, her hand remained in his. She didn't pull away. Luke dared to look at Bridgette. She was watching him. Their gazes met and held. He moved closer to her, so close that he could smell the lightly floral scent of her shampoo.

She inched forward, closing the distance between them. He slipped his hand to the small of her back and pulled Bridgette closer still.

Luke bent to her. His lips hovered above Bridgette's. Their breath mingled, becoming one.

The door opened with a bang. "Are you two in here?" Neil called out. "Mom needs the serving stuff and we all want another beer."

Bridgette slipped out of Luke's arms at the same moment her brother entered the kitchen.

Neil stopped short. Drawing his brows together, he asked, "What's going on here?"

Sure, Bridgette was a grown woman. It was also true that Luke had dated her when they were in high school. It was also a fact that nobody—Neil included—wanted to see their sister kissed by any dude.

"Um…" said Luke.

"Who got hurt?" Neil asked, gesturing to the first-aid kit and bloodied towel.

"I cut my finger," said Bridgette, holding up her injury as proof. "Dry off the flatware and I'll finish up. Luke, beer's in the fridge, help yourself."

Had she really let the moment slip away in an instant? Was Bridgette's heart racing like Luke's? Or had she not been moved by the moment at all?

BRIDGETTE STOOD ALONE in her parents' kitchen. From the window, she had a clear view of the entire lawn that sloped down to the lake.

Everyone had gathered around the table, bathed in the glow of a dozen candles. Her eye was drawn to Luke, and her lips began to tingle with the kiss that never happened. In the quiet kitchen, Bridgette admitted, if only to herself, that she was attracted to Luke.

It was more than his blue eyes, or strong arms, or broad shoulders, or tight ass, that drew her in. It was him. His smile. His willingness to lend a hand, no matter the personal inconvenience. Like the old saying went, they didn't make them like Luke Walker anymore.

Then again, could she really give her heart away again?

Hadn't Bridgette learned her lesson? Everyone she ever truly loved would one day die.

The back door opened and closed. "Bridgette. Are you still in here?" called Jordana.

"In the kitchen."

"What's keeping you?" Jordana asked. "You know Mom won't let anyone eat until we're all together, and no offense, but I'm starving."

"I didn't mean to keep people waiting. Let's go."

Jordana said, "Wait a second. You look spooked. What's the matter? Is it because your car was vandalized?"

"I'm fine," said Bridgette. "But let's go. I really don't want people hungry on my account."

Without a word, they walked out of the house and across the patio.

"Why are you so jumpy tonight?" Jordana asked.

"Why are you so nosy?"

"I'm your big sister and a cop. It's kind of my job."

Bridgette gave a quiet laugh. "Coming back home has made me realize how many secrets we try to bury in the past."

"Like how you feel about Luke Walker?"

"Jeez, that's pretty blunt."

"Like I said, I'm your big sister and a cop. Being blunt comes with the territory, too."

"For your information, I don't feel any way about Luke."

"You used to."

"Yes, as in the past. Besides, I'm still not sure how I feel about Henry."

"You loved your husband." Jordana placed her hand on Bridgette's shoulder and pulled her to a stop. "But he really is in the past. Luke Walker is right here, and I can see how he looks at you. How you look at him."

Despite herself, Bridgette scanned the group gathered around the bonfire. Luke was talking to her father and brother, Ty. Looking up, his gaze met hers. He lifted his beer in a salute. She waved back.

"See?"

"No," said Bridgette, shrugging off her sister's touch. "I don't see anything."

She stalked away, thankful to leave the conversation behind. Especially since Jordana had been right. Luke had awakened emotions in Bridgette she thought had died with her husband.

Chapter Ten

Night draped its velvety cloak over the sky. The meal had been served and enjoyed. After the table was cleared, dessert was brought out—an obvious choice of a s'mores bar. Luke watched Bridgette and Yvette catch their marshmallows on fire and then giggle, much like schoolgirls.

"Hey, Luke," said Brooks. "I'd like to introduce you to my girlfriend, Gwen Harrison."

Gwen, a lithe redhead with a warm smile, held out her hand to shake. "It's a pleasure to meet you."

Dex, cocktail in hand, stood nearby and snorted.

Brooks rounded on the older man. "What in the hell is your problem?"

"You know you can do better, right?" Dex asked.

"What'd you say?" Narrowing his eyes, Brooks stepped forward.

Holding up a hand, Dex slurped his drink. "My boy, I've been around a long time and I know a tart when I see one."

"Tart?" Brooks lunged forward.

Luke didn't think; he acted. Stepping between the

two men, he placed his palms on Brooks's chest. "Calm down, man."

Brooks tried to brush his hand aside. "You heard what Dex said to Gwen. How am I supposed to be calm?"

The chatter from the other partygoers fell away, leaving the night completely silent except for the crackling bonfire.

"It's late," said Luke. "Everyone is tired. Dex has been drinking. But you're right, he was out of line."

Brooks tried to step forward again. "He is out of line and someone needs to put him back."

Luke, his hand still on Brooks's chest, shoved him back a little. "How is getting into a fight with your dad's business partner going to make things better? Is Gwen going to like you more? What about your mom? Or your sisters? Do they need to see you get violent?"

Brooks, a bowstring pulled tight, let the tension lessen. "I guess not."

"Then come on," said Luke. "Go roast a marshmallow. Everyone will feel better with something sweet."

Dex, seemingly oblivious to the problem he'd caused, walked away.

Brooks nodded and turned to Gwen. "You okay?"

"I'm shocked," she said. "Offended. I've never met Markus Dexter before, so I don't know why he has a problem with me."

"Dex is the problem," said Brooks.

Luke took that as his cue to give the new couple a moment alone. He walked away from the bonfire and into the darkness.

"Luke, wait." He didn't have to turn around to know who'd spoken. It was Bridgette. Slowing his gait, he waited as she jogged to his side. "Where are you going?"

"I guess I just needed a minute alone."

"Everyone can be overwhelming, that's for sure," Bridgette said. "It's part of the reason I wanted to live in town. I need quiet, and sometimes it's impossible to think around here."

She paused. He said nothing. His gaze on the ground, Luke gave a noncommittal nod.

After a moment, she continued, "I just wanted to make sure you're okay and thank you for stepping in. You did a great job defusing a situation that could've gotten real ugly real fast."

He dug the toe of his shoe through the grass. "You're welcome," he said.

She stood at his side a moment longer.

What did Bridgette want? What should he say? Should he bring up what happened in the kitchen? Should he try to kiss her again?

"Well," she said with a sigh. "I don't want to interrupt your time alone."

Bridgette turned to go. He should just let her walk away. True, Luke's life was far from exciting, but Bridgette came with complications. More than the feelings she aroused in him, she had a large and messy family. Moreover, if his guess was right, she was still dealing with her grief after the death of her spouse. Wasn't he content with his dull, predictable life? Hadn't he had enough drama as a kid while dealing with his father's illness?

If all of that was true, why did he call to Bridgette? "You know, you can stay if you want. We can be alone together."

She laughed and the sound filled his chest. "If we're together, then we wouldn't be alone, would we?"

"I suppose not," said Luke. "But I really do like your company. In fact, I don't know of anyone else I'd rather be with."

"Oh," she said. She stepped backward as if surprised by what he'd said. "That's quite a compliment."

"It's true."

"Until earlier this week, we hadn't spoken in decades. You can't know anything about me. I could have changed."

"You haven't changed that much, Bridgette."

She shook her head. "I'm not so sure about that."

A burst of laughter erupted from the party. Whatever issues had been brewing before seemed to have been forgotten.

"Have you had any luck getting an animal shelter involved in the Boo-fest parade?"

"To be honest, I haven't had time. The beginning of each case is always involved. But I promise to look into it tomorrow."

"I wasn't pressuring you," said Luke. "Just asking because I want the downtown festival to be worthwhile. Who knows, maybe we can expand to the winter holidays or do something for spring."

"Sounds like you really love the town."

"Of course," said Luke. "It's my home. Don't you love Braxville, too?"

She shrugged. "Like you said, it's home. But *love*? I don't know. It seems like there are so many things I didn't notice when I lived here last."

"Like what?"

"Well, I'm sure you heard, but two bodies were found on one of the old construction sites."

"I heard about that," said Luke. "Do the police know anything?"

"You'd have to ask Yvette," said Bridgette. "She's the one working on the case."

Luke knew he never would but nodded. "Is that it? Are there any other secrets lurking in the darkness?"

Bridgette shrugged again. "Maybe."

Her evasive answer covered Luke's arms with gooseflesh. *Maybe?* "How's your work? What brought you to Braxville?"

"There's a cluster of cancer cases in town. Several men have developed esophageal cancer. Statistically, it's impossible for all of these cases to be random."

She kept talking, but her words grew faint, as if she were faraway. His chest tightened, making it hard to breathe. "Esophageal cancer?"

"That's what I said." Bridgette laid her hand on Luke's shoulder. "Are you okay? You look like you're about to get sick."

A bead of sweat trickled down the side of Luke's face. He wiped it away. "My dad was sick, back when we were kids."

"Yeah," said Bridgette. "I remember." Even in the

dark, Luke could tell that the color drained from her face. "Oh, no. Don't tell me that your father had esophageal cancer."

"He did."

"Luke, I'm positive that the state hasn't identified him as being part of the cluster. Still, it's my job. I have to speak to him."

"I can arrange that. What should I do? Bring my dad to your office? Do you want to come to his house?"

Bridgette glanced over her shoulder and looked back at the party. Suddenly Luke wanted nothing more than to go home.

"My family owns a fishing cabin on Lake Kanopolis," Bridgette said.

Luke remembered the property well. He'd lost his virginity to Bridgette under a cottonwood on that very same lake. "I know."

"We can go there tomorrow morning. It'll give us some privacy."

"Can we make it after two o'clock in the afternoon? That's when the store closes for the weekend," he said. There were so many other thoughts taking shape in his mind. Things he wanted to say but shouldn't. Things he wanted to ask for but wouldn't.

"Two o'clock works just fine," she said. "Let's go back before someone comes looking for us."

"Hold on for one more minute," said Luke. Sure, he was about to step over the line, but tonight he didn't care. "What can you tell me about the cancer cases?"

"At the moment, not much."

"Is that because it's confidential."

"Right now," said Bridgette, "I'm just trying to understand what all the victims have in common. It's that one thread—a simple thin thread—that will run through the life of each man. We will find that thread and follow it until it leads us to the cause."

"You know, my dad was diagnosed with cancer when I was just a kid. In a way, I lost my childhood to the disease. For a long time, I was mad. Mad at my dad for getting sick. Mad at my mom for needing me to take on extra responsibilities around the house. Mad at God for letting everything happen. Mad at myself for, well, being so damned angry." He paused and drew in a breath. "But I really didn't think there was anyone to blame."

Luke tilted his head back. Stars, a thousand pinpricks of light, shone through the eternal blackness of the night sky. "And now you're telling me that someone or something might be at the root of all this suffering?"

"I want to be very careful with what I say next, Luke. I don't know that your father belongs in the cancer cluster." She sighed. "From what you've told me, there's enough evidence for me to investigate further. That's it."

"I have no right to ask this of you, Bridgette," Luke began. "Promise me that you'll figure out what's happening in Braxville. Even after all these years, you're still the smartest person I know."

"Getting to the bottom of all of these cases is why I'm here," she said. "It's my job and I will make things right for everyone in town."

He took a step toward her. And then another. And

another. Luke was so close that he could hear her breathing and see the pulse thrumming at the base of her neck. "Promise me," said Luke, "that you'll find out what happened in our home. Find out what happened to my father."

She looked down. For a single moment, time stopped and Luke was positive that she was going to refuse his request.

What had he been thinking? He never should have asked anything of her, yet he had. And once Bridgette said no? Well, would he ever be able to face her again?

"For you, I promise to do my best and never give up," she said.

"Your best is more than enough," said Luke.

Still, she stood close. All he had to do was lift a finger and he would touch her. He remembered the feel of her skin. She'd been soft and warm. In her arms, he came to understand what it meant to be a man. And it had nothing to do with discovering sex. Being a man meant protecting those you loved. It meant showing up even if you didn't feel like it. It meant always being an example worth following.

Another burst of laughter erupted from the party. Bridgette looked over her shoulder and the moment was gone.

"Come on," she said. "Let's make a s'more before everything's gone."

Without speaking, they returned to the party. Luke had been so focused on their past that he hadn't actually realized what he wanted from Bridgette. But he knew now.

It was a future.

Then again, Bridgette was still a grieving widow. Did that make Luke a fool for wanting more?

THE FLAT TIRES on her car and the tussle between Brooks and Dex notwithstanding, Bridgette considered the annual Colton bonfire a success. In fact, she was sincerely sorry when the evening ended, and not counting the minutes until the family event was over.

As she waved goodbye to her parents, Bridgette realized that she hadn't spoken to either one about Colton Construction's possible connection to the cancer cases. Sure, she'd been distracted by Luke, but really, Bridgette knew there was more.

She felt as if she were trapped between the proverbial rock and a hard place. She didn't want to upset her parents or seem disloyal to the family.

Then again, several of the men in her investigation were former employees of Colton Construction. It wasn't a detail she could ignore. In fact, she'd be neglecting her duty if she didn't investigate.

With Luke at her side, they returned to his truck. He opened the passenger door and Bridgette slid into the seat. After rounding to the driver's side and getting in, he started the engine and drove down the long drive and took the road back to Braxville.

"I was thinking about tomorrow," said Luke. "If you want, we can ride together. No sense in taking two cars."

"Especially since mine might not be fixed yet," she added.

"True," said Luke with a nod.

Headlights sliced through the night and the outside world passed in a shadowy blur. The purr of the engine and the rumbling truck were enough to lull Bridgette into a trance.

"About your car," said Luke.

"Yeah," she mumbled as her stupor neared sleep.

"I think I know what happened. What I don't know is why."

Adrenaline rushed through her veins. She sat up. "What do you mean?"

"Do you remember the woman you saw on the street the other night?"

"Your ex-girlfriend? Julia?"

"That's the one."

"What about her?"

"After you came over, I called her mother and told her that Julia had been hanging out at all hours. Her mother was shocked. Julia said she had been at work. I think Julia was upset that I'd contacted her mother, and slashing your tires was retaliation. What I don't get is why would she vandalize your car? Why not damage my truck?"

"That might not be much of a mystery," said Bridgette. "I saw her at the coffee shop the next morning when I grabbed breakfast for the two of us. Megan said your name when I picked up the order. Julia overheard, I'm sure of it."

"And then?" Luke coaxed.

Bridgette's face burned with a blush. Thank goodness the cabin was dark. "And then I told Julia that you and I dated in high school."

"Is that all you said? And how did that come up in conversation, anyway?"

"I might have let her believe that I spent the night with you, as well."

"You what?" Luke jerked the wheel as he gaped at her. They rumbled over the shoulder, kicking up a cloud of dust. Righting the truck, he smiled and shook his head. "I can't believe you implied that we'd been together. What were you thinking?"

"I guess that was the problem," she said. "I wasn't thinking at all." Bridgette stared out the window at the miles and miles of plains that stretched out forever.

How could she have been so stupid with Julia? Speaking to Luke's ex had been a rash decision that went against her cautious and thoughtful nature. "I was trying to help," she began. "You told me that she'd been lurking around your store for months. I hoped that if she thought you'd moved on, then she'd do the same."

"If she's the one who flattened your tires, I'd say she hasn't moved on at all."

"Obviously not," said Bridgette. "I didn't mean to make matters worse, but it seems like I have."

"Julia's never been destructive before," said Luke. "The fact that I don't know what else she might do bothers me."

"It does a hell of a lot more than bother me." She leaned back in the seat and rubbed away the tension between her brow. "Maybe it would be best if I just moved back to my parents' house."

"You can if you want, but I was thinking of something else."

"What else can I do? Are there other apartments to rent in Braxville?"

Luke stared straight ahead and worked his jaw back and forth. "Well," he began. "You can stay with me."

JULIA DROVE IN the dark. The headlights on Luke's truck cut a wedge out of the darkness. Yet driving without lights—or even being seen by Luke—wasn't Julia's main concern. It was Bridgette Colton. The other woman's silhouette was unmistakable in the passenger seat.

Hands trembling, Julia gripped the steering wheel so tight that she feared it would break. Sweat dripped down the back of her shirt. Her head throbbed and her stomach roiled. But it was no malady of the body.

Julia was stricken with disbelief and heartache.

Were Luke and Bridgette really an item?

Luke had taken Bridgette to her parents' house. He'd stayed. He was bringing her home. It was almost as if they were on a date. Had Julia caused this to happen? Had her ploy to get Bridgette to move back home only brought her closer to Luke?

It seemed impossible. Yet, in front of her, in the cabin of Luke's truck was the proof. As they drew closer to Braxville, subdivisions branched off the main road. Above, streetlamps spilled pools of light across the asphalt, giving off enough illumination for Luke to see her car.

If he did, what then?

She didn't want a repeat of the encounter with her

mother. Letting her foot off the accelerator, Julia turned into a nearby neighborhood. Small houses sat behind chain link fences. In the distance, a dog barked.

Julia found a house that was dark except for a sconce above the door, and she parked at the end of the drive. Turning off the ignition, she leaned back in her seat. She had time to wait. She knew where he was going.

What she didn't know: Was there anything beyond friendship between Luke and Bridgette? She intended to find out.

Chapter Eleven

As Luke turned his truck onto Main Street in downtown Braxville, Bridgette was exhausted both in body and spirit. Seemingly, a million different problems filled her mind. A night of uninterrupted sleep would help her sort out the answers.

But there was one issue that she couldn't escape.

How did she feel about Luke?

Bridgette glanced at him as he drove. Silvery light from the dashboard turned the angles of his face sharper, his eyes a deeper shade of blue. In the light, his lips were the color of spilled wine and she imagined the feeling of his mouth on hers.

This was no adolescent memory.

It was an all-too-real adult fantasy. Her pulse began to race, and Bridgette looked away.

"What's on your mind?" he asked.

Damn. He'd caught her staring. What was she supposed to say now? "I was just thinking about how Braxville looks exactly the same as it did when I was a kid. In reality, everything is different."

"Or maybe you're just noticing new things for the first time," he said.

"Maybe," said Bridgette as Luke parked his truck at the curb. His grille was next to her rear bumper. "Will my car be safe here tonight? I'll have it towed in the morning."

"I hope so," he said. "Like I said, usually crime is low in Braxville."

True, she and Luke were having a conversation. So far, neither one of them had said much of anything. Although the air in the cabin was warm, the hair on Bridgette's arm stood on end. She glanced at Luke again. Her eyes were immediately drawn to his lips a second time.

Luke interrupted the silence. "I meant what I said before. You can stay in my apartment if you'd like. My sofa is comfortable enough." He paused, "I promise not to be a slob in the bathroom."

Bridgette laughed. "I'm sure you'd make a fabulous roommate."

"So you'll stay with me?"

"I moved out of my parents' house because I'm a grown woman and I need my own place. How would moving in with you keep me independent?"

"It's more for your safety," he said.

"I know," said Bridgette. "Truly, I do. I appreciate your concern and offer. But you're right across the hall. If I need anything, I can come to you."

"Of course," said Luke. "At least let me look through your apartment and make sure everything's in order."

Bridgette wasn't sure if Luke's precautions were justified or not. "Thanks," she said. "That'd be great."

In less than a minute, they stood in front of Bridgette's apartment. She opened the door. The room beyond was dark as pitch. Luke flipped a wall switch and a table lamp glowed, filling the room with light.

A blanket was draped across the end of the sofa. A plate, filled with crumbs from her morning bagel, sat on the kitchen counter. A mug, with the dregs of her coffee, sat in the middle of the plate. "It looks like it did when I left for work," she said.

"Mind if I check out the bedroom and the bath?"

Bridgette hadn't unpacked, much less made a mess worthy of embarrassment. "Help yourself," she said.

Luke disappeared through the single door and she moved to the window. Bracing her palms on the sill, she looked down onto the street below.

Luke said that Julia had been lurking outside his store for months.

Was she watching them now?

"Everything looks good," he said, stepping into the living room.

Bridgette used the mirrored glass and looked at Luke without turning around. "Thanks again for checking out my apartment. And for driving me to my parents'. And staying at the bonfire, even though my family can be nutty."

Luke slipped the tips of his fingers into the pockets of his jeans. "Everyone's family is a little crazy. Still, you Coltons are good people."

Bridgette wasn't sure how to respond and returned her gaze to the street below. She half expected to see Julia standing on the sidewalk, but the road was empty.

"Well, I better get going," said Luke. "Tomorrow's a busy day at the store."

Maybe it was just a bunch of kids who'd flattened her tires. Maybe the destruction had been random. Maybe Julia had nothing to do with the damage done to Bridgette's car. If that was the case, why did Bridgette suddenly loathe the idea of being left alone? "Let me make you a cup of tea," she said. "It's the least I can do."

"The food and the company tonight were more than enough, but thanks."

"Sure," she said, turning back to the window. "It's late. I understand."

There, just across the street, in the recessed entrance to a hair salon, Bridgette saw something. Movement? A flash of color where there should only be shadows? She sucked in a breath. With her pulse racing, she took a step back.

"What?" Luke asked as he moved to her. He was so close that his chest brushed against her back. She liked the heat from his body. Liked the feeling of his hard muscles next to her skin. Liked that being near Luke reminded Bridgette of what it meant to be a woman.

He asked, "What is it?"

"I'm not sure," said Bridgette. "I thought I saw something."

She moved back to the window. Her breath fogged the glass, and she wiped it away with her sleeve. "In the doorway across the street, something caught my eye."

Luke stood behind her, his hand resting on the small of her back. "What'd you see?"

"That's just it. It was only a glimpse of…whatever. It startled me."

A cat darted out from the doorway and sprinted down the street, its fur gleaming in the streetlight.

Bridgette laughed. "I guess I did see something."

"Your property was damaged," said Luke. "It's totally natural to be on edge."

She pivoted where she stood, coming face-to-face with Luke. Her fingers itched with the need to touch him. She reached up and then paused with her palms halfway to his chest. What was she thinking?

Balling her hands into fists, Bridgette forced her arms to her side.

"You know," said Luke, moving closer to her. "I might just take that cup of tea."

"Let me put water on to boil," she said, yet she didn't move.

"Maybe you should," he said. His voice was low and deep, and sent reverberations through her chest. He leaned to her. His breath washed over her cheek.

She moved closer still. Their lips were close but not yet touching.

Then Bridgette reached up and ran her fingers through the short hairs at the nape of Luke's neck.

"Are you sure you want to do this again? Get involved with me?"

"To be honest," said Bridgette, "there's only one thing I know. Only one thing that I want."

"Oh, yeah?" he asked. "What's that?"

"I want you," she said, "to kiss me."

BRIDGETTE'S INVITATION WAS all Luke needed. His mouth was on hers, and his world shrank until it filled the apartment, and Luke and Bridgette were the only two people who mattered.

Moving his hand from her back upward to her hair, he wrapped his fingers in her long tresses. Luke pulled back on her head, exposing her throat. He licked her neck. Sucked on her earlobe. When she let out a mew of delight, he returned his lips to hers. Slipping his tongue inside her mouth, Luke explored, tasted and conquered.

"Luke," she said into his mouth, their breath becoming one. "Oh, Luke."

He pressed her into the window, his hand traveling from her hair to her stomach. He worked his fingers under the hem of her shirt, just to see if she felt as soft as he imagined.

She was.

His fingers traveled farther up her stomach, and the tips of his fingers grazed the lace of her bra. Luke pressed against the fly of his jeans. He wanted Bridgette. And it wasn't just tonight. He'd always wanted her. Hers was the face that came to him in dreams and fantasies alike.

And then the window exploded. Glass rained down as a piece of concrete skittered across the floor. Luke went numb for the span of a heartbeat. Time slowed as he recognized danger. Pulling Bridgette away from the window, they dropped to the floor. He covered her with his body.

"What the hell just happened?" she asked.

Luke didn't have an answer. Rising up, he glanced out of the window. The street was empty—except for a lone figure running down the road.

Even from his vantage point, he could clearly see the retreating form. Moreover, he knew exactly who had broken the window.

It was Julia.

"Son of a bitch," Luke growled. His hands shook with rage. He'd honestly tried to be reasonable with her, and it hadn't done either one of them any good.

"What's going on, Luke?" Bridgette asked, her eyes wide. "What happened?"

Holding out his hand, he pulled Bridgette to her feet. "It was Julia. Looks like she threw a piece of concrete through the window." Bits of glass sparkled in Bridgette's hair. He dusted them away. "Are you hurt?"

She drew in a shaking breath. "Just startled, that's all."

"I don't know what to say," he said. "Obviously, I knew that Julia had an unhealthy attachment, but I never imagined she'd be destructive, much less violent."

"I guess everyone's full of surprises," she said with a wry chuckle.

He supposed that Bridgette keeping some of her sense of humor was a good thing. Yet Julia's behavior was no laughing matter, especially since her animosity was directed at Bridgette.

"Grab whatever you need for the night," said Luke.

"Why?"

"There's no way I'm letting you stay here alone.

You can crash at my place tonight. Tomorrow, we can figure out what to do next."

Bridgette looked at the door leading to her bedroom, to the chunk of concrete on the floor, and then back at Luke. He could well imagine the arguments she was forming. She was a grown woman. Julia was now long gone. Even if Luke's ex came back, she couldn't get into the stairwell that led to the apartments.

Before she said a word, Luke held up his hand. "I don't want to fight with you, but I insist that you keep yourself out of harm's way. This apartment isn't safe for you—not tonight anyway."

To his surprise, Bridgette nodded her head. "You're right. Give me a minute and I'll be right back."

And then Luke was alone. He pulled the phone from his pocket and placed a call that he had never intended to make. It was answered after the second ring. "This is Detective Reese Carpenter."

"Hey, it's Luke Walker. I have a problem and I need your help."

BRIDGETTE NEEDED ONLY a few minutes to pack an overnight bag. She returned to the living room and set the bag on the floor. Luke stared at her, his jaw tight.

"Everything okay?" she asked.

"You know Reese Carpenter?"

"Of course. He's Jordana's partner on the police force."

"I called him about Julia," he said. "At first, I thought she was only lovesick, but this is more than I can deal with—and I definitely can't ignore what she's done. Not when she's threatening you."

Bridgette wasn't sure how to feel. Was she terrified that she was now a target of Luke's ex-girlfriend? Or was she touched by Luke's caring and concern?

Like always, Bridgette needed more information.

"What's Reese going to do?"

"Come here," said Luke. "I suppose he'll get pictures of the damage. Take a report. And, most important, he's going to talk to Julia." Whatever he was about to say next was interrupted by the pinging of a message on his phone. Luke glanced at the screen. "He's here. You'll be okay while I let him in?"

"Of course," said Bridgette, though her heart raced at the idea of being alone even for a few seconds. Folding her arms across her chest, she continued, "Go ahead. I'm fine."

Luke didn't bother to shut the front door, and the sound of his footsteps on the staircase were unmistakable.

"Thanks for coming, man," said Luke as he opened the door.

Bridgette recognized Reese's deep voice. He replied, "It's my job. Let's chat here for a minute. Can you tell me anything more than what you said on the phone?"

"Not really. Julia, the woman I dated over the summer, continued to hang around after we broke up. I told her to stop. She didn't. I figured she'd have to get bored eventually and go away, right?"

"I'm guessing that you were wrong."

"Bridgette Colton rented the apartment across the hall on Tuesday."

Reese asked, "As in Jordana's little sister?"

"The same. Anyway, Julia has taken a great disliking to Bridgette. Earlier, all four of Bridgette's tires had been slashed. Then tonight, someone threw a brick through Bridgette's window."

"Someone?"

"I saw Julia running down the street."

"But you didn't see her throw the concrete."

"No," he said. "But it's not hard to figure out what happened."

Reese asked, "And you didn't see her tampering with Bridgette's car, either. Correct?"

"You're correct," said Luke.

"Since you didn't see what happened to either the car or the window, I can't charge Julia with anything," said Reese. "What I can do is ask around. Maybe some of your neighbors or the other business owners saw something."

"If they didn't? What then? Are you saying that Julia will just get away with what she's done? Believe me, I know she's guilty. I have all the proof I need," said Luke.

"Calm down, man. There's a few things I can do with Julia even if I'm not going to arrest her or charge her with a crime."

"Like what?" Luke asked.

"I'll run her name through the system and see if she has any outstanding warrants."

"I doubt she does," said Luke. "So, what happens after that?"

Reese continued, "If she doesn't have a record, I'll stop by her house and have a chat. Hopefully, a visit from the police will help her to understand the seriousness of her behavior."

"Hopefully?" Luke echoed. "I just want to make sure that Bridgette is safe, you know."

"You two used to date, isn't that right?" asked Reese.

"Back in high school," said Luke.

"Is she the ex-girlfriend who got you all worked up the other night?"

Luke mumbled something that Bridgette couldn't hear. He continued, "She was my first love and is still a special lady. It's my job to keep her safe."

"That's noble of you," said the detective. "But I'm the expert in safety. Let's take a look at the damage. Then I'll talk to Julia."

Treading lightly, Bridgette moved across the room and shut the door. Undoubtedly, she hadn't been meant to overhear the conversation between Luke and Reese Carpenter. Then again, what was she supposed to do with what she now knew?

Did Luke really have feelings for her?

And what about the kiss?

Bridgette had spent the last two years clinging to the past. Now she had no idea how to feel about having a future. Especially one that might include Luke Walker.

JULIA FEARED THAT she would retch. How could she have been so stupid?

In all honesty, she didn't even remember throwing the damned piece of concrete—a chunk of sidewalk that had broken loose. Hell, she barely remembered picking it up.

All she recalled was the weight of the slab in her hand. The rough edges biting into her palm. The heat of anger consuming her as Luke embraced Bridgette.

Then the concrete went airborne. As it sailed across the street, Julia had felt a sense of relief, as if she truly had launched her fury. It slammed through the window and she froze for an instant.

Christ, who knew that she had such power and aim?

Without a backward glance, she'd sprinted from the scene. What else was she supposed to do?

Had she done more damage than breaking the window?

Had Luke been cut by a shard of glass? Had the heavy concrete hit Bridgette?

Julia pulled into her driveway, opened the car door, leaned out and emptied her stomach. Everything she'd eaten splattered across the ground. Wiping away the last of her spittle with a fast-food napkin, she asked herself again how she could have been so stupid.

The flickering light from the TV filtered around the edges of shades drawn over the front window. Damn. Despite the late hour, her mother was awake. Julia had messed up badly.

Would her mother be able to tell?

And if she could, what would she do?

Turning off the ignition, Julia stepped from the

car. Her legs ached with each stride as she walked to the house.

"That you, Julia?" her mother called from the adjacent living room.

Julia busied herself with hanging up her coat and her purse, not daring to look in her mother's direction. "It is, Momma."

"Have fun at your friend's house?"

"I did, Momma," said Julia. "I'm going to get some dinner and go to bed, though. I'm real tired."

"Dinner? I thought you said that you were going to a barbecue."

Is that what she'd told her mother? Damn, Julia couldn't remember what she'd said. Sure, just a few hours had passed, yet it seemed like days since she'd last spoken to her mother. "It was, but the sauce didn't sit right with me."

"I didn't make you a plate," her mother said. "But if you give me a minute, I can get you a sandwich."

"Don't worry," Julia interrupted. "I'm just going to grab a bowl of cereal, or something."

Outside, a car's engine idled.

The neighbor's dog barked.

Julia, standing next to the coatrack, froze.

Of course, someone could be outside for a million different reasons. Yet, Julia's palms began to tingle, and she knew the truth. She'd been seen by Luke or Bridgette. They'd called the police.

Tonight was not going to end well.

She opened the front door again. There, at the curb,

was a Braxville Police Department cruiser. A man with dark hair sat in the driver's seat.

Julia stepped outside.

"Where are you going?" her mother called after her.

"I forgot something in the car," Julia yelled over her shoulder. "I'll be right back."

"Are you going outside without your coat?"

Julia shut the door on her mother's question.

Standing on the stoop, she waited as the man stepped from his vehicle. "Are you Julia?"

For a moment, she considered lying though she knew better. Her ruse, once discovered, would only make matters worse. She gave a quick nod of her head. "I am."

"I'm Detective Reese Carpenter, with the Braxville Police. Can I ask where you were tonight?"

"I know what I did was wrong," she began. "And honestly, I'm sorry."

"What did you do that was wrong?" he asked.

Did he want her to confess? Or was the police officer here for an entirely different reason? Had she already said too much? No. Detective Carpenter coming to her house was no coincidence. The more honest she was, the better it would be. Wasn't that what the doctors at the hospital always said?

"I got mad and threw a chunk of concrete at a window. I'm pretty sure the window broke, but I started running as soon as I heard the crack."

"Anything else?"

Well, she was in for a penny, she might as well be in for a pound. "I sliced the tires on Bridgette Colton's car," she said, suddenly too tired to lie anymore. "I dated Luke Walker over the summer. I really thought that he was the one. We broke up and, well, he started dating someone else. Like I said, I was upset."

"You know that destroying property is a crime? You can be criminally charged for what you did tonight."

"I know," said Julia. Tears burned her eyes. Would crying help her cause? "I really am sorry. I'll pay for the damages, if that helps."

"You may very well end up being sent a bill, but that's not for me to decide." The police officer exhaled. "What I want is for you to stay far away from both Luke Walker and Bridgette Colton. If I hear that you've bothered either one of them, even a little, I'm coming back. Our chat will be different next time. You won't receive a warning, and when I leave, you'll be coming to the station with me. Got it?"

"Got it," said Julia. Was that it? Of their own accord, the corners of her mouth turned up. She pressed her thumb to her lips, hiding the smile.

"Try to have yourself a good night and remember what I said."

"I'll stay away from Luke and Bridgette."

The police officer drew in a long breath and opened his mouth, ready to say something else. With a shake of his head, he slipped back into his car and closed the door. As he drove away, Julia's knees went weak. She held on to her house for support, thankful that there'd been no real consequences.

Turning, Julia opened the door and stepped inside. Her mother—and her wheelchair—blocked the entryway. Even in the darkness, Julia could see that her mother's mouth was pressed into a colorless line.

"Was everything that I just heard true? Did you really break a window and flatten somebody's tires?"

"If you heard all that," Julia began. Her hands went numb and the back of her knees began to sweat. "Then you heard me say that I was sorry. You heard me admit that I'd gotten mad and also promise not to bother Luke anymore."

"What about his girlfriend?"

Julia recalled the scene on the windowsill. Bridgette's mouth pressed onto Luke's like a sucker fish on a dirty tank. Julia's face burned as her chest filled with shame and rage. "Her, too."

"You have to listen to the police officer, Julia. There are worse places to go than the hospital."

Julia snorted. "I doubt it."

"Like jail," said her mother. "Jail's worse than a hospital."

"I know, Momma," she said, leaning on the wall. "I'm going to bed now."

"I thought you were hungry. What happened to having some cereal?"

"I've lost my appetite," she said, pushing from the wall and walking down the short hallway.

"You need to be careful," said her mother.

Laying her hand on the doorknob, Julia turned. The TV was still on. Light spilled into the entryway, casting her mother in flickering shadows. "I'll be careful," Julia said.

"And you need to leave Luke Walker alone. You know that."

Julia opened the door to her room. "I heard the police officer," she said. "And I heard you." With that, she pushed the door shut and turned on the light. Luke's face was on every inch of her wall. Tracing a finger over a picture, she spoke. "You don't have to worry," she said. "I won't abandon you."

Chapter Twelve

Bridgette woke in a bed that she knew wasn't hers. In an instant, moments from last night came back like a wave crashing against the shore. Her car being vandalized. The party at her parents. The kiss with Luke. The brick coming through the window. The visit by the police. And, finally, the arrangement for her to stay at Luke's apartment, at least until the window was fixed.

Luke insisted that Bridgette take his room and she'd been too tired to argue. Like a gentleman, he slept on the sofa. She inhaled. The sheets smelled like fresh-cut lumber, spice and the out-of-doors. They smelled like Luke.

Dropping her feet to the floor, Bridgette stood. She twisted her tresses into a bun and secured her hair in place with a band. With one more stretch, she wandered from the bedroom. The living room and adjacent kitchen were empty, and a single sheet of paper sat in the middle of the coffee table.

It was a note from Luke.

His handwriting had changed little over the years.

Good morning, his note began. Bridgette smiled, imagining that he was far too chipper for the early hour.

I'm at work but help yourself to anything you find in the kitchen. Coffee's fresh. There are towels in the bathroom. Stop by if you get bored. I'll see you this afternoon.

She set the note back on the table, inexplicably sad she had woken up to an empty apartment.

With an entire morning to fill, she made a plan: First things first and she called a local garage to collect her car. After arrangements for a garage to tow her car had been made, she turned her attention to the Boofest. Thanks to Bridgette's old roommate, the Braxville Boo-fest was about to get help from a very popular TV show. More than that, Bridgette hoped to help some well-deserving pets find their forever home.

She read through the binder he'd been given and ninety minutes later, Bridgette had written a short press release. After that, she showered, got ready for the day and finished a Google search. With an address written on the back of her note, she locked the front door and descended the stairs to the street.

Walking past the hardware store, she peered into the window. More than a dozen customers stood in line at the counter. She was happy to see the place so busy. All the same, she'd hoped to catch a glimpse of Luke.

Pressing her lips together, she recalled the feeling of his mouth on hers and a shiver of desire danced along her skin. What would have happened last night if Luke's ex hadn't shattered the window?

Then again, Bridgette knew. She'd have woken up with him in the bed, not on the sofa.

It brought up another question. How would she have felt about their lovemaking this morning? Was Luke a mistake she'd soon regret?

With a shake of her head, she started walking.

"Good morning," a voice called out. She recognized it at once and stopped. It was him.

The door to the hardware store was open and Luke stood on the threshold. "I wanted you to know that I got a text from Reese Carpenter," Luke said. "He stopped by Julia's house last night. She admitted to throwing the concrete that broke the window. She also said she was sorry for overreacting and promised to leave me— and you—alone."

"Thanks for the update," she said. "I'm glad that everything got sorted out with your ex."

Luke said, "Me, too." He paused. "Where are you headed?"

Bridgette looked at her note and read the address. "Is that Perfect Pets Dog Shelter?"

"I want to see if we can get some of their dogs to participate in the parade."

"I'll go with you," said Luke. "I know the shelter's director."

Of course he knew the director. Luke Walker knew everyone in town. "What about your store. It looks busy."

"My dad helps out on Saturday mornings. He'll be okay for a few minutes."

Sure, having Luke help with introductions would be great. All the same, that meant they'd be spending more time together. It wasn't that she disliked Luke; in fact, it was the complete opposite. Luke was attractive, smart, considerate and hardworking. He was everything she admired in a man.

And that was the problem.

Luke was damn close to being perfect. And Bridgette was damn close to losing her heart to him again.

Would that be such a bad thing?

Then again, how would he feel once he knew why their sweet summer love had turned sour?

THE MORNING SKY was clear and bright blue, promising a sunny fall day. All the stores in the downtown were open and filled with patrons, leaving Luke more than a little pleased.

Perfect Pets Dog Shelter was located two blocks from the downtown shopping district, where businesses and residential properties started to blend. Located in a renovated Victorian mansion, a wooden cutout of a dog hung from a light pole at the gate.

"Here we are," said Luke, gesturing to the brick walkway.

Bridgette turned to the walkway and he followed her to the porch. They opened the front door and the sound of happy barking greeted them.

Steven Faulkner, the director of the shelter, looked up from a reception desk that sat in the one-time foyer.

"Luke," said the older man, getting to his feet. "Good to see you. What brings you by today?"

Hand on Bridgette's back, Luke said, "Let me introduce you to my friend and the newest chair of the Boo-fest parade, Bridgette Colton."

"Colton, eh. Are you one of Fitz and Lilly's kids?"

Bridgette smiled and stepped forward. "I am," she said, shaking hands with Steven. "It's a pleasure to meet you."

Luke continued, "Bridgette has an idea for the Boo-fest parade, but we need your help."

"Well, you've got me intrigued," said the older man. "What can I do?"

Bridgette spent a few minutes outlining her plan of partnering with the shelter to have dogs attend the Boo-fest and participate in the parade. She concluded with the opportunity to have them featured on the popular TV show, *Good Morning, Wichita*. As she ended her speech, Bridgette asked, "What do you think?"

Steven was nodding and smiling, which Luke assumed was a good sign. "I think that you've come up with a great way to get much needed exposure for the shelter. And even better, a way to get some of the animals into their forever homes. I'm sure we can have a few at the parade, provided we pick the right ones."

"Of course," said Bridgette. "We'd only want dogs who are comfortable with a crowd and lots of attention."

"Let me give you the grand tour." Pointing to a winding staircase that led to the second floor, Steven said, "I have an apartment upstairs and then also run a low-cost vet clinic on Thursday mornings."

"You're a veterinarian?" Bridgette asked.

"Semiretired. My wife, Helen, and I always wanted to run a dog sanctuary. So, when I sold my practice, we remodeled the house and opened the shelter."

"That's a great retirement story," said Bridgette. "Where's Helen now?"

"She's in Kansas City, Missouri. Our oldest daughter just gave birth to another baby. A grandson."

"Congratulations," said Luke as Steven beamed with pride.

"Anyhow," said Dr. Faulkner, "follow me." He ushered them through a set of metal doors that led to the back of the house. All the walls had been knocked down on the main floor, leaving a single room with more than a dozen pens lining each wall. Most of the pens were occupied with barking, happy dogs.

Kneeling next to the first pen, she reached her fingers through the wire door. "Hello, boy," she said. A white-and-black dog with a short coat sniffed her fingers.

"That's Pocco," said Steven. "He's as sweet a fella as there is, but a bit shy. I don't think he'd enjoy being a part of the parade."

Bridgette rubbed the dog's ears. "We won't stress you out, then. Will we, boy?"

"He's taken a liking to you," said Steven. "I'm glad to see that. He's been at the shelter for months, mostly because he's wary of strangers."

"Pocco knows a friend when he meets one," said Bridgette.

Since her return to Braxville, Bridgette had appeared to be serious-minded and competent. She'd shared with him that she was in town to do a job and had no intention of failing. Yet, in that moment of her kneeling next to the dog's cage, Luke saw another version of Bridgette. One that was vulnerable, open and, above all, caring.

His chest filled with an emotion he dared not examine.

An hour later, Bridgette and Luke had a list of ten dogs with the personality needed to be in the parade. Bridgette had also texted her friend, the TV producer, pictures of the dogs, along with pertinent information—breed, age, gender, name.

On her way out of the shelter, Bridgette stopped once again to visit Pocco. "Goodbye, boy. I'll see you real soon."

The dog's tail was a blur and he gave a happy bark.

"He really does like you," said Steven. "I rarely get him to say anything."

"If you ever need a dog walker, I'll volunteer."

"I can always use the help," said Steven. "In fact, he's due for a stroll if you want to take him out now."

"I'd love to," said Bridgette.

Luke had promised his father that he wouldn't be gone long. He really should get back to work. Then again, he wasn't about to miss a chance to take a walk with Bridgette.

"Care for some company?" he asked.

"If you can spare the time."

"For Pocco," said Luke as Steven hooked a lead to the dog's collar. "Anything."

The sun rose in the sky, warming the air. Without

speaking, they walked down the sidewalk and turned into a residential neighborhood. Nose to the ground, Pocco snuffled as he walked.

"Hopefully," said Bridgette, "Someone will adopt this guy, too. It breaks my heart to see a good dog go overlooked time and again."

"Sounds like you have a passion for helping shelter dogs."

"For the most part, they're uncomplicated creatures. All a dog wants is to have someone to love and to be loved in return." He sensed she had more to say and waited for her to speak. "Two years ago, I was in a very low place. When Henry died, I lost more than my husband. I'd lost my future, along with all the plans we'd made. I'd lost my past, too, because of the history we shared."

"You were out of hope," he said.

"I've never thought about it that way, but I guess you're right." They walked another block in silence. Bridgette spoke again. "I threw myself into work for several months. It's what I'm good at, after all. Yet, I knew I needed to do more. At the same time, being around people was exhausting."

"Is that when you started volunteering at your local shelter?"

"A lot of dogs make great company. With a dog, I can just be. At least they don't ask too many questions."

"And how are you doing now?"

Bridgette shrugged. "Before I came home, I thought I had balance in my life."

"You don't?"

"Let's just say that family can make things more complicated."

"What about plans for your future?" Luke asked. "Do you know what else you want from life?"

"No." She exhaled. "With Henry, I knew I wanted kids."

"What about now? Do you want kids? Do you want to get married again?"

Bridgette glanced at her smartwatch. "We better get Pocco back to the shelter. It's getting late."

He wasn't a fool. Luke knew that she wanted to get rid of him. And he also knew why. He'd asked too many questions—questions that Bridgette didn't want to answer.

They turned at the corner, rounding the block and heading back to the shelter. At the end of the street, he glimpsed the back of a blue sedan as it drove away.

His heart began to race. Had it been Julia? Was she still stalking him despite being visited by the police?

THE TRIP FROM Braxville to Lake Kanopolis took less than thirty minutes. For the entire drive, Paul Walker regaled Bridgette with stories, much to her delight and Luke's embarrassment.

"And then there was the one time we went hiking," said Mr. Walker. "Luke was about three years old. He'd stopped wearing diapers and there was no bathroom for miles. So, when he had to go, there was only the woods."

"Thanks, Dad," said Luke. For comfort's sake, they'd taken Paul's SUV. Luke drove. His father sat in the passenger seat and Bridgette rode in the back. "That's enough personal history for the day. Remember, Bridgette and I went to school together from kindergarten to graduation. She doesn't want to hear all of this."

"No, you can keep telling me about Luke," said Bridgette. "I didn't know him when he was in preschool. The stories are cute."

"Don't forget humiliating," added Luke.

Using the rearview mirror, she stole a glance at him. Sun shone on his face, turning his skin golden. Bridgette could almost pretend that the outing to the fishing cabin was just that—an outing. But she couldn't ignore Luke's connection—through his father—to her investigation.

"Well," said Mr. Walker. "If you really don't want me to, then I guess I won't."

Luke exhaled. "Fine, finish the story."

Mr. Walker smiled. "Where were we?"

"In the woods and without a bathroom," Bridgette said.

"That's just it," said Mr. Walker. "My wife had worked so hard to get Luke potty trained that he wouldn't do anything because he wasn't in a bathroom."

"Uh-oh. What happened?"

"We convinced him that it was okay because it was outside, which made everyone happier that day."

"I feel like there was another day when people weren't as happy," said Bridgette.

"You'd be right. Like the next day, when my wife took him to the park."

Bridgette started laughing. "Oh, no."

Luke was laughing, too. "Oh, yes."

Luke turned up the long drive leading to the fishing cabin. Sun shone on the water, and Lake Kanopolis sparkled like a carpet of diamonds. Pulling up next to the back door, Luke put the SUV in Park.

Using a key that she'd gotten from her mother, Bridgette opened the back door. An alarm started beeping. She entered the code—Yvette's birthday, something everyone could remember.

The house, used every weekend in the summer, had been closed for the colder months ahead. Shades were drawn, leaving the interior dim. Sheets were draped over the furnishings. The air was stale and cold.

"Come on in," said Bridgette.

Paul, his back stooped and his steps slow, walked into the house. He looked up and gave a low whistle. "That's quite the ceiling."

Bridgette followed his gaze. The ceiling, repurposed from an old bank, was made of hammered metal tiles. "Glad you like it. Mom made Dad save it from a renovation he did years ago.

"Let me give you the tour, which I can do from right here." She pointed to a set of stairs, tucked behind the front door. "Those lead to the master suite. The door to the right goes to a second bedroom. The door on the left is a communication room. It's PI stuff, so don't ask too many questions. We do have a landline, but no cellular service. And this," she said, striding across the room and pulling open the drapes to a large window that overlooked the lake. The sun hung low in the afternoon sky.

"What a great view," said Luke. He stood right behind her, the heat from his body warming her skin. Why, then, was she covered in gooseflesh?

She remembered the last time they were at the lake together. It was the night before she left for college. They'd sat under the cottonwood tree and watched the sun set over the lake. As the sky darkened and the stars came out, their kisses grew more passionate. They'd had sex. It was a few moments that even now Bridgette recalled as painful and exhilarating. Funny, how she remembered the hitch in her breath as Luke entered her with a singular clarity. Yet, she couldn't recall the trip from the fishing cabin to her home later that night. As he kissed her good-night, they swore to keep in contact.

It was a promise neither of them kept beyond the first few months of the semester.

What would he say if he knew why she stopped keeping in touch?

Stripping a sheet from the chair, she said, "Give me a second to clear off the furniture and I'll get a fire started in the hearth."

"Point me in the direction of the woodpile and I can get the fire started," said Luke.

"It's behind the outbuilding," she said. "Just to the left of the back door."

As Luke left, Mr. Walker settled onto a bar stool at the kitchen counter. "This is a lovely place," he said.

Bridgette had spent her life being told she had access to lots of nice things. It always filled her with a mixture of pride and embarrassment, leaving her uncertain how to respond. It was true today, and she said, "I was told there was a big flood downtown, about twenty-two years ago."

"Oh, yeah," the older man said with a shake of his head. "It almost wiped Braxville off the map."

"Did you help with the cleanup, Mr. Walker?"

"Call me Paul. And, sure, I helped. My store was all but destroyed. Then again, there was me, owning the one hardware store in town. I was able to order a lot of what folks needed."

"What about the cleanup? Did you help?"

"Oh, yeah, everyone in town really pitched in." He paused. "Luke told me that there are a bunch of men who developed esophageal cancer. Do you think that there was something in those floodwaters that made us sick?"

"It's a possibility," she said, thankful that Luke had explained everything to his father beforehand.

"What other possibilities are there?" he asked.

"To be honest, Mr. Walker, that's why I'm here."

"Paul," he said again.

"An old habit dying hard, I guess," she said with a blush.

"What's this I hear about old habits?" Luke asked as he came into the house, his arms filled with firewood.

Her gaze followed as he passed, her middle filled with a fluttering. Luke was undeniably a handsome man. It was no wonder that they'd kissed last night or that he had been her first lover. Yet, there was more to him than a really nice bod. Luke Walker was a genuinely kind person.

"I was just trying to get Bridgette to call me Paul instead of Mr. Walker," said Luke's dad. "As hard as it is for you to call me Paul, it's harder for me to realize that both of you are grown-ups now."

"All right, Dad," said Luke, adding in a good-natured eye roll. Setting the stack of wood next to the hearth, he began to arrange sticks and logs.

Bridgette turned her attention back to Luke's father. "I have several questions to ask. They're all procedural. I'm trying to get an idea of your health history while looking for a link between you and all the other folks who are part of the cluster."

"Ask away," he said. "I'd be grateful for any information that you can give me."

As with all her cases, the weight of responsibility was heavy on Bridgette's shoulders. Yet, this case was different—it was too close to her home, literally. For one instant, she asked herself the unthinkable. What if more evidence surfaced that Colton Construction was involved? Could she really be impartial?

Chapter Thirteen

Before leaving Braxville, Bridgette had started a file.
She removed it from her bag and flipped it open. The
first sheet was the health questionnaire she'd already
mentioned. She got his height, weight and age before
moving on to the rest of the items covered.

"Are you a smoker?" she began.

"No."

"Ever smoked?"

"Does trying twice when I was a teenager count?"

"Not really," said Bridgette, but it was her job to
take note of everything.

"Prior to your cancer diagnosis, did you drink alcohol?"

"Sure."

"How often."

Paul puffed out his cheeks, blowing out the air in a
single gust. "A beer or two a week."

"Any illegal drugs?"

"Never."

For the next thirty minutes, she asked questions
about his health. As expected, there was nothing of

note. Next, she moved on to his work history. Like the two generations of Walkers before Paul, he had helped his father run the hardware store. "I worked there six days a week from eighteen years old to the age of fifty-eight," Paul said, his chest expanding with pride.

"What changed when you turned fifty-eight?" Bridgette asked.

"He retired," said Luke. These were the first words he'd said in nearly half an hour. Once Luke had gotten the fire started and sat quietly in the adjacent living room.

"Why'd you retire at such a young age," Bridgette asked. Sure, it was an intrusive question, but intruding into all parts of Paul Walker's life was the only way to discover the truth.

"To be honest," said Paul, "I tire easily. It's hard to get through an entire day without needing a nap."

"Did you seek any medical opinion as to your lethargy?"

"The doctors ran a whole host of tests," said Luke, rising from the living room and coming to take a seat next to his father. "They checked for sleeping disorders, anemia, Lyme disease and found nothing wrong."

Paul added, "In the end, the doctor felt the cancer made me old before my time."

Bridgette couldn't help but think of Ernest O'Rourke and how he looked older than his years. Try as she might, Bridgette couldn't ignore the connection to Colton Construction. Despite the fact that she'd asked once before, she couldn't help but ask again. "And the only job you've ever held was at the hardware store?"

"The store is part of our family," he said with a sigh.

It was then that Bridgette noticed dark circles ringing Paul's eyes. His shoulders were stooped, and she figured now was the time he needed a rest. "Why don't you go to the sofa and enjoy the fire. I packed a cooler with sandwich fixings. It's in the SUV. We can eat before finishing the interview."

Opening the back door, Luke held it for Bridgette as she passed. "I'll help."

The sun was low on the horizon. The water of the lake reflected the sky, making it look as if there were two worlds, one stacked atop the other.

They returned to the cabin with the cooler. Stretched out, with his eyes closed, Luke's father snored softly.

"I didn't mean to wear him out," she said, a twinge of guilt in her chest.

"It's not you, but now you can see why he retired."

"He's lucky that you were able to take over the hardware store," said Bridgette.

Luke shrugged. "You know how it is with family-owned businesses."

She did. Sort of, at least.

"It's a nice time for a walk," said Luke. "Want to go while Dad naps?"

"Absolutely," said Bridgette as he grabbed a denim jacket and slipped it on.

Without discussion, they wandered toward a trail through the woods. It was a path she knew well. Dried leaves carpeted the forest floor and crunched underfoot. "When I was a kid, my brothers and I pretended that elves and fairies lived in these woods and left out

food. We were convinced elves took everything because it was always gone in the morning."

"Sounds like a nice childhood," said Luke.

"Ty and Jordana, being older and wiser, said we
were dumb kids who didn't know better."

"Wow. That's harsh," he said.

"One night, I snuck out of the house to see what was
taking the food we left."

"And what'd you find?" Luke asked.

"Raccoons," said Bridgette with a laugh.

They'd walked over half a mile, and there, in the
middle of a clearing, was a well. The casing was
green with moss and lichen. The stones were worn
smooth from time and the weather. The crossbar was
askew, and the only thing left from the rope was a few
blackened strands. A wooden bench sat nearby, and
Bridgette took a seat. "That night I kind of grew up.
But to this day, I still think that this place is magical."

DENSE WOODS ENCROACHED on the glade, the trees at
the peak of their autumnal glory. Luke stood next to
Bridgette, resting his foot on the bench's crossbeam.
Her palms ached with the need to reach out and touch
him. She slid her hands under her thighs.

He said, "I can see why you thought this place was
magic, the raccoons notwithstanding."

She laughed. "You better watch out—I'm starting
to like all your corny jokes."

"I'm not afraid, you know." He sat next to her, his
thigh brushing against hers. "Should we talk about last
night?" he asked.

"The kiss?" she asked, moving her leg closer to his.

"Yeah. The kiss. Was it just a kiss, or is there more?"

Bridgette had asked herself that same question more than once. She hadn't come up with an answer, which seemed to be an answer in itself. "I'm glad we've crossed paths again, Luke. You are a sincerely kind person."

"Uh-oh," he said. "Every good friend-zone speech begins with those exact words."

"I'm sorry," she said. "There's too much history between us, and I can't see repeating the same mistakes."

Luke's spine stiffened. He moved his leg and they no longer touched. "A mistake? Is that what I am to you—a freaking mistake?"

Damn. Bridgette's chest contracted.

Then memories of that day returned to her with a clarity that stole her breath. Bridgette was a freshman in college, just nineteen years old, and away from home for the first time in her life. She'd locked herself in one of the stalls of the communal bath and leaned against the metal wall. She stared at the plastic tube in her hand. A *plus* sign appeared in the results window of the pregnancy test.

She didn't need to read the directions. She knew what it meant. She was pregnant with Luke Walker's baby.

She had wrapped the pregnancy test in half a roll of toilet paper and shoved it deep into the garbage can by the door. Her eyes burned. Thank goodness that her roommate was in class. Bridgette couldn't have faced anyone else.

All the same, she couldn't suffer through the moment alone. She had to call, well, someone.

Her mother? Lilly was near to perfect and wouldn't understand how Bridgette—smart as she was—would make such a dumb mistake.

Jordana? Yvette? Sure, her sisters cared, but what could they have done?

Bridgette had known there was really only one person for her to call. Sliding up the face of her phone, she'd typed a series of numbers.

"Hey," said Luke, answering after the second ring. Her chest had hurt, making it hard to breathe. "Bridgette, is that you? Are you there?"

She'd wiped her eyes and put a smile in her voice. "Luke, how are you?"

"Lousy," he'd said. "I'm working, like constantly. You know my dad. He's not feeling too hot and can't work too much. I had to drop out of my intro to engineering class at the community college. This is total crap."

"I'm sorry, Luke. That does sound awful."

"It is." He had paused and huffed a breath. "What's worse, I'm actually worried. What if something's wrong with my dad again, you know?"

"I know," she said. In that moment, Bridgette had made a decision. She wouldn't burden Luke further.

"Did you call for a reason? Or just to chat?"

"Just to chat, I guess."

"Listen, I love the sound of your voice and I miss you, babe. A customer just came in. I gotta blow. Laters."

She never even got a chance to say goodbye. Before

she could speak, the line was dead. Her stomach had contracted, bending her almost double. As the pain ebbed, Bridgette tried to tell herself that it was all a normal part of pregnancy.

Then again, she knew better.

Her period had started later that night.

And she had been left with a single question. *What if I had said something to Luke? Would things have turned out differently?*

Then she was back in the present. He was sitting beside her as the last light of day slipped beyond the horizon.

"Listen, Luke," she began. "I hadn't meant to imply that there's something wrong with you."

He looked over his shoulder, his eyes narrowed. "Did you hear that?"

"No," she said, following his gaze. "Hear what?"

"There's something in the bushes." Luke rose to his feet and walked toward a copse of trees with scrub clinging to the base of their trunks.

"Elves?" she joked. "Or is it a raccoon."

"It definitely sounded like someone walking through the woods. Bigger than a raccoon and more real than an elf."

"This is all private property," said Bridgette. "Nobody else should be out here."

"Key word—*should.* Stay here," he said. "I'm going to check it out."

His sudden alarm left her heart racing. Bridgette stumbled after him. "You aren't going to leave me all by myself."

He paused and worked his jaw back and forth. Bridgette could tell that he wanted to argue. She didn't wait for what he planned to say, and she strode toward the tree line. Luke caught up with her. Grabbing her arm, he pulled back gently. "At least let me go first."

They walked into the woods. The spindly branches of trees rose to a sky of soft blue. Dried leaves covered the ground and crunched with each step taken. As the sun began to set, the air held a chill. "Maybe you just heard the wind in the trees," Bridgette suggested, even though she hadn't recalled a breeze blowing.

"Maybe," said Luke, his tone guarded.

"Well, whatever you heard is obviously gone now."

He turned a slow circle, scanning the forest. "I guess you're right. We should head back."

Side by side, Luke and Bridgette retraced their steps. Her earlier foible sat heavy on her chest. "You aren't a mistake," she said with an exhale. "There are just things that happened between you and me, things that make our past complicated. Do you understand?"

For a long moment, Luke said nothing. Then he grumbled, "Understand? Not at all."

"Can you trust me that we had complications and those scare the hell out of me?"

"Oh, so now I'm a complication?" His tone was as hard as flint.

"No, that's not what I meant, either." They'd returned to the clearing with the bench and the well. "We should just head back to the fishing cabin. If your dad wakes up, he'll wonder where we've gone."

Luke reached for her arm, pulling Bridgette to a

stop. "Not a chance. It sounds like there's something important I need to know—and you haven't told me."

Bridgette shook her head and shrugged off his touch. "Forget I said anything."

"You've dropped more than one cryptic hint, Bridgette. Whatever the problem was, I have a right to know."

"The last time we were together at Lake Kanopolis," she began.

"The night before you went to college, you mean?"

"We, well, had sex."

"I remember that, too."

Bridgette couldn't find the right words. Then again there was nothing complicated about what she needed to say. "I got pregnant."

Luke went pale. "You what?"

"About two months after I went to college, I realized I was pregnant."

"Why in the hell is this the first time I'm hearing about a baby?"

"I called you," she began. "Your father was sick, forcing you to drop out of school. I couldn't add to your concerns. I decided to call you later and then…" Her voice caught with emotion. She shrugged.

"And then," Luke prodded.

"And then." Bridgette's eyes stung with unshed tears. She tried to blink them away, but they slipped down her cheeks. "I lost the baby and there was nothing more to tell."

Luke looked at the ground and shook his head. "I never knew."

"Of course not," said Bridgette, wiping away tears with the side of her sleeve. "I never told you."

"Have you ever told anyone? Or have you been living with this secret your entire life?"

She shrugged again.

"Your sisters?" he asked. "Your mom?"

With a shake of her head, she said, "No, none of them."

"You told your late husband, right?"

For the first time in her life, she realized telling Henry had been a betrayal of Luke. "I'm sorry. I just thought that after the miscarriage there was nothing else to concern you. I know now that I was wrong. I should have said something to you at some time."

Luke stepped toward Bridgette and wrapped his arms around her shoulders. He pulled her to him. She laid her head upon his chest and inhaled. His scent, the sweet smell of fresh-cut lumber and the musky scent of his skin, overwhelmed her senses. His hands rested on the small of her back. Her breasts were pressed against his pecs. To be held by Luke reminded Bridgette of how long she'd gone without the company of a man.

"I'm not mad," he said, his words washing over her.

Lifting her chin, Bridgette looked up at Luke. "What are you, then?"

"Sad, I guess. I wish things would've worked out differently."

In the days and weeks to come, Bridgette wasn't sure how the kiss began. Had she placed her mouth on Luke's first? Or was it the other way around? What she did know was that their lips were pressed together, their tongues in a tangled dance.

He gripped her breast, rubbing his thumb over her nipple. Despite her layers of clothes, she hardened under his touch.

"Oh, Luke," she moaned.

He placed a line of kisses on her throat and she began to burn from within. Desire consumed her. She splayed her hands across his chest, his heartbeat racing beneath her palms. Bridgette reached for the hem of his shirt and pulled it up, exposing a line of his abdomen. She ran her fingers over his flesh.

He gripped her ass, pressing her to him. He was hard and wanted her as much as she wanted him. She lowered her touch, feeling his length through the fabric of his jeans. He let out a low growl.

"You like when I touch you like that?" she asked, nipping his bottom lip with her teeth.

"God, yes," he breathed.

She worked the buttons of his fly loose and reached into his jeans, stroking the silky skin of his sex. It had been so long since she'd touched anyone in an intimate way. For a moment, Bridgette wondered if she'd forgotten how to give—or receive—pleasure. A bead of moisture clung to the head of his penis. She collected it with the tip of her finger and glided her palm down his shaft.

He claimed her mouth with his, and this time the kiss was hard and urgent. "God, you're so sexy and that feels fantastic," he said, grabbing a handful of her hair. "But I want to make you feel good, too."

"I can wait my turn," she said.

"Or we can do this together."

"Out here? In the woods?" She worked her hand up and down his length, and Luke hardened with her touch.

"Who's here to see us?" he asked, unfastening the top button of her pants. He pulled down the zipper and reached into her jeans and then her panties.

Bridgette was already wet, and he slid his finger over the opening of her sex. His touch sent a shock wave of pleasure through her body, and she trembled with desire. "Do you like it when I touch you like that?" he asked, echoing her earlier question.

"Yes," she said. She parted her thighs, giving Luke more access. Bridgette could feel herself slipping away and expanding at the same time. She was becoming one with a feeling as old as time, while experiencing something that was wholly new.

The climax crashed down on Bridgette with the force of an avalanche and left her breathless. How long had it been since a hand other than her own had brought her pleasure? Then again, she knew the answer.

The last time she had been touched was two years ago. For the first time, she no longer needed to cling to the past. The question was—what did Bridgette want to find in her future?

Chapter Fourteen

Luke wanted one thing in the world—to make love to Bridgette Colton. He slipped his finger inside of her. Her muscles clenched and pulsed as the last of the climax rippled through her body. She continued to touch him, working her hand up and down his shaft. The pleasure was exquisite, yet it wasn't enough to satisfy his need.

"I want you," he said, his mouth on hers. "Tell me you want me, too."

"I want you, Luke. I want you inside of me so bad."

It was all the invitation he needed. From his wallet, he took out a condom. Then Luke pulled down his pants, just enough to free himself. As he rolled on the condom, Bridgette kicked off one shoe and stripped out of one leg of her pants.

He sat on the bench. She sank down on Luke, taking him in one stroke. His nuts tightened, warning Luke that he was ready to climax. That wouldn't do. He wanted to take his time with Bridgette, to savor the moment as she rode him.

Long and slow, she moved down and back up, until

just his tip was inside of her. Luke looked to where their bodies met and became one. The tightening in his balls was an excruciating bliss.

Wrapping his hand through her hair, Luke pulled back on her head, exposing her neck and bringing up her breasts. He kissed the skin of her throat while working his hand into her shirt, her bra. He twisted each nipple between his finger and thumb and smiled as she moaned with pleasure. Her strokes became faster, more frantic. Her breathing came in short gasps.

Luke lifted her shirt, exposing her breasts. He took one of Bridgette's nipples in his mouth, rolling it with his tongue. She cried out as she came, and Luke could hold on no longer. A prickling began at the back of his neck, traveling down his spine. It ended with his climax, which came hard and fast. As his pulse slowed and the sweat from his brow dried, Luke gently kissed Bridgette's lips.

"That was magnificent," he said. "You were magnificent."

"You aren't so bad yourself," said Bridgette, nuzzling his neck. "I'd forgotten how good this could be."

Sure, he wondered if Bridgette meant sex in general or, specifically, making love to him. But he knew enough to not ask, to just appreciate the compliment— and the way she fitted perfectly in his arms.

He wound his fingers through hers. "I'm glad we found each other again," he said. "And that you're back home."

"It's just while I complete this investigation. Then I'll go back to Wichita."

Luke had a bad feeling about where Bridgette's head—and heart—might be as far as he was concerned. He swore, if only to himself, that he'd give her all the space she needed and not push for anything more than this moment.

Bridgette wiggled off his lap and sat on the bench. Slipping into her pants, she refastened her jeans and put on her shoe. Retying the laces, she said, "I can't make any promises to you about the future. All I can offer you is the next few weeks, and if that's not enough, well, then…" She let her words unravel the thread that tied his heartstrings together.

"I understand," said Luke, a throbbing in his chest. Hadn't he known from the beginning that any connection with Bridgette was fleeting? Being with her was like holding sand in his grip. The tighter he squeezed, the more of her slipped away.

All the same, he had hoped for a different answer. More than that, he thought the news of the pregnancy lost had brought them closer. Now it seemed as if Bridgette was less accessible than ever.

Then again, he had other more immediate problems. Like what to do with the used condom? Thank goodness he had a few crumpled napkins in his jeans pocket and a plastic bag from the store in his jacket.

Bridgette turned away and gave Luke a moment of privacy while he got cleaned up. Luke stood and shoved the plastic bag deep into the back pocket of his jeans. He'd throw the whole mess away once he got a minute.

Maybe his thoughts about Bridgette were too harsh.

Before making love, he hadn't asked for any promises—and she hadn't given any.

The sky was orange, with pink at the edges. Soon it would be full dark. "We better head back. I'm sure my dad's awake by now."

"And he's worried about us?" Bridgette offered.

They walked away from the bench and the well, their fingers were close but not touching. Luke dared not take Bridgette's hand in his own although he wanted to all the same.

"Dad, worried?" Luke echoed with a chuckle. "I doubt it. I think he's helped himself to the food you brought, and we might not have much left for our own sandwiches by the time we get back."

Bridgette folded her arms over her chest and gave a small laugh, as well.

"Cold?" he asked.

"A little," she said. Luke slipped out of his coat and draped the jacket over her shoulders. "Thanks," she said with a smile.

Luke looked away. There, in the distance, he saw the glint of a light. He stopped. "What's over there?" he asked.

"The woods," said Bridgette.

"No houses? No neighbors?"

"No. The Coltons own acres of this land."

Luke went cold and it wasn't from the chilly night air. He jogged toward the light. Then, unmistakable in the silence of the woods, was the sound of a car's engine revving.

JULIA STARED THROUGH the ocular lens—the binoculars trained on Luke. His lips were pressed together. He scanned the woods. She would have sworn he was too far away to hear when she started the engine.

She'd been wrong.

Dropping her foot on the accelerator, she pulled hard on the steering wheel. The car jostled over the rutted track as the wheels dipped over the lip of a ravine. She slammed her foot on the brake and jerked the gearshift into Reverse. Slowly the car inched backward. She put the auto in Drive and turned the car back toward the road. With the grille finally facing forward, she sped down the bumpy track that wound through the woods. The front fender of her car rose as she crested a hill. For a moment, Julia was suspended in the air, and then the tires slammed down. Julia hit the seat and her teeth cracked.

She pressed her foot onto the accelerator harder. The undercarriage of her car mowed down a small tree. The engine whined as the car shimmied.

Dammit.

Dammit.

Dammit.

What had she broken now? Or maybe the question she should be asking was whether the car was able to get away.

The track leveled off and the shaking stopped. The squealing engine quieted at least a little.

Last night she had told the police officer that she'd never bother Luke or Bridgette again. Certainly, following them to the lake, trespassing while spying on them in the most intimate moment, would be considered bothering.

What did that mean for her? Would the police be waiting when she got home?

Would Julia be sent back to the hospital? Or worse, jail?

The forest thinned and the track widened. Her headlights caught an opening in the tree line and, beyond that, a sliver of road. Turning onto the blacktop, Julia knew that she was out of the woods, at least in the literal sense.

Yet, there would be consequences—horrible costs— for what she had done.

As she drove, her pulse slowed. As the road stretched out like a long, gray ribbon, her mind wandered. She'd been horrified and fascinated as Luke had made love to Bridgette Colton. Lips. Arms. Legs. All tangled together.

In the moment, Julia tried to look away—really, she had. In the end, she was helpless to do anything other than watch.

The sight had sent her pulse racing. As she drove, Julia knew that she'd felt more than lust at the sight; there was rage, as well. The anger began to smolder until it was the white heat of a flame, and Julia knew that someone was about to get burned.

SPRINTING THROUGH THE FOREST, Luke hurtled over a felled tree. His toe caught the decaying wood, breaking it into a thousand splinters. Ducking under a low branch, he pressed forward. Thorny bushes reached out, scratching his face and hands as he ran.

He didn't care.

Someone had been in the woods. He wasn't going to let them escape.

Behind, he heard Bridgette's labored breathing as she struggled to keep up. He pushed his legs to go faster, determined to place himself between her and whatever danger might lie ahead.

The path the car had taken was easy to follow. The tires chewed up the undergrowth and had mowed down dozens of small trees and bushes. He ran up an incline and skidded to a stop. There, in the dying light, lay a dented hubcap.

Bridgette came up a moment later. Gripping her knees, she bent over to catch her breath. "Who was it? Did you see the car?"

With a shake of his head, Luke said, "They're gone now." Sidestepping to the bottom of the hill, he picked up the metal disk. It told him nothing, yet he held it up for Bridgette to see. Continuing, he said, "But whoever it is, they lost this."

Starting up the hill, something else caught his attention. Dropping to a knee, he ran a finger over the damp dirt. Luke rubbed a finger with his thumb. The scent and viscosity were unmistakable. "Motor oil."

"My guess," said Bridgette, from her spot atop the hill. "The car came over this ridge and landed hard. It lost the hubcap and cracked something in the undercarriage." Luke gaped and said nothing. She added,

"Remember, I grew up around a lot of construction sites. And, I am an investigator."

Unable to hold back his smile, Luke said, "I guess you are both. Now let's get out of here. I don't think whoever it was is coming back, but I don't want to hang around and find out if they do."

"Whoever?" asked Bridgette. Luke reached the top of the ridge. "You don't think your ex-girlfriend was spying on us again?"

Luke couldn't lie to Bridgette. "It could be a random person, but I doubt it was anyone other than Julia."

"Which means she saw us while we, well, you know...."

Luke clenched his teeth together. "I should have showed more restraint, Bridgette. I'm sorry that you were put into that situation."

"It's not like you were alone or I didn't have some kind of say in the matter."

"So, you aren't mad?"

"At you?" she asked. Shaking her head, she continued. "Not at all. I am furious with Julia. She's gone too far this time."

Luke said, "I'll call Reese. It'll be easy to see if Julia is missing this hubcap."

"You'll have to wait until we get back to town. There's no cellular coverage at the fishing cabin. Mom's rules, so we can all unplug and connect."

Luke glanced at his phone. "I have three bars," he said.

"Are you joking?" Bridgette asked, looking at his screen. "That's weird. Just don't tell Mom."

He actuated the speaker function before placing the call. Reese answered. "Luke, what's up?"

"It's Julia again." Luke took a few minutes explaining what had happened with the car on the private road, along with the suspicion that it had been Julia. "I found a hubcap," Luke said. "Can you check and see if she's home, and if her wheel's been damaged."

"I'm on it," said Reese. "Did anyone get hurt?"

"Spooked is all," said Luke, leaving out any intimate details of what Julia might've seen.

"I'll get back to you after paying Julia a second visit," said Reese.

"And then what?" Bridgette asked.

"If her car's missing a hubcap, I'll bring her in to the station. If we can prove that it came from her vehicle, she'll be charged with trespassing, vandalism, and several other minor crimes. Hopefully, it's enough to convince your ex that she needs to end her obsession."

"I appreciate anything you can do," said Luke, ending the call. Then to Bridgette, he said, "Now, we have to let the police do their job." He paused. "Speaking of jobs, did you learn anything from my father?"

Luke and Bridgette retraced their steps. The sky was a deep shade of violet, and lights from the Colton fishing cabin shone through the dark.

"Do you remember anything about a flood when we were kids?"

"Sure," he said. "We were in grade school when it happened. I remember helping my dad with one job or another—gutting buildings, hauling away debris."

"It seems like a lot of people were involved in the

cleanup, including several of the other victims. With all the older buildings downtown, it's possible that carcinogens were released into the floodwaters."

"It makes sense."

Bridgette nodded. "And yet, there's something I don't like about that theory. You just said that you were part of a cleanup crew, but you're healthy. If there was something caustic in the water—say arsenic that was used as a wallpaper base—why are there only half a dozen cases from decades ago? I'd expect to see hundreds." She continued, "And it does nothing to explain why there are men who weren't around for the flood and are now getting sick."

Luke didn't have an answer for either of her questions. As they approached the house, his father opened the door. "There you are. When I woke up, you were gone."

"We just went for a walk," said Luke, not willing to share much more with his father.

"What's that you have in your hands?" he asked. "Is that a hubcap?"

Luke opened the rear liftgate and threw the metal disk into his father's SUV. "Just something we picked up in the woods."

"Well, come on in," said Luke's dad. "I saw the sandwich fixings and have nice enough manners to wait for you all."

Bridgette laughed. "Luke said that you'd have eaten everything before we got back."

"Really?" Luke asked with mock indignation. "You're going to throw me under the bus?"

"I'll admit to snacking a little," said Luke's father. "But now that you're here, let's get some food."

Within minutes, everything for a meal had been set on the counter. While throwing away the bag with the condom and cleaning up, Luke took a few moments to think. He'd only been gone from the fishing cabin for an hour—and yet everything had changed.

He'd made love to Bridgette Colton. And there was no denying his feelings to himself—he had come to care for her once again. No, that wasn't true. He'd always cared about her. Yet, did sex mean they had a future together?

Years ago they had created a life. Despite the fact that the pregnancy had ended, Luke liked the idea of Bridgette being the mother to his children.

And then there were other concerns that were far less pleasant.

His ex-girlfriend was more determined than he had ever imagined. Moreover, Bridgette was obviously the target of Julia's wrath.

It meant that Bridgette was in danger, not just now, but until she left Braxville.

Chapter Fifteen

Dinner at the lake house, cleanup and the ride back to Braxville were all uneventful—something that brought Bridgette a great deal of gratitude. Life had been more problematic than ever since returning home. Now Bridgette had to parse out her feelings for Luke.

No, that wasn't true.

She knew how she felt.

What she didn't know was if she wanted to act on those feelings? First, she'd lost a child and then a husband. Was Bridgette ready to try for love again?

At least she had more anecdotal evidence that the cancer had been caused by something in the flood waters. True, there were holes in her theory, but for the moment it was the most solid one that she had.

Since Paul Walker had only worked at the hardware store, he couldn't have been an employee of Colton Construction. It meant that her family's business was in no way connected to the cluster.

She was more relieved about that fact than she cared to admit.

As he had done before, Luke drove his father's SUV.

He returned to Main Street, and from there, Paul would drive himself home.

Bridgette opened the door and slipped out of the large auto. Luke and his father did the same, and they all stood near the grille of the SUV, headlights illuminating the empty road.

Wind swirled around the corner, creating a dust devil of leaves and debris. Bridgette shivered with the cold. "Thank you for taking the time to meet with me," she said. "You've been very helpful."

Paul said, "Getting cancer changed my life. In some ways, I'm a better man because of everything I went through. I appreciate my family and friends more. I look at every day as a gift. But the illness has taken a physical toll." With a shake of his head, he continued, "If you can figure out what caused me to get sick, I'd surely appreciate it."

"I promised your son that I would do just that," she said.

"Well, you kids have a nice evening. Luke, I'll be in touch." As Paul rounded to the driver's side and opened the door, he said, "And, Bridgette, tell your dad I said hello. I kind of miss old Fitz. He used to come by the hardware store back when the construction company wasn't as big as it is now." Before she could comment, Paul continued, "And then there was the time when they renovated the mall downtown. Business was slow at the store, so I worked for your dad on that job. A good man but a hard boss."

Bridgette could not recall getting from the street to Luke's apartment. When she finally became aware of her senses, she stood in the middle of his living room. The light from several lamps filled the room. Her head throbbed with each beat of her heart. She was deaf to every sound beyond her rushing pulse and her own breath.

"What's the matter?" Luke asked. He had ahold of her arm and led her to the sofa, where he gently guided her to sitting. "Should I call someone? Your mom? One of your sisters? A doctor?"

His touch was warm. His hand was strong. She said nothing.

"You okay?" he asked.

Bridgette was far from okay. "Can you turn off one of the lamps?" she asked. "It's too bright in here."

Luke flipped a switch by the door. Two of the lights went dark. "Better?" he asked.

"Much."

"So," he began, taking a seat next to her. "What happened?"

Leaning her head back on the sofa, Bridgette pinched the bridge of her nose. "To be honest, I don't know."

"You were talking to my dad and you turned pale. You were able to walk, when I led you up the stairs. But as the old saying goes, the lights were on, but nobody was home."

"That about sums it up, I guess." Bridgette tried to laugh, but there was nothing funny about her situation. The sound came out as a snort.

"Let me get you a glass of water."

Luke filled a glass with water from the tap. Returning, he set the glass on the coffee table. "Drink," he said.

She lifted the cup with a hand that trembled. Water sloshed over the rim and soaked into the sleeve of her sweater. After taking a sip, she set the glass down. "Better," she said. "Thanks."

"Can you tell me what happened out there now? I still think I should call someone," he said, reaching inside his jacket for his phone.

"Don't," she said, her hand on his wrist. "Your father told me something that was... Oh, I don't know."

"Was it upsetting?" Luke offered.

"I'm not sure what to call how I feel. What's the word for upsetting times a thousand? He gave a bit of information that proves a supposition about the cancer clusters."

"Does it have to do with the flood?"

"No," said Bridgette with a shake of her head.

"What is it then?"

Before she could decide what to share or not, her phone rang. She fished it from her pocket and glanced at the screen. It was her coworker, Rachel. "I have to take this," she said to Luke, while swiping the call open.

"Rachel, what's up?"

"I wanted you to know, I've gotten one of the disks open."

"And?" Bridgette's heart hammered against her chest.

"It looks like the data is password protected. Until we can get around that, we won't be able to access any of the information. I like to think that I can do everything on a computer, but right now I'm stumped." She paused. "My recommendation is that we send the disks to the state IT department. They have tech I don't have at the office."

"You only need a password?" Bridgette asked.

"Finding the right code is a lot harder than *only*."

"I'm on my way," Bridgette said.

"What are you going to be able to do?"

"My mother set up the disks. I might be able to figure out what password she used."

"I'll see you soon."

Bridgette ended the call and rose to her feet. Like she was suddenly standing on the deck of a ship in the middle of a storm, the room seemed to pitch to the side. Her vision darkened at the edges. Luke's strong hand gripped her arm.

"I'm not asking if you're okay again. Obviously, you aren't." He pulled her toward the sofa. "Sit back down."

The floor leveled and Bridgette inhaled, her vision clearing. "I need to go to my office," she said.

"Tonight?"

"Right now."

"I'm not letting you leave until we know what's going on. Your health is more important than your job, Bridgette."

"This from a man who does nothing but work," she said, trying to pull her arm from his grasp. It didn't work.

"If you can make a joke, then I guess you are feeling

a bit better." Luke's grip loosened, but he didn't let go. "Then again, I know how you'll be safe."

"How's that?" she asked.

"I'm going to go with you."

Bridgette didn't have time to argue with him, especially since she suspected that she was suffering from shock. Being escorted by a capable friend made sense.

"All right," she said, acquiescing to his demand. "Let's go."

Luke held Bridgette's arm as they walked down the flight of stairs. Outside, a cool breeze blew droplets of rain. The wind and the water revived her, at least a little, and her thinking cleared.

"My truck is parked behind the store," said Luke. "Let's get it and I'll drive you."

"My office is only a few blocks away. Besides, the walk will do me some good."

"Are you finally going to tell me what's going on?"

"At the very beginning of the investigation, I had a suspicion," she said, walking down the street. "Several of the men who got sick used to work for my father's company. Then the investigative team learned about the flood, and in a way being exposed to carcinogens in dirty water makes perfect sense."

"But then my father mentioned that he worked for Colton Construction," said Luke.

"Moreover, three men from the original cancer cluster not only worked for my dad but on the renovation of the downtown mall, as well."

"And you were kind of traumatized once you put all of those pieces together," said Luke.

"I was able to get all employee information from my mother, who used to be the office manager. The tech was pretty old, so it's taken some time to get the disks open."

"There could be other things that connect all the men in the cluster beyond Colton Construction."

"Thanks for trying to make me feel better," she said as they approached City Hall. At this time of the night the building was locked, and Bridgette swiped her ID over a sensor. The latch clicked and she shouldered the door open. Automatic lights switched on as they walked down the corridor, illuminating their way.

Her office was on the second floor. The door was unlocked, and she walked in. The old boxy computer still filled the conference table. Rachel wore her hair in a ponytail and sat in front of a monitor. Looking up as Bridgette walked in, she gave a wan smile. "That was quick," she said.

"I'm renting an apartment a few blocks away for now." Stepping aside so Luke could enter the small work space, Bridgette continued, "This is Luke Walker." She paused, not entirely sure how to categorize their relationship. "A friend."

"I know you," said Rachel, getting out of the chair and giving Luke a wide smile. "You own the hardware store downtown."

"I do."

Was Rachel flirting with Luke? A hot flash of anger and jealousy sprang up in Bridgette's chest. She immediately tamped it down. She had more pressing worries than her love life.

As she slipped into the seat just vacated by her co-worker, Bridgette's mouth went dry. Was she really about to do this? The screen was gray, with silver lettering. The cursor blinked in a field of lighter gray. Password.

"The key is six characters. It can be numbers, letters, a combination," she said. "Don't worry about locking yourself out. I was able to override that part of the system."

"For my mom," said Bridgette. "Six characters means a date. I'm going to start with the most obvious one first," she continued while typing. "My parents' anniversary."

Six dots appeared, shimmied and disappeared.

Incorrect password.

"My dad's birthday," Bridgette said, entering the date.

Incorrect password.

She tried her mother's birthday, and the birthday of Bridgette and each of her siblings.

The message, *incorrect password*, flashed on the screen again and again.

"Try Colton," Luke said. "That has six letters."

"Good suggestion," said Rachel.

Bridgette turned back to the screen and typed.

Incorrect password.

She used all capital letters. All lowercase letters. Nothing worked.

"It could be random. Or another word. Maybe the name of one of your siblings. Or a pet," said Rachel.

"There are a few things I know about my mother,"

said Bridgette. Lacing her fingers behind her head, she stared at the computer. "The password won't be random, and it'll be related to family. I don't think she'd use a name of one of the kids because she'd feel guilty about the five others who she didn't pick." It gave her an idea and she typed *T-J-B-N-B-Y.* "The first letter for everyone's name," she said, hitting the enter key.

Incorrect password.

"Can you think of anything else?" Luke asked. He leaned forward, his arm grazing her shoulder. An electric charge ran up Bridgette's arm.

"No," she began. "I have one last idea," she said, typing out six numbers. It was the birthdate for her uncle, Shep. "Let's see if it'll work."

The password field disappeared, and for a moment the screen went black.

"What happened?" Bridgette asked. "Did I do something wrong?"

"I don't know," said Rachel. "I'm not used to this operating system. Maybe my override wasn't as secure as I thought."

Then rows of text scrolled up the screen.

"I think we're in," said Rachel.

Bridgette's hands were cold and damp. She pressed her palms into her thighs to keep them from trembling. The text stopped scrolling and a menu of documents filled the screen. She opened one titled Employee Contact Information. There was a list of names, along with dates of employment. Bridgette found the ones she expected to see. Ernest O'Rourke, the foreman. His buddies—Tom Cromwell, Bill Warner. Paul Walker was on the list, having worked for Colton Construction during the mall renovation. Bridgette glanced at the whiteboard and the list of men who were part of the cancer cluster.

One by one, she found them on the official list of past employees.

"Do you know what this means?" Rachel asked.

Bridgette did know and all too well. "Colton Construction is definitely the point of contact for everyone who got sick."

JULIA HAD NO place to go, no safe place to stay. She knew with every beat of her racing heart that Luke had called the police. The cops would be waiting at her home, ready to cart her off to jail.

What would she say?

How could she defend against what she'd done?

She'd die before being locked up again.

If that were the case, why couldn't she leave Luke alone?

She drove, without destination, as images from the woods played over and over in her mind. This time, it was Julia who straddled Luke.

Why hadn't he made love to Julia? Or even kissed her for that matter? Did he think she was too pure?

Luke was her soul mate. They were destined to be together. Julia had to make him see that truth.

But how?

A sensor sounded.

Ding. Ding. Ding.

Damn. The gas gauge leaned lethargically to the

side. Empty. Julia knew that the time had come, and she turned for home. Maneuvering the car onto her street, she held her breath. Where Julia expected to see a police cruiser, there was nothing.

Pulling into the driveway, she turned off the ignition and stepped from the car. Her eyes burned from staring at the road, and her hands ached from gripping the steering wheel. She stood and her knees creaked like the hinges of a long-neglected door. She hobbled up the walkway, not sure why her house looked different. She tried to put the key into the lock, and the teeth scraped against metal.

Why hadn't her mother turned on the lights? Was something wrong with Momma?

Her pulse began to hammer against her ribs as a million awful thoughts filled her mind at once. She fumbled with the key, dropped it. With a curse, she knelt on the darkened concrete and blindly groped for the key.

Her fingers brushed against the cold metal. She stood and tried once more. This time, the key slid home and she turned the handle, opening the door.

The TV in the living room was dark. A single light, above the stove, blazed in the kitchen. No savory aromas wafted through the house.

"Momma?" Julia called out.

Nothing.

The house was dark and cold as a tomb.

"Momma?" she said, louder this time.

Nothing.

Rushing to her mother's bedroom, Julia opened the door and flipped on the overhead light. The bed was made. A set of pajamas was laid out across the pillows. Tears stung Julia's eyes as she rushed to the adjacent bathroom.

Empty.

The hall bath was empty, as well.

In each room, Julia turned on lights, calling out her single word. "Momma?"

"Momma?"

"Momma?"

The metallic taste of panic coated her tongue. Her legs were heavy, her arms were limp.

She couldn't fall apart, not when her mother needed her. What Julia had to do was think. Dammit, think.

What facts did she know? Her mother wasn't home. Her mother couldn't drive. She didn't visit neighbors. Aside from Julia, Momma really didn't have much except church on Sunday.

Had the ladies from church stopped by to collect Julia's mother? Was she right now in the church hall, eating cookies and drinking punch? If that was the case, why hadn't her mother left a note?

Maybe the plans had been made earlier? Had Momma told Julia, who then had forgotten?

There was nothing to be done beyond go to church and check for herself.

She strode toward the door. Passing the hall bath, Julia caught a glimpse of herself in the mirror.

Mud was smeared across her cheek. A dried leaf clung to her hair. There was a stain on her rumpled shirt, along with a rip on the knee of her pants from a tumble that Julia didn't recall taking. She needed to find her mother, but first she'd get cleaned up and change.

Pivoting, she raced to her room. Pushing the door open, Julia stopped on the threshold and sucked in a breath.

There, sitting in her wheelchair, was her mother.

"Momma, there you are. Thank goodness you're okay."

Nothing.

"Did you hear me calling for you? I was really worried that something bad had happened to you."

Nothing.

Her mother worked her jaws back and forth. Her eyes were red rimmed and watery. It was then that Julia noticed other details.

First, her walls were stripped bare.

Every picture of Luke was gone. The tickets from the movie they'd seen had disappeared. The napkins were gone.

Julia's small metal wastepaper basket sat in front of her mother. In one of her mother's hands was a bottle of rubbing alcohol. In the other, a box of matches.

"You promised to leave Luke Walker alone," her mother said.

"I did," said Julia, stepping forward and peering into the garbage can. Every bit of the shrine she'd built was inside. "I have."

"That nice policeman stopped by today," her mother said. The temperature in the room seemed to plummet and Julia began to shiver.

"What'd he say?" she asked, her voice shaking.

"He wanted to know where you were. He was wondering because someone was trespassing out by the Coltons' fishing cabin today."

"I can explain, Momma," she began.

"I'm done with your lies." With a shake of her head, Julia's mother dumped the entire bottle of rubbing alcohol into the waste basket. She struck a match, the scent of sulfur dioxide hung in the air. Her mother let go of the lit match. It tumbled end over end, the flames blue and orange, until it landed in the can.

Whoosh. Flames consumed every memory, every moment spent with Luke.

"Mother," Julia screamed. "What have you done?"

"I'm giving you a clean slate," said her mother. "You need to get over this obsession. You're clinging to a relationship that isn't rooted in reality. It's just like before, but I'm not going to let you go on any longer."

Julia reached for the can. The metal was hot and burned her skin. She screamed, jerking her hand back and tipping the can over. Sparks struck her mother's pants. The cloth immediately caught fire.

"Julia," her mother yelled. "Help me."

She lunged forward, ready to grab a blanket and smother out the flames.

Then she stopped.

"Why should I?" Julia asked, her jaw tight. "You were the one who started the fire. Now, you can burn in hell."

Chapter Sixteen

Cold wind whipped around the corner. Bridgette wished she'd worn something warmer than a sweater and jeans. Folding her arms across her chest, she walked faster, wanting nothing more than a hot cup of tea and a night in her own bed.

"Penny for your thoughts?" Luke asked, opening the door that led to the apartments above the hardware store.

"I need about a million dollars' worth of answers," she said. "I can't ignore the connection between Colton Construction and the cancer cases. But what I don't know is what I need to do next."

"We," he said. "What we need to do next."

They'd reached the landing and stood between the two doors. "This is my job and my responsibility," she said. "It's my family. I have to take care of the problem."

Luke nodded, although she wasn't sure that he was agreeing or simply acquiescing.

Bridgette continued, "I just don't know how."

"This can't be the first time you've found a connection between a business and an illness."

"It's not," she said. They were inside. The wind no longer blew, yet Bridgette still shivered and her voice trembled.

"What did you do then?" he asked.

She hesitated a moment, drawing in her arms closer to her chest. "I closed down the business. It's a matter of public safety."

He said nothing. Then again, what was there to say?

"I should go," she said at length, turning for the door to the apartment she had rented.

Reaching for her hand, Luke pulled her to a stop. "The window hasn't been fixed yet," he said. "And we have every reason to believe that Julia was spying on us in the woods."

"I know what you're implying, that I can't stay alone," she said. "Don't worry about me. I'll be fine."

Luke shook his head. "Fine isn't good enough for me."

He still held her hand. His flesh was warm. His grip was strong. She recalled the feel of his palms as they had skimmed her body. His mouth on hers. The waves of pleasure that moved through her body as she came.

"I'm a big girl," she said, letting her fingers slip through his grip.

"I know just what kind of girl you are," he said, stepping toward her. "I know you are capable, smart—and sexy as hell. But here, in my house, it's my job to protect you."

Bridgette swallowed, trying to think of something to

say. She was saved by the trilling of Luke's cell phone. He removed the phone from his pocket and glanced at the screen. Brows drawn together, he swiped the call open. "Yes?"

Bridgette was less than a foot away from Luke. In the small space she could hear everything the caller said. "This is Nancy, Julia's mother."

"Why are you calling from the hospital?" he asked. "Is everything okay?"

"There was an accident—and a fire," the woman said. To Bridgette, the older woman sounded weary and worried.

"Did Julia have anything to do with either?" Luke asked.

"Just tell me," said the woman. "Have you seen her? Has she tried to contact you?"

To Bridgette, the non-answer was answer enough. What had Julia done to her mother?

Nancy continued, "I just want to know that she's safe."

"If I see her at all," said Luke. "I'll call Detective Carpenter. But what about you?"

"The doctors are taking care of me now. I'll be spending the next few nights with a friend from church." Julia's mother paused. "My daughter's not a bad person. She just gets these ideas and can't let them go, that's all."

"I'll call if I see or hear anything," said Luke, and he ended the call. Then to Bridgette he said, "That was Julia's mother."

"I heard everything."

"I know you want to be independent. I also know that I'm not letting you stay by yourself, not with Julia out there—" he gestured to the locked door at the bottom of the stairs " —somewhere."

Bridgette shook her head. "Running to someone who can keep me safe feels like giving up. Then it means that Julia has disrupted my life and won."

"If she hurts you," he said, "she's won as well." He opened the door to his apartment. "Let's finish this conversation inside."

When was the last time someone had cared about her well-being, much less insisted that they keep her safe? "I'm sure the police will find Julia soon. But I'll stay with you tonight."

"With me?" he asked, his voice low as they crossed the threshold and Luke closed the door behind them.

Bridgette had meant that she'd sleep on the sofa. But the frantic sex in the woods hadn't sated her desires as she hoped. In fact, taking Luke as a lover had awakened longings that Bridgette had tried to bury with her late husband.

"Would that be so bad?" she asked, casting a glance at the window. The shades had already been drawn and there was no chance that they might be seen from the street below. Continuing, she reached for his hand and ran a finger over his wrist. "Would you mind terribly?"

Whatever she was about to say next was cut short. Luke reached for Bridgette, pulling her to him. Her breasts were pressed against his chest. She wrapped her arms around his neck, running her fingers through his hair and pulling him closer.

He was already hard, and her pulse began to race. She wanted—no, needed—Luke inside her.

Bridgette splayed her hands across his chest. His heartbeat resonated under her palms. She rocked her hips forward, savoring the feel of his length. She wasn't so stupid as to think that having sex for a second time in a single day wouldn't deepen their relationship. And Bridgette didn't know what she wanted from Luke, or life—beyond the moment.

Was it fair to him—and to her?

Did she care?

His mouth moved to her throat. His kisses were hot and ignited a fire inside of her. Bridgette moaned.

Luke claimed her mouth with his. She closed her eyes and let the kiss take away all her worries.

His touch was no longer making up for time lost or regret for the past. Now it was all about dominance and surrender.

Luke lifted Bridgette's shirt, exposing her flesh, and brought it over her breasts. He bent his head to her chest, running his tongue between her cleavage. He pulled one breast free from her bra's cup and scraped his teeth over her nipple.

The sensation sent a shock wave of pain and pleasure rippling through Bridgette. She looked down to her own body. Her skin was slick and wet. Her nipple was pink and hard. Luke's tongue swept over her breast and Bridgette's knees went weak with desire.

"Take me," she said.

Flicking his tongue over her breast once more, Luke smiled. "I will, just not now."3 As he spoke, he worked his fingers down the front of her pants and into her panties. A second finger joined the first, and she opened herself up to take him in all the way. He continued, his blue eyes locked with hers. "Earlier, we were rushed. Now, I intend to take my time."

Time? Bridgette felt as if she were a ticking bomb, and without Luke she might explode. He continued to work his fingers inside of her, her muscles clenched as he rubbed the top of her sex. Her climax came quickly and left her breathless. She clung to his shoulders as her heartbeat slowed.

"Kiss me," she whispered.

He placed his mouth on hers as he slipped his hands from her pants. He painted Bridgette's lips, still wet with her musk.

Bridgette circled her tongue around one finger and then the other. She took him in her mouth and sucked. He growled with pleasure.

His gaze met hers, and Bridgette's heart began to thunder in her chest. Luke kissed her once more before tugging on the hem of her shirt and pulling it over her head. He opened the clasp on her bra. The straps slid down her arms and the undergarment dropped to the floor. It landed on top of her shirt. With his lips pressed to her lobe, he whispered, "Take off your pants."

His words danced along her skin until gooseflesh covered her skin, his eyes so intense she could do nothing beyond obey. She stripped until clad only in her panties.

Bridgette wasn't embarrassed by her body. Sure, she could spend a few more hours at the gym, but she knew that her long legs were strong. Her rear was tight—for the most part.

Yet, standing in the middle of the room, naked except for a pair of underwear—with a crotch that was wet from her orgasm—left Bridgette shifting her weight from one bare foot to the other.

"God, you're beautiful," said Luke. "I could look at you all day."

As he watched her, she studied Luke in return. His shoulders were broad. The beginning of a beard covered his cheeks and chin. The fly of his jeans was stretched tight over his erection. She dropped her gaze.

"Look at me," he said again. She lifted her eyes. "Are you uncomfortable being watched?"

Bridgette flipped a lock of hair over her shoulder. "No."

Luke gave a small smile. "Are you lying?"

She shrugged. "I'm not sure."

"I've thought about you over the years," he said. "My fantasies always started out the same. You are standing about where you are now, wearing nothing but your panties."

Running a finger from her throat, between her breasts, she asked, "What else do I do when you think about me?"

"Touch yourself," he said.

Bridgette cupped her own breast, feeling the weight in the palm of her hand. She stroked her thumb over her nipple. In the two years since being a widow, Bridgette had touched herself more than once, yet that was always the most private of moments. What was she willing to do with Luke watching?

Then again, didn't she want to be a fantasy made into reality?

"Like this?" she asked.

"Like that," he said.

She moved her hand lower, skimming her palm over her abdomen and sliding a finger under the fabric of her panties. Her sex was swollen, and the slightest touch sent a surge through her body. She rubbed, unable to control the sensation that built and grew. Closing her eyes, she moaned.

"Look at me," he said, his voice not much more than a whisper.

Bridgette opened her eyes and met Luke's gaze.

"Come here," he said, gesturing to the sofa.

She walked to the edge of the couch.

"Sit," he said. "And spread your thighs."

She did his bidding, light-headed with lust and the game they were playing. Luke knelt on the floor, between her legs, and stroked Bridgette's thighs. His touch was torture—she wanted more of him, needed more.

She fondled her breasts, flicking a thumb over each nipple.

"Don't look away," he said. His breath warmed her core. "I always want you watching."

"Always," she whispered back, as he pulled aside her panties and placed his mouth on her.

BRIDGETTE SQUIRMED BENEATH Luke's mouth. She wanted to close her eyes and just feel the rush of sensations. But she kept her gaze trained on his eyes as he worked his tongue over her sex and used his fingers inside of her.

In that moment, she left her body, unable to distinguish between her physical self and emotions. She rose higher and higher, leaving the apartment and Braxville and the whole state of Kansas behind. Still, Luke was always there—always watching. His blue eyes became her North Star as she exploded, shattering into a thousand pieces.

Gulping deep breaths, she re-formed into something—someone—brand-new. As if being loved by Luke Walker had rearranged her somehow. She had little time to wonder how. He stood, his gaze never wavering from hers and stripped out of his shirt. Next came his pants—his sex was hard. He rolled a condom down his length and positioned himself over Bridgette.

She tilted her hips, and he entered her slowly. She gasped with pleasure as he withdrew with the same deliberate movements, until just his tip remained inside. Bridgette gripped his ass, urging him to go deeper, harder, faster. She looked down to the point where they joined. Him, inside of her.

They were separate but fitted together perfectly.

"Look at me," he said.

Bridgette was transfixed with the sexes joined and she dragged her eyes away. "Why?"

Luke drove into her hard. "I never want you to think of anyone other than me when we're together," he said, slowing his strokes. "For years, I've wondered about you. If you're happy or sad. If you've seen the latest movie—and what you thought about it."

Bridgett reached up and stroked his face.

"Tonight is about more than making fantasies become real. Tonight is about claiming you as mine—even if it's just for a few hours."

Luke's breathing increased. His strokes became harder and faster. Bridgette didn't know that it was possible, but she felt another climax building, a storm gathering in her belly. She cried out with her passion a moment before Luke threw back his head and growled.

For a moment, they stayed on the edge of the sofa, covered in sweat and panting. As Bridgette's pulse slowed, she moved out from under Luke. "That was amazing," she said.

"I've said this before, but I'll say it again," said Luke. "I'm glad you're back home." He stood. "I gotta take care of the condom. Stay where you are."

Bridgette took advantage of the moment alone and redressed in her panties and Luke's flannel shirt. She stretched out on the sofa. For the first time, she noticed that the apartment was chilly. A blanket was draped over the back of the couch and she pulled it over her shoulders and legs.

For a moment, she stared at nothing.

Hadn't she vowed not to get involved in life in Braxville? Wasn't she just back for a few weeks to do her job? Her family's involvement in the cancer cases was a problem she hadn't anticipated.

And what about Luke?

And as sleep came to claim Bridgette, even she had to admit that Luke Walker would be an easy man to fall in love with for a second time.

Chapter Seventeen

Bridgette woke, warm and with a feeling of being safe, cherished and loved. For years it was how she began each day—waking in the arms of her husband, Henry. For a moment that reality was as thin as a thread, and she felt as if her husband were still alive. Then the thread snapped, and she lost him all over again. A boulder of grief pressed down on her chest and her eyes burned, filling with tears.

Tears leaked down the side of her face, wetting her hair. Bridgette knew that her first thought upon waking had been right—she was safe and, well, at least cherished. She had fallen asleep on Luke Walker's sofa, and he had joined her. In fact, he slept beside her now, with his arm over her waist.

He was warm and solid. His light snores relaxed away all her tension.

Yet, an ache remained in her chest—the exact spot that hurt every time Henry came to mind. But this time, the pain was bearable. As if maybe—just maybe—the worst of her grief was in the past.

And if that were the case, did she dare to hope for a future?

Luke stirred and drew a deep breath.

"Good morning," he said, placing a kiss on her shoulder.

Bridgette snuggled deeper into his embrace. "Good morning," she said, memories of their lovemaking surrounding her like a fog.

"You looked so peaceful last night, I decided to join you out here."

"I don't mind," she said. "I miss waking up next to someone." She turned to face him and placed her hand on his cheek. "This was nice."

"So, I was thinking that we should spend today here," he said.

"On the sofa?" she asked, teasing.

"If you want…" he began. "Or we can move to the bedroom. Or the shower."

For the span of a heartbeat, she thought about ignoring her job and her duty. She couldn't. Stifling a curse, she sat up. "I can't."

"Can't what?"

"I can't just spend the day with you," she said, rising from the sofa. Her clothes lay across the floor. Stepping into her pants, she continued, "I need to talk to my father about how Colton Construction is the cluster's point of origin." Bridgette paused. "I should probably call Elise Willis, as well."

"The mayor?" Luke sat up. The blanket fell to his lap, revealing his chiseled chest. Bridgette's mouth went dry and she looked away, searching for her socks.

"Why do you want to talk to the mayor?" Luke asked.

"Colton Construction is one of Braxville's major employers. Aside from the economic impact on the town, we very well could have a health crisis."

Luke scratched his chin. "I hadn't thought about the economic impact." He shook his head. "It's hard to imagine folks wanting to visit Braxville if they're going to be exposed to toxins."

"Then you aren't going to like my second concern any more," she said. "All the men who got sick worked at the mall renovation. There's evidence that the carcinogens might be there instead of with the construction company. Elise and I need to discuss if it can safely remain open."

"Shut down the mall before the Boo-fest?" asked Luke. His voice rose an octave. "How is that supposed to make the town look?"

"Responsible," Bridgette snapped. Fully dressed, she grabbed her bag from the coffee table and found her phone. "I'm going to send Elise a text and see when she's available."

After pulling up Elise's contact, Bridgette sent a short message.

I know it's early, Bridgette typed. But we need to meet—today if possible. Important.

Elise replied immediately. I heard you were back in town. Is there something wrong with Neil?

More than being the mayor of Braxville, Elise was also the ex-wife of Bridgette's brother. Bridgette should have anticipated the question. She replied with two words. Work related.

The reply came in seconds. My office in an hour?

It gave Bridgette plenty of time to get ready and collect her data. See you then.

"What'd she say?" asked Luke. Clad only in his boxer shorts, he rose from the sofa.

"I'm meeting her at City Hall in an hour."

"Correction. We're meeting her," said Luke.

"I understand that you're concerned since your father's now part of the cancer cluster. I can't allow family members to be part of the investigation."

"If that's what you think," he said, "then you don't understand at all." Before she could comment, Luke continued. "Julia is still out there, somewhere. Because of me—and our involvement—you're a target for her anger." He paused. "I have no idea what she might do next. Either way, it's my job to keep you safe. Until she's found and getting the help she needs, I'm your new shadow."

IN LESS THAN an hour, Bridgette was headed to City Hall. As promised, Luke Walker came with her. As always, he wore a flannel shirt and a pair of jeans. It was perfect for the crisp fall weather, and Bridgette had selected an aqua-colored sweater, jeans and boots.

It was Sunday, which in Braxville, meant that none of the businesses were open except the coffee shop. Occasionally, a car drove past. Otherwise, the downtown area was empty and silent.

"I'd forgotten how nice the slower pace of a small town can be," said Bridgette. "In Wichita, there's always busyness and noise. You have to drive anywhere you want to go." She drew in a breath of cool air. "Like I said, this is nice."

Luke hummed an agreement and said nothing more.

She wondered what had him preoccupied, but she had concerns of her own.

A single metal door bisected the back wall of City Hall. Bridgette used her keycard to open the automatic lock. The door clicked and she pushed on the handle.

Without comment, they rode the elevator to the third—and top—floor. The mayor's suite took up a quarter of the story. Elise's personal office overlooked the town park. There was a large wooden desk, along with a bookshelf in the corner. There was also a wine-colored velvet sofa and a matching set of chairs.

"It's good to see you," said Elise, giving Bridgette a quick hug. Elise wore jeans and a button-down blouse. Her dark blonde hair had been pulled into a low po-nytail. The mayor looked like she always did—smart, competent, and ready to work for the betterment of the community. "And you, too, Luke." He got a hug, as well. "I have to admit, I was surprised to see your text. You said it's important and work related."

"I recognize this," said Bridgette, running her hand over the sofa's arm.

"You should," said Elise. "Your mother gave me all of this furniture when she redecorated a few years ago." She paused. "Now, have a seat and tell me why you're here."

Bridgette dropped onto the sofa and Luke took a seat in one of the chairs. Elise leaned her hip on the corner of her desk and faced them both. "I'm actually here because of my parents," Bridgette began.

Drawing her brows together, Elise said, "I thought this was business related."

"It is," said Bridgette. "The Kansas State Department of Health has assigned me to investigate a cancer cluster in Braxville."

"I've been briefed."

"Then you know that I'm in charge of the investigation."

Elise nodded. "Have you learned anything?"

"Unfortunately, I have." For a beat, she was at a loss for what to say. "Every one of the cancer victims worked for Colton Construction."

Elise sucked in a breath and leaned back. "Are you sure?"

Bridgette had a file with copies of all her paperwork. "I'm positive," she said, holding out the folder to Elise.

For several minutes, the mayor flipped through the pages without comment. Closing the file, she shook her head. "What do you do next?"

"I have no choice. Colton Construction needs to be closed down," she said, her chest tightening with each word. "We should consider closing down the mall, as well."

"It will devastate the local businesses if people are worried that they might get sick by going downtown," said Luke. It was the first opinion he'd offered since they'd arrived.

"They should be worried," said Bridgette.

"As far as I'm concerned," said Elise, "public safety is my top concern."

"If there is something in the mall that's making people sick," Luke began, "why are there only a dozen cases of cancer?"

"What do you mean?" asked Elise. "I thought we'd be happy with just a few cases and not a town epidemic."

"I know what he's getting at," said Bridgette. "Hundreds of people go through the mall each day. Thousands in a week. People work there, spending hours of their day. If that's the case, why would only twelve of them get sick over a span of two decades?"

"Exactly," said Luke.

"For now," said Bridgette, a headache forming behind her eyes, "we'll test air and water quality in the mall. Until we have results, it can stay open. But if there are issues, I have the authority to close down the facility and I'll use it. No questions asked. Agreed?"

Luke nodded. "Agreed."

Elise asked, "What are you going to do about Colton Construction?"

"There's a strong connection to the cancer cases. Until I know that the office compound is safe, I have to close them down and start testing," said Bridgette. "I'm going to visit my dad as soon as we're done here."

"Shouldn't someone else make that visit?" Elise asked.

"No," said Bridgette. "This is my investigation. This is my demand. I'm not putting that responsibility onto anyone else."

"It's also your family and could cause a real dispute between you and your parents." Elise paused. "And there's another problem I can see."

"Which is?" Bridgette asked, her headache intensifying with each beat of her heart.

"If Colton Construction is absolved of culpability in the end, the investigation could look like a sham because you are in charge."

Jaw tight, Bridgette said, "I'm a professional. I can handle it."

"Like you said, it's your decision." Holding out the file Bridgette had brought, she continued, "You'll keep me apprised of any findings?"

Rising to her feet, Bridgette took the folder. "I will, and thanks for meeting with me, Elise. It's good to see you."

"You, too." Elise opened her mouth, seeming to consider what to say next. With a shake of her head, the mayor snapped her jaw shut.

"What did you want to say?" asked Bridgette.

Elise said, "It's nothing."

"It's obviously something. We need to be able to communicate to make it through this investigation. Please, ask me anything."

Elise folded her arms. "How's Neil? I haven't heard from him in a while and, well, I was just wondering."

"I saw him on Friday," said Bridgette. "He was in good spirits. Should I let him know that you asked about him?"

Elise chewed on her bottom lip. "No," she said after a beat. "I'm happy he's doing well."

The conversation wrapped up quickly. Luke and Bridgette left City Hall, and within minutes they were walking down Main Street. "I hate to impose," said Bridgette. "I need a ride to my dad's office. My car was towed yesterday and won't be ready until tomorrow."

"I meant what I said earlier. Until the police find Julia, I'm your shadow." Luke shoved his hand into the pockets of his jeans as he walked. "Why go to your dad's office? It's Sunday morning. Won't he be at home?"

Bridgette shook her head. "Ever since I can remember, Dad's gone to work on Sunday mornings. He says he gets more done if the office is empty."

Luke nodded and they continued to walk. "Are you okay with all of this?" he asked.

Bridgette didn't need him to explain what *all of this* meant. She knew. Moreover, she'd been asking herself the same question.

Could she really be an impartial investigator?

Running Colton Construction was more than her father's job. It was her family's legacy. In a way, the company defined who Bridgette was or, at least, who she had been.

They were at Luke's truck and he unlocked the passenger door before pulling it open. "I'm not sure I'm okay with anything right now," Bridgette said, her tone more resolute than her heart. "But I do know that I have a job to do—and I intend to do it."

DRIVING ON FUMES, Julia had left her house in the middle of the night and parked at the back of an abandoned warehouse more than a mile outside of town. From there, she began to walk, terror dogging each step.

Julia was terrified that she'd killed her own mother. Terrified that every passing minute brought her closer to being arrested by the police. Terrified that she'd spend the rest of her life locked up—either in jail or a hospital.

After more than an hour of walking, she realized that her feet had taken her someplace safe. Colton Construction.

Julia had a key to an annex building where the mail was sorted and office supplies were kept. There was a sofa in the room, a coffeemaker and, most important, heat. Despite her constant movement, her hands had turned white with cold and her face was numb.

It was on that same sofa and in that same room that Julia jerked awake. For a moment, she sat up, blinking. Morning sun streamed through the slats of metal blinds. A cup of coffee sat on the floor, a film of creamer floating atop the mud-brown liquid.

Casting a weary gaze around the room, Julia wondered what had woken her suddenly. She heard the low rumble of an engine. Someone had come. But who? Was it the police? Tiptoeing to the window, she pulled aside the blinds and peered into the parking lot.

Dazed, she stumbled back.

Bridgette and Luke, here?

How had they found her?

Sure, there were security cameras on the property. It's just that Julia thought she had avoided them all.

Scanning the room, her heart hammered against her

chest—a wild animal trying to break free. There was no way to fight, no way to escape, nothing for her to do beyond give up.

Yet, giving up was something that Julia refused to do.

FITZ COLTON HAD been true to his habits. Aside from Luke's truck, there was only one other vehicle in the parking lot of Colton Construction—the gleaming, white pickup belonging to her father.

"Looks like he's here," said Luke.

Dry-eyed, Bridgette stared out of the window and nodded. "There are two things I value the most," she said. Looking over her shoulder, her gaze met Luke's. "My family and my professionalism. I just never imagined having to choose one over the other."

Luke put the gearshift into Park and turned off the ignition. "You could still have someone else speak to your father. Elise? Somebody from the Kansas Department of Health?"

"I can't shirk my responsibilities," she said. "Shutting down Colton Construction for testing will make my father mad." She paused, knowing that her projection wasn't quite right. She corrected herself, "He'll be humiliated. It's better if the news comes from me."

Luke removed the key. "You know your dad. You may very well be right."

"Besides, he'll want to know what's made everyone sick."

Luke nodded. "You could be right about that, too." Yet, his tone told Bridgette that he thought she was definitely wrong. After a beat, he added, "If you'd rather that I stay in the truck and wait, I can."

"No," she said, maybe a bit too quickly. "I'd like it if you came with me."

Luke nodded. "Are you ready?"

"No," she said. "But let's go."

Bridgette and Luke crossed the parking lot. The main entrance was closed and locked, but as Bridgette and Luke approached, her father opened the door. He was dressed in a dark blue golf shirt, with the Colton Construction logo embroidered on the chest and a pair of jeans.

"Morning," he said, pausing on the threshold. "I saw you on the security camera as you drove up. It's a pleasant surprise to have you drop by and see me."

"Daddy," said Bridgette, her voice small. She held the folder out to her father and continued. "We need to talk."

Her father stepped forward. The door closed and the lock clicked. Taking the file, he drew his brows together and flipped through the pages. "Where'd you get these documents?" he asked, his tone hard.

"Mom had an old box with disks. She gave them to me."

He held out the folder. "It's sad that so many folks in town have gotten ill."

"Daddy, it's not just people in town. It's people who worked for you. Colton Construction is the common thread between the men and their illness." She drew in a shaking breath. "They all worked at the mall renovation, too."

He held the file out farther, implying that if she took the folder all of this would simply go away. Bridgette forced her hands to stay at her sides.

With a shake of his head, her father sighed. "Like I said, it's sad."

Bridgette's pulse raced until it echoed in her ears. "More testing has to be done," she said. "For now, the mall will stay open. I've already talked to Elise."

"Elise Willis?" her father spit. "You talked to her? Really? Why?"

"She's the mayor, and it's her job to protect the public's safety." Another breath. "Colton Construction has to be closed down for testing."

"Closed down? To hell with that plan. Elise hates our family, you know. Your brother Neil, most of all. She'd do anything to get under his skin—including this." He shook the file like an accusatory finger.

"It's not Elise's decision." After folding her arms across her chest, Bridgette met her father's glare. "It's mine."

Her father let out a bark of a laugh. "You had me going for a minute. All this paperwork looks legitimate."

"It's no joke, Daddy. There's something that's making people sick—really sick. It's my job to find out what's wrong and fix it. Until then, this property isn't safe."

"Your job?" Her father's face grew red. A vein appeared on his forehead and began to throb. "What is your job when compared to your family?"

"You need to know what's happening to your employees," Bridgette began. "These folks are your responsibility."

"Don't tell me what I need, missy." Rivulets of sweat ran down her father's face. "I'm your father, dammit. I provided you with that fancy college degree so you could, what? Turn around and use it on me the first chance you get?"

"Mr. Colton," said Luke. "I don't think that Bridgette is being disloyal. What we all want is to find the truth."

With a grimace, he said, "I just want every damn one of you to stop telling me what I want and if you try to close down my business, I'll sue."

"Daddy," said Bridgette. "Be reasonable. We just need to run some tests."

Whatever else she planned to say was forgotten. Her father gripped his shoulder and fell to his knees before toppling, face-first, onto the ground.

Chapter Eighteen

"Daddy!" Bridgette dove for her father.

Luke was right behind her. "Can you hear me, Mr. Colton."

The older man's complexion was red. Sweat streamed down his face, dampening his shirt. "I'm fine," he said, struggling to sit up. "I just got light-headed."

Luke knelt at Fitz's side and pushed his shoulder back down. "Don't try to get up. I'm concerned you're having a heart attack," he said. "Do you take any medications for chest pain?"

With a shake of his head, Mr. Colton said, "No."

To Bridgette, Luke said, "In the glove box of my truck, there's a first-aid kit with aspirin inside. Go and get it."

She returned a moment later, first-aid kit in hand. Luke had already dialed 9-1-1. As she found the foil packet of aspirin, the ambulance was dispatched to their location.

"Here, Daddy," Bridgette said, handing her father

two white pills. "You're supposed to chew and swallow these, okay."

Fitz Colton popped the medication in his mouth and began to chew. "They taste like garbage."

"Hopefully, they'll protect your heart," said Luke.

The color in the older man's face had turned from bright red to chalky white. In the distance, the ambulance's siren could be heard.

"Hear that, Daddy? Help's on the way."

Fitz Colton reached for his daughter's hand. "Call your mother and tell her what happened. Can you do that for me?"

"Of course," said Bridgette.

The ambulance sped into the parking lot and stopped next to the front doors. An EMT with a medical kit jumped from the passenger seat. The driver rushed from the front of the vehicle and pulled a stretcher from the ambulance's rear.

"Excuse us," said one of the EMTs, shouldering Bridgette aside.

As the paramedics began to work on Fitz, Bridgette moved to the edge of the sidewalk. Luke followed.

Rubbing her brow, Bridgette said, "I can't believe that I gave my father a heart attack. How can I live with myself if anything happens to him?"

"Hey," said Luke, resting his hands on her shoulders. "You didn't cause anything to happen."

"How can you say that?" She shrugged, trying to rid herself of his touch. Luke tightened his grip. She continued, "You saw how upset he got when I told him it was my decision to close down Colton Construction for testing."

"If your father had had a heart attack, it was bound to happen. If we hadn't been here, there's no telling how things would have turned out."

"I need to call my mother," she said.

"You don't believe me, do you."

"I don't know what to believe," Bridgette said.

Luke let his hands slip down her arms. "Fair enough."

He stepped aside, giving Bridgette a private moment to speak to her mother. As she ended the call, one of the EMTs approached. "We're taking your father to the hospital for an evaluation."

"We'll be right behind you," said Luke.

They jogged to the truck as the ambulance's lights began to strobe. Bridgette slipped into the passenger seat. "Thank you for taking me to the hospital," she said.

"You don't need to thank me, you know that."

"It seems that I'm turning out to be more trouble than I'm worth."

Putting the gearshift into Drive, Luke maneuvered the truck out of the parking lot and followed the ambulance. "You aren't any trouble at all," he said, knowing that he was dangerously close to losing his heart to her—a woman from his past who didn't want to be a part of his future.

BRIDGETTE COULD NOT recall a worse day since her husband, Henry, had died in a car crash. In fact, it was all too familiar. The quiet corridors of the hospital. Worry, a hard kernel, took root in the pit of her stomach. The stench of antiseptic and stale coffee. The hum of fluorescent lights overhead that reflected off tile floors.

She sat in the waiting room, flanked by her mother and Yvette. Everyone had come to the hospital—all three of her brothers, Gwen Harrison, Jordana and Clint, Yvette, Shep. Through it all, Luke stayed. Hour stacked upon hour until she was positive that time would tumble to the ground.

By midafternoon, Dr. Jamapal, a woman not much older than Bridgette with coal-black hair and large, dark eyes, entered the waiting room.

"Mrs. Colton," she said, addressing Lilly.

Bridgette's mother stood. "What happened? How is Fitz."

"Your husband had a blockage in an artery leading to his heart. This broke loose this morning, causing a myocardial infarction. In other words, your husband lost blood flow to his heart and had a heart attack."

"How is he, Doc?" Ty asked.

"At the moment, he's resting."

"What's his prognosis?" Jordana asked.

"He has other blockages that need to be surgically removed. Then, given time to rest and the right rehabilitation, your father can live many more years." She continued, "He was lucky today. If he'd been alone or not have had aspirin administered so quickly, we would be having a very different conversation."

"I'm glad that everything has turned out in the end," said Brooks.

"This isn't the end," said Dr. Jamapal. "But it's not a bad outcome for now. You all can visit your father. The room is small so you might want to take turns. Remember, it's important that he remain calm."

"Thanks, Doc," said Ty. And then the doctor was gone. When the family was alone, Ty said, "There's a lot we have to be thankful for—especially that Bridgette and Luke were with Dad when it happened."

"Yeah, thanks," said Neil. "How'd you even think to give him aspirin?"

"It wasn't me," she said, shaking her head. "It was Luke."

"Because I own a small business," said Luke, "I'm always vigilant about medical emergencies and how important those first few seconds can be."

"It seems like we all owe you our thanks," said Brooks. Then he asked, "Do you two want to go and see Dad first?"

Bridgette shook her head. Her throat was tight, making it hard to breathe and harder still to speak. "You guys go ahead with Mom," she said.

Lilly placed her hand on Luke's shoulder. "Thank you." Then she was gone, leaving Luke, Bridgette and her sisters.

"Are you going to tell me what's going on or not?" Yvette asked. "You haven't said more than two words since we got here, Bridgette."

Her eyes burned. She dropped her gaze to the floor and said, "I should probably go. Luke's been carting me around all day, and he doesn't have this time to waste."

"That's a lame excuse," said Yvette. "And you know it. Spill."

"Dad and I had an argument," said Bridgette. "I'm the reason he had a heart attack."

"You aren't the reason," said Jordana. "You heard what the doctor said. If Dad hadn't gotten immediate care, things would have been worse. It's basically a miracle that you were visiting him when you were."

Bridgette was sick of secrets and always skirting unpleasant truths. "You don't get it," she snapped. "I wasn't just visiting Dad. I was at his office for work." She paused, drew in a breath and met her sister's gaze. "There's a strong link between Colton Construction and the cancer cluster that I'm investigating. The company needs to be closed—at least temporarily—while the state does some testing."

Yvette went white and stumbled backward, as if struck. "And that's when he had the heart attack?"

Bridgette echoed her sister's words, "And that's when he had the heart attack." She dropped her gaze to the floor once more. "So, you can't say that I'm not responsible because, obviously, I am. It was stupid of me to think that I could be the one to deliver such devastating news."

"That's one problem about being a Colton," said Yvette. "Colton Construction is such a big part of life in town that we never really escape it. You know how they found two bodies in the wall of that old warehouse?"

"Of course," said Luke. "It's been all over the news."

"There are people in the police force who don't

think I can be unbiased. They want me to recuse myself from the case."

"You can't be serious," said Bridgette. Anger flowed through her veins. "I'd like to talk to anyone who suggests you aren't completely professional."

"I appreciate your support," said Yvette. "But what I'm saying is that in Braxville, you're a Colton first."

"I know," said Bridgette. For a moment, it felt as if the walls of the small waiting room were moving closer, inch by inch. "I have to get out of here before Mom and the guys come back."

"I understand," said Jordana. "I'll explain to Mom later. And you," she said to Luke. "Take care of her."

"I will."

Bridgette was already gone and striding down the long corridor.

Jogging to catch up, Luke gripped Bridgette's elbow. "Where are you going without me?" he asked.

"I just had to get away."

"I know all of that was hard," he said. "Especially since you are so determined to find out about the connection between the construction company and the cancer cases."

Bridgette nodded as she walked even though she wasn't sure if Luke was right. Bridgette had learned that some things were more important than discovering the truth.

It was her family.

OVER THE NEXT WEEK, Bridgette developed a routine. In the morning, she went to work. She and Luke spent an hour at lunch taking Pocco, the shelter dog, for a walk. She had dinner with Luke while they worked on the final plans for the Braxville Boo-fest. Since Julia was still at large, she stayed in Luke's apartment.

Bridgette had become more than a guest. She and Luke now shared the master bedroom.

For her, the week had been perfect. There were only two minor—okay, make that major—issues. First, Bridgette had yet to speak to her father. He'd had surgery and was still hospitalized. She had not stopped by to see him, nor had he asked to speak to her. His silence was death by a thousand cuts.

And that brought about her second problem.

Megan Parker's husband had been diagnosed with esophageal cancer. The news had made the rounds in Braxville. Chuck, Megan's husband, was also an employee of Colton Construction.

Bridgette continued to hope that her father's business wasn't involved. The evidence said otherwise. She knew that her job was not worth her relationship with her father. There were other competent people who could take over the investigation. Moreover, as imperfect as Fitz Colton was, he was also her dad.

She woke on Saturday morning, Luke's arm draped across her chest. Her limbs were still loose from the previous night's lovemaking, but her chest was filled with a steely resolve. She didn't care that it was the weekend. Today was the day.

After the parade, she'd call her boss at home and recuse herself from the cancer cluster—the consequences to her career be damned.

Luke stirred, stretched. The covers fell down to his waist, revealing the hard muscles of his stomach and chest. He opened one eye and smiled. "Good morning," he said.

Bridgette couldn't help but smile in return. She stroked his cheek. The short hairs of his day-old beard tickled her palm. "What's got you so happy?"

"I love waking up next to you," he said. "And today is the Braxville Boo-fest. Aside from bringing lots of folks to town, after today I'll be done as the chairman of the festival."

"You think they'll let you go?" Playfully she snapped her fingers. "Just like that? Trust me, Luke. You are a natural-born leader. Honest. Charismatic. Organized. Before long you'll be president of the downtown business association or, worse, mayor."

"I don't want Elise's job, especially with everything that's going on in town with the cancer cluster." He sat up and ran his hands over his scalp, leaving his hair standing on end. "By the way, how's that going. You haven't mentioned anything in the last few days."

"I've made a decision," Bridgette said, rising from bed.

"Oh, yeah? What's that?"

Slipping into a pair of jeans as she spoke, Bridgette said, "I've decided to recuse myself from the case."

"You what?" Luke asked, an edge to his voice.

She slipped a black turtleneck sweater over her head, feeling the heat of irritation rise in her chest. Who was he to take a tone with her? "This case is connected to my family's business. I wanted to think that I could be impartial, but honestly I can't. Every bit of information I uncover leaves me wondering how it affects my father's health. If I'm distracted, I can't be successful."

"So, that's it?" Luke asked, throwing off the covers and getting to his feet. "You're quitting?"

Anger rolled off him in waves, like a hot wind swirling over sand dunes. Bridgette stepped back. "Quitting?" she echoed. "No, of course not. I'm recusing myself from the case."

"Which is a fancy word for quitting."

"What in the hell is your problem?" she asked.

"Cancer ruined my dad's life. You promised me that you'd figure out what happened."

Bridgette searched the floor for her shoes. Where in the hell had they gone? "So, your dad is the only one whose health gets to matter?"

Her argument dampened some of the flames in his fury. "Of course not. That's not what I said—or at least, that's not what I meant."

Pressing her fingertips to her own chest, she continued, "My father had a heart attack. He's in the hospital right now. It's all because of my involvement in the case and the fact that I had to close down his business. Not to mention those cold homicide cases." She waited a beat and then another. "I've lost a child, a husband. I'm not burying my father."

"What upsets me is that you promised to find out what caused everyone to get sick. You said that this was your top priority. You swore to me that you would see this thing through—no matter what. And now, just because things are a little rough, you're done?"

"You're putting words in my mouth."

"But not the sentiment."

There, her shoes were tucked into the corner behind the open bedroom door. She grabbed both boots and sat on the bed's edge. Working her foot into her shoe, she continued, "Besides, it's not as if the case is going to go away. The Department of Health will assign someone else to lead the local team."

"It just won't be you," said Luke, his tone more weary than combative.

Shaking her head, she said, "It won't be."

"Who then?"

She lifted one shoulder and let it drop. "I have no idea, but I'm going to go now. I think we need some time apart, don't you?"

"No," said Luke. "I think we can disagree and still get along."

"I just need a few minutes alone, then," she said. "We have a busy day ahead of us and have to work together to make the parade successful. That won't happen if we're quarreling."

Luke nodded. "Understood."

"I'm going to take Pocco for a walk, first. Then I'll get ready across the hall. I'll meet you at the coffee shop and get ready for the TV interview." She glanced at her phone for the time—6:45 a.m. "At eight o'clock."

Blankets were strewn on the floor. While tossing them back onto the bed, Luke nodded. "See you then."

Without another word, Bridgette left the building.

It was the first time in days that she had truly been alone. After years of widowhood, she'd gotten used to her own company. Had being around people so much set her on edge?

Or was the fight with Luke more? Did they really see the world differently? If so, what did that mean for their future? Certainly, she'd be ordered back to Wichita after her recusal. Maybe that wasn't a bad thing.

Maybe it was time to return Luke Walker to her past. And this time, leave him there.

JULIA LEANED OVER the steering wheel, straining to see out through the grimy windshield. She had spent the past week in the mail annex of Colton Construction. Closing down the offices had provided her with the perfect place to hide. For days on end, she'd lived on single-brew coffee and stale snacks.

It gave her time to think, to worry, to plan. She'd heard every word spoken between Bridgette and her father. She'd watched all of the state employees conducting tests and had been able to avoid them all.

She knew that Colton Construction had been closed down because of a connection with several cases of cancer. She also knew it was her job to reopen the company.

On Wednesday morning, she woke covered in sweat with her hands trembling. She'd had a dream that left her breathless. It was then that she knew what to do. She took her time going through all the mail that stacked up day after day. She compiled a folder full of documents and bided her time.

It was the morning of the Braxville Boo-fest and Main Street was already busy at 6:45 a.m. She'd parked around the corner. Using the binoculars, she watched the doorway leading to the apartments located above the hardware store.

There were cars parked on both sides of the road. Lights were on in every store, and the windows were decorated with pumpkins, scarecrows, witches and ghosts. Vendors were setting up booths that offered everything from apple cider and doughnuts to custom-created wreaths to antiques to headbands that looked like bat wings and twinkled with purple lights.

None of the activity interested Julia. In fact, the commotion offered the perfect cover. The door opened and Bridgette stepped onto the street. She wore her long hair in a ponytail and shoved her hands into the pockets of a jacket.

Julia expected her to head directly for the coffee shop. Instead, she walked down the street before turning the corner and disappearing from view. Julia started the car and circled the block, not daring to drive down Main Street, where she'd certainly be seen and recognized.

By the time she made her way to the street where Bridgette had been, the other woman was gone. She beat her hand on the steering wheel. "Dammit. Dammit. Dammit all to hell and back," she said, her curses matching the cadence of her heartbeat.

Still, she couldn't have gotten far.

Unless Bridgette had been picked up by someone

else. If that were the case, the other woman could be anywhere by now.

Yet, Julia wasn't about to give up—not when she was so close to solving everyone's problems.

On her second circuit through the neighborhood, Julia's luck changed for the better. Bridgette, holding the leash of a black-and-white dog, strode down the street.

"Where did the dog come from?" she asked, knowing what the doctors would say about Julia speaking to people who weren't really there. Then again, the dog wasn't important. What mattered was that she had finally found Bridgette Colton.

Pulling up to the next block, Julia parked and left the car running. She grabbed the folder and stepped from the car.

"Hey, Bridgette," Julia called out. "We need to talk. Do you have a minute?"

Stumbling to a stop, the other woman met Julia's gaze. "You," she said, the single word an accusation.

Julia waved the navy blue folder with the golden Colton Construction logo embossed on the cover like a flag of surrender. Julia said, "I have something you need to see." She was careful to keep her other hand tucked in tight to her leg.

"Do you know how much trouble you've caused?" Bridgette asked. "My car. The apartment's window. Trespassing at my family's lake house."

"I know. I know." Walking toward Bridgette with the folder in her outstretched hand, she continued, "There's something you need to see. It's about Colton Construction and the cancer cases."

Eyes wide, Bridgette blanched. "How do you know about that?"

"I work in the mail room and found some documents you need to see."

The dog began to growl, a low rumble coming from its chest.

"The company has been closed. If you worked there, you'd know that."

"I had an incident with my mom," said Julia, her throat tight. "I've been staying in the trailer because I can't go home. I've seen all the DOH workers taking samples and running tests. I've heard everything you've said to one another. Then, I started looking." She held out the folder farther. "This is what I found."

"What is it?" Bridgette asked, not bothering to step forward.

"I'm not sure," Julia said. "I think it will exonerate your father and Colton Construction of any wrongdoing."

"You do?" Bridgette's face brightened until she almost smiled.

Moving toward Julia, she held out her hand and took the offered folder. The dog began to bark in earnest. "Stop it, Pocco," said Bridgette. "Behave."

Scanning the first few pages of the file, Bridgette drew her brows together. "I don't understand," she began. "None of these documents are connected in any way."

Julia kept her other hand hidden though it trembled. And then, she slipped out of her own body. Like a marionette, her physical self was controlled by an unseen puppeteer. She watched from a distance, breathless with anticipation.

Did the puppet master have the nerve to act?

If Bridgette realized what kind of danger she was in, she didn't show it. Not until she saw the tire iron did her eyes go wide. She screamed—the noise swallowed by the dog's continual barking.

Metal connected with bone and flesh. An arc of blood came off the iron, a comet's tail of gore. Bridgette's eyes rolled into her skull. Falling backward, she hit the ground.

Julia stared at the body and asked herself a single question.

What do I do now?

Chapter Nineteen

Luke Walker held his phone. His grip was so tight he thought the metal and plastic cell might crumple in his hand.

"Have you heard anything yet?" Elise walked across the coffee shop, cup in hand.

The news crew from Wichita had arrived and set up for the interview. Three director's chairs, with the station's logo emblazoned on the seat back, were in a semicircle. Lights shone on the makeshift set, where a blonde anchor read over notes.

Glancing at the screen, he read the long line of messages sent.

I'm here.
At the coffee shop.
Are you on your way?
It's 8:15. Where are you?
Elise just showed up.
The news crew is here. Text me back

And finally, I know we parted ways mad, but don't bail on me now.

There were no replies.

"Nothing," he said.

"It's odd," said Elise. "Bridgette's always seemed so reliable."

With a shake of his head, Luke said, "We argued this morning before she left."

"What about?"

"It doesn't matter now, but I think she might have gone back to Wichita."

"Did she say that?" Elise asked.

Luke opened his mouth, ready to say yes, and then stopped himself. "Not really. She was the one who suggested putting our disagreement aside until after the Boo-fest. Then again," he began, but let his words trail off.

"Then again what?"

He finally gave voice to his fear. "Then again she could have changed her mind."

"It's doubtful. Bridgette is a lot of things—capricious is not on her list." Elise took a sip of coffee and looked out of the window. "I'll be honest, I'm a little worried. Where was she headed after leaving your apartment?"

"She said she was going to the shelter to walk one of the dogs," he said. "I expected Dr. Faulkner to be here by now, too."

"Maybe there was a problem," suggested Elise.

"I'll call," said Luke, opening his phone's app.

The bell on the coffee shop's door rang, and the old

vet—led in by three dogs on leashes—entered. "Sorry I'm late," he said. "I was waiting for Bridgette to come back with Pocco. When she didn't, I figured she'd kept him with her, and they were both here."

"Bridgette's not with you?" Luke asked, his annoyance quickly morphing into alarm.

"No," said the older man. "I haven't seen her since before seven o'clock this morning."

"Excuse me," said the anchor. "Do we have everyone we need for the interview? We go live in three minutes, and you still need to get on your mics."

Luke turned for the door while talking to Elise and the veterinarian over his shoulder. "You both do the interview."

"Where are you going?" Elise called as he pushed open the front door.

"To find Bridgette."

The minute Luke's feet hit the sidewalk he began to sprint. He knew the route she took with the dog. As he ran, he came up with a dozen possible scenarios of what had kept her from her appointment at the coffee shop. Too bad none of them were good.

Three blocks from the shelter, Luke skidded to a halt. Huddling near a fence stood the dog Pocco. The animal's tail was tucked between his legs and he shivered.

"Hey, boy," said Luke, holding out his hand.

Head down, the animal approached. Luke ran his fingers through the dog's short fur. Bridgette was nowhere to be seen.

She'd never abandon her charge while on their walk.

If that was true, where had she gone? Why was she gone?

Luke wrapped his hand around the dog's lead and stepped forward. He stopped, his eye drawn to the seam between street and curb.

A rainbow shimmered atop an oil slick.

Taking a knee, he touched the ground. The oil was still viscous, which meant it wasn't an old stain. His thoughts immediately went to the fresh motor oil they'd found in the woods. He still didn't have any solid evidence that it was Julia who'd been spying that day. Then again, his ex-girlfriend had disappeared soon after, so who else could it be?

And if Julia's car had dripped oil on the street, it meant only one thing—she had Bridgette. Luke had never made a wager, but he'd bet that Bridgette hadn't gone with Julia willingly. The cold hand of dread gripped his heart, his pulse sluggish. He also wasn't the kind to panic, and he pulled the phone from his pocket. He placed a call. It rang twice before being answered by voice mail.

"You've reached Bridgette Colton. I'm not available right now. Leave me a message and I'll get back to you soon."

Cursing, he ended the call.

Phone still in hand, he called Bridgette's sister, Jordana.

Luke had begun to walk again, his hand still wrapped in Pocco's lead.

"It's me, Luke," he said, when voice mail answered.

"I think there's something wrong with your sister and I need your help."

He ended that call and placed another, this one to Yvette. It also went to voice mail and he left the same message. Luke placed a call to Bridgette's brother, Brooks Colton. No luck. Then, he called his buddy with the police department, Reese Carpenter.

"Dammit," he said out loud. "Why won't anyone answer their phone?"

The dog looked up and cocked his head. They stood beside Luke's truck, which he had moved away from the downtown festivities to the parking lot of a nearby bank.

For the moment, he'd assume the unthinkable. Julia had kidnapped Bridgette.

Hell, by now, they could be out of state and Bridgette would be gone forever.

No. That wasn't how Julia thought. Everything was a sign. Every place held meaning. Opening the door, he said to the dog, "Come on, boy. Bridgette's missing and we need to find her."

Pocco jumped up and settled into the passenger seat.

Luke turned the key in the ignition and the truck's large engine rumbled to life. He had an idea of where Julia might've gone. He only hoped that they weren't too late.

BRIDGETTE'S MOUTH WAS DRY, and her head pounded. She pried her eyes open and saw nothing but darkness. She lay on a floor covered in rough carpeting. The scent of motor oil and exhaust hung in the air. Somewhere close was the constant drone of an engine.

"What the hell?" she mumbled through cracked and bleeding lips. Pushing to sitting, Bridgette's head collided with a solid wall, and she slumped onto her stomach again. The aching in her head intensified, and she touched her scalp. Her fingers found a patch that was wet and sticky.

She was bleeding.

What had happened? And, more important, where was she?

Bridgette tried to think and remember. Memories came to her in bursts, like the flash of a camera. The walk. Julia's arrival. The folder full of papers, along with a promise of more information about the cancer cases. Then there was the attack—brutal and brief.

Drawing a lungful of hot air, Bridgette counted to ten and then exhaled. The pain in her head lessened, creating room for her thoughts. First, she knew that she wasn't in a room, but rather the trunk of a car. The rumble of the engine and the jostling of the wheels as they turned were unmistakable.

Which meant that Bridgette had been abducted while unconscious. She knew very little about how to survive a kidnapping other than what she learned in a self-defense class taken in college. Then again, the little bit she remembered might be enough.

The inside of every trunk was equipped with a safety release installed for just such emergencies. Flipping to her back, her hand danced along the lid. She found a plastic handle and pulled.

The latch opened. Blinding and bright, light struck Bridgette in the face. The tires kicked up a rooster tail of dust as the car rumbled down a dirt road. Bridgette didn't waste time with thoughts that might make her lose her nerve. Rising to her knees, she rolled out of the car.

She hit the hard ground at the same moment the car skidded to a stop.

Bridgette's shoulder hurt. Her forearm was scraped and raw. Blood dripped from the side of her hand, and her ankle throbbed with each beat of her heart.

As she struggled to stand, Bridgette cursed. She should have taken a moment to find the car's tire iron. At least then she'd have a weapon, a way to fight back.

"What the hell do you think you're doing?"

She recognized Julia's voice and began to run. Bridgette's ankle collapsed. A tremor of pain ran up her leg as she tumbled to the ground. Julia stalked toward her.

She held the tire iron in her hand, and Bridgette realized she would have searched in vain for it.

"Come back here, you bitch," the other woman said.

Scrabbling backward, Bridgette asked, "Why are you doing this?"

"You know," Julia said.

She was right, Bridgette knew. "Luke," she said.

"You should have just left him alone. I tried to warn you, but you stayed and stayed and stayed." Her face twitched with each word. Foam clung to the corner of her mouth; the tire iron hung in her grip. "He loved me. We were perfect together and you ruined everything."

It was then that Bridgette understood. Julia was more than immature and committed to being bothersome. The other woman was truly obsessed. The life she lived, including her feelings for Luke, had not been rooted in reality. That fact made her dangerous and deadly.

Bridgette knew one thing. She was too injured to fight off another attack. If she wanted to survive, she needed to use her wits. "I'm leaving for Wichita on Monday," she said. "After recusing myself from the Braxville cancer case, I'll be gone. Luke's mad at me. Why don't you just leave me here and go. I won't say anything about what happened."

Julia paused, considering the offer.

Bridgette exhaled a breath she didn't recall holding. Had her argument worked? Had she gotten through to the rational part of Julia's mind?

Then the other woman's face hardened, storm clouds covering a blue sky. "No," she said, her eyes turning black. "It's too late."

"Too late," Bridgette began, as terror gripped Bridgette's throat and her words came out as a squeak. "Too late for what?"

"Too late to let you live."

Grabbing Bridgette by the arm, the other woman pulled her to her feet.

Bridgette's vision exploded in a flash of white. The pain from her head injury made it hard to breathe and harder still to think. Yet, she had to get away from Julia.

Marshaling all her strength in her shoulder, she

swung her arm in a wide arc. Her fist connected with the side of Julia's head. The impact sent the other woman staggering back and her grasp faltered.

Bridgette didn't take in her surroundings and began to run.

A road led through a heavily wooded area. She clambered over a rotted tree trunk. In a flash of memory, she recalled Luke jumping over the very same log. That meant they were in the woods near her family's lake house.

Pain radiated through every part of Bridgette's body. She shoved all her discomfort aside and forced her legs to move faster. Bushes and shrubs on either side of the trail passed as a blur.

Ahead, Julia stepped out from behind a tree. Her dark hair was wild, and tendrils obscured her pale face. Her shoulders were hunched forward. In her hand was the tire iron. Bridgette slowed, spun and began to run the other way.

Sweat streamed down Bridgette's face, stinging her eyes and blurring her vision.

Then a pain exploded in the back of her head. She knew she'd been hit once again while stumbling forward. As she fell, the forest floor disappeared and a bottomless chasm opened. Bridgette continued to fall, surrounded by nothingness.

She tried to scream but could make no sound.

Her eyes were heavy and her limbs were weary, aching all the way to her bones. Sleep called to her with a siren's song.

Yet, if she gave into the desire for rest, she would

never wake again. Forcing her eyes to open, she saw the sky and dappled sunlight streaming through the tree-tops that towered above. There were hands under her arms. The ground was rough at her back as she rolled over twigs and stones.

She was being dragged. But where was she being taken?

A beam of light caught her in the face. The light seared her pupils and she screwed her eyes shut. She tried to pry her lids open. It didn't work.

Then she was falling again.

This time she didn't care.

The blackness was inviting and seductive. It was the open and waiting arms of a lover. She longed to be lost in the oblivion it offered.

Then for a moment Bridgette went cold. She felt a breeze on her face. She was weightless and out of control.

She landed on her back.

Icy water slapped her in the face. All the air was driven from her lungs. Her mouth filled with cold and slimy debris. She began to cough. Her arms and legs swung out in wild arcs.

It was then that all of Bridgette's faculties returned.

She was at the bottom of a well, the same one she had loved as a child. This time there was no magic to save her. She was trapped. The walls were covered in slick black slime, making climbing out impossible.

Treading water, Bridgette looked up. The sky, a blue disk, was visible at the mouth of the well. The opening was less than a dozen feet away—it might as well have been miles.

Standing in the sunlight and looking down was Luke's ex—Julia. With a smile, the other woman flipped the metal door closed. It hit the well's stone lip with a clang, surrounding Bridgette in darkness.

Important life moments rushed by. Luke's face filled those memories more than once. His was the touch she craved, and his voice was the one she longed to hear. Sure, she'd only been back in Braxville for little more than a week. But she'd known from the beginning that she and Luke were meant for one another.

How could Bridgette have let his love slip away for a second time?

Paddling her feet, she treaded water to stay afloat. Her arms ached and her legs were heavy. She could feel the cold water pulling her down.

Nobody knew where she'd gone—or maybe even suspected that she was missing. It was here, at the bottom of this well, that she was going to die.

LUKE PRESSED HIS foot on the accelerator as the speedometer climbed to seventy miles per hour. Eighty. Ninety. He completed the half-hour drive to Lake Kanopolis in less than fifteen minutes.

Swerving onto the short drive leading to the Colton fishing cabin, he slammed on the breaks, the grille of his truck inches from the wall. With the engine still running, he leaped from his truck and sprinted to the door. He turned the handle—it didn't budge. Lifting his foot, he made ready to kick in the lock. His phone rang. Standing upright, Luke removed the phone from his jacket and checked the caller's ID.

It was Elise. The reception was lousy, with only a single bar of coverage.

Swiping the call open, he said, "Tell me you have Bridgette with you."

"No, that's why I'm calling. Where are you two?" she said, her words filled with static. "The festival has started, and we need our chairperson."

"You have to take care of this without me," he said. "I'm at the Coltons' cabin."

"Did you just say the Colton lake house?" she asked. "What? Why?"

Luke took only the briefest moment to tell her about finding the shelter dog on the street along with the suspicions that his ex-girlfriend had something to do with Bridgette's disappearance. He ended the story with, "I had a feeling that Julia brought Bridgette out this way, but it doesn't look like anyone has been at the house since we left last week."

"Lake Kanopolis is huge," said Elise. "Bridgette could be anywhere."

Luke searched the expanse of water. A veil of fog hung over the surface, and he couldn't help but wonder what was hidden in the depths. Yet Julia wouldn't have simply taken Bridgette someplace random. That was why the fishing cabin had come to mind. It was a special place for Bridgette and Luke's relationship.

"I'm not leaving until I have a chance to look around," he said. "You'll take care of the Boo-fest for me?"

"Of course, and I'll find Jordana. We'll get the police looking for both Julia and Bridgette in case either one is still in town."

Luke didn't bother thanking the mayor or even ending the call. He turned off the truck's ignition and began to run. Frantic barking jerked him to a stop. He didn't have time to deal with an animal. Then again Pocco might be able to help. Retracing his steps, he opened the passenger door.

Jumping to the ground, the dog began to snuffle.

"Do you have her scent, boy?" he asked, picking up the lead that still trailed from the dog's collar.

Pulling on his leash, the animal forced Luke to run in order to keep pace. By the time they reached the well, Luke's breath came in ragged gasps. The metal door was closed, but the rusty chain had been shattered, and pieces were scattered on the ground.

Pulling free of the leash, Pocco began to whimper and paw at the ground around the well.

Luke raced forward and lifted the heavy metal door.

There, looking up from the gloom, was Bridgette Colton.

HOLDING TIGHT TO the webbed fabric, Luke dangled Pocco's lead into the well. Bending at the waist, he stretched down. Bridgette reached upward, her fingertips grazing the leash.

"You can do it," he said. "Just a little higher."

"I can't," she said, batting at the handle. Her touch sent the leash into a lazy circle.

Dammit. Bridgette was right. She was reaching up as far as she could. If he bent down farther, they'd both end up in the water. He had rope in his truck, but he dared not leave her alone.

It was then that Luke realized he didn't need a rope—only something strong that could make the leash a bit longer.

"Hold on a second," he said. "I know what to do."

Bridgette looked up. Her wide eyes were filled with terror but also hope. "You aren't leaving me here, are you?"

"I'll be right here the whole time. I promise."

Luke straightened and unbuckled his leather belt. He wrapped it through the leash's grip, creating a loop that Bridgette could grab. He lowered the lead and Bridgette took hold of the belt. He began to pull.

Bridgette rose from the water. She pushed her feet into the wall of the well, transferring some of her weight and helping her ascent.

Upward she rose, inch by inch. Stone bit into Luke's middle. White-hot pain filled his shoulder. His legs trembled with fatigue. He ignored the pain and continued to pull.

Bridgette was mere inches from Luke. He reached to her. Her fingers interlocked with his. With all his strength, Luke hauled her out of the well. He toppled back and Bridgette landed on his stomach. She was cold and wet. Her body trembled, not solely from the chill.

"I thought I was going to die," she said, her voice thick with emotion. "How did you find me?"

"I found him," said Luke. After helping Bridgette to sit up, he hooked his thumb toward the dog. Head down and eyes up, the dog approached. Reaching out, Luke ruffled Pocco's ear. "He was alone on the street. That's when I knew something had happened to you. I saw a fresh oil stain on the ground, just like we saw in the woods. I figured Julia was involved. I had a hunch that she'd come to the lake."

"Thank goodness you listened to your instincts." She drew in a deep breath. "It was Julia. She said she had information about the cancer cluster and how Colton Construction wasn't involved. It was all a ruse. She told me that she worked in the mail annex—had been hiding there while the offices were closed—and had found some paperwork. She even had a Colton Construction folder and everything. I wanted to believe and didn't worry about being careful."

Luke's phone began to ring. He glanced at the screen. "It's your sister," he said, handing over the phone.

"I still can't believe you have coverage all the way out here," Bridgette said, swiping the call open. For a moment, she spoke, giving her sister the details of what had happened. It was hard for Luke to listen. He never should have left Bridgette alone, especially since he knew that Julia was dangerous.

She ended the call just as the sounds of sirens could be heard in the distance. "Yvette said she called the ambulance."

"That must be them," said Luke, helping her to stand. He held her close until the EMTs arrived and Bridgette was moved to the rear of the ambulance, where she was evaluated.

He stepped away and placed a call to Reese Carpenter. Pocco ambled next to Luke and sat as the phone began to ring.

"Luke," he said. "What's up?"

"I have Bridgette with me, but Julia needs to be found before anyone else gets hurt."

"Every police officer in the state is looking for Julia right now."

"Bridgette mentioned that she'd been hiding in the mail room at Colton Construction for the past week. It's a trailer located at the rear of the property."

"I'll check it out now."

"Thanks, man," said Luke. "I appreciate it."

After ending the call, he approached the ambulance. Bridgette sat on a stretcher in the rear cabin with the back door open. "What'd the EMTs say?" he asked.

"I need to be evaluated further at the hospital," she said. "I'll call you once I know anything."

"Are you trying to get rid of me?" he asked.

"Today is the Braxville Boo-fest. You've worked hard to make it successful. Certainly, you want to be there. It's important."

"You are important to me, Bridgette." He paused. "If you want me leave you alone, tell me. Otherwise—I'm going to be with you now and later."

"Luke, I…"

Before she could continue, one of the EMTs approached. "Excuse me, sir," the other man said, slamming the door shut. "We have to take the patient to the hospital."

Lights strobing and siren wailing, the ambulance sped away.

Luke watched as the ambulance rumbled over the woodland track. Were the police on the way, ready to search the woods and the lake for Julia? Or would they come to the well and collect evidence? He assumed so, but for now, it was silent.

Birdsong filtered through the woods. The sun climbed higher, warming the morning and promising that it was going to be a perfect fall day. Luke had confessed that he wanted a future with Bridgette. What would she have said if they hadn't been interrupted?

The dog leaned into his leg, giving a contented sigh. "What do you think, boy?" Luke asked. "Should we go after her?"

Pocco looked up as Luke spoke.

"I agree completely," he said to the dog. "We can't give up now."

Chapter Twenty

Julia had no place else to go and returned to the mail annex. Her brow was covered in sweat and her pulse resonated in her skull. She sat in the corner, her knees pulled up to her chin, and wondered how long she would feel sick.

Was this a fleeting sensation?

Or would Julia be overwhelmed with guilt for the rest of her days.

She hadn't meant to kill Bridgette and that was a fact.

Yet, there was another fact, one that Julia couldn't avoid. The other woman was most certainly dead by now.

And dead was dead. There were no do-overs.

For the first time in months, the scars on Julia's wrist began to itch.

She scratched, her nails leaving red welts on her skin.

"Julia Jones, this is Detective Reese Carpenter with the Braxville Police. Come out of the trailer with your hands up." The voice boomed through a PA system.

Dammit. She should have left her car at the old warehouse and not driven back to Colton Construction.

"Julia," he said again. "You have to come out or I will come in and get you."

She crawled across the floor, careful to stay below the windows. There, on the shelves, was a box cutter. Still on her knees, she reached up and grabbed the knife.

Julia scuttled back to her corner. She looked at her wrists. The lines were already there. She pressed the knife's tip to her flesh. Harder. Harder. The blade sliced her flesh and her arm began to weep blood.

The door opened with a bang.

Reese Carpenter and Jordana Colton stood on the threshold. Both had their guns drawn.

"Put down the knife, Julia," said Jordana, hand lifted. "You don't want to hurt yourself or anyone else."

"Don't I?" Julia spit. "I hurt my mother. I killed your sister. I'm a bad person." She shoved the knife deeper into her arm. There was a flash of pain, white-hot, and blood began to drip onto the floor, soaking into the dirty carpeting.

"My sister's not dead," said Jordana. "And your mother misses you. She wants you to come home—not die."

"Momma?" Julia asked. Her resolve wavered.

She should have never let her guard down.

Before she realized that he'd moved, Reese Carpenter had Julia's wrist tight in his grip. The flow of blood was now a trickle. She was on her feet, her back pressed to his chest. The knife lay on the ground, surrounded by a puddle of blood.

BRIDGETTE WAS EVALUATED by Dr. Jamapal, the same physician who had seen her father only days before. The diagnosis: a mild concussion, scrapes, bruises, a cut to her scalp that needed stitching, and hypothermia from being submerged in the cold water.

Considering everything that she'd endured, Bridgette was lucky to be alive.

"I'm keeping you overnight for observation," said the doctor. "The man who followed the ambulance, Luke Walker, is in the waiting room. Would you like to see him?"

"Sure," said Bridgette, pushing up to sitting.

The doctor left, and a moment later the door opened. It wasn't Luke who entered the room—it was her father. He was still a patient at the hospital and wore a robe over a set of sweats.

"Daddy?"

"Hey, honey, I heard you were here. Can I come in?"

She bit her bottom lip, stanching her tears of love and disappointment. "Of course," she said. "I'm sorry that I haven't stopped by this week. I feel, well, responsible for what happened. More than that, I was worried that you blamed me for your heart attack."

"To be honest, until I heard that you'd been attacked, I did blame you. Then I realized that there's nothing more important than you and my other kids."

"I've decided to recuse myself from the investigation. I tried to be a good scientist and not let anything other than the facts form my opinions. But you and your health are important to me—as is our relationship."

"I'm not asking you to step away from the case because of me."

"You didn't have to ask," she said.

Her father sat on the edge of her bed. Rubbing a hand over his chin, he exhaled. "You know, there's something I should probably tell you about what's happening in town." The door opened. Fitz Colton stopped talking.

Luke stood on the threshold. "Sorry for interrupting," he said. "I thought you were alone."

"I just had to check on my baby girl."

"Well, I'm glad you're both here," he said. "I got a call from Jordana. She and Reese found Julia."

"Really? Where?"

"She was hiding in the mail room of Colton Construction, just like you said."

"Colton Construction?" her father echoed. "What in the world is happening?"

"Julia worked in the mail room, but there's more to the story," said Bridgette. "It sounds like there's a lot for us to discuss."

"Do you need a minute?" Luke asked, hooking his thumb toward the door. "I can give you some privacy."

Bridgette's dad stood. "I'm the one who should be going. I'll call your mother and give her an update. I'm sure she'll be down to visit shortly. I just wanted to see you first."

"Daddy," she said as he reached the door. "What was it that you wanted to tell me?"

He waved her question away. "It'll keep. You get some rest."

Luke moved to Bridgette's side and took her hand in his. "How are you feeling?" he asked.

She answered his question with one of her own. "If you've been here, then where's Pocco?"

"My dad stopped by and picked him up. If I know my dad, he's probably sharing a sandwich with the dog right now."

Bridgette laughed. "He's a good dog. I wish he would find his forever home."

"Funny that you'd say that. I'm pretty sure that someone plans to adopt Pocco."

"Really? Who?"

Luke shrugged. "Me."

"You?"

"We made a pretty good team in finding you." He lifted her hand and placed a kiss on the inside of her wrist. "But you never answered my question. Honestly, how are you?"

"I'm sore. I'm tired. I'm thankful to be alive." Yet, there was more to talk about than her health. "When I was in the well," she began, "I thought there was no way I would ever get out. There were a lot of things for me to regret. The one that came to mind again and again was that I never would be able to see what the future would hold for you and me."

"Future?" he echoed, reaching for her hand.

"I realized something important," she said, unwilling

to stop speaking now that she'd begun. "Over the years, I'd lost people I loved—the baby, Henry. I thought that the best way to avoid pain was to live behind an emotional wall. With you, I couldn't hide. I'm happy to be alive because it gives us another chance." She paused, bit her bottom lip. "That is if you'll have me."

"Bridgette, I loved you when we were kids and I've never stopped. All this time, there was something missing in my life. I now know what it is," he said.

"Oh, yeah, what's that?" she asked.

"You."

Luke leaned forward, placing his lips on hers. The kiss was tender, loving and meant to last a lifetime.

* * * * *

COMING SOON!

We really hope you enjoyed reading this book.
If you're looking for more romance, be sure to
head to the shops when new books are
available on

Thursday 3ʳᵈ September

LET'S TALK
Romance

For exclusive extracts, competitions
and special offers, find us online:

 facebook.com/millsandboon

🐦 @MillsandBoon

📷 @MillsandBoonUK

Get in touch on 01413 063232

MILLS & BOON

THE HEART OF ROMANCE

A ROMANCE FOR EVERY KIND OF READER

MODERN

Prepare to be swept off your feet by sophisticated, sexy and seductive heroes, in some of the world's most glamourous and romantic locations, where power and passion collide.
8 stories per month.

HISTORICAL

Escape with historical heroes from time gone by. Whether your passion is for wicked Regency Rakes, muscled Vikings or rugged Highlanders, awaken the romance of the past.
6 stories per month.

MEDICAL

Set your pulse racing with dedicated, delectable doctors in the high-pressure world of medicine, where emotions run high and passion, comfort and love are the best medicine.
6 stories per month.

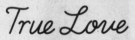

Celebrate true love with tender stories of heartfelt romance, from the rush of falling in love to the joy a new baby can bring, and a focus on the emotional heart of a relationship.
8 stories per month.

Indulge in secrets and scandal, intense drama and plenty of sizzling hot action with powerful and passionate heroes who have it all: wealth, status, good looks…everything but the right woman.
6 stories per month.

HEROES

Experience all the excitement of a gripping thriller, with an intense romance at its heart. Resourceful, true-to-life women and strong fearless men face danger and desire - a killer combination!
8 stories per month.

DARE

Sensual love stories featuring smart, sassy heroines you'd want as a best friend, and compelling intense heroes who are worthy of them.
4 stories per month.

To see which titles are coming soon, please visit

millsandboon.co.uk/nextmonth

JOIN US ON SOCIAL MEDIA!

Stay up to date with our latest releases, author
news and gossip, special offers and discounts, and
all the behind-the-scenes action
from Mills & Boon...

 millsandboon

 millsandboonuk

f millsandboon

It might just be true love...

MILLS & BOON

MODERN

Power and Passion

Prepare to be swept off your feet by sophisticated, sexy and seductive heroes, in some of the world's most glamourous and romantic locations, where power and passion collide.

Eight Modern stories published every month, find them all at:

millsandboon.co.uk/Modern

Sensual love stories featuring smart, sassy
heroines you'd want as a best friend, and
compelling intense heroes who are worthy
of them.

MILLS & BOON
MEDICAL
Pulse-Racing Passion

Set your pulse racing with dedicated, delectable doctors in the high-pressure world of medicine, where emotions run high and passion, comfort and love are the best medicine.